The Whale at the End of the World

John Ironmonger was born and grew up in East Africa. He has a doctorate in zoology and was once an expert on freshwater leeches. He is the author of *The Good Zoo Guide* and the novels *The Notable Brain of Maximilian Ponder* (shortlisted for the 2012 Costa First Novel Prize and the *Guardian's* Not the Booker Prize), *The Coincidence Authority*, *The Whale at the End of the World* (an international bestseller) and *The Many Lives of Heloise Starchild*. He has also been part of a world record team for speed reading Shakespeare, has driven across the Sahara in a £100 banger, and once met Jared Diamond in a forest in the middle of Sumatra.

Follow him on Twitter @jwironmonger

The Whale at the End of the World

JOHN IRONMONGER

Previously published as *Not Forgetting the Whale*

First published in Great Britain in 2015 by Weidenfeld & Nicolson
This paperback edition published in 2021 by Weidenfeld & Nicolson
an imprint of The Orion Publishing Group Ltd
Carmelite House, 50 Victoria Embankment
London EC4Y 0DZ

An Hachette UK Company

1 3 5 7 9 10 8 6 4 2

A CIP catalogue record for this book is available
from the British Library

ISBN (Mass Market Paperback) 978 1 4746 2341 4
ISBN (eBook) 978 0 2976 0822 6

Typeset by Input Data Services Ltd, Somerset

Printed and bound in Great Britain, by Clays Ltd, Elcograf S.p.A.

www.orionbooks.co.uk
www.weidenfeldandnicolson.co.uk

'Whatsoever therefore is consequent to a time of war, where every man is enemy to every man, . . . there is no place for industry . . . no knowledge of the face of the earth; no account of time; no arts; no letters; no society; and which is worst of all, continual fear, and danger of violent death; and the life of man, solitary, poor, nasty, brutish, and short.'

Thomas Hobbes — *Leviathan*

PART ONE

Can you catch Leviathan with a hook?

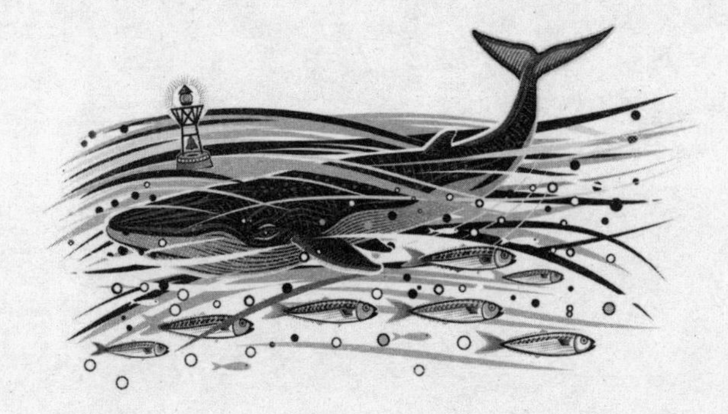

Prologue

In the village of St Piran they still speak of the day when the naked man washed up on Piran Sands. It was the same day Kenny Kennet saw the whale. Some say it was a Wednesday. Others seem sure it was Thursday. It was early October. Unless it was late September; but almost half a century has passed since the events of that day, and the turmoil of the days and weeks that followed, and no one, at that time or since, thought to write it all down. So memory is all we have, fragile though this may be. There are some in the village who claim to recollect every detail, as if perhaps it happened last week. They would have been young when these things happened, and their stories are part of a web of tales that echo of the old days, and the world as it was, and they all tell of the naked man, and they all tell of the whale.

Many who shared in these events are no longer with us. Old Man Garrow is long since dead. So too is Dr Mallory Books, and Martha Fishburne, and the Reverend Alvin Hocking, and Jeremy Melon, and many of those who helped to rescue the whale. But their stories survive and they are told by the children and the grandchildren of the villagers, by neighbours, and by friends. They are told too at the Festival of the Whale held in the old Norman church every Christmas Day. So if you should ever find your way to St Piran (which might be hard to do), you will hear the story in the streets and in the bars; and if you should stop a villager or two, and ask, they might sit you down upon a bench with a view out over the swell of the ocean, and there they might recount the tale, about the beach, and about the whale, and about the naked man. They might, perhaps, walk you down along the ancient harbour wall and the rocky path around the headland to where the shingle and the sands begin, and there they might show you the rock where Kenny Kennet stood when he saw the whale; and just a clamber away they will point out the stretch of sand where the man named Joe was found. They might look out to sea, to the uninviting rocks that garland the beach like a giant's necklace. 'How,' they might ask you, 'could any man float among all those and not be cut to shreds?'

'It was an unconventional entrance.' That's what Jeremy Melon, the naturalist, would say of Joe Haak's arrival in St Piran, when he gave the annual address at the Festival of the Whale. 'Trust Joe to get carried naked onto the beach by a whale! Other people ask for directions and drive politely onto the quay in daylight. But not Joe. Oh no. Joe wants to make a dramatic entrance. So he sneaks into town in the middle of the night, swims all the way out to sea, and rides back in on a bloomin' great whale.' And every time Jeremy Melon told this tale he would bow his legs wide like a cowboy straddling an enormous horse, and he would swing one arm as if holding a lasso. You could picture Joe mounted on the great beast, steering it through the rocks and up onto the sands. Jeremy would know, as well as anyone, that very little of that story was true; but there were tiny fragments of truth in there somewhere, and fragments of truth are often all we need to help us understand reality. Jeremy's story would make people laugh – even those who had known Joe Haak. And that, in the end, was what mattered. 'Sometimes exaggeration can be closer to reality than truth,' Demelza Trevarrick the novelist would say. And it seemed to Jeremy Melon that this was the way St Piran preferred to remember Joe Haak. They didn't want the serious Joe, the geek who had spent his life bent over his computers, working out the mathematics of Armageddon. They didn't want the slick, spoilt city boy who wore silk ties and drove fast cars and earned more in a month than they could earn in a year. They didn't want the Joe that none of them had known – the insecure, troubled Joe, the Joe beset by demons, the solitary Joe that lurked in the darkness fighting his private fears. None of these is the man they remember at the Festival of the Whale. The man they celebrate was a *hero*. He was a prophet. He was the man who saved the world. And if you live in the village of St Piran, then St Piran *is* the world – for you at least. And so, the years have passed, and the real memories of the man called Joe have become confused with the stories. There would be children at the Festival of the Whale, listening to Jeremy Melon speak, who would now always picture the young Joe Haak, naked, astride a whale, and perhaps, when all who knew him have died, this will be the image that remains.

1

The day Kenny Kennet saw the whale

It was Charity Cloke who saw him first. Just seventeen she was then, so fresh of complexion that her cheeks shone like clover honey. They would say in St Piran that she was 'late to blossom', but a summer of soft Cornish sunshine and warm Atlantic winds had swept away any lingering trace of adolescent spots, and scowls, and rolls of baby flesh, and the girl who took to the beach with her dog on that October morning (or was it perhaps September?) was truly a girl no longer. 'Trees that are late to blossom,' Martha Fishburne would say, 'often blossom best.' And Martha was a teacher, so she would know.

Charity Cloke was walking her dog along the strip of dry shingle that ran between the beach and the cliffs, just above the litter of seaweed discarded by the tide. The few autumn holidaymakers who might, on a warmer day, have ventured onto the sands were muffled up, walking the clifftops instead. The beach was all but deserted. To hear the stories now, you might believe that half the village was there, for many claim to have seen the man, or to have helped him away from the sea, but when you sort through the accounts, and when you listen carefully to who saw what, only five people, including Charity Cloke, can be said, beyond doubt, to have been there that day; six, if you include the naked man himself.

There was Kenny Kennet, the beachcomber. He was prowling the shingle at the east bay looking for mussels, and crabs, and flotsam, and driftwood. He would, if the finds were good, turn the driftwood into works of art he could sell to next summer's tourists. The mussels and the crabs he would cook up, and eat. And the flotsam – well – that would depend upon whatever he found.

Old Man Garrow the fisherman was there, but, as villagers would say, Old Man Garrow was *always* there. He would sit on a bench for much of the day when the weather was fine and the winds were low, his knitted hat pulled over his ears, and here he would smoke his pipe and gaze out across the waves, drawn by the swell of the waters and the slap of the salt spray and the call of the herring gulls; and here, perhaps, he would dream of the years when the ocean was his home.

Aminata Chikelu, the young nurse, was there. She worked the night shift at the cottage hospital in Treadangel, so the morning on Piran Sands was, in a sense, the *evening* of her day. Aminata would unwind, when the morning was fair, with a walk along the narrow path that hugged the coast. Here she could let the stresses of the night shift evaporate away. 'What do you *do* in the hospital at night?' people might ask; 'I watch sick people sleeping,' she would say. And so she did, out on her rounds with her dim torch and shoes that didn't squeak, checking the drips, and the drugs, and the pulses of her long-stay, elderly and (often) dying patients. Few of us live quite as intimately with death as nurses do; and the Cornish coast, Aminata would tell you, was one of the places where people *came* to die. There are worse places to live out your twilight years. But would you imagine, if you swapped your city home for a cheap retirement cottage by the sea, that one night you might exhale your final breath within the antiseptic confines of an overheated hospital ward, with no one to hold your hand or watch your parting but a willowy nurse from Senegal? And even for those possessed of sufficient imagination, it might be hard to picture a fairer face, or a softer voice, or warmer hands to ease their passing than those of Aminata Chikelu. She was blessed with the coffee-and-cream complexion that spoke of a cocktail of genes within her ancestry, a little bit of Africa and a little bit of Europe, and a little bit of who-knows-where; a hybrid confection that had favoured her with the perfect combination of features, dark sub-Saharan eyes, thick hair that she wore beribboned in braids, a slight Celtic nose, and a beguiling gypsy smile.

Last of all on the sands that day was Jeremy Melon the naturalist and writer. A lean and singular figure, Jeremy came to the cove, or so he would tell you, for *inspiration*. Sometimes he would set up an easel and daub at a canvas with watercolours, but this was never especially his thing. Words were his thing. Stories were his thing. More often he would pick his way across the bay at low tide, contemplating the creatures in the rock pools, imagining the stories of their lives. How curious it must be, he would think, to be a worm, or a fish, or a seashell, in a pool. At high tide your life would become a part of the great ocean that girdles the planet. You could come and go as you choose. You could sail out on a wave and float or swim to the beach at Port Nevis, or over the seas to Tahiti. Then the very next moment, the tide has abandoned you; the sea withdrawn; and now you occupy a fragile kettle of water with no refuge from the desiccating powers of the sun, or even from beachcombers such as Kenny Kennet who might scoop you into a bucket and fry you. One day, Jeremy Melon would think, he could write a story about this.

Six people then, and one dog; and one of the six was lying naked, face up, and looked to be drowned.

People would ask of Charity Cloke, 'was he as beautiful . . . you know . . . *down there*?' and they would flick their eyes suggestively downwards. What they meant, of course, was, 'was he as beautiful below the waist as he undoubtedly was above it?' And Charity Cloke would respond with a coy smile, and her honey cheeks would blush. 'I'm not telling,' she would say, and she would lift her eyebrows just so – happy to be possessor of such intimate information, but never inclined to share it.

Above the waist, the man on the sand would be said, by

many, to be beautiful. Cold from the sea, his flesh seemed translucent, his blue veins like a secret map beneath the pale paper of his skin, his hair strewn across his face like wet wheat after a storm. But what the villagers who mooted the subject with Charity Cloke already knew (because the rumours had clearly told them) was that the naked man had exhibited, on that day, a physiological phenomenon quite unusual for any man drawn from cold water. Dr Mallory Books would use the proper medical term when explaining this to Charity. The man from the sea, he would say, was 'priapic'. Very cold water, he told the young woman, can, in some circumstances, cause vasodilation. And vasodilation can result in the reaction that Charity Cloke observed. Don't worry, Dr Books told her, the tumescence was involuntary. 'These things don't last long,' he said. And sure enough, within minutes of his arrival at Dr Books's little surgery in Fish Street, the effect had receded, the man's erection subsided, and Miss Cloke's further blushes were spared.

You could, if you were a visitor to St Piran, piece together the sequence of events on Piran Sands and the village of St Piran that autumn day by overlaying the stories told by Charity Cloke and Kenny Kennet, and Jeremy Melon. You could add to these the reported accounts of Casey Limber the net-maker, and Dr Books, and Old Man Garrow. If you were to do this, you might, with some confidence, be able to unravel the true course of events on the day when everything started.

You could begin with Kenny Kennet, the beachcomber, picking among the rocks at the east end of the bay with his plastic sacks, his pond nets, his oddments of equipment. These were rocks he knew well. He had been scouring this cove, and a dozen others around the coast, for fragments of the sea's discarded treasures for ten or fifteen years now; since leaving school, if his account is to be believed. His hair, rarely cut, was dreadlocked, coiled and stiff, like strands of rope bleached by the salt and the wind; now that the days were growing cooler he held the unruly locks in place beneath a linen gendarme cap. He wore jeans from Oxfam rolled up to the knee, and a Guinness T-shirt, and a pointless cotton scarf. He was bent, prying mussels from a rock with a flat-bladed knife, when, on an impulse, he straightened up, scrambled a dozen feet or so up the headland and, from this commanding position, gazed out towards the sea.

What was he looking for? 'Nothing in particular,' he would say. This was simply something he did. He was hoping for drifting debris perhaps, for floats he might sell back to the lobstermen for the price of a glass of beer, or for scraps of net for Casey Limber.

What he saw, however, was the whale.

At first it might have been a dolphin. Or even a harbour seal. It slipped into view like a shadow beneath the waves, like the grey-green hulk of an ancient wreck, rolling slightly, sucking the sunlight from the water. It seemed to Kenny as if a hand had waved in front of the sun, sending a slice of darkness scudding along the deep. And then with barely a ripple, the leviathan sank, and was gone.

The water was dark and deep at the headland. Kenny Kennet knew that, but he'd never seen a dolphin quite this close to shore. He stared at the empty stretch of sea, reflecting on what he had, or hadn't, seen. It must have been a dolphin, he thought. Unless . . . unless perhaps it was a whale? There was a sheen now to the water where the giant shape had been, as if a thin film of glass had been left upon the sea. The beachcomber turned his face away to see if anyone else was there who might confirm his sighting. And, just a hundred yards or so away, was Charity and her poodle.

'Hey!' Kenny waved both arms. 'Hey.'

His cry caught the attention of Charity Cloke, and also of Aminata Chikelu, who was further up the shore, and of Jeremy Melon too, who was still exploring rock pools.

'Hey,' Kenny called again. 'I think I saw a whale!'

'A what?' shouted Charity. Jeremy and Aminata were too distant to join in the exchange.

'A whale.' Kenny made a beckoning gesture.

Charity Cloke broke into a run across the sand towards the headland. There were several spits of rock to negotiate.

'Quick!' Kenny could see the shape again, emerging slowly from the depths.

'I'm coming.' Charity used her hands to steady herself around a spear of barnacle-encrusted rock.

'Quick.'

In the ocean the leviathan was surfacing. The tide appeared to be rising with the beast, a waterfall of spume and foam was flooding from its flanks. Now it was a discernible shape, a striated barrage balloon flexing and rippling. Could it be a submarine? The thought struck Kenny, but in an instant the suggestion was dispelled as the great grey back of the cetacean surged above the surface, and with a monstrous snort a plume of water flew from its blowholes.

'Oh my God!'

A few yards from the shore Charity Cloke was screaming.

'It's all right,' called the beachcomber, his eyes transfixed by the whale. 'He isn't going to hurt you.'

But Charity wasn't screaming at the whale.

Later, Charity would say that it wasn't the man's nakedness that caused her to scream. Nor was it his prominent erection; his 'priapic state', as Dr Books had called it. 'It was just a shock,' she would say. 'I came around the rock, and there he was – lying there. I thought he was dead.'

The man on the beach may not have been dead, but he was certainly cold, and very still. Jeremy Melon was the second to arrive on the scene. If anything, Jeremy seemed even more shocked by the man's appearance than Charity had been. Then Kenny came down from his rock still flushed from his encounter with the whale.

'What the . . .?'

'I think he's dead,' said Charity.

Three people now stood looking at the body on the sand, and not one dared touch him. It was the terrible inertia of crisis that held them back. The immobility of indecision. It was a man . . . of course; his terrible tumescence was proof of that; but his skin was so white and so bruised with sand that at first, Charity had thought, he may have been a porpoise. Or a seal. Or a dead thing dredged up from the depths and deposited like debris on the beach.

'Who is he?' Kenny asked, as if knowing this might help.

'I've never seen him before,' said Charity.

Jeremy shook his head slowly. 'Me neither.'

'Should we . . .' Charity started.

'Do what?'

'Give him the . . . kiss of life?'

The pause was awkward. Neither of the two men seemed anxious to administer such a therapy.

'I'll do it,' said Jeremy, after a moment. He was sinking to his knees.

'No. I'll do it,' called a voice from behind. Aminata the nurse, glowing from her run across the beach, had arrived. She pushed between them and dropped to the sand. 'Hold his arms for me.'

They did as they were told. The castaway was cold and soaking wet; he hadn't been out of the water for long. Perhaps the surge-wave from the whale had driven him ashore.

'Get him onto his front. We have to empty his lungs.'

This was a team activity now. They flipped the body over, ignoring the impact this would have on his erection. Aminata thrust her palms down hard on his back. Water spluttered from his mouth. She pressed again. He seemed to choke.

'I think he's alive,' Aminata said. 'He didn't have much water in his lungs. Flip him back.'

Clumsily they turned him over.

'I think he's breathing,' Kenny said.

'Let's make sure.' The nurse squeezed shut the man's nostrils and closed her lips around his mouth, exhaling into his lungs. His chest rose, and then, as she released her hold, his chest fell. She blew again.

'He's definitely breathing,' Jeremy said.

'One more time.' Another lungful of warm Senegalese air expelled into the cold alveoli of the man who wasn't dead. And this time, as Aminata released Joe and his body fell slowly away, their lips seemed to separate reluctantly, like the desperate mouths of parting lovers.

'He's freezing,' said Charity.

'It's the cold that's kept him alive.' Aminata was peeling off her coat. 'But all the same, we have to warm him up. Let's put this on him.'

'Where did he come from?' Kenny asked.

'Does it matter? Here. Give me a hand.'

'He needs some . . . trousers,' said Charity. It was as close as she would get to referencing the man's condition.

'He's not having mine,' said Kenny.

'He can have mine.' Jeremy pulled his belt loose. 'Don't worry. I'm decent.'

'More decent than he is,' said Aminata.

They pulled Jeremy's trousers over the castaway's wet legs. Jeremy, in his windjacket and boxer shorts, surveyed their handiwork. 'Now,' he said, 'we'd better get him to Doctor Books.'

Old Man Garrow, sitting on his rock, tapping down the tobacco in his pipe, watched the foursome struggle to lift the man. At first each rescuer took a limb, dangling the stranger sack-like between them, but this proved cumbersome. They stopped and made a basket of their arms and slung the man between them. It wasn't elegant, but it was easier.

Garrow tapped his pipe on the rock. 'Did ee zee yon whale?' he asked, as they made their ponderous progress up the sands.

'I saw him,' said Kenny. 'He was as close to me as you are now.'

'Ees bad news,' said Garrow, rising heavily to his feet. He gave a deep and throaty cough. 'Ee shawn't be this close.'

'No,' said Kenny. 'Mr Garrow, we have to take this man to Doctor Books.'

'A whale in the cove, ees bad.'

'Yes,' said Kenny. 'We have to go.'

'Fishermen in't goin' to like it.'

'I don't suppose they will.'

'It wasn't a fish-eating whale, Mr Garrow,' said Jeremy. 'From what I could see, it was a fin whale.'

'A fin whale, is it?'

'They don't eat fish. It's a baleen whale.'

Aminata broke in. 'Mr Melon, much as we'd all like to stand around and discuss the biology of whales, I really think we need to get this man to the doctor.'

'Of course. Of course.'

The path along the beach at Piran Sands leads around the rocky headland and then turns immediately inland onto the great granite stones of St Piran village harbour. Here a pair of sea walls reach out like protective arms holding away the ocean from the unimposing strip of low whitewashed buildings that line the quay. It was around this headland that the rescue party stumbled with the body of the stranger suspended awkwardly between them. On the dockside they drew the attention of every villager with a view of the harbour. Casey Limber the net-maker was the first to spot them. He had been walking along the harbour wall in the direction of the beach when he came upon them. They were soon joined by Jessie Higgs the shopkeeper, and the fishermen Daniel and Samuel Robins, and the landlord of the Petrel Inn, Jacob Anderssen, and two of the girls who packed fish, and Captain O'Shea the harbour master, and Polly Hocking the vicar's wife and Martha Fishburne the teacher, and a dozen more if we are to believe the stories.

'Who is he?' was the cry from many, anxious that the body from the sea might be a lover, or a brother, or a cousin, or a son.

'We don't know,' Jeremy told them.

'A stranger then?'

'Indeed.'

Behind the stretcher party came Old Man Garrow, waving his walking stick in one hand, his pipe in the other. 'Eez an omen, I'm tellin' ee. Eez a bad sign.'

Eager for more information, the villagers settled upon Garrow. ''Twas a whale,' he told them, waving with great exaggeration. 'Ee came from the waters like a devil from the deep. Bigger'n a house ee was. Bigger'n a row of houses.'

This report was confusing. 'What are you talkin' about, Old Man Garrow?' someone said. 'That in't a whale. That's a man.'

'An 'ansum one,' said someone else. This may have been Polly Hocking, the vicar's wife.

''Twere a WHALE, I tell ee,' cried the old fisherman. 'I saw 'im. Ee come out the sea, and ee looked at me with 'is eye.'

This revelation was considered with suspicion by the crowd on the quay.

'You were nowhere near the whale,' offered Kenny Kennet, keen, now that the conversation had turned to the whale, to ensure that his own part in the events did not get overlooked. 'I was right next to him.'

'I saw ee as close as I see you,' said Garrow.

'Can we please get this man to the doctor?' said Aminata.

'Here, let me help.' This was young Casey Limber. He stepped in to relieve Charity of her share of the burden, but so strong were his arms that he lifted the unconscious man clear and carried him alone.

And so the crowd swept along the harbour keep, past the fishermen's houses that fronted the quay, into the narrow square, and up along a narrow cobbled street to the door of a terraced cottage. Many of the people who had joined the original four on the dockside attempted to follow them indoors. 'Are you ill?' demanded Jeremy of Mrs Penroth the lobsterman's wife. 'No? Then please stay outside.'

The door of the house in Fish Street closed behind them and the collective of interested bystanders were left in the road with their theories.

2
The teeniest tiniest toe

'A country is no more'n a body,' Martha Fishburne would say to the children in the Primary School at St Piran. 'Your big cities, they're the heart, and the lungs, and they're the brains. They're the eyes and the mouth and the ears. They do all the thinkin' and they do all the speakin'. Now your roads and your railways, out they run, and they're the arteries, and they're the veins, carryin' all the nourishment back to the cities. And all the towns and villages, well, they're the bones, they keep the country standin'. And the farms and the factories, they're the muscles; they do all the work. They do all the liftin' and all the carryin'.'

'And what about us?' the children would ask. 'What about St Piran?'

'Us is no more'n a tiny pimple on the tippety-tippetiest-tip of the teeniest tiniest toe,' Martha would tell them. 'Us is never visited, never seen, never even thought of.' She would fix the children from the oldest to the youngest with the sternest look she could summon. Then she would let her face break into a very wide smile. 'And that's just the way we likes it.'

It might be hard to explain to a stranger, exactly, or even approximately, where to find the village of St Piran. It lies beside the sea at the end of a headland, a tight clutch of narrow houses, balanced on the hillside, pressed up hard against the twist of the lane that cascades down the slope to the harbour. It's a small place, more a hamlet than a village, its face bent towards the wilderness of water, its back ever turned to the squat finger of land upon which it lies. There is only one road that leads down to the village. How could there be more? The same road, of course, leads back, and it is a route that is absurdly easy to miss. There was a signpost once, off the long road from Treadangel to Penzance, before a bad bend, and just over a hill. The sign read 'St Piran 3½ miles', but that, it appears, was a falsehood, for it was painted over to read 'St Piran 4 miles'. Another hand later amended this to 'St Piran 4¼'. Later still the sign disappeared altogether; stolen, some would say, for the scrap metal.

The loss of the road sign did not, as far as anyone could tell, have an impact on the village. Few even noticed it was missing. Only the hardiest holidaymakers would travel this far; most preferred the big surfing beaches of Newquay, or the quainter fishing ports of Looe, Mevagissey, or Fowey. Those who did make it all the way to St Piran, to rent one of the cottages up on the clifftop or to stay in the Bed-and-Breakfast with Hedra and Moses Penhallow – well, these folk were the determined ones. They would drive triumphantly onto the harbour and stumble exhausted from their cars, waving their map-books to evidence their success. 'We found you,' they would crow, 'we found you!'

For these intrepid visitors, the great achievement of the journey never appeared to have been the hours of motorway travel from wherever they might call home to the Channel coast at Exeter, or even the two and a half hours from Exeter to the toes of Cornwall. The highlight was the lane – the 4¼ miles of roadway that wound and coiled this way and the other from the Treadangel road to the sea. Could this really be the right road? The hedgerows are awfully high in this part of Cornwall, so just when you thought you'd crest the brow of a hill and see the village ahead, the lane would swoop down another dip, or swing around another bend. Not far from the start, the route narrows to a single track. Here, in the gateway of Bevis Magwith's farm, was the place where many a casual visitor would give up and turn around. For those who didn't, there would still be three miles to go without so much as a signpost, or a greeting, or the glimpse of a distant steeple.

No wonder, then, that the villagers of St Piran had long abandoned the hope of earning a living from passing tourists. Apart from the Penhallows' B&B overlooking the harbour, and the rocky little beach, and Kenny Kennet's dubious works of art, there was very little to attract them. Parking could be difficult; there were only six spaces in the Pay-and-Display car park on the quay, and many casual summer visitors would find themselves driving back up the lane to Treadangel without once getting out of the car. The village store sold little more than a basic selection of groceries; it had no room for postcards, or beachwear, or souvenirs. The Petrel Inn was dark and poky, and altogether uninviting. There were no boat tours, no crazy golf, no restaurants, not even a decent café. Hedra and Moses Penhallow would advertise 'Cream Teas and Coffees', but their front room contrived to look so unappealing, with its faded net curtains and cheap Italian ornaments, that even in the height of summer there were never many takers.

On the day when Kenny Kennet saw the whale, when the naked man appeared on Piran Sands, there was one solitary car in the Pay-and-Display car park. A white Mercedes coupé. It was locked. Jeremy Melon peered through the windows. 'Nothing,' he said to Polly Hocking, the vicar's wife.

'What are you looking for?'

'I'm not sure.' He straightened up. 'Something to indicate who might own it.'

'You think it might belong to him? The man from the beach?'

Jeremy nodded. 'How else did he get here?' he asked.

'Perhaps,' suggested Polly Hocking, who had a flair for the dramatic, 'he was washed off a ship.'

'Possibly.' Jeremy tried the boot. 'Or maybe he drove here early this morning, went for a walk, decided to take a swim, got caught by the tide . . .'

'Stark naked?'

'It isn't unheard of. Maybe he forgot his Speedos.'

'Should we call the police?'

'Perhaps,' said Jeremy. He turned away from Polly to look out over the harbour. 'But not yet. We should wait until he wakes up.'

'His parking ticket will run out soon,' Polly said.

Jeremy shrugged. 'When was the last time we had a traffic warden in St Piran?'

Over the end of the harbour wall where the breakwater starts, out of view of the village, Charity Cloke sat hard up against the stone, ignoring the dampness of the sand. Casey Limber sat alongside her. They avoided each other's gaze. Instead they focused on the heavy rolling waves, and the diving of the herring gulls.

Why had Casey Limber been out by the headland that morning? He had no reason to be there, unless perhaps he was out looking for Charity Cloke – and there are some who say he was, although Casey denies it to this day. Some say that the net-maker was *following* Charity, but that sounds like stalking. The fair explanation might be that Casey was hoping for a chance encounter with Charity. Perhaps they would come upon one another in the secluded cove, and there he might politely raise his hat and issue a cheerful 'hullo'. They might talk, and one thing might lead to another, and who knows where these things might take them? For these are, indeed, the kind of plans that young men lay for girls, especially for late blossomers, and those as fair as Charity Cloke. And as things happened, the chance encounter did come about; and while it wasn't quite the rendezvous that Casey might have planned or imagined, one thing did eventually lead to another, and the outcome for Casey (and for Charity as well) might fairly be described as positive. We make our own luck, as Martha Fishburne would say.

'What a strange day,' said Casey. He felt so close to Charity that he imagined he could hear her heartbeat.

What goes on in the mind of a girl like Charity Cloke?

Casey might have wished he could read her thoughts, or at the very least decipher her expression.

'Let's go for a walk,' he had said as they left the doctor's house in Fish Street, and instead of dropping her gaze and shaking her head as she might have done the day before, she had nodded. And so they trailed out along the quayside, her poodle in tow, and here they had ended up, watching the broken rhythm of waves and spray against the ancient rocks.

'Do you think he'll be all right?' Charity asked.

'We've done all we can. He's in good hands. If anyone can fix him, then Doctor Books can.'

'He's not a real doctor any more.'

'Of course he's a real doctor. He's just retired, that's all. Doesn't mean he won't know what to do.'

'Do you think they'll call the ambulance?'

'Perhaps.' Casey stretched his long legs out. 'Last time they called an ambulance out here was when Dorothy Restorick was having her baby.'

'I remember.' Charity smiled.

'It took four hours to get here.'

'Five – some say.'

'And by the time it came, the baby was weaned.'

They laughed, and for an instant turned their faces to catch each other's eyes.

He was older than she, but not by much. He came from Port Nevis in Roseland, and he'd mended nets in Mousehole, and he'd danced with girls on the beach in Newquay where the boys wear very little and the girls wear even less. Now he was living in St Piran all by himself, in the two small rooms over the harbour master's house. His father was still mending nets back home, but there wasn't call for two grown men to share the trade in one small village, so here was Casey Limber, let loose on St Piran, lean and tall like a young spruce, with dark Spanish eyebrows and a gentle way of talking.

'Have you ever seen a man like that before?' she asked him.

'Like what?' he said, mischief hidden in his words.

'Washed up, on a beach,' she said, but she couldn't hide her smile.

When he kissed her, it wasn't planned. It didn't happen because he'd edged too close, or snuck his arm around her. It was more like the swoop of a shearwater into the dark swell, like a magnetic pull, like gravity that toppled his body towards her and drew her face towards his. Had the unexpected vision of Priapus on the beach awoken something within her? Their lips met and when she inhaled it was the sweet smell of the net-maker that she drew into her lungs.

So little time had passed since the naked man arrived, since Kenny Kennet saw the whale. Yet already things had begun to change. Charity knew this, as she breathed in the essence of Casey Limber. She knew that if this were yesterday she wouldn't be falling beneath the tender branches of Casey Limber's spruce. She wouldn't be feeling the dampness of the sand all the way up the back of her pinafore. But yesterday wasn't today.

'All things must pass,' the Reverend Alvin Hocking would say. 'All things must pass away.'

In her imagination Charity saw the man again, so white and so bruised, so wet and so cold, his erection like a flagpole aimed towards the cliffs. 'Don't let it trouble you,' Dr Books had said. Did it trouble her? She didn't think so. She knew about the workings of the human body. She had a brother – all of fifteen – and she had seen him in every pose imaginable.

Although not, perhaps, in that one.

'All things must pass,' she whispered, as Casey Limber's tongue began to explore her lips.

He drew back and looked at her.

'Every day is a new one,' she said. 'I don't know if I really knew that before.'

'Of course it is,' he said, and he kissed her again.

'But this day is newer than new. We need another word to describe this day.'

'How about perfect?' he said.

'No, that isn't the right word.' She folded herself down onto the sand, the last of her resistance gone, and she kissed him back. 'But it will do.'

3

Always a good start

'The first thing you should know is, I'm not a proper doctor.'

He lay between crisp cotton sheets, dry now, and warm. His eyelids felt gummed together.

'That is to say, I *am* a proper doctor. Just not practising any more.'

He forced open his eyes, looking for the source of the words. He turned his head.

'Anything I do, I do as one human being to another. There's no contract. I'm not NHS. If you're unhappy with any of this then all you have to do is get up and walk out.'

In the corner of the room, by the doorway, stood an indistinct figure. The figure was talking.

'God knows you never retire when you live in a place like this. The chaps up at Truro keep telling me I should simply turn people away. One of these days, they say, some ungrateful blighter is going to sue me, and then where will we be, eh? In the poorhouse, I suppose. So of course I say I'll stop seeing patients. Then, the next thing I know, in comes some poor wretch with a nail through his foot, or a fish bone in his throat, and what am I supposed to do? What about the Hippocratic oath? Someone gets dragged in here, half-drowned and frozen – what then?'

The figure stopped talking for a moment to take a long and exaggerated drag on a short cigar. He blew out a lungful of smoke with a cough. 'So if you want a proper doctor you need to get your sorry arse out of that warm and comfortable bed and get yourself down to Truro where the doctors like or not will kill you.' He took another toke on his cigar. 'They usually do.'

Joe Haak blinked. Where was he? Whose bed was this? He tried to focus on the man who was speaking, but the effort made his eyes feel sore. He squeezed them shut.

'So what's it to be then? Take your chances here with the quack, or walk all the way up the lane for the three-twenty bus and hope you get to Truro before they all go home for the night?'

'Where am I?'

'Good question. Very good question. Do you want a map reference? Or will a postcode do?'

'A name would help.' He was trying to recall the events of yesterday. There had been a journey. A long one. He'd been in the water. His name had come out of a hat. What hat? He tried to lift himself up but his muscles felt absurdly weak.

'What, my name? Or the name of this godforsaken hamlet?' The doctor who wasn't a proper doctor took another puff of his cigar and then screwed what was left of the stub into a small glass dish. 'My name is Books. Mallory Books. I should say Doctor Books but if I did you might sue me.'

Joe's tongue felt unreasonably large in his mouth. 'Why should I sue you?' Could the doctor understand his words? They'd sounded to his own ears like 'why chewed I chew who'. He tried again to open his eyes. If he held them open just a slit, maybe they wouldn't sting so.

'Who knows?' The doctor clearly had an ear for difficult speech. 'For keeping you alive maybe? Not everyone welcomes this blessed state we call life.'

'Ah.' Joe sank back down onto the pillows. He was alive then. He felt an unexpected surge of relief at this thought. 'Have you . . . kept me alive? I mean . . . really?' Hab oo kebbed be alibe? I been weerly?

'Me and a few others. Seems you owe your life to a girl called

Charity, a nurse called Aminata, and some willing porters. All I did was keep you warm.'

'Thank you.' Joe closed his eyes again and felt for a moment as if he might be drifting. 'We've drawn lots,' a voice in his head was saying. 'And it's you, matey boy. It's you, matey boy.'

When he reopened his eyes the doctor had disappeared. He slept.

'I thought you might want something to eat.' Dr Books was back at his bedside. The room was darker now. 'Soup? Sit up. It'll do you good.'

'Thank you.' This time he sat up with less effort and his tongue seemed to have shrunk back to its normal size. 'Where am I?'

'Didn't we do that question?'

'Did we? I don't remember the answer.'

'Very few people do.' The doctor slid a tray onto the bed. Hot soup and a mug of tea.

Joe clutched at the tea and drank it in half a dozen gulps. How had he come to be so thirsty? He made a start on the soup. When he looked up, his eyes no longer stung. 'So, where am I?' he asked again.

The doctor lowered himself into a wing-backed chair. 'Tell you what,' he said, 'I'll trade you an answer to that question for an answer to one of mine.'

'OK.'

'What in God's sorry name were you doing down on the beach in nothing but your birthday suit? At this time of year?'

Birthday suit? Joe suddenly felt embarrassed. Stripping off had seemed almost natural at the time. Daring perhaps, but hardly shocking. The sea had been dark and the beach deserted. He had felt the shock of the bitter cold water. 'I'm not really sure.'

'Then why don't we try this one. Who are you? Where are you from?'

'We've drawn your name out of the hat, matey boy,' said the voice in his head. 'You're taking the fall.'

He felt his heartbeat rising.

'Who are you?' asked the doctor again.

'Who am I?' he echoed faintly. Did he even want to answer that question? 'The police have tracked the man down to a small village in Cornwall,' a news reporter was saying in his mind. 'He gave himself away when he revealed his real name to a doctor who immediately informed the authorities.'

'What's your name?' The doctor reached into the inside of his jacket and drew out an old-fashioned pen and a small leather-bound notebook. 'I'll write it down.'

'Do I have to answer?'

'Always a good start,' said the doctor. 'They taught me that in medical school. Establish the identity of your patient. Not that you are my patient, of course. I'm just an ordinary citizen doing you a favour. So . . . name?'

How easy it would be to give his name. It was just a name. A simple combination of letters. A 'J', an 'O', an 'E'. He could say his name, and then perhaps it would all be over.

'This is the easy question. They get harder.' The doctor tapped his notebook with his pen. 'You are, at least, English. Or should I say British? One of the chaps thought you might be a foreigner, fallen off an oil tanker or something.'

'An oil tanker?'

'Or something, but you're not. So . . . name?'

He tried to stutter something, but failed. His tongue seemed to be swelling again. He could invent a name, of course, but that would require imagination.

'You don't know your own name?' There was a trace of impatience in this.

What would be a good name? John Smith? Far too obvious, even though there had been two John Smiths at the bank where he worked. How, he wondered, would they fare in these circumstances? Would they need to invent a more realistic name? But thinking about that wasn't helping his predicament. The name Merkin Muffley popped into his mind; but would the doctor recognise the film reference? Possibly. Surely there were other names? Perhaps it was the trauma that had sealed off his mind. But it might equally have been discomfort with the very idea of dissembling. Joe Haak wasn't an untruthful young man and dishonesty wasn't in his nature. This may have been a residue from the Danish Lutheran values imparted by his father. Or the more gentle English hippy creed that he'd learned from his mother. But either way, a mental censor had intervened. Joe found himself shaking his head.

'Do you know where you come from?'

Where do any of us come from? The subject required some thought. If he couldn't lie to this doctor, perhaps he could close his eyes and wait for the questions to pass.

The doctor set down his pen with a sigh. 'Amnesia then? Is that what this is?'

Amnesia would be blissful. You're taking the fall, matey boy. How wonderful never to recall those words. 'Amnesia?' he echoed.

But the doctor took his reply as an assertion. 'Amnesia. I see. Well, let me tell you something, Mr Jason Bourne, or whoever you want to pretend to be. You've read too many books; seen too many films. Amnesia is an invention of fiction writers. It doesn't exist – not in the sense that you think it does. No one ever wakes up forgetting their own name. If they do, they're lying. Serious brain damage can do very nasty things to a man's memory, but apart from a few cuts and bruises, your body and brain seem to be happily intact. I don't for one minute believe you have amnesia, Mr Naked-Surfing-Man or whoever you are. So I'm about to ask you the question again.' Dr Books made a snorting noise and took up his pen. 'Are we ready?'

Joe reopened his eyes.

'Shall we start with a simple yes-no question? Do you know your name?'

Joe nodded, very slowly.

'Excellent. Are you going to tell me?'

'I suppose I shall have to.'

'Good,' the doctor said. 'Please don't play any more games with me if you want to keep on enjoying my soup. Is that your car in the Pay-and-Display car park? The white one?'

'Yes.'

'Where are the keys?'

'I don't know. At the bottom of the sea somewhere. In the belly of the whale. Who knows?'

Books gave a chuckle. 'So there *was* a whale! And we all thought Kenny had made it up.' He lifted himself out of his seat.

'Joe. My name is Joe.' He held out a hand and the doctor took it.

'Delighted to make your acquaintance, Joe. Are you going to tell me where you're from? Or what you were doing down on the beach?'

Joe gave a long sigh. 'Did they teach you that at medical school as well?' he asked. 'Do you need to know everything? Are we to have no secrets?'

'To be honest,' said Books, 'I can barely remember anything they taught me at medical school. It was all so long ago.' He wrote down the name 'Joe' in his notebook. 'Is there any point asking for a surname? No? Very well. I can't call you "Joe Doe" because that would sound stupid. "Joe Soap" will have to do.' He wrote this down and then snapped the book shut. 'This may turn out to be the shortest medical note I've ever recorded.' He collected up the soup plate and the mug. 'You are a guest in my house,' he said. 'Tonight is on me. From tomorrow I will start to charge, ten pounds a day. Soup will not be included. Neither will tea. Do we have an understanding?'

'Yes,' said Joe, nodding gently. 'I think we do.'

'I have some clothes that no longer fit me. I shall bring them down for you.'

'Thank you.'

A comfortable pause settled upon them. 'The City,' Joe said, after a while.

'What?'

'You asked where I came from. I'm from the City.'

'Penzance?' the doctor asked.

This made Joe laugh. 'No. The City of London.'

'Ahh. That City.'

'And my name is Haak. Joe Haak.'

'I see.' Dr Books left the room, but then he was back. 'I could run to some rice pudding,' he said. 'From a tin.'

'That would be lovely.'

4

It's a bloody fin whale

As he stepped out from the doctor's house on the grey autumn morning after his unconventional arrival in St Piran, Joe could already feel a dissonance about the place. There was, it seemed to him, a discomforting misalignment in reality in this village – like a variation in gravity, or a change in the composition of atmospheric gases. Perhaps the brief coma from which he had emerged had unsettled the balance centres in his brain. Leaving the house felt like his first foray into an alien world. How curious, Joe thought, that a location should possess a *feel*. He had heard architects discussing a *sense of place*, as if there were some alchemy in the soil, or a confluence of ley-lines that could endow a site with mystical properties. A sort of geographic feng-shui. The idea had always struck Joe as unlikely, but something about this village seemed to confirm such beliefs. It nestled so comfortably in the crook of the hill-side, the winding streets and granite walls echoing the natural contours of the rock cliffs beyond. Indeed, it might be hard to imagine this bay without the village, as if these low walls and slate roofs were part of the local geology, features hewn out of the rock face by the sea and the wind.

Just a short distance away from the doctor's front door, and already Joe's internal compass was trying to come to terms with this new place. There was no road noise. No hum from a thousand engines, no grinding gears, no horns. Yet it wasn't silent. Seagulls brayed high on the rooftops, aerial sentinels marking out the landscape with their cries. There was the sound of the ocean, the heaving swell and motion of water and wind. A rope and canvas were flapping somewhere, slap-slapping with the breeze. He inhaled and there were the familiar Atlantic smells of salty air, wet sand, seaweed and fish scales. If ever there were a recipe to dissolve anxiety from the bones, this village seemed to possess it. He turned to walk down the hill. Something was stirring within his bloodstream. He felt an urge to explore, to walk down to the seashore, to feel the crunch of shingle beneath his feet. Maybe he could find his clothes, his wallet, his car keys. Maybe he could seek out the spot where he had walked so stubbornly into the cold waves.

It all looked so different in daylight. The only view he had had of this village had been cast in the monochrome glow of his headlights. St Piran had loomed into sight at the end of a tortuously winding lane, and not a light had been shining from the grey row of houses that had greeted him. There was no further he could drive. He had pulled up on the quay at a quarter to five in the morning and had sat for a while, listening to the sounds of the sea, breathing in the same aromas as he was breathing now. Yet how desolate and friendless it had appeared then. St Piran had felt, on that first encounter, like the condensation of despair into stone, the furthest-flung outpost of an empire of melancholy. The granite rocks along the wharf seemed as friendless and abandoned as he was. But today there were colours and textures; there were lime-washed walls and trails of moss along the stones, yellow lichens in the pointing, and pale blue front doors. He walked down the street into a small square. The weather wasn't especially kind today. There was a stiff wind and the first cold lashings of a winter squall. The sky was as grey as a battleship. But someone in the square called out a cheerful 'hullo', and Joe turned his head instinctively in case the greeting had been intended for him. A square-faced woman in an apron had emerged from a narrow shop and was offering him a smile.

'Good morning.'

There is something infectious about a smile, and Joe found

his own expression lightening. They would all be at work now, he thought. His colleagues. Neatly arrayed in rows at their desks, hunched over computer screens, or barking commands into telephones. If there was still work to be done. If the doors hadn't been locked on them, if the building wasn't swarming with accountants and regulators and policemen. Either way his name would be common currency by now, even among people he had never met. Maybe even here, he thought. Maybe the news had reached this village before he did.

Around the corner from the square was the harbour, and there was his car, sitting alone in a small car park. He walked towards it and tried the door. Locked. Never mind. Where would he drive to, even if he could? Lying low felt like the best strategy. So now might be a good time, he thought, to make some plans. He could walk around the end of the wharf to the beach, and there, perhaps, he could clear his head and work out what to do next.

But even this plan seemed to elude him today.

A woman bustled past him, plump and cheerful in a floral dress. 'Good mornin', my 'ansum,' she said as she passed.

'Good morning.' He turned to watch her go. Her face had been rosy and weathered. She had nodded at him as if she knew him.

Could desolation be so short-lived? Could a greeting from a stranger be sufficient to lift his spirits from the dark foreboding he had experienced when he first stepped onto this quay? Joe inhaled deeply. He had some thinking to do. In a perfect world he would be furnished with a whiteboard and a selection of coloured pens. He would have an Americano coffee and a choice of pastries. He could start to list the issues at the top of the board, and work down with options and arrows. He could write up the question '*How much trouble am I in?*' Beneath that an arrow would lead to 'massive trouble' and an alternative arrow to 'moderate trouble' and then an option box – go left for 'turn yourself in to the police' or go right for 'run!'

Or was he fleeing from ghosts? Were they phantoms entirely of his own imagination?

Along the headland the pathway snaked around an outcrop of rocks then gave way to sand and shingle. This was the beach. He had discovered it in darkness, had sat on the damp shore watching the first glow of sunrise. At dawn, compelled by a sudden desire, he had stripped off his clothes and walked into the sea. The sharp pain of the cold Atlantic waters had been almost cathartic.

The cliffs afforded very little shelter against the wind that was blowing up the beach, and the sea spray made the rocks slippery underfoot. Joe pulled the doctor's old duffel coat tighter around his middle and lifted up the hood. There was no one on the beach, as far as he could see, apart from a beachcomber bent over the rocks, wrapped in a fisherman's coat and sou'wester against the inclement winds. Joe walked down towards the tideline and skirted around the long spit of rocks that ran out into the sea. They were hard to climb, slippery and salty. He tried to remember where he had left his clothes, but nowhere looked familiar in the daylight. The rain and the spindrift were in his eyes. The sea was as grey as iron.

And then something caught his eye, in among the rocks, further up the shore. It looked like a column of spume rising from a patch of water very close to the tideline. He slid clumsily down the rocks and made off along the beach. A memory was stirring within him. Surely it couldn't be there? Right off the sands? Was the water deep enough for a whale?

Then there it was, unfeasibly large, thrashing in the shallows, smacking the surface with its colossal tail.

The beachcomber had seen it too. He was running towards Joe, his arms waving.

Joe broke into a run. The whale was partly in the water and partly out, submerged halfway up its girth, twisting and splashing in the foam. Black and grey it was, striped with white, and scarred all the way down its flank like a survivor of a great battle. A murky film of red ran through the water; blood from an injury perhaps.

'What in God's name is it?'

The beachcomber in the yellow sou'wester had stopped, transfixed, a few short paces behind him. 'It's a whale. A bloody great fin whale.'

A high wave was rolling in towards the beach. As it caught the whale, the beast batted its tail against the swell and, like a huge corrugated barrel, it came scudding head first out of the water and up the sand.

'Look out!' Joe found himself scrabbling backwards up the shingle. 'It's going to beach!'

The ocean wave that had surged onto the shore now sucked away back down the sands and the whale was abandoned, head and front flippers beached, its tail still waving in the water.

'Oh shit!' the beachcomber shouted. 'Oh, sweet Jesus. The bloody thing's beached.'

It was to his credit that Kenny Kennet, who lived from the gleanings of the seashore, did not react to this whale as an economic gift from the deeps. Instead his only instinct appeared to be to protect the beast, to shepherd it safely back into the water.

Yet there was something fearful about the whale, still alive, still breathing, huge and dangerous. It could roll and crush a man in a moment.

'We have to help it,' Joe said. 'We have to help it back into the water.'

Kenny was looking at him strangely. 'I know you.'

'You do?'

'I carried you from the beach just yesterday. We found you over there.' He nodded in the direction of the east cliffs. 'We thought you were dead.'

'You saved my life then?' said Joe.

'In a manner,' said Kenny. Just as it was not in the character of the beachcomber to see profit in the whale, nor did he appear to seek anything from this stranger.

'Thank you.' Joe turned his attention back to the floundering creature on the sands. 'We need to do something. We can't just leave it here.' Yet even as he spoke these words, Joe could feel a sense of helplessness enveloping him. What could anyone do for a beast this large? 'I'll stay here with it. You go and get help.'

Kenny was hesitating. A great judder came from the lungs of the beast and a blurt of spray from the blowhole, and the creature's body seemed to sag a little lower on the sand. 'You go,' Kenny said. 'They'll more'n likely believe you. Me, they'll think it's one of my stories. They know me too well.'

Joe seemed to be equivocating.

'Go,' Kenny urged. 'Go on.' It was something like a command.

'It's no good. We'd need an army,' Joe said. 'It will take at least fifty men to move this whale – a hundred maybe.'

'You'll find them in the village. Go quick. The tide's going to turn in about thirty minutes.'

A sudden gust of wind brought a high wave rolling up the beach and both men had to scramble back. For a brief moment the situation looked promising for the whale. The beast appeared to lift slightly as the surge caught it, but if anything, the wake left it even further up the beach. As it settled, its great head turned slightly, dropping down towards one side, and Joe found himself looking into its eye. A dreadful message of hopelessness seemed to emanate from the heart of the animal itself.

Did Joe Haak recognise its feeling of desperation? Did he reflect that, even for a whale, desolation might be short-lived? When Jeremy Melon spoke at the Festival of the Whale, years after these events happened, he would touch on this moment in Joe's life. Jeremy would cast it as a tipping point, one of those rare instants when the decisions a person makes can determine the direction of their lives from that moment on. 'Most of life,'

Jeremy would say, 'is like driving on a motorway. We have no choice but to keep moving forward. The only control we have is over the speed of travel. But every now and then we pass an exit. We have just an instant to decide. Stay on the highway and nothing will change. Or turn off and find yourself in an unfamiliar town. Over the course of just a few days,' Jeremy would say, 'Joe Haak would turn off the highway several times. He would walk away from his bank. He would walk into the sea. He would make the decision to rescue the whale. Joe was not a procrastinator,' Jeremy Melon said. 'Joe was the kind of man who made choices. He made choices and he lived with the consequences.'

Was it as simple as that? In the case of the whale, some credit must be due to Kenny Kennet, who urged Joe on. Yet at that moment of vacillation, facing the forbidding prospect of raising an army from behind the closed doors of a strange town, Joe looked into the eye of the fin whale. There is not so much that separates us, Joe thought. We are both mammals. We breathe the same air. We enter this world through a bloody birth canal, we struggle to cling on to this fragile, ephemeral moment of magic called life. And then one day we exit. We could both have gone the same way, Joe thought. On this same stretch of sand.

'I'll go,' Joe said.

5

A dead fish already

Polly Hocking, the vicar's wife, would say that the first startling thing she would remember from that autumn morning was the sight of a young man in a duffel coat (that was several sizes too large) tearing down the quay towards the village, flailing his arms like a madman. The thin sound of his calls was almost completely whipped away by the wind, but he was clearly shouting nonetheless. He grabbed at the shoulders of the first person he passed, who as chance would have it was Old Man Garrow, and Polly could see an animated conversation taking place with a great deal of pointing. Then the young man turned and ran on. Old Man Garrow, with an uncharacteristic turn of speed, made off up the quay towards the headland without once looking back.

'Whatever is going on out there?' Polly asked.

She was in the little café, the front room of the Harbour Bed and Breakfast owned and run by Hedra and Moses Penhallow. She was taking tea with Demelza Trevarrick. Tea was a safer option than coffee in the Harbour B&B.

'My dear, it'll just be a tourist who has lost his dog, or some such.' Demelza was a writer of romantic novels. To her there was no particular drama if a holidaymaker happened to wave his arms around on the quay. She stirred sugar dreamily into her tea.

'He seems to be in quite a state.' Polly stood up to get a better view through the window.

'He's young – like you. The young are always in a hurry.'

'I'm never in a hurry.'

'My dear, of course you are. You were married at seventeen. If that isn't impetuous I don't know what is.'

'He's heading this way.'

Demelza straightened her hair. 'I'm not going outside to look for a dog in this weather,' she said.

The young man had caught up with Daniel and Samuel Robins. Polly and Demelza watched them through the window. There was more waving and pointing, and then the two fishermen also set off at a run in the same direction.

'Could there be a fire or something?' Polly asked.

'On the beach? There's nothing to burn.'

'Well, there's something exciting them all. Do you think it might be a shipwreck?'

'Darling, it'll be nothing. Nothing whatsoever. Boys just get excited.' Demelza Trevarrick had lived sufficient years in St Piran to understand that the tranquillity of the village was almost geological in its permanence.

'I do believe it's the young man we found on the beach,' Polly said.

'My dear? I didn't know it was *you* who found him.'

'You know what I mean.'

The door of the café burst open and the man was standing there sodden, windswept, and badly out of breath. 'I could do with your help, ladies,' he said.

'My dear! And we haven't even been introduced.'

'We need a hundred people,' Joe said. 'There's a whale on the beach.'

'Good gracious!' Demelza was rising slowly to her feet. 'You'll be lucky to find twenty. This isn't Penzance, you know.'

Alerted by the commotion, Moses Penhallow, red-faced and wheezing, emerged from the kitchen in his apron. 'A whale?' he snorted, when all had been explained. 'It won't be a whale. A porpoise maybe.'

'Whatever it is, we need your help.' Joe was already out of the door. 'Is there a church bell in the village?' he called back over his shoulder. 'Or a klaxon?'

'They don't ring the church bells any more. They're unsafe.

Go and see the harbour master.' Polly Hocking pointed up to the cottage on the cliff edge. 'He'll send up a rocket.'

'Thanks.'

'We'll round up more people.'

St Piran isn't a large community. The population, Dr Mallory Books had confidently informed Joe, was three hundred and seven. 'The winter population,' he had said. 'Three hundred and eight,' Joe had replied with a smile. That was yesterday. Today the prospect of coaxing enough of those souls from their homes on a miserably inclement day did not seem encouraging. Joe took the stone steps up to the harbour master's cottage two at a time.

Captain Abel O'Shea was hard of hearing. They would say, in St Piran, that he was deaf. 'Deafer'n a nail,' Martha Fishburne would tell Joe some days later. The old harbour master stood in the doorway of his cottage like a sentinel while Joe repeated the story.

'A what?' he said when the young man had finished.

'A whale.'

'A wheel?'

'No, not a wheel. A whale! A bloody great whale.' Joe held his arms out wide to illustrate the size.

A young man came bounding down the stairs inside the cottage. He had, it seemed, heard most of the exchange. 'He wants you to send up the rocket, Captain.'

'The what?'

'I'll do it.' The young man reached past the harbour master and held out his hand. 'I'm Casey Limber.'

'You're one of the people who rescued me?'

'I carried you – just a short way.'

'Thank you.'

'You won't understand this, but it should be me thanking you.' Casey grinned. 'I'll explain when you have time for a beer in the Petrel. Meantimes I'll send up the rocket.'

'Thanks.'

'That's where they pack the fish.' Casey pointed to a warehouse on the harbour edge. 'There'll be a couple of girls in there. Then try the school.'

'The school?'

Casey pointed. 'Get Martha to send word to all the parents. It'll be the quickest way.'

'OK.'

If you were to take, let us say, a young denizen of a large capital city, and set him loose in a hamlet of three hundred or so souls – especially a forcibly isolated place such as St Piran on the tippetiest tip of the teeniest toe of the country – well, you might expect some natural distrust to betray itself in the community. You might anticipate some animus, some hostility even. The face of a stranger might stir up feelings of dissension. You might forecast a general reluctance to comply with his undertakings. If you were to set the city boy loose with an urgent instruction – for example, to recruit one hundred volunteers for an enterprise that most would find fanciful in the extreme, such as rescuing a whale on a day when the wind was high and rain unrelenting – you might not wager on any great success. Yet there was, from the first moment, something about the young man in the duffel coat that seemed to neutralise any opposition. Perhaps it was the freshness of his face, the youthful way that he ran from house to house, the insistent manner in which he made his case. Martha Fishburne, the teacher, would say it was his smile. Polly Hocking, the vicar's young wife, would talk about his eyes. Jessie Higgs at the village shop would recall the boyish way he came bounding through the door and fixed her with an imploring look. 'He was a self-assured young man,' Jeremy Melon would say. 'Dashingly handsome, but seemingly unaware of it.' To the inhabitants of St Piran, Joe Haak had a confidence that belied his years. His eyes shone with an intensity – and an intelligence – that disarmed the small community. As the whoosh and bang of the maroon rang around the little cluster of buildings that called itself a village, a retinue of local people was already setting off towards the headland. The recruitment process that began with one arm-waving man had, in just a few minutes, transformed into a cascade. Residents ran home and knocked on doors. In a very short time men and women in waterproof coats and sensible footwear were spilling out of the houses all the way up Harbour Hill and Fish Street and from the bungalows on East Cliff Way. 'It was a matter of critical mass,' Joe would later explain to Mallory Books. 'Like the way that one particle in an explosion will set off two more, and those two set off four, and then you have an exponential flood of particles in no time at all.'

On the beach, Kenny Kennet was worried about the whale. Its body seemed to have shrunk since the beaching, or at least flattened under the weight of its own blubber. It had stopped its quivering and thrashing and now lay motionless, resigned to immobility on the sand. The tide was almost at the turn. The beachcomber had a small hand-spade among the tools of his trade. He started to scoop away the sand. It wasn't easy. Each wave would undo his work, but perhaps, Kenny thought, if he could allow more water underneath the whale, this might help it to slide back down the beach.

Old Man Garrow was the first on the scene, his walking stick abandoned. 'Eez no way you can 'elp 'im,' he called to Kenny. 'Oive seen this before. Eez a dead fish already.'

If anything, this information seemed to make the beachcomber dig faster. 'He in't a fish.'

'Well, whatever ee is, eez a dead'un.'

'Help me shift this sand.' Kenny flung a bucket at the old fisherman. 'If we can dig underneath him, maybe we can float him out.'

'Float 'im out, is it?' said Garrow, but he sank to his knees by the very flanks of the whale and started to scoop handfuls of sand into the bucket. ''Twon't work, I tell ee.'

As if in response the whale gave a shudder, and a ripple rolled down the length of its side.

''Twon't work.'

The villagers started to appear. In twos and threes they came, in family groups, the young and the old. Dr Mallory Books was there in an old tweed coat. Demelza Trevarrick, aloof, with a cigarette in a silver holder, looking for material, perhaps, for her next romantic novel. The girls from the fish packers glad of the interruption; the boys from the boats happy to be part of an adventure. The Magwith boys from the farm were there, half a dozen wives from the houses at the top of Harbour Hill, Dorothy Restorick with her baby in a pushchair, Martha Fishburne the teacher, plump and fresh-faced with half a dozen primary school children in tow, Jacob and Romer Anderssen from the Petrel Inn; there were fishermen and farmhands, the employed and the unemployed and the long since retired. The vicar, Alvin Hocking, was there, along with his young wife Polly, and Charity Cloke, and Casey Limber, and the deaf harbour master, and the B&B owners, and Jessie Higgs from the shop, and the Shaunessy boys who did the milk round and delivered fish to the cannery, and Jeremy Melon the writer and naturalist, and the local plumbers, and decorators, and Aminata Chikelu the nurse, experiencing a second successive surreal end to her working day.

After a while it might have been easier to list those from the village who weren't there that morning. There were some who worked away – in Treadangel or Penzance, teenagers away at the high school, some who were simply too old or infirm, and just a very few who missed the commotion altogether. The rest of the village of St Piran, it seems, had taken themselves off to the cove. And if anyone had chosen just that time to visit, to brave the 4¼-mile track from the main road, well, they would have found a ghost town; doors shut fast, businesses abandoned, as if a hurricane had swept through and relieved the place of its population. Which, in a sense, it had.

6

No one could have pulled that hard

'The fin whale,' Jeremy Melon would tell the crowded public bar at the Petrel Inn that night, 'is the second-longest whale in the world. The only whale that is longer is the blue whale; and the blue whale is the biggest animal that has ever lived. Ever.' Ale made Jeremy Melon eloquent. 'You will find the fin whale in every ocean on the planet,' he told his fellow drinkers. 'From the cold waters of the Arctic, to the great Southern Ocean, and everywhere in between.'

'Even here in St Piran,' someone would quip. 'Even on land.' This caused laughter.

As the crowds had arrived on Piran Sands, there was a danger, just for a while, that the whole event might turn into a carnival. The rain, miraculously, stopped. No one in the melee had seen a whale before – at least, not at such close quarters – and no one knew quite what they should do, or even what they were supposed to *try* to do. Kenny Kennet, faced with the familiar faces of his home town, had found his grasp on leadership slipping away. Some of the boys were trying to push the whale. Others were digging at the sand. Most were standing awestruck, frozen by indecision. There was a cacophony of vacillation.

'Wait. STOP! Everybody stop.' Joe found himself issuing the cry.

From anyone else this call might have become engulfed in the general frenzy of instruction and counter-command, but this was the voice of the stranger. It was an unfamiliar voice.

'We won't achieve anything if we're all working on different things. We have to work together.'

There was a murmur of assent.

'Does anyone know exactly what time high tide will be?'

'Twelve minutes,' came a confident voice.

'So this is what we're going to do,' Joe said. 'We're all going to dig for seven minutes. We're going to get as much water as we can underneath her belly. That way she'll slide better. Then in seven minutes' time we're all going to heave together in time with the waves. We're going to lift her out. OK? Will someone volunteer to be timekeeper?'

'I will!' One of the schoolboys with a watch.

'Shout every minute until we get to seven,' Joe said. 'Are we all ready? Then DIG!'

A pack of willing hands surrounded the whale. On hands and knees they started to widen out the trench.

'Does anyone have any ropes?' Joe called. 'Fetch them. Quick! You have seven minutes. Tarpaulins too, if you can find any.'

Several boys sprinted off in the direction of the village.

Joe fell to his knees to help with the digging. The flank of the whale rose dangerously up above them, like a rock face pitted with barnacles and engraved with a pattern of deep parallel stripes that ran from nose to tail. The position should have felt perilous, but somehow it didn't. Joe scooped a double handful of sand from beneath the creature's belly, and flung it behind him, then another. The effort seemed pitiful. One of the farm boys was digging alongside him. Together they scrabbled at the sand like rabbits at work on a burrow. With each new wave the sea would coil, cold and promising, into the space; but all the same there was a sense of futility about the enterprise. How could they ever hope to float out an animal this big?

'Six minutes,' called the timekeeper obligingly. As if in recognition of the hopeless nature of the task, the whale issued another shudder and a snort from its blowholes, and the communion of diggers gave a chorus of cries.

The water was cold, and hands were inadequate tools. By the

time the five-minute call had sounded Joe's fingers were sore, but the villagers kept on digging. There was a terrible sense of urgency now, of desperation even.

'Urge them on,' said Kenny to Joe in a whisper. 'They like you.'

'Keep digging, everyone!' It seemed a cruel exhortation with his own hands so reluctant to dig. But all the way down the long flank of the whale, a column of kneeling villagers obeyed.

Demelza Trevarrick was one of the few still standing. She was talking to the whale. 'Be strong,' Joe could hear her saying. She was stroking its face. 'We'll get you out.'

'I doubt if he can hear you,' a man said. Joe would learn that this was Jeremy Melon. 'Its ears won't be tuned for sounds in air. All it can hear are underwater vibrations.'

'He can hear my vibrations, can't you, my lover?' Demelza addressed the whale.

'No, he can't.'

'I'm calming him down.'

'You're doing a very good job,' said Joe, not wanting to foment a revolt.

'Four minutes.'

It looked just possible that a shallow channel of water might be filling up beneath the colossal beast. It could never be enough to float it, but it might just create a slipway down the slope to the sea.

'We're getting there,' shouted Joe with excitement in his voice. 'Keep digging.' He rose to his feet and scuttled around to the far side of the whale to inspect the progress; there another line of willing diggers, more flying sand and shingle. If anything, this side was deeper.

'This side is doing brilliantly!' he called. His hands were numb as he dropped to dig some more.

Three minutes.

Two.

'Look out!' A full wave washed all the way up the beach and over the top of the channel, catching the diggers unawares. The whale wobbled alarmingly.

Joe made a decision. They could wait no longer. 'Everybody stand up. We're going to push.'

There were no objections. Cold, exhausted, and very wet, the gaggle of helpers struggled to their feet. There was a distant cry. Around the headland path ran four of the village boys carrying a tangle of ropes and a large canvas sail.

'Good lads!'

The village had become a team. What followed was an almost miraculous example of human beings working together with all the precision of a colony of ants. No one required instruction. The potential of the canvas sail and the ropes had been grasped in an instant. Hands reached out and started to lash ropes onto the corners of the sail. It could have been rehearsed. The sail was draped over the breast of the whale and pulled down tight into the sandy channel.

'Grab hold of the ropes!'

They didn't need telling.

'Now HEAVE!' Like a single organism the villagers of St Piran threw their weight against the ropes. The sail drew tight around the whale.

'HEAVE. HEAVE.'

Could they be facing the dreadful prospect of failure after all their work? The whale refused to budge even an inch down the sand, its massive weight anchoring the front of its body completely on the beach.

'OK. We have to wait for a wave. Not just any wave. We have to wait for another big one. Everyone take the strain.'

There was a collective leaning on the ropes.

'Wait. Wait. Wait.' Joe tried to gauge the waves. 'Wait . . .'

'We should go on this next one,' someone called.

'No, not yet.' Joe had seen another, bigger wave behind. 'Don't pull – not yet.' He could see the wave starting its long break all along the shore. 'Wait for my command. Ready . . . Ready . . . HEEEEEAVE.'

They would say in the bar of the Petrel Inn that night that every person on the beach was invested at that moment with a superhuman strength. So often was the tale told in St Piran that one by one many of the villagers themselves came to believe it.

'It was like the way a mother can lift a tractor off her child,' said one of the Magwith boys.

'It was a miracle,' said Demelza Trevarrick.

'It isn't possible that we could have pulled that hard,' said Kenny Kennet. 'No one could have pulled that hard.'

And yet, somehow, they did.

There was a kind of hysteria in their strength. The first sign of movement from the whale fed the frenzy. Men strained so hard against the ropes that blood vessels stood out on necks and foreheads. (In the Petrel they would show each other their hands, burned from hauling on the ropes.) They cried out like a single creature, men and women alike. They gritted teeth and tested muscle and sinew as they leaned all their weight against the ropes. And all of a sudden, with a primordial shudder, the whale was sliding down the channel of water and the wake was up around their knees.

'One more pull!'

They heaved again, but now they had to follow the whale into the ocean. This time the cry became a cheer.

'Push!'

Joe had dropped the ropes, and now he was pushing the front of the whale with the flat of his cold hands. Its skin felt rough but warm to the touch. Dozens of hands joined his and the crowd surged around him to push.

Then all at once the water shelved away deeply, and the creature was afloat. A new cheer arose. For the whale, it was as if something had awoken it from an unexpected slumber. It began to roll.

'Everyone get back.'

The whale arched and twisted.

'Careful!'

Who would have thought a beast so big could move so fast? It seemed to sink beneath the water, and then, with a huge thrash of its tail, it turned, sending a fresh cascade of water up the beach.

'Mind out!'

One old man seemed transfixed by the great leviathan. Up to his waist in water, he stood unmoving as the whale spun round. The tail of the animal rose as if preparing for a slap of monumental force on the sea and the hapless figure of Old Man Garrow who stood beneath it; but then, with the gentleness of a circus dolphin, the whale checked its motion. Its tail glided down, and some would say that it caressed the old fisherman as he stood there, the flukes of its tail sliding softly down the old man's face.

Then, with a lurch, the whale slid into the dark waters of the cove.

They stood and watched. A wet, cold huddle of men and women and children, knee-high in the foam.

'Go for it,' someone shouted, and someone else gave a long whistle. The leviathan had sunk beneath the surface like a dark shadow. For a while they watched the cove, expecting perhaps that it might return. Then far out in the bay, way beyond the protection of the rocks, a fountain of spray erupted from behind the roll of a wave.

'Thar' she blows!' called Kenny Kennet. Somebody whooped, and Jeremy Melon started to clap, and pretty soon they were all applauding, their numb hands beating out the rhythm of celebration.

7
What do people die of?

'Did you read about the bank?' Joe asked Dr Books.

'Which bank?'

'Lane Kaufmann Investment Bank. Did it make the news?'

'What news?' asked Books. They were in the saloon bar of the Petrel Inn, each of them nursing a beer. Most of the crowd that had been there to celebrate the rescue of the whale had drifted back to their homes. A dozen or so remained. Joe sat at a table with the doctor, and Jeremy Melon, who was drinking glasses of merlot, and Demelza Trevarrick, who seemed like a fixture stretched out on a seat that should have accommodated three.

'He never watches the news,' said Jeremy. 'In fact he doesn't even have a television. And he never buys a paper.'

'Really?' Joe was surprised.

'Not a lot of point down here,' Books said gruffly. 'So some politician gets found in bed with some footballer. So what? After a while you realise that it's never going to affect us. And it isn't even interesting.'

'I saw the news,' said Jeremy. 'But nothing about any bank.'

'Did it go belly up?' said Books. 'They all seem to these days. Nothing's safe any more.'

'They needed us,' purred Demelza, caressing her Bloody Mary. 'We would have gotten them afloat.'

'By golly yes,' said Jeremy, rising up in his seat at the thought. 'We'd have dug a ruddy great channel and heaved them back into the sea.'

'It was my bank,' Joe said.

'Your bank?' asked Demelza, surprised. 'Did you *own* it, darling?'

'No, no.' Should he even have started this conversation? Joe took a mouthful of beer and reflected on the curious difference in perspective between London and St Piran. Wasn't there a continuous ribbon of tarmac connecting one to the other? Didn't the cold economic fall-out of one cause a dust storm in the other? When London sneezed, didn't this community at the very least cover its face? It seemed not. An event that had swept like a tsunami through the capital just forty-eight hours ago had caused barely a ripple here.

'It wasn't my bank. Not in *that* sense. I was an employee. I worked there.'

'That would explain the car, darling,' Demelza said.

'We used to have a bank in St Piran,' said Books. 'A long time ago, mind. It was a branch of Lloyds if I remember.'

'It would have been a retail bank,' Joe said. 'Not an investment bank.'

'Do you remember the chap who used to manage it?' said Jeremy. 'What became of him? Tall bloke from Truro?'

'Dreamy eyes,' said Demelza.

'Bad feet,' said Books. 'Problem with his arches.'

Joe nodded slowly. He took another sip of beer. 'Anyway,' he said, lamely. 'Lane Kaufmann. I used to work for them.'

'I always distrust institutions with two names,' offered Demelza. 'When you have two names, you have conflict. One partner always resents the other. I understand that, you see – I'm an observer of human nature. Two partners will never march in step. It goes against all natural instinct. In the end the hatred gets so great that either one of them might bring down a whole company just to spite the other.' She smiled. 'Like Dyer and Wilson.'

'The butchers in Treadangel?'

'You remember what happened to them?'

'Who could forget?'

Joe found himself tapping his empty glass on the table. 'Anyway,' he said, 'they went bust. So far as I know. Anyone want another?'

'I'll have one if you're buying,' said Jeremy.

'I'm buying, but Mallory's lending me the money.'

'Never one to say no,' said Books.

'My dear,' murmured Demelza, and she leaned suggestively towards Joe. 'I thought you'd never ask.'

Was this little foursome to become his coterie of friends in St Piran? Joe had barely been in the village for two days, but already he seemed to be settling into a niche of sorts. There might, he thought, have been a label on his forehead detailing the particulars of his new identity. He was the castaway who had washed up on the beach. He was the man who had rescued the whale. He was the lodger who lived with the doctor. He had drifted into the gravitational fields of Jeremy Melon and Demelza Trevarrick – both more than a dozen years his senior. Jeremy, in particular, had assumed a genial responsibility for his welfare. Perhaps his role in carrying Joe from the beach had afforded Jeremy a more proprietorial interest in the young man than the dozens who had helped with the rescue of the whale. After the incident with the whale was over, and most of the villagers had returned to their daily routines, Jeremy had walked Joe around the village pointing out the sites of interest (of which there were very few). They had shaken hands with dozens of people, and Joe had learned some of the names and forgotten many more. 'There'll be a celebration at the Petrel tonight,' Jeremy had confidently predicted, and sure enough, soon after sunset, the little inn had been heaving with villagers, crammed in shoulder to shoulder along the bar, all anxious to renew acquaintance with the young man who had choreographed the rescue, and to share their own stories from the beach. Jacob Anderssen, the landlord of the inn, a square-shouldered man with mutton-chop sideburns, had thrust a beer into Joe's hand as he'd entered the pub. 'This one's on the house, young man,' he'd exclaimed. So it was that Joe Haak, in the space of forty-eight hours, had transitioned from a desk-bound functionary in a dark corner of a City bank to hero in a tiny community hundreds of miles away.

Later, after the closing-time bell had sounded, Joe helped Mallory back up Fish Street to his house. The doctor may have been well into his retirement, but he seemed to have retained some capacity for ale. They stood in the little hallway on the flagstone floor and Joe helped the old man with his coat.

'You'll join me for a whisky,' Mallory Books said. It sounded more like a command than a request.

'Ought you to have another?'

The doctor made a theatrical expression of surprise. 'Are you concerned for my health?'

'Not especially. I just thought . . .'

'Well, you don't need to.' Books disappeared into his clinic room and re-emerged with a bottle and two glasses. 'Strictly on prescription only,' he said, leading the way into the living room. 'Clynelish,' he said. 'Sixteen years old. You'll like it.'

'I'm not much of a whisky drinker really.'

'Then you have a great deal more to learn than I feared.' Books popped out the cork and poured two generous measures. 'It's a North Highland malt. Just about as far from here as you can drive before getting your tyres wet.'

'Thank you.'

The two men settled into armchairs.

The doctor swilled the pale spirit around in his glass and took a long sniff of the bouquet. 'Have a go of that,' he said.

Joe did the same. 'It smells good.'

'It does an' that.' Books took a sip and closed his eyes, relishing the moment. 'Here's how I see it,' he began softly. 'Someone in the Lane Kaufmann Bank – a trader or something – took a very dodgy position on . . .' he waved his glass '. . . something, shares, I suppose, but they lost an awful lot of money. So they doubled the stake on another thing. Then they were sweating, waiting for the share prices to rise. Or fall. Or something. But they didn't.'

'So you *do* read the news then?'

'I have a radio. That stock fell too. Or the wrong stock rose. So they tried another. And then another, but it seems that the market wasn't in the mood to oblige them. Everything they touched turned to dust.'

Joe was nodding gently. 'Not exactly. But something like that.'

'I'm guessing. I didn't hear any news about your bank as it happens, but lots of banks seem to be in trouble this week. You're probably not the only one to have made a run for the coast. The countryside is probably full of parked-up Mercedes. You're just the first to make it this far. But I can picture you as a rogue trader. You have that manner.'

'Do I?'

'Oh yes. You're a risk taker.'

'No.' Joe shook his head. He couldn't reconcile this description with his nature. 'Truly I'm not. I'm normally the cautious one.'

'Really? Well, maybe you're just impetuous.'

'Impetuous?' Joe swilled the whisky around in his glass, uncomfortable with the adjective. What did that even mean? Rash? Foolhardy? Reckless?

'You make quick decisions and then you act,' Books said.

'Is that a good quality or a bad one?'

The doctor was surveying him. 'I suppose it depends upon the quality of the decisions.'

'I suppose it does.'

'Deciding to rescue the whale could have been a bad decision. But you made it anyway. And saw it through. And in the end it was the right thing to do.'

The vapour from the Clynelish was drifting beyond Joe's sinuses into his head. 'Thank you.'

'Anyway, shares have been a big story this week if you listen to the news. Breaking all records, I believe, and not in a good way. Lots of banks in trouble. Lots of investors too. Seems like you're in good company.' Books took a sip of the whisky. 'This really is good. Have you tried it yet?'

Joe allowed himself the smallest taste. His head was already spinning. It must have been all that beer in the Petrel. 'I'm feeling a little dizzy.'

'Of course you are, but where were we? Ah yes. Banks. I've never really trusted them. Have to use them, of course. No choice. But whose interests drive them, do you think? Is it ours, the customers who bank with them? Or is it the directors with their million-pound bonuses?'

Joe savoured the single malt and let it sting his gums. His breathing was heavy, he noticed. This happened when he drank too much. He should stop right now. 'We weren't really a retail bank,' he said, rather too loudly. 'But you have a point.'

There was a comfortable silence, the kind that only a very good whisky can enable.

'I was thinking,' said Joe. 'I should like to rent your room on a more permanent basis.'

'You would be very welcome,' said Books. 'My accommodation charges are twenty pounds a day.'

'Yesterday you said ten pounds!'

'Yesterday you weren't a rich banker and a fugitive from justice.' Dr Books smiled slowly. 'I'm eighty-one years old,' he said, as if this wasn't a change of subject. 'I came to this village in . . . ooh . . . I forget the year but it was more than half a century ago. Long before you were born. Anyway. A funny thing happens when you live in a small community for fifty years. You see the whole human lifespan. You see people celebrating their eightieth birthday, and you remember how you knew them when they were thirty. You see people die in old age, and you can picture them in their twenties. And you see babies being born, and you see them grow, and you see them halfway to a hundred.'

Joe nodded. The whisky was making him even more dizzy.

'I've seen a lot of people come, and a lot of people go,' said Books. 'But I don't think I've ever seen a newcomer make such an impact in twenty-four hours as you have, Mr Joe Soap.'

'It's Haak. Joe Haak.'

'Ah yes, so it is. Foreign name?'

'My father is Danish.'

'Well, Mr Haak. You've shaken this village up.'

'Is that a compliment?'

'It's an observation.'

'I think I should be going up to bed.' Joe made to rise from his chair.

'Not yet.' Books held up the bottle, and without being asked he dropped another finger of spirit into the younger man's glass. 'We have one or two more details to sort out first.'

'Details?' Joe found himself picking up the glass.

'How do people die? Do you ever think about that?' The old man leaned back in his chair. 'In a village of three hundred people you're going to have three or four deaths a year. Five or six in a bad year. All the same . . . do you know how people die?'

Joe shook his head.

The doctor gave a grim smile. 'Circulatory diseases, they're the biggest. I'm talking about the heart packing up mainly. Two a year maybe. Cancer. That's a pretty big killer. One a year. In a bad year. Respiratory conditions? They're common enough too. Accidents? I've seen some bad 'uns. I've seen old folks and I've seen infants and I've seen everything in between, but here's the thing: I've never seen a suicide. Not in fifty years. And I hope never to.'

There was a silence. Joe looked deeply into his drink.

'Are we clear on this?'

The young man exhaled slowly. 'It wasn't suicide,' he said, at last.

'Oh no? What was it then? A cry for help?'

He tried to think back. How long ago it all seemed. Had it only been a day or so? What had been going through his mind? Plasma screens showing red, red, red. Voices raised. Faces turned towards him. Expressions of horror, despair. 'You're taking the fall, matey boy. You're taking the fall.' That terrible sinking feeling, like a cannonball in his gut weighing him down, blood leaking out of his veins, his body deflating. Oh God!

He put down his glass and rested his face in his hands. 'I had a bad day,' he said. 'It was a very bad day. I got in my car, and I drove. I drove and drove. Until I ran out of road. Any further and my tyres would have been wet.' He gave a weak smile.

'And then?'

'Then I walked down to the sea.'

'And then?'

Joe shook his head slowly. 'I sat for a while. I watched the sun coming up.'

'And then what?'

'I think I kept on walking.'

'What about your clothes?'

'I left them on the beach.'

'I see.' The doctor was rolling his lips. 'So you were planning to come back then?'

Joe sank a little deeper into his chair. 'Yes. I think I was. But I really don't know. I hadn't thought that far ahead. I remember swimming out. I thought perhaps there was a risk that the cold might kill me, but I wasn't really planning on dying. I didn't even think about it. I think perhaps I was testing myself. That's all. I've heard about people who ended their lives by walking into the sea. Didn't Virginia Woolf do that? But it isn't that easy. You have a tendency to float – an instinct to swim. I don't know how anyone could deliberately inhale seawater. Imagine that decision. That point when you overcome all the resistance of your throat and your lungs and you suck the water in. I just don't think your body lets you do it. Anyway, after a while I'd had enough. I decided to swim back, to find my clothes, and get myself together. So I turned back, but I was further out than I'd realised. And the cold was getting to me. I couldn't feel my hands or my feet. I struck out, but my limbs would hardly move, and now there seemed to be a current dragging me out even further.'

'You wanted to know how it might feel to be close to death,' suggested Books. 'You wanted to be *that* close.' He held up two pinched fingers. 'But you didn't want to cross over. Is that it?'

Joe sat silently, bobbing his head. 'Perhaps you're right,' he said.

'So what saved you?'

Joe closed his eyes. 'You'll think I'm mad . . .'

'Oh, I wouldn't flatter yourself. I've never seen a suicide and I've never seen madness. Not true, clinical madness. I've seen my share of crackpots and numbskulls, of course. You might turn out to be one of those.'

'Maybe I will . . . I heard a voice.'

'Someone calling?'

'No. Not a real voice. A memory of a voice. Perhaps I should say I *remembered* a voice.'

'And whose was it?'

It hadn't really been a voice, more of a whisper. Just three quiet words blown into his ear a long time ago. With his eyes tight shut he could imagine himself back there, leaning across to hear the words, straining his ears in fear of missing them. 'I remember being so cold in the water,' he said, 'feeling sick, feeling faint. I couldn't make any headway, so there may have been a current against me. I was starting to panic. That was when I heard the voice. Or I remembered the voice. And then there was something in my way. I didn't know what it was at first; but of course I do now. It was the whale.'

'You saw the whale?'

'I saw a great wall of darkness push past me and that was when I felt myself going underwater. I saw her eye.'

'And then?'

'That's all I remember.'

'How far out were you?'

'I can't tell. Maybe a quarter-mile.' Joe offered the old doctor a smile. 'I'm really not suicidal, Doctor Books. And I'm not mad. Maybe you were right with that first word. Maybe I'm a little . . . impetuous. Besides, I'm too young to die. And I have a promise to keep.'

'A promise?' Books looked at Joe over his glass. 'What kind of promise?'

'It doesn't matter. It isn't important. But it's the kind of promise that I really need to be alive to keep.'

'I see.' The two men sat and contemplated, in the way that late-night drinkers often do. 'I had a wife once,' the old doctor said when enough silence had passed.

'Did she . . . pass away?'

Books gave a garrumph. 'No. She still lives, as far as I know. She just couldn't take living here. She put up with it – with me – for over ten years. She moved away thirty-nine years ago. The last I heard she was living in Fleetwood with a tree surgeon. Fancy name for a woodcutter.'

'I'm sorry,' Joe said.

'No need to be. I only told you so you'd understand. I live a pretty solitary life. Set in my ways, if you like.'

'Do you have any children?'

'A son. He's twice your age and I hardly ever see him. You're in his bedroom.'

'Thanks.'

'She filled her coat pockets with stones,' Books said.

'Who did?'

'Virginia Woolf.'

'Ah.'

'And on that note,' Books finished his drink, 'I think we should retire.'

8

Go short on Estonian Steel

The desks on the fifth floor at the Lane Kaufmann Investment Bank were made from glass. It was part of a design engineered to be futuristic. The trading screens were recessed into a sheer glass wall, and the daily-dashboard screen, with its dials and bright alerts, was projected along panes of softly frosted glass above the desks, so that no one could miss the smallest detail of the day's trading. Digital counters clicked as shares went up, or slid down. Soft beeps would sound every time profits rose by £10,000, or an urgent, rasping sound, like the squawk of an injured owl, would warn when takings fell by an equivalent amount. On a good day the voices of the traders would rise in pitch to the rhythmic beep . . . beep . . . beep of a rising market, the zeros would roll around on the screens, and somewhere a trader would whoop. 'We're half a million up,' Janie Coverdale would call, and someone would cry, 'Yes!' Phones would ring and traders would shout numbers into them. Faces would glow. Teeth would show.

On a bad day the squawking owl would stalk the traders like a malevolent spirit. 'Oh shit!' Janie Coverdale would say, as profits fell another hundred thousand pounds. 'Hold your nerve, boys and girls,' she would call down the anxious lines of traders, 'New York opens in twenty minutes. Get ready for the bounce back.' On these days faces were stern as statues. Traders would bang phones down on their glass desks in frustration, and peck furiously at their keyboards. Squawk! Down another ten thousand. Squawk. Ten more. 'OK, get out of Canadian Solar, get out now. I don't trust it. Switch to shipping. Someone get me twenty million Olsen Sea Freight.

Go short on Microsoft. Short on Phillips. Short on IBM.'

As he sat listening to the ocean, Joe closed his eyes and pictured the trading floor. Even trying to imagine it made his pulse race. He had worked for the short-traders on the fifth floor – Janie Coverdale's floor. Short selling was a complex trading process, and a risky one. The rewards could be astonishing if they read the market correctly, but dismal if they foundered. Short-traders were the scavengers of the investment community, feeding on the carrion flesh of ailing companies. They would borrow shares from brokers, and straight away would sell those borrowed shares. Then they would cross their fingers and wait. What they wanted, what they *always* wanted, was for the businesses to fail, and for prices to fall. The further the fall, the better, as far as short-traders were concerned. Once the price had fallen enough (was it ever enough?) they would buy back the shares at the new, lower price, return them to the broker that had lent them, and pocket the difference. It was an absurdly simple way to make a whole lot of money. Many institutions frowned on short selling. There was often, on the trading floors of the Square Mile, a sense of disquiet about the practice, a feeling of unease. Could it be right to profit from the implosion of a dying business? Not everybody thought so. Some countries banned it, but on the fifth floor at Lane Kaufmann, in among the leveraged and exotic deals, it was bread and butter. While brokers and traders all across the City watched and prayed for rising prices, Janie Coverdale and her team would seek out shares in free fall. If prices should happen to rise, then the traders on the fifth floor would start to sweat. The sight of fingers sliding around the inside of a trader's collar was as accurate a sign of distress as the displays on the daily-dashboard.

The key to short selling was market intelligence; and intelligence was the only commodity of any true value in the money markets. It was the singular edge that one trader could have over another. 'I saw it coming,' a trader would say, four small words that betrayed hours of detailed research and a trail of deductive reasoning. 'I *saw* how a tropical storm in the Bahamas would damage the prospects for bananas, which would dent the profits of the Caribbean freight company that ships the bananas, which would delay their promised order for new shipping, which would depress the shares in a South Korean shipbuilding conglomerate, which might delay their decision to acquire a steel mill in Estonia.' This was the cascade of logical presumptions that fed marketplaces from London to Shanghai. So if 'Go short on Estonian Steel' was the shout that followed the forecast of a Caribbean hurricane, most of the traders on Janie Coverdale's desk would need no explanation for the reasoning. Even if they couldn't immediately join the dots, they would understand that dots were there to be joined. 'Go short on Estonian Steel' would ripple down the line of traders. Phones would be lifted and keyboards would clatter.

Joe had been walking along the coastal path and had found the bench where Old Man Garrow had been sitting on the morning that Kenny Kennet first saw the whale. Today it was bright, and Joe settled to enjoy the view. A light offshore breeze held the promise of a pleasant, if blustery, day. He looked over to the stretch of beach where, only yesterday, they had rescued the whale. Nothing remained of the earthworks, the channel, the heaps of sand; all had been levelled by the unforgiving tides. A visitor to the beach would find no sign of the great community effort that had taken place here. Not a footprint, not an echo. Had it really happened? Joe found himself musing. There, on another slope of the beach, was the spot where Charity Cloke had found him. Already his life felt strangely connected to this little cove, this sheltered stretch of shingle and sand.

Above the trading screens at Lane Kaufmann shone the information screens; Bloomberg, and Reuters, and CNN, and Sky News, their silent ticker-tape laden with coded messages for the moneymakers of Wall Street and London. Watching these screens had been Joe's job . . . part of his job. Joe had never been a trader; he was an analyst. His task had been to join the dots. Yangtze Motors announce the acquisition of an engine builder in India, says the ticker-tape. 'What does that mean?' Janie Coverdale would rest her hand on Joe's shoulder. 'My blue-eyed boy,' she would say. 'Find me a short.' And Joe would let his fingers fly over his keyboard, testing his models.

'It might be bad news for Anglo Emirate Holdings.'

'Why so?'

'They own forty per cent of SKO Components in Mumbai – in fact they only recently bailed them out – and SKO provide parts to Vinus Patel, who were also on Yangtze Motors' hit list, and I'm guessing this decision leaves them high and dry.'

'Got it,' Janie might say. 'What's Anglo Emirate's exposure?'

'Half a billion.'

'OK. Let's short them big.' Janie would hug Joe and call the instruction to the traders. 'Well done, Blue-Eyed Boy,' she would say.

'You should wait to see if the stock falls before you say that.'

'Oh, but it will. It will.'

A hand fell on Joe's shoulder, and he gave a start.

'Did I give you a shock?'

He turned around to see a young woman, her face familiar from the rescue effort of the day before. He rose to his feet and took the proffered hand.

'I'm Polly Hocking. We haven't been properly introduced.'

'I'm Joe,' he said.

'Joe . . .?' She was waiting for a surname.

'Just Joe. Joe Haak if you insist.'

'I see.' She offered him a smile. 'May I sit with you?'

'Of course.' He moved up the bench to make room, and Polly Hocking settled down beside him, resting delicately on her thighs, her leg pressing almost imperceptibly against his.

'You were wonderful yesterday.' She offered him a beguiling

smile that belonged somewhere on the spectrum between admiration and teasing, but on such brief acquaintance he couldn't decipher it further.

'You weren't so bad yourself,' he said weakly, and they both laughed.

'I have something of yours.'

He raised his eyebrows. 'You do?'

She reached into a basket. 'I'm guessing these belong to you.' A pair of pinstripe trousers, newly pressed. 'Kenny Kennet found them on the rocks. I washed them for you. And these.' She drew out a set of car keys and rattled them. 'I've never been in a Mercedes.' She smiled wider, an easier smile to interpret. 'Are you going to take me for a spin?'

They drove out of the Pay-and-Display car park on the quay, back up the long Cornish lane towards the Treadangel to Penzance road. 'I'm very low on fuel,' he told her.

'There's a petrol station in Treadangel.'

'How far?'

'Just a few miles.' Polly Hocking settled herself comfortably into the deep leather seat and started fiddling with some of the controls. 'I've always wanted a sports car,' she said.

'This isn't really a sports car.'

'What does this button do?'

'It's the MP3 player.'

'Can we have some music?' She twisted a knob. 'Is this the radio?'

'No. That's the heater.'

'How about this?' Music burst from hidden speakers.

'Please.' He reached out a hand and killed the sound. 'I'd rather not.'

She gave him a look and withdrew her hand from the dashboard. 'Did I touch a nerve?'

'No.' But he pulled the car up at the entrance to Bevis Magwith's farm. 'I think we should turn around.'

'Already? But we've only just set off.'

'I know. I'm sorry.' He started to reverse, and Polly gave a pout.

'Spoilsport.'

He turned the Mercedes back down the lane towards St Piran and gave a sigh. 'They might be looking for me,' he said.

'Who might?'

'The police, maybe.'

'Are you a criminal?'

'I don't feel like a criminal.'

'Well then, you're not one.' She laid a soft hand on his knee and gave it a squeeze. Very gently he lifted her hand away.

'Sometimes,' he said, 'it doesn't matter what you feel like. Sometimes the law has a different opinion.'

The lights were bright on Janie Coverdale's floor at Lane Kaufmann, all along the high windows where the traders barked numbers into telephones, but in the corners, where the analysts bent over their displays, it was a dimmer, murkier world, lit by the pale glow of liquid-crystal screens. This was Joe's domain, away from the high-octane decisions and frantic voices of the traders; his world lay in the tangle of wires behind the screens, his contribution coded into algorithms, databases, lines of code and Boolean logic. He had learned to filter out the voices – Janie Coverdale's sharp commands, the low persuasive tones of the bond salesmen spinning scenarios to customers in Lombard Street, or Singapore, or Hong Kong, the triumphant whoops of traders following the rising beep of the ticker, or the groans from the desks when the numbers turned bad. For Joe the sounds dissolved into a hum of white noise.

Sometimes Janie Coverdale would slip away from the traders and find her way into the gloomy world of the analysts. She would slide up softly behind Joe when his whole attention was afloat in an ocean of numbers, and she would rest her hand on his shoulder and make him jump. 'Joey, my Joe, my blue-eyed boy.' She would lean over him, so close that her bosom would brush his face, but her focus was on his screen. Only ever on his screen. The bosom thing was accidental. Or incidental. Janie Coverdale, thin as a snake, thrice married, thrice divorced, desired by half the young men on the trading floor, rued by most of the others, would slide an arm around Joe's shoulder so that he could smell the fresh sweat of her armpits, could inhale her intense organic pheromones. 'What do we have here, Joey boy? What do we have?'

There was an alchemy to calculating the roll and swell of the sea of numbers that were stocks and shares. The analysts were the shamans of their day; they were the sorcerers and astrologers who could forecast the future. 'How does this work?' Janie would ask. 'What is *this* doing?' And Joe would run a finger down his screen and pick out a number here and another one there. 'Look,' he might say, 'NovaQuest Labs are down, BSAF Biotech are down, Ambire Chemical are down, well down.'

'And that means?'

'This program looks at the patterns of share prices over the past twenty-five years of trading. It tells me that every time these indicator stocks have all dropped together, then within hours we've always seen corresponding falls in pharma stocks – up to five-point falls. This figure here . . .' he slid a fingernail along to pick out a number, 'this is our confidence level. Eighty-eight per cent.' And Janie would squeeze his shoulder, and sometimes she would plant a kiss on his cheekbone, and the slower and softer the kiss, the happier she would be with his insight. She would straighten up and direct her focus on the sharp young men in the light. 'Julian . . . short me some pharma stocks. Astra Zeneca. Not too many. Keep it below the regulation limit. Half a million.' She would wag a forefinger at the traders, would run her tongue around her lips, and then click her way back across the floor in her Christian Louboutin shoes without once looking back at Joe.

There was an evening once, how long ago? Five years? Six? An evening when the trading day had closed, when even the keenest traders had left their desks for the night, when Joe was still hunched over his screen, working late, scrolling through a thousand lines of code, and he felt the familiar soft hand on the back of his neck and smelled the blowsy scent of female perspiration.

'Janie?'

'My blue-eyed boy.' She rolled up an empty chair and sat alongside him. 'What are we doing here so late?'

He tapped a pen on the table. 'The last three stocks we shorted lost us money.'

She wagged her head slowly, gave her sly smile, walked her fingers down his shoulder. 'And what are we doing about it?'

He leaned back in his chair. 'Trying to understand it,' he said. He made an effort to return her smile. 'There's a weakness in our approach.'

'A weakness?' Step by step her manicured nails were pacing down his chest. He tried to ignore the bullet holes they left.

'We rely too much on historical patterns,' he said, 'but every hedge fund and investment bank has the same numbers we have. Every trading floor in the City is running the same analysis. They all have the same computerised trading systems. We can't *all* short the same stock. That's why the regression analysis is failing.'

She pulled her hand away, heavy with gold rings from lost lovers, and stroked her fingers through his hair. 'That's the stock market for you,' she said. 'Shares rise and they fall. Fortunes are made and fortunes are lost. And the sharpest brains and the cleverest men and the biggest fortunes have fallen on the simplest of calculations. Which way will this share price move? Will it rise? Or will it fall? Why can't we calculate such a simple thing?' These words she almost whispered with a puff of scented breath in his ear, and he shrank just enough for her to feel it. Now she pulled back and examined him. 'What do you have for me, Joey boy? What do you have?'

In the glove compartment of his car he found his wallet. He was solvent again. He left the car in the Pay-and-Display and walked with Polly Hocking along the harbour. 'Let me buy you coffee,' he said, 'to make up for such a short drive.' They picked their way over the coiled ropes and nets and dropped into Hedra Penhallow's B&B, where they squeezed together on a floral divan.

At Lane Kaufmann the coffee was freshly roasted and ground from Arabica beans; a girl called Amelia was the barista, frothing the milk for the cappuccinos, tapping down the coffee cartridge tap tap bang. That's how important coffee was on the fifth floor. Forty-eight employees and their own barista. Amelia would know exactly how they liked their coffee, and precisely how often. Joe would drink a latte first thing, skinny, served in white bone-china with a double espresso shot to wake him up. At a quarter past nine his used cup would be whisked away and in its place a fresh Americano would appear and with it a pastry or a fat-free muffin. Sometimes he didn't even notice the wraith-like barista wafting up behind him, swapping the cups around. In the afternoon he drank tea, Earl Grey, with just a dash of milk. In the early evening it was time for another latte. He would look up, perhaps thinking, now is about time for a drink – and Amelia would be gliding towards him, cup in hand.

'Shall I show you the church?' Polly asked. They climbed together up Cliff Street and she let him into the back of the churchyard through the swing gate. 'It's a kissing gate,' she told him, but his attention was on the clock tower and he let the gate swing back so she had to catch it.

'Will you look at that beautiful church,' Joe whispered to himself. It was a line from his memory – one that brought a smile to his lips. 'How old is this church?' he asked Polly.

'Old,' she said.

They picked their way among the stones. 'Eighteen sixty-five,' he said, reading a gravestone. 'Eighteen forty.' He was looking for the oldest. 'Seventeen something.'

At Lane Kaufmann the analysts would write computer code

as fast as a courtroom reporter writes prose. Their brains were wired this way. Joe would sketch a flow-sheet onto a flip chart, his fat pen flying this way and that, and the boys would write the code.

How long ago it all seemed now. Five years since they had started work on the system that would change everything. But at the time it had been little more than another day in the office. 'This box here,' Joe would say, 'this is a commodity – any commodity. This line here is the dependency. Shell Oil is dependent on shipping. Shipping is dependent on security. Security is dependent on defence spending in this country and this one, and in that one there.' His hands would draw the lines and the boys would code. Rodney Byatt and Jonathan Woodman and Manesh Patel and the small team of programmers who worked with them – they were the wizards who turned his ideas into pinpoints of light on computer screens. 'We need to *model*,' he would tell them, 'we need to model every dependency that every stock has with every other. It isn't enough to know that water-supply companies depend upon rain. Imagine a company as a planet – an orb – floating in a dark universe of hidden forces. What are the secret gravities that pull and push this planet, what drives the tides?' He would toss his marker pen from hand to hand, enjoying the look upon their faces. 'Imagine,' he would say, 'an artwork in a gallery where ten thousand balls are suspended in a giant cube above your heads, each one connected by threads to a hundred others. Each ball is a business, and every thread describes a link, a relationship, a crucial conduit through which money and custom flows. Now imagine an event.' He turns to catch their eyes, these boys who will convert his words into computer magic. 'An oil well catches fire in the Gulf of Mexico. We have to cut some threads. Picture it.' He holds up imaginary scissors and snips an imaginary thread. 'Snip.' He smiles. 'Snip.' They are used to his flights of fancy, these program writers. He talks in words but they understand in numbers and decision trees and database markers and screen drivers. They talk of Java and HTML and SQL operators, of field identifiers and messages and strings. Joe, who understands this complex dialect, bats their questions back. They sit in a huddle around their desks on the fifth floor. They are the 'quants', treated with suspicion by the traders, who don't like to believe that mathematicians and computer programmers can make investment decisions that rely on the subtleties of human behaviour, but increasingly offered respect by the bank's directors. Amelia hovers with coffee. Tap tap bang. Another cappuccino. In the background the landscape of telephone voices and ringtones, and Janie Coverdale calling instructions to the dealers.

'This is my husband, the vicar.' Polly Hocking said. A white-haired man had emerged from a side door of the church to meet them. His thin weathered face was familiar from the beach. Joe, in his reverie, was still listening to the voices of a far-away investment bank. He snapped back to the present and extended his hand.

'Pleased to meet you.'

The handshake was as cold as seaweed. There was no smile. 'You're the fellow with the whale.'

'Well, it wasn't my whale exactly,' Joe said, but Polly Hocking's husband had already turned away.

'You missed the Bible study.' The vicar was talking to his wife. 'You were supposed to do the flowers for the chapel. Did you do them? Aileen Magwith called and said she saw you tearing out of the village in a sports car. A sports car!' His tone was uncomfortably hostile in the presence of a stranger.

'I wouldn't call it a *sports* car,' said Joe.

The Reverend Hocking let his head swivel slowly in Joe's direction as if he had quite forgotten he was there. 'Wouldn't you?' he said acidly. 'Does it matter?'

'It would matter to an insurer,' Joe said. In his mind he saw the patterns spiralling out, the threads of connectivity. The car insurer is dependent upon drivers. Drivers depend upon cash for fuel. The price of fuel rests on demand and supply. Supply needs proven reserves and political stability. Why did his mind always do this? Had all those years on the fifth floor implanted thought patterns in his brain that couldn't be broken? He held up imaginary scissors. Snip.

The vicar was looking at him with a mixture of distaste and contempt. He moved his lips as if to speak, but no words emerged. Instead he turned to Polly. 'Would you explain to this young man that you have responsibilities in the church,' he said. 'I shall expect you in the vestry in two minutes.' He was engulfed by the doorway from which he had appeared.

'Awkward,' said Joe. He could suddenly feel the imprint of Polly Hocking's hand upon his knee where she had rested it in the car.

'That's OK.'

He was seeing her for the first time. The very first time. How had he missed looking at her? Somehow they hadn't faced each other. Not exactly. She had slid down beside him on the bench overlooking the sands, he'd walked beside her, had sat with her in the car, his eyes on the road, had squeezed alongside her in the tea room of the B&B, and somehow, all the time, he'd been looking away, his attention drawn elsewhere. His view of her had been the edge of her nose, the turn of her cheek, the curtain of her hair. But now the soft shape of her face was in front of him. He could see the downy hairs on her upper lip, the little frown lines around her eyes, a faint pattern of freckles, an expression of anxiety etched across her forehead. When she swept an unruly strand of hair away from her face he could see the way she had done it a thousand times before.

'Thank you for the ride,' she said, and suddenly he was the guilty party. Why had they turned back so soon? What had he been worried about? Why had he lifted away her hand? He should have left it there. Where might that have led?

A block had appeared between his brain and his voice box.

There was nothing he could say now that would make any sense.

Polly raised a slim finger. She was going to touch him – maybe just a touch upon his face. It was to be a tender gesture, yet a teasing one, an action with no meaning unless he chose to see one. With the swiftness of thought he caught her arm and her finger was suspended just an inch from his face.

'Polly . . . are you coming?' The cantankerous call of a hidden husband.

Her eyes were as soft as a watercolour. Her blink was in slow motion. They were so close now that Joe could feel her breath upon his face. 'Wait . . .' he found himself saying. Where had that word emerged from? What did he have in mind?

She held his gaze. 'I have to go.' It was a whisper.

He released her hand. Her fingertip was still there, frozen on its journey. Now she could touch him and, if she did, she would own him, every beat of his heart would belong to her.

'Polly . . .'

'I have to go.'

And all that was left to them was the flicker of her eyes and the warm compassion of his gaze.

Then she was gone.

'Polly Hocking.' Joe whispered her name to be sure of remembering it. He lifted his hand to his face to stroke the spot where her finger had come so close to touching him. 'Polly.' She had slipped into part of his mind like an uninvited dream. 'Polly Hocking.'

In Janie Coverdale's office were paintings of the Charente, skies that were painfully blue, sunflowers that burned the eyes. She had an ottoman settee in white leather that looked altogether too fragile to take the weight of two. When she seduced him, that one and only time, she wouldn't permit him a single button of her blouse. She slid her pencil skirt up to her waist in a concertina of fine fabric, and rolled her stockings down to her knees. Her face told him that this would be her final concession to undress. She lay back on the white leather to wait for him. He would know what to do. It was, he imagined, a rite of passage on the fifth floor. The well-worn route to Janie Coverdale's office. The late-evening working. The locked door. The smell of success. The circles of mutual sweat.

Afterwards, with her fabrics smoothed back and every trace of their encounter erased, Janie unfastened her topmost button. 'Just to keep them guessing,' she said, as if anyone might still be there to see them. She leaned towards him to whisper in his ear and he strained to hear whatever tender message she might have. 'Tomorrow,' she said, blowing softly, 'I want to see the new model.' For a heartbeat he struggled to interpret her words, so she pulled away and raised a precisely plucked eyebrow. 'The computer model,' she said. 'The network? The one you promised?'

'Of course.' He had pulled his pants back up too quickly. They felt uncomfortable around the tops of his legs. Would it be impolite to readjust?

'Tomorrow,' she said. 'My blue-eyed boy.' She swept her phone up from the desk and started to click the keys, scrolling down through messages. 'Can you let yourself out?' she said.

9

That thing in Saudi Arabia

He had to get hold of some cash. For a start there was his rent to pay to Dr Books. He needed clothes. More food. He hankered for a computer. But might they be looking for him? Would they spot his car on the open road? Were the police computers programmed to zero in on a white Mercedes? And what about his bank account? Could they have frozen it? Would they be tracking it?

He drove to Bevis Magwith's farm, parked, and walked the mile to the main road. His car was too conspicuous. There would be a bus; Books had mentioned one. Sure enough there was a bus stop but no indication of how frequent the service might be. He waited. Maybe he had just missed one? He contemplated walking, but if he did, then the laws of nature would demand that the bus should sweep by moments later. He sat on the insufficient bench and ruminated. How had he ended up here? *Why* had he ended up here? He wasn't responsible. He told himself this. So why not wander back to his car, drive to a police station and hand himself in? He rehearsed the scenario in his mind. 'I'm Jonas Haak,' he would say. 'I'm the man you're looking for. The chap who brought down that investment bank. I'm here to take the fall.' He would hold out his wrists for the handcuffs.

Could he do that? Or would he break? 'I didn't *really* bring it down. I didn't make the trades. You need to talk to a Mrs Coverdale.' He might nod at them knowingly. 'Talk to Colin Helms. Talk to Julian McEvan. They pressed me,' he might say. 'They pushed and pushed me. They went too far.'

It was good the first time they had run the model. They

didn't do it with real money. Janie brought Colin Helms down from the ninth floor to see it. Colin was a lumbering bear of a man with a nose like the beak of a raptor and hair the colour of a thunderstorm.

'Show him what you can do,' Janie purred to Joe.

'I've seen this sort of program before – a hundred times,' Colin Helms said. He seemed more interested in Janie than in the software.

'All the same,' Janie said, 'I think you should see this one.'

'I don't like the *look* of it,' Helms said as Joe and Manesh fired up the system. 'The colours are dreadful.' And he laughed at this as if it was hilarious.

'We haven't focused on the UI,' Manesh said. 'This is a DB viewer.'

'Aargh, too much, too much,' said Helms with fake dismay.

Joe came to the rescue. He alone spoke both the dialect of the programmers and the language of the ninth floor. 'Don't worry about the look of it,' he said reassuringly. 'We're not aiming to sell this software. It doesn't have to look nice. It doesn't have to be robust. It just has to work.' He hit some keys. 'Give me an event.'

'What kind of event?'

'Anything from the news today. Preferably breaking news. That's the beauty of this program. It doesn't just look at share price connections, it looks at everything. Unemployment in Italy. Elections in Romania. Wet winters in Spain.'

Helms laughed. 'My wife's had a boob job.' He guffawed. 'Try putting that in.'

Janie leaned forward, looking serious. 'That thing in Saudi Arabia,' she suggested.

'Good one.' Joe took the mouse and clicked. 'So CNN started reporting about half an hour ago that a Saudi government minister was found dead in his apartment and Riyadh is blaming it on Iran.' The screen displayed a slider. 'This lets us set the temperature of the relationship between Saudi Arabia and Iran.' He clicked and dragged the slider down. 'Let's say it's just one degree frostier. Nothing to frighten the camels.' At the bottom of the screen, numbers were populating a table.

'What are these?' Helms was suddenly interested.

'They're forecasts. Ranked by the scale of the opportunity. We're looking for shorts.'

'Hmm.' The senior man shifted his seat closer to the screen. 'Oil stocks all down. Metals. Shipping. Nothing you wouldn't guess at, though. Can you scroll down?'

'Of course.' The table slid up the screen.

'Stop. What's this?' Helms stabbed at a line on the screen. 'Marshall and Oakes? I own shares in them. These guys import cotton, for God's sake. What does that have to do with Iran and Saudi?'

'I have no idea,' Joe said. 'It's a complex algorithm. You either trust it or you don't.'

'But your system is predicting a nine per cent fall in their share price. You can't just follow that without knowing why.'

'We'll never know why, Mr Helms,' Joe said. 'There could be a thousand connections and if they all move just one per cent, that leads to five hundred that shift by two per cent, and maybe a few dozen by three per cent, and somewhere in all that mathematics is poor old Marshall and Oakes down by nine per cent.'

'Well, I don't believe it.' Helms pulled out his phone. 'Someone call up their stock.'

There was the parp of a car horn. Alongside the bus stop a car had pulled up and the window was gliding down – behind it was the wide smile of Jeremy Melon. 'Looking for a lift?'

At the cashpoint in Penzance Joe tried to conceal his face from the hidden cameras. He slid in his card, punched in the PIN, and waited for alarm bells to ring. What service do you require? Cash, he told it. He asked for five hundred pounds. Inside the bank, wheels whirred, counting out his money.

His heart was fluttering. Surely the sirens would sound any moment now.

They found a department store where he bought four pairs of jeans and half a dozen shirts, a Fair Isle jumper, a comfortable jacket, and a winter coat, socks, trainers, stout shoes, and underwear. He paid with his card. Nobody pounced. He stocked up on toiletries.

'Quite a shopping spree,' Jeremy remarked as they carried the haul back to the car.

'I'm not done yet. I need a computer and a mobile phone.'

'I have an old laptop you can borrow.'

'Thanks, but I still need a phone.'

'I wouldn't bother.' Jeremy threw the shopping bags into his car. 'There's no signal in St Piran.'

'No signal?' Joe looked astonished.

'We're in a bit of a dip, apparently. There's nowhere they could put a mast. Or something. Fancy a beer before we set off?'

Joe cocked his head, listening for the wail of sirens. 'Not here,' he said. 'Somewhere closer to home.' Home? What a curious word to use. How could this remote place be home?

Manesh swivelled his screen. 'Marshall and Oakes,' he said.

'That's the current price?'

'Down six points.'

Colin Helms was licking his lips. 'Who else was on that list?'

Joe started scrolling. 'Gemtech – we forecast eight per cent drop, KKL Polythene, China Tech . . .'

'Stop.' Helms held up a hand. 'Check those prices.'

Manesh was ahead of him. 'Gemtech down five, China Tech down seven, KKL down four.'

'Fucking hell.' Helms was out of his seat.

'Marshall and Oakes are down two more.'

'Shit.'

Jeremy and Joe drove to the harbour at Port Nevis. Joe bought sandwiches in the Bell and Anchor. It was warm for an autumn day. They settled down with a pint each of Merryweather cider on a table overlooking the harbour.

'I'm having a strange day,' Joe told Jeremy. 'My head seems to be spinning. I can't stop thinking about things. They're going round and around in my mind.'

'What sort of things?'

'Work.' Joe looked into his glass.

'I get that too.'

Joe looked up. 'You do?'

'Oh yes. I'll have an idea for a story and I find I can't think about anything else all day. It's the imagination working overtime.'

Working overtime. Working late. Janie Coverdale rolling up her skirt. Cold pizzas and computer code. Stepping over drunks in the doorway. Small talk with the taxi driver. Share prices up. Brokers cheering. Share prices down. Klaxons braying.

'I don't think it's the same thing.'

'Ah.'

He was noticing something. What was it? More of the dissonance he had experienced in St Piran. Fishing boats in the harbour. A man mending a net. A couple walking hand in hand along the harbour wall. The sharp kaleidoscope of reflected sunlight on the water, the rhythmic breaking of waves against the sea wall. Time. That's what he was noticing. Time was moving at a different rate here. A man could sit with a cider and look out over the ocean and the hands of the clock would sweep around the face and no one would call out his name. Did they have 'time' in the City? Was it the same phenomenon? Did moments softly evolve and drift down like soap bubbles in Threadneedle Street? Did clocks stop?

'How does it work? This goddamned computer system. Tell me how it works.' Colin Helms had gone back upstairs and had returned with a silver-haired man whose face was as lined as a map. They didn't sit down. 'Show us again,' Helms demanded.

There were stress demons lurking in the corners of the room;

Joe could feel them watching, turning up the controls on his heartbeat. He began to tap the keys.

'Every brokerage house in the City has something like this,' the new man said thinly. 'What makes this one so different?'

'We use natural language processing,' Joe said. 'A semantics engine. We used it to build the model. It's like a citation index. It reads the financial press.'

'It reads? . . . What do you mean, it *reads*?'

He should have been able answer these questions easily, but there was an intimidating seniority radiating from Helms and his colleague, especially from the older man. For a moment he was disarmed. 'It reads,' he said, raising his shoulders as if the question had been a foolish one. An unfortunate gesture. He dropped his shoulders and tried to look more serious. 'Pretty much like you and I do. Just a lot faster.' Manesh would have said 'Backspace/Erase', a familiar expression among the quants. It meant, 'oops, that came out wrong – let me try again'. Joe sank into his seat. He could feel sweat breaking out around his collar. 'I mean it's connected to the web and it reads every financial article out there. The *Financial Times*, all the dailies, the *New York Times*, *The Economist*, the *Harvard Business Review* – over three hundred online publications in a dozen languages; it's reading over ten thousand financial articles a day, plus press releases and announcements. It has a historic database of over twenty million press reports and that's just the financial press. It also reads the mainstream news.' He was gabbling now.

The silver-haired man raised his hand ponderously like a schoolboy.

Joe stopped. The encounter was making him feel ridiculously nervous. 'Yes, sir?'

The man spoke quietly. His voice seemed to emerge from a watery place within his lungs. 'Explain to me, Joe,' he said, 'that is your name . . . Joe?'

'Joe Haak, sir.'

'I'm Lew Kaufmann.' The old man held out a hand as limp as laundry. 'Tell me, Joe Haak. I've never heard of a computer that could make sense of the written word. Not on this scale.'

'No, sir. And nor does this one. What this program does is look for proximity of terms. To start off we were simply [illegible]ing financial articles for company names. If two companies are mentioned in the same press report, then how many words separate them? The closer they appear, then the more likely is that there will be some kind of link between them. A thread. There are over forty-five thousand listed companies around the world, not including investment funds, and fifty-four national stock exchanges, so that was a lot of data right from the start. But then we did something clever. We widened the net. Now we started to include other words – water, fuel, election, conflict, Syria, Japan – and soon we were tracking twenty thousand nouns. Then we added value statements – adjectives such as "good" or "bad", "booming", "falling", "out of fashion", "controversial", "healthy", "misleading" – thousands of words and expressions. We're growing the list all the time.'

'Well, I'll be damned.' Colin Helms and his colleague looked stunned.

'We don't even need to add new expressions any more. The computer does it for us. It recognises when a word or phrase appears in more than one article and it starts to index it.'

Lew Kaufmann was looking at the screen with an intense expression.

'But that, alone, was still no smarter than a dozen other electronic trading systems here in the Square Mile. The really clever thing,' said Joe, feeling a little more relaxed now, 'was to marry all that data to the stuff we already had. All the information we've been collecting for years showing how share prices are related. That was the difficult bit to do, but it was the key. Now we could look at the way share prices had moved historically and see how those movements related to the threads we picked up in the press reports at the time. When we added that to the r k, it meant the computer could try to forecast what woul appen to shares in the wake of any event. And we don't eed to feed it the event either. It should pick it up on the re wires all by itself.'

What do you reckon, Lew?' said Helms. He was smiling dely, as if the whole thing had been his idea.

The man with the deeply lined face was nodding slowly. 'How long did it take you to develop this?' he asked.

'Five years, sir.' The stress demons seemed to be retreating.

'Good,' the old man said. 'So it could take a while for any other bank to catch up?'

'Unless they're already working on something similar.'

'Good answer.' Kaufmann turned to look at him closely. 'What does this thing say about human nature, son? Where does that fit into your . . . equations?'

It wasn't a question Joe had expected. 'I'm not quite sure what you mean, sir . . .'

'I was just curious,' the old man said, perching on a corner of the desk, and letting out a sigh like a deflating tyre. 'Do you know why those boys and girls out there . . .' he gestured towards the trading desks, '. . . why they distrust computer trading? It's because every trade they make relies on an understanding of human nature. And computers don't understand us. They don't understand people. That's what they believe.'

'I know, sir.'

'Do we really understand why people buy this share rather than that one? Buyers don't always behave logically. They buy out of sentiment. Or they buy out of habit. Or they buy because they recognise a brand. And they sell because of fear. Or because a brand has been tainted. Or because a chief executive used an inappropriate word in a speech.'

'Yes, sir.'

'But ultimately, Joe, there's something stronger than all these things. That's what those traders out there understand and I'm not sure whether computers can. Do you know what that is?' He raised a furrowed eyebrow.

'I'm not sure, sir . . .'

'Self-interest, Joe.' Kaufmann rested a hand on his shoulder. 'Greed. The competitive desire to look after yourself and the other guy can go hang. That's what drives the markets, young man. So do you have a way to set the degree of human self-interest? That's what I need to know.'

Joe exhaled slowly, feeling the weight of the banker's hand on his shoulder. The stress demons seemed to be returning. 'I understand that, sir, but our approach allows for it. We don't include any value judgements of our own.' He was watching Kaufmann for any sign that the old man might disagree with this, but the banker's face seemed impassive. 'We don't need to program any rules for human behaviour. We depend upon the experts who write those thousands of articles. If the financial press takes a view on human self-interest, then their views will feed into the model. So you see, we do rely on the judgement of humans, just like the traders out there on the desks. It's just that our information comes from a thousand experts. We read their advice and we weigh it against all the others'. We don't take any position of our own on how people will behave.'

The old banker looked thoughtful. 'Could you include *my* views in your analyses? Or do I have to write a column for the financial press before your computer will take any account of my opinions?'

Joe's neck was starting to sweat, and his throat felt dry. 'This system will be great,' Manesh had often said to him, 'until the guys upstairs get their hands on it.' Joe nodded slowly. 'If you were to email me a short memo any time that you wanted to influence the system, I could make sure the system reads your views.'

'I see.' Kaufmann seemed to be reflecting on this. 'And would you assign particular . . . *weight* to my views?'

Joe turned to look at Kaufmann, and for a moment there

was eye contact between the two – the young man and the old. Joe hesitated. His reply, when it came, was almost a whisper. 'Not . . . willingly, sir.'

Colin Helms weighed in. 'That's not what he means, Lew. He's joking . . . aren't you, Haak?'

But Kaufmann lifted his hand from Joe's shoulder and held it up to silence Helms. 'One minute, Colin. Now, Mr Haak, correct me if I'm wrong, but I understood that I was the one paying for this computer system.'

The fifth floor seemed to have fallen silent. Where were the ringing phones? The raised voices of the traders? Where was the tap tap bang of the coffee machine?

'I'm not refusing, sir.'

'Just unwilling, eh?'

Joe could see the expression on Colin Helms's bear-like face; his dark eyebrows were almost quivering.

'The thing is, Mr Kaufmann, one reason this system works so well is because we don't try to interfere with its reasoning. We don't try to steer it in one direction or another.'

'You prefer to trust the judgement of the masses over the judgement of one expert? Is that it?'

'Yes, sir.'

Kaufmann rose slowly to his feet. 'How much are we paying you, son?' he asked.

Joe grimaced. 'Just a quant's salary, sir.'

'Well, you just doubled it.' The old banker placed a wizened hand on Joe's shoulder. 'When do we start using this thing in anger?'

Noise had returned to the fifth floor. 'We're running tests for three months,' Janie said.

'Make that one month. And I want a report on my desk every evening to tell me what our trading day would have been if we'd used this system rather than the ones we're using now.'

'Yes, Mr Kaufmann,' said Janie.

'Does it have a name, by the way?'

'A name?'

'Certainly. Like Windows? Or Facebook?'

'Right now,' Joe said, 'we're calling it LKTestDB3.'

'Not exactly catchy,' said Kaufmann. 'How about "Cassie"? That's my granddaughter's name.'

'An excellent name,' Joe said. 'I christen it Cassie.'

'And you,' said Mr Kaufmann, pointing at him with a narrow finger, 'just doubled your salary twice in two minutes.'

They left the inn at Port Nevis and strolled back to Jeremy's car.

'You've been very kind to me,' Joe said.

'Not at all. You've livened up the village.'

'All the same.'

They drove out of the village and onto the Treadangel road. 'I'm feeling a lot better,' Joe said. 'I think I've been suffering from . . . I don't know . . . post-traumatic stress.'

'Good Lord!' Jeremy said. 'It sounds as if you've been at war.'

At war? It felt rather like that. 'Well, maybe that's the wrong expression. I just feel like . . . a violin string that's been pulled so tight that one pluck will snap it. But now it's being tuned down. Loosened. Does any of that make sense to you?'

Jeremy Melon was smiling. 'Oh yes. When I first came to St Piran I felt the same. I was an academic then. That was sixteen years ago.'

'What made you stay?'

'It's complicated. I taught biology to university students in Leeds. I wasn't very good at it.'

'I'm sure you were.'

Jeremy shook his head. 'Kind of you to say so, but I wasn't. I couldn't take the stress. I'm a lot happier now. I don't earn so much, of course. I write school textbooks on natural history. That just about pays the bills. I contribute to a few encyclopaedias. I write some short stories. I teach some adult education classes. That's it really.'

'You dropped out of the rat race . . .'

'Yes.' Jeremy turned to look at him. 'That's exactly what I did. Mind you, it wasn't quite as straightforward as it sounds.'

'That's mysterious . . .'

Jeremy changed down a gear and swung the car into the lane to St Piran. 'I fell in love . . . with one of my students.'

'Oh dear.' Perhaps, Joe thought, St Piran had become a destination for life's refugees. We run away from stressful situations and this is where we end up. Any further and the tyres would be wet. 'Still,' he added, 'that isn't illegal or anything? Not at university?'

'No,' Jeremy agreed. 'Unethical maybe. Anyway, the student never knew.'

'You kept your feelings a secret?'

'Of course. The university would never have approved.'

'I don't understand. Why did you have to leave, then?'

'I didn't have to leave. But one night I just got in my car and I drove.'

'That's a sad story,' Joe said.

'No it isn't. It has a happy ending. Here I am in St Piran. I've never had to run away again.'

They had reached the entrance to the Magwith family's farm where Joe's car was parked. 'I should drop you off here then?'

'Yes please.'

Jeremy pulled up and let the engine idle.

'What became of the student?'

'He's a high-flying civil servant in the Foreign Office, I believe. A wife and two children.'

Joe swung open his door. 'Can I ask you something?'

'Ask away.'

'Do you know Polly Hocking?'

'Of course.' Jeremy's eyes narrowed. 'What's this about, Joe?'

'Nothing really. I just wondered, what is she like? Is she happily married? That sort of thing.'

Jeremy reached forward to turn off the ignition key and the car fell silent. He was nodding slowly to himself. 'Are you asking me if Polly's off-limits?'

He shouldn't have started this. Jeremy's open confession had emboldened him, but perhaps he had gone too far. 'No. Of course not. It was a silly question.'

Jeremy made no move to restart the car.

'Although perhaps . . . maybe I was thinking that. But not because of . . . anything. I was just . . .' What? 'I was just confused by her.' That was certainly true. He couldn't remember being quite so confused by a woman.

'Has she been flirting with you?'

Joe shook his head. 'Not flirting . . . *exactly*.'

'She's very good at that.'

'At what?'

'At not flirting *exactly*.'

'Maybe I'm misreading the signs. I mean, maybe the body language is different here . . .'

Jeremy rested a hand on Joe's forearm. 'Can I offer you some advice?' he said.

'Yes please.' Advice would be good. But somewhere behind his eyes he could picture her face, that strand of hair, those freckles . . .

'Talk to Demelza,' Jeremy said. Joe waited for more, but Jeremy seemed to have spoken.

'That's it? That's your advice? Talk to Demelza?'

'She's a romantic novelist. She understands affairs of the heart. What do I know? I write books about barnacles. There isn't much I couldn't tell you about the humble barnacle, but when it comes to love . . . I wouldn't even listen to my own advice.' Jeremy lifted his hand away. 'Demelza's the expert.'

'Right.'

'Did you know that the barnacle has the longest penis in the animal kingdom?'

'Really?'

'Up to eight times its body length.'

'Well, there you go.' Joe lifted himself out of the car. 'I didn't even know barnacles had a penis.'

'You've learned something new. The next time we're down on the beach I'll show you. The world's largest dick.'

'Thank you, Jeremy.' Joe was laughing now.

'Talk to Demelza.'

'I'll think about it.'

10

Does the roof come down on this?

In the morning on Piran Sands the veil of mist that shrouded the great Atlantic had started to dissolve and the salty breezes of another world were rolling up along the shingle. To Joe it seemed as if the nightmares that belonged in another place and another time might dissipate away here, in wisps like sea fog. Sitting on the bench, Joe could see Kenny Kennet with his sack of driftwood pottering among the rocks at the water's edge. Charity Cloke was there, arm in arm with her young man, walking the sands with her dog. Was that Aminata the nurse resting on a rock with a book? It delighted him that he was learning their names. Casey. That was the name of the net-maker walking out with Charity. He mouthed the name silently. Faces that, a week ago, were so unfamiliar. A village that had heaved and strained and dug to release a whale.

'Jacob Anderssen the landlord,' he whispered silently. 'Samuel Robins, the fisherman. Hedra Penhallow at the B&B. Polly. Polly Hocking.' And as he spoke her name, there she was, coming around the headland with a young man by her side. Who was he? They were too far away to tell. Yet he could almost see the glow on Polly Hocking's cheeks. She sways a little when she walks, he thought. And she sweeps her fingers through her sandy hair and pulls the disobedient locks back over her ears.

She hadn't seen him, and all at once he didn't want to be seen. He turned away from the beach and found a rough footpath leading towards the cliff. She might spot him disappearing, but she would never know that he had seen her. It was a scramble, steep in parts, over the rocks and through the gorse. Concealed behind an outcrop, he looked out again at the ocean. How can we share our lives on this planet with such a monstrous body of water and yet live from day to day without ever thinking of it? Well, the villagers of St Piran didn't know such ignorance. They lived their lives by the rise and fall of the tides, by the shoaling of the mackerel, and the breeding cycle of lobsters and crabs.

Should he go back to the City? Their anger might have turned to worry by now. He had friends who would be frantic. Would his father know? Papa Mikkel would be in his cottage near Copenhagen raking over his vegetables, or maybe still in his summer lodge, on an island way up past the Sound of Oresund. Joe had a sister too. Brigitha. Just thinking about her made him smile. Little Brigitha with the golden plaits, with braces on her teeth, with pink plastic spectacles. She was older than he was, but that was how he pictured her still. Where was she now? Somewhere in Lithuania the last time he heard. How had they lost touch so? Joe rested on a tussock of grass and contemplated his life. He could climb into his car and drive back to the real world. No need for goodbyes. Perhaps he should. Nobody here would miss him. Maybe no one was looking for him at all. He might be overplaying his role in events at the bank. Maybe his contribution was barely remembered. Maybe he was little more than collateral damage. Maybe the threats of the traders – *you're taking the fall, matey boy* – were simply without substance. Perhaps Colin Helms and Janie Coverdale had accepted all the blame. He wouldn't have a job, of course, but he had money in the bank. He had skills that somebody would buy. He could even play the markets himself. He could use Cassie. What was keeping him here in this soporific hamlet where time ran at half-speed? Nothing.

He half rose from his hiding place but then heard a voice calling his name. 'Joe! Joe!' Beneath him on the sands Polly Hocking was waving. The young man who had walked her onto the beach had vanished.

'Polly.' He returned the wave. Now there was nothing to do but clamber back down the path to greet her while she stood at the foot of the hill and swayed, her hands clasped behind her back. And as Joe drew closer he watched her face blossom into the widest smile he could imagine.

'I come bearing good news,' she said, and she swung away so that he had to follow her down to the shoreline where the shingle met the path.

'I like good news,' he said.

'Good.' And she swung her hips and flicked her sandy hair.

'Who was the man?'

'What man?' She tipped her head to one side. 'Have you been spying on me, Joe Haak?'

'Certainly not.' He tried to sound offended. 'I just . . . thought I saw you with someone.'

'I think somebody is jealous.'

'Don't be silly. You're a married woman.'

She gave him a serious look but it was hiding a smile. 'Are we going for a drive today?' she asked.

'Where to?'

'Anywhere.'

'Why?'

'Don't you want the good news?' She spun round and ran a few steps backwards. 'Come on, Mr Sports Car,' she called to him.

'Does the roof come down on this?'

'No. It isn't actually a sports car.'

'Shame.' She pressed a switch and the window slid down. 'Can we go further than Bevis Magwith's farm today?'

'Only if you tell me the good news.'

'Ah, that,' she said. 'I called up a friend of mine in Penzance. He's a policeman.'

'And . . .?'

'He's never heard of you.' The wind was whipping up her hair. 'How fast does this go?'

'Very fast. What do you mean, he's never heard of me?'

'I mean you're in the clear.'

'Are they looking for my car?'

'Nope.'

He started to feel a little unsteady. 'I'm . . . in the clear?'

'You are In. The. Clear.' She was beaming as if this made her the happiest woman on Earth. 'Let's celebrate.'

He felt the accelerator beneath his foot. A surge of freedom. 'How would you like to celebrate?'

'Champagne does it for me, honeybird.'

They found a seaside restaurant that had seen better days. The carpet was worn around the door and the paint was yellowing. 'I've always wanted to eat here,' she told him. It was a little early for lunch. They had champagne, and crab sandwiches. She sat looking out over the bay, swaying along to the piped music, and it seemed to Joe from Polly's breathing that a legion of demons was feuding within her, each one of them seeking release. They barely spoke. Afterwards he ordered strawberries and tried not to watch her too closely. Was that a tear in her eye? He turned away, and when he looked back, it had gone.

She was beautiful. How had he failed to notice this? It wasn't the steely beauty of the City traders, the professional cold beauty of Janie Coverdale, or the expensive beauty of the girls on the ninth floor, enhanced by perfect teeth and precision hair and designer wear. It was a more organic form of beauty, less sharp, less cosmetic. She radiated it like the warmth from the embers of a fire.

'I had a crush on him,' she said as they were collecting up their things to go. 'Alvin. When I was a schoolgirl. He has quite a way in the pulpit.'

'Ah.' Joe nodded. He was positioning her on a mental graph. The y-axis would be beauty. On that scale she would be right at the top. But the x-axis would be unobtainability; far at the end, she would join a crowded field of beautiful, unobtainable girls.

'He's quite a bit older than me. Twenty-six years. It didn't seem to matter. Not really. He told me if I wanted him, then I should have to marry him. He said it was the only way.'

They took a scenic way back. Joe stopped at a petrol station for fuel. It wouldn't matter now if they caught him on the CCTV. He had already spent enough on his credit cards to raise the alarm if they were looking for him. And he hadn't thought about Lane Kaufmann once in almost an hour. Apart from a vision of Janie Coverdale in her raspberry suit, sitting alone in a police cell, her skirt rolled up tight like a condom.

11
How will it all end?

But his dreams were still on the fifth floor. Even awaking to the shriek of gulls and the scent of freshly landed lobsters and the calling voices of village children, even so the images inside his eyelids were of the glass desks, and the dashboards, and the Milanese suits, and the newsfeeds from CNN. He blinked, inviting in the sunlight of a new day, and the images were gone. But the ghosts lingered. I should stay here, he thought, until I can wake one morning and discover that I've dreamt a different dream. How long would it take to banish memories that were burned into your psyche? Perhaps Mallory Books could answer that.

He showered and dressed, enjoying the feel of freshly unwrapped clothes. He had slept late. What was the time? Nine fifteen. He found himself shaking his head slowly. By this time he would have been at his desk for over an hour. Amelia Warren would be drifting by with his Americano and a *croissant aux amandes*. That would be welcome right now. What would become of Amelia, he wondered. He imagined her in Starbucks, still tap-tap-banging down the coffee grounds. He found himself thinking about his team. Manesh would walk into a job with another City bank. He had a file of offers waiting. Jonathan Woodman and Rodney Byatt – they would be OK. Manesh might take them with him. Perhaps they were all at Citigroup or Barclays Capital already, but what about the juniors? Would they be at home now scouring the situations vacant pages of the *Evening Standard*? He felt uncomfortable.

There was an evening a while back when he was clearing his desk to go home, pulling on his coat, folding up his laptop, when a man appeared by his side. It was the silver-haired man from the upper echelons of the twelfth floor.

'Mr Kaufmann?' Joe said in surprise. 'Are you looking for someone?'

'I was looking for you, Joe.'

They took the lift together and found a wine bar in Lombard Street. They sat in a dark corner; the place was full of bankers sharing obituaries of a day of trading. Joe ordered a diet cola. Kaufmann a Chardonnay.

'What did you want of me, Mr Kaufmann?'

'Lew,' said the silver-haired man. He laid a bony hand on the table. 'Tell me about Cassie.'

It was the conversation Joe had expected. 'So far so good,' he replied. They had run their month of trials. Not long enough really, Joe thought, but investment banks were urgent places. Answers were always wanted *now*. In truth Janie had been staking investments on the recommendations of Cassie well before the month was over. 'We've had one or two little glitches,' he said. This was the programmer in him speaking. 'But it's settling down.'

'I've seen the reports,' Kaufmann said. He was smiling. 'We've seen twelve consecutive days of positive trading from the fifth floor.'

'They're calling it the Computer Aided Share Selection and Investment Engine,' Joe said. 'Hence CASSIE. It fits.'

'Excellent,' said the senior man. He liked this. 'I'll tell Cassie.'

They tasted their drinks. 'Tell me,' said Kaufmann. 'Are you an economist?'

'No, not really. I'm a mathematician. I studied the modelling of complex systems.'

'Interesting.' Kaufmann was leaning across the table as though their conversation might be clandestine. 'I was hoping you might be.' His face was uncomfortably close to Joe's, but Joe felt unable to retreat. 'What does your clever computer model tell you,' he asked, 'about the future? Not today. Not tomorrow. I mean what does it tell you about next year? About the next fifty years?' His breath smelled vinegary. Joe tried not to inhale.

'Nothing really, sir. Cassie is designed to look forward a few dozen hours. No more. We built it to forecast price movements over just a few days.'

'I see.' There was a sense of disappointment in his tone. 'But you could look further forward? There would be nothing to prevent it?'

'In theory, no,' Joe said. 'But small errors would compound. Accuracy would drop off. It's the butterfly effect. After a while our forecasts would be no better than chance. We can see into the future, but only a short way.'

Kaufmann exhaled through his teeth. 'Then let me ask you a very simple question – as a mathematician. How will it all end? What will become of all this?' He held out his hands like a supplicant drawing an imaginary cage over the City of London and all of its banks and institutions and exchanges. 'All of this?'

'I'm not sure what you mean.'

'I mean . . . do we carry on growing for ever? What do you think? There are four scenarios, Mr Haak, and that, I suppose, has to be one of them. Let's call it "scenario number one". Endless growth. If we come back in a thousand years will the whole of England be a forest of glass and steel, full of businesses all making money, and traders buying and selling shares? Will the FTSE reach a million?' He let his hands sink. 'Or do we go with scenario two? Let's call it the "steady state scenario". Does it all level off where we are now? Does London in ten centuries look much as it does today? Are we still driving around in petrol-powered cars, watching plasma televisions, reading the *Sunday Times*, going off to see the tennis at Wimbledon, taking holidays on the Algarve?' His hands dropped lower. 'Or do we decline slowly? That's scenario number three. Do we reach a point at which demand for commodities gradually exceeds global supply, and we all get slowly, measurably poorer? Do we descend a shallow staircase from this world of glitter and light, step by step, all the way back to the Stone Age?'

'I don't know.'

'But you must have an *opinion*, Joe Haak? Mr Mathematician? You're the man who built the model. You know better than anybody how these things work.' There was something of a steely glint in Kaufmann's eye.

'I guess there must be some limit to endless growth,' Joe said, cautiously.

'You *guess*?'

This was starting to feel like a test. 'Maybe it'll oscillate,' he ventured, moving his hands to describe a sine wave. 'Growth and then contraction and then growth . . . and so on.'

'Now you're cheating, Joe.' Kaufmann looked disappointed. 'You're avoiding the tough question, but let's assume that you're right, and the world economy vacillates like a wave, you still need an answer. What is the general trend if we even out your oscillations? What is the direction of travel? Is it up?' He lifted his thin hand to his shoulder. 'Level?' He smoothed an invisible plateau. 'Or down?' He drew the descending stairway.

A familiar feeling of stress began to invade Joe, like an invisible gas drawn in through his fingertips, diffusing up his arms and into his bones. Was there a right answer to this interrogation, or was Lew Kaufmann merely seeking an opinion? 'Nothing can grow indefinitely,' he found himself saying.

'Good.' The old banker was moving away just slightly, building a pyramid with his fingers.

'If we're stuck for ever on this planet, in this solar system, then the very best we can hope for is to find a level of economic activity that is sustainable in terms of resources . . . and then to level out.' Joe was gabbling. He found himself looking the old man directly in the eye. 'At some stage,' he said.

Kaufmann was nodding slowly. 'The very best we could hope for,' he echoed.

'Yes, sir.'

'Have you heard of Dr Pangloss?'

Joe shook his head. 'I don't think so, sir.' He hesitated. 'The name seems familiar . . .'

'You need to read more, young man. Dr Pangloss was a friend of Candide, a creation of the French author Voltaire. His fundamental weakness was a profound belief that we live in the best of all possible worlds. It's always been a popular theory. After all, if God created the world, and God is perfect, then this must be the most perfect of worlds. Dr Pangloss would say that we all have ears and noses so that we can all wear spectacles upon them.'

'Except that in the most perfect of all possible worlds we wouldn't suffer from poor eyesight in the first place,' Joe said.

Kaufmann gave a wheezing laugh. 'So you don't believe we live in a perfect world, Joe?'

Joe shook his head. 'Probably not.'

'So you reject scenarios one and two. Where does that leave us?'

'Slow decline?'

Kaufmann leaned back towards him. 'Or are we overlooking something? Is there a fourth possible future? One that we never like to think about? One that Cassie could foresee?'

Joe could feel his pulse quickening. This conversation was beginning to feel like a strange initiation into a dark global secret. 'What future would that be?' he said, but he already knew Kaufmann's answer.

'Collapse,' Kaufmann said, and he pulled his engraved face away, watching for Joe's reaction. 'But you knew that, didn't you, Joe? You're a mathematician. You know what happens to complex systems. Sudden, dramatic, catastrophic collapse.' His words hung over the table. 'Have you ever heard it said that our society is only three square meals away from anarchy?'

'I have heard that expression. Yes.'

'Do you believe it?'

Joe shrugged. 'I suppose so. If people are hungry, well, anything could happen.'

'Law and order could break down?'

'Probably.'

'How long would it take?'

Joe leaned back. His head was swimming. This was why Lew Kaufmann had appeared on the fifth floor, it was why he'd brought him here; it was probably why Kaufmann had raised his salary. This was the question he wanted answering. Joe needed to be cautious. 'On the whole, systems are pretty resilient,' he said. 'If one supplier fails another one pops up to take its place. If one source of a commodity dries up, another one appears. The prices may change, but social networks and institutions adapt.'

Kaufmann was watching him closely, his hands folded as if in prayer. 'Have you ever played that game with wooden blocks? I play it with my granddaughter. You build a tower of blocks, and then, one by one, you take turns removing a piece.' He mimed the cautious removal of a wooden block. 'What is surprising is how long the tower remains standing. You see, it's just like the economy. It's resilient. It has redundancy built into every level, but the point comes when you release a block – just one little inoffensive piece – and crash, the whole edifice tumbles down.' With his hands he created the catastrophe. 'You see, it doesn't decline slowly. It doesn't sink down into a comfortable approximation of a smaller tower. No. It collapses. Bang.' He looked at Joe for a long moment. 'Could that happen to us? To our tower? Our society? Our civilisation?'

'It hasn't happened yet.'

'Which doesn't mean it couldn't.'

'I suppose.' Joe was silent for a moment.

'Imagine you're a turkey,' the old man said, smiling as he let Joe contemplate the image. 'Life seems good to you. The farmer feeds you more than you can eat. He looks after you, keeps you warm, protects you from predators. And every day is much like the day before. If you, as a turkey, had to make a forecast for tomorrow, what would it be?'

Joe smiled. 'More of the same.'

'Exactly. You could only base your conclusion on what had come before. So you'd say tomorrow will be fine. We'll be warm and well fed. Because you don't know that tomorrow is the day before Christmas Eve.' He leaned across the table towards Joe. 'And if anyone asked you if tomorrow might bring disaster, you'd say exactly what you said to me just now. It hasn't happened yet.'

'I suppose so.'

'How much food is there on supermarket shelves?' Kaufmann asked. 'How much fuel is there in petrol station forecourts? A lot less than you'd think. Businesses don't carry ruinous levels of stock. Not any more. It doesn't make financial sense. We walk into a supermarket and we see all the aisles groaning with food, and we imagine, somehow, that it could feed a city for a year, but we're so wrong. They stock much less than most of us care to imagine. Most big petrol forecourts need nightly deliveries. They have twenty-four hours of fuel in their store tanks – not allowing for any panic buying. And most supermarkets operate "just-in-time" ordering. It's all worked out by computer. The new stock arrives just as the old stock runs out, and every night they have to replenish most of their inventory. How long would it be, do you think, until enough people had missed three square meals?'

'Well, if you put it like that . . . maybe a week? Or two weeks?'

'And do you think there are any conceivable circumstances that could interrupt deliveries for that long?'

Joe dropped his gaze to consider the question. 'It would have to be something global,' he said.

Kaufmann nodded. 'I agree. It isn't easy to imagine any developed country sliding into collapse as long as the international supply routes and systems are still functioning. So make it global. What would it take?'

Joe shook his head. 'I don't really know.'

Kaufmann lifted his glass and finished his wine. 'I want you to ask Cassie,' he said. He was getting to his feet.

'Cassie?'

'Yes. I don't know how you would do it. Just find a way. You're a bright boy, I'm sure you can think of something.' He clapped a leathery hand on Joe's shoulder. 'Find out what unsavoury combination of circumstances would need to occur for the whole Tower of Babel to collapse.' He held Joe's gaze. 'Do you think you can do that?'

'It isn't what Cassie was designed to do . . .'

'Then change the design.' Kaufmann's eyes had narrowed. This wasn't a suggestion.

'Repurpose the software?'

'If that is the technical term, then yes. Please don't misunderstand me, Joe. This is important. I will add your name to the bank's bonus scheme in recognition of your work. But there is another thing . . .'

'Yes, sir?'

'This must stay between us. You and me. No one else.'

'But my programmers . . .'

'. . . don't need to know. Be creative. Find a way to conceal this from them.'

Joe sucked on his lip. 'I'll try, sir.'

'Good boy.' Kaufmann gave a satisfied grin.

This is how he works people, Joe thought. He catches them late, and unawares. He pins them in the corner of a dark wine bar and extracts promises that might never have emerged under neon lights across a meeting table.

'My office. Any time,' Kaufmann said. 'Now I must go. I'm meeting my granddaughter Cassandra for dinner.' And he steered Joe out into the twilight of Lombard Street.

12
But that was her curse, don't you see?

'She was the daughter of the King of Troy – King Priam,' Jeremy Melon said. 'She had an affair with Apollo and he rewarded her with the gift of prophecy.'

'Darling, it wasn't a gift, it was a curse,' said Demelza Trevarrick. 'She spurned Apollo, so he cursed her. Would anyone object if I lit a cigarette? Just a teensy little one? There are only the four of us here and it's too damn cold to smoke outside.'

'Five if you count Jacob.' Jeremy pointed to the landlord of the Petrel, who was drying glasses behind the bar. 'You should really ask Jacob.'

'Anyway, I would object,' said Books. 'Filthy habit.'

'My dear, *you* smoke those dreadful cigars. They stink the place out. My little teeny cigarette won't harm anyone. Let them send a policeman. They'll never find us.' She drew a silver cigarette case from her bag and tapped out a single cigarette. '*And* they might send that dreamy policeman from St Just – the one with the bushy eyebrows. He could arrest me any time.'

Joe coughed. 'You were saying,' he prompted. 'About Cassandra?'

'Cassandra was also Jane Austen's beloved sister, let's not forget that,' Demelza said, hunting in her bag for a lighter.

'She was Hector's brother,' said Jeremy. 'She foresaw his death at the hands of Achilles, but nobody believed her.'

'But that was her curse, don't you see?' Demelza said. 'Apollo gave her the gift of prophecy, but arranged matters so that no one would ever believe her. Just like a man, if you ask me. They can't bear a woman to know anything they don't.'

'Demelza, you can't tar all men with your bigoted brush,' said Jeremy.

'Why not? Apollo was a prick.' Demelza flipped the lid off a silver lighter and drew the flame up through her cigarette.

'A fictional prick,' said Books. 'Let's not forget that.'

'How did we get on to this subject anyway?' asked Demelza.

'I was explaining about my computer system,' Joe said lamely.

'. . . and you called it Cassandra?'

'No, we called it Cassie. But that isn't really the point. I was trying to explain why I had to run away. Why I left the City.'

'So you were, my dear, so you were. Please go on. We are hanging on your every word.'

Would it always be like this? This village was trapped in a bubble, hardly able to see beyond its own narrow boundaries. Here in St Piran a news story from neighbouring Treadangel would be treated as almost exotic, and events in Penzance were really too distant to be worthy of discussion. How could he persuade them to listen to dire warnings from London? Or even to understand them?

'Would you like to know my theory?' Demelza asked. She blew a thin trail of smoke across the table.

'As long as it's a genuine theory and not another plot for one of your novels,' Jeremy said.

Demelza looked at Joe. She had the thin, bohemian demeanour of an artist, Joe thought. He could imagine her in Paris smoking Gauloises in a dingy Left Bank café, reading her poetry to a little collective of acolytes. She must have been beautiful once, a decade or so ago, even desirable – but only in a gaunt, almost Gothic way. Now she seemed to see herself as a kind of Daphne du Maurier character, exiled in Cornwall and pouring her soul into darkly romantic stories.

'I shall tell you,' Demelza said. She drew another lungful from her cigarette and let it percolate into her system, breathing it out with a sigh of satisfaction. 'It's a girl.'

'Here we go,' Jeremy said.

'What's a girl?'

'The reason you ran away from London. No . . . hear me out . . .' She raised a hand to silence any protest. 'The real Cassandra isn't a computer. She's a woman. A colleague perhaps. I dare say her name isn't Cassie . . . but what you've done here, darling, is you've conflated your feelings for this girl with your anxieties around your silly computer . . . am I right?'

'No.' Joe shook his head, but he couldn't help smiling at the idea and this seemed to encourage Demelza.

'She spurned your advances, darling, isn't that it? She took your honest protestations of love and she threw them in your face. But what was the final straw? That's the mystery we have to solve. What did she do, darling, that upset you to the point that you should try to drown yourself in the sea?'

'I didn't try to drown myself . . .'

'Was it another man, darling? Did she show up one day with another man wrapped around her like a disreputable stole?'

'No, of course not.' But his smile was fading. So much for Demelza the expert. This wasn't what had compelled him to flee, to drive like a madman out of the City all the way to the ends of the earth.

Had there been a girl? There had been a succession of girls.

'What was her name, dear?'

Could she still be there in his deepest psyche? Could he really be running from her?

'She'll have *you* believing it before you know where you are,' Jeremy said, breaking the spell. 'She's a good storyteller, our Demelza.'

'Was it a broken heart, darling – or just a disappointment?'

A disappointment. Definitely a disappointment. 'It wasn't a girl,' he said.

'Well then,' Demelza said. 'If it wasn't a woman, then there is one simple solution to our problem. We need to find a lover for Joey boy.'

'Really . . . no . . . I'm not . . .'

'I'm looking to you two for suggestions.'

'Elizabeth Bartle,' the doctor proposed. 'I've always thought she was a lovely girl.'

'Lovely she may be,' Demelza said, 'but she's way too old for our Joe.'

Our Joe?

'Besides,' Jeremy said, 'she smells of fish.'

'You get used to that sort of thing, though,' Mallory said. He looked at Joe. 'Lovely girl, Elizabeth Bartle. Works in the fish packing station. I'd propose to her myself if I wasn't twice her age.'

'My dear, you're closer to her age than Joe is.'

'How about Aminata Chikelu?' offered Jeremy.

Demelza held up a thoughtful finger. 'Now *she* would be good. She could be just the match.'

'She's Senegalese,' said the doctor.

'Why should that count against her?' asked Jeremy.

'It doesn't. But one day she'll want to go back to Senegal. And she'll break his heart all over again.'

'I really don't have a broken heart.'

'She's pretty,' Demelza said. 'Lovely little figure on her.'

The men murmured agreement with this.

'And she's the right age,' Demelza continued. 'But she is noisy. Very noisy. We have to bear that in mind.'

'How is she noisy?' Joe was curious now.

'My dear, she's a noisy *lover*,' said Demelza. 'When she was seeing that doctor from Falmouth you could hear them at it all across the village.'

'He wasn't a doctor,' Mallory protested. 'He was a physiotherapist.'

'Same thing,' said Demelza.

'It isn't.'

'I remember you could hear her yelling,' Jeremy said. 'I was in Jessie's shop once when she started up. It sounded like somebody strangling cats.'

'Never a good quality in a lover, especially in a small village,' Demelza said. 'And she works nights. When would they have their moments of passion?'

'If they had any moments of passion we'd all know about it,' Jeremy said.

'Who said I was looking for moments of passion anyway?' said Joe.

'My dear,' said Demelza, '*everyone* is looking for moments of passion. And for some of us, moments are all we ever get.' She sucked suggestively on her cigarette.

How had it come to this? How had he become trapped in this surreal conversation? How was it that the dream that replayed incessantly in his head was afforded such minimal attention here in this bar with these people? In the bars and coffee shops of the Square Mile there would be talk of little else. His own name was probably as well known now as that of Lew Kaufmann. It was that chap Joe Haak, they would be saying. They gave him too much power. Too much leeway. And yet, of course, he had no power at all. No real power. He had run from the Lane Kaufmann building without even stopping to grab his jacket, his computer, or his mobile phone. He had found his car in the lock-up at Blackfriars and had gunned along the underpass onto the Victoria Embankment, his eyes dissolving with tears. 'What do we do now?' Janie Coverdale's words were ringing in his ears. 'What do we do now?'

'Hold it. Hold the position. Hold it.' That's what he'd told them, but they closed down with a forty-million-pound loss on Monday night. When the markets opened on Tuesday they were down another sixteen million. Still. They'd seen worse, they had all seen worse, but it was wretched. 'Keep your nerve,' Joe told them. 'Cassie is never wrong.' But dear God, was she wrong! 'They're closing down our floor,' Janie called out at lunchtime on Wednesday when losses hit two hundred and twenty million. Her voice was like the wail of a martyr facing the first lick of the flame. 'Close down all the trades.'

'We can't!' Just one voice on the whole of the fifth floor and it was his voice. It was him. Joe Haak. 'We *can't* close down the trades.'

'We have to, Joe. We have to cut our losses now.'

Now every face on the fifth floor was turned his way. The anxious expressions of the brokers. They hadn't slept. The agonised face of Janie Coverdale. Even Amelia the barista. They were all looking at him. Nobody ever looked at the analysts. They were the invisible people. But not today. Not Joe.

'We need twenty-four hours. It *will* turn around. Every one of these stocks is set to dive. We just need to hold our nerve.'

Janie looked more drawn than he could ever remember. 'They're closing us down, Joe. I'm sorry. The bank won't take the risk. Colin Helms has told us to clear every short position. The market is rising too fast.'

'Then call Kaufmann,' he said. He had never noticed an echo on the fifth floor, even after eight years, but today his voice seemed to bounce between the walls. 'Call Kaufmann. Call Kaufmann.'

'No, Joe. We're closing down.'

'Then I'll call him.'

'No.' Her hand was on his phone. She had deep lines beneath her eyes. 'What does Cassie say?' It was almost a whisper, but it too echoed among the glass desks.

'Twelve hours.'

'Too long. If the market rises another point it'll sink us. We can hold another hour.'

'And then what?'

'If the prices fall, we all breathe again. We recover the best position we can. We set light to your fucking computer and we go back to doing this with pen and paper and we never get into this position again.'

'And if the market keeps on rising?'

'Then Lane Kaufmann goes belly up and we all go to jail. That's what usually happens. We'd be breaking a direct order here and God knows how many regulations. So tell me what Cassie says our position will be in one hour?'

'The market should be sliding. One point down at least.'

'Not enough.'

'But then at least we can hang on.'

There was a silence on the fifth floor. You could hear forty-five people breathing. Janie turned back to the traders. Her pause was so long it was painful. 'You heard what the man said, boys and girls. Stay off those phones for sixty minutes. Twiddle your thumbs. Write your wills.'

And now the only sound was the clack of Janie's heels as she tacked back across the office into the light.

Jeremy lived on Fish Street just two doors up the hill from Mallory Books. They squeezed through his little front door. The hallway was cluttered with his painting apparatus – easels, palettes and half-finished canvases. 'Do mind all of this stuff,' Jeremy said. 'I keep meaning to tidy it away but I don't have much room, you see. These were fishermen's cottages once upon a time, and I don't suppose they needed a lot of space.'

'I don't imagine they did a lot of painting,' Joe observed.

'Probably not.' Jeremy was rummaging in a cupboard. 'Ah. Here it is.' He retrieved a computer from a heap of discarded goods. 'I knew I had it somewhere.'

Joe surveyed it, wishing that he'd obeyed his instincts and bought a new laptop in Penzance. Still. The thought was there. 'Thanks, Jeremy.'

'Not at all. It's a good one.'

'I wonder if Mallory has wireless broadband.'

'Not a chance, but Jacob at the Petrel does. That can be your office.'

My office, Joe thought. He had never had an office. Not a private one. He tried to picture his glass desk at the bank. Was it possible that the memories were fading?

He found a corner at the Petrel with a power socket and a half-reasonable wireless signal. To appease Jacob he bought a pint of Seagrass and left it warming slowly on the table. The computer was slow, the software was old, but then he had all day. No one was measuring his time. No one was calling his name, demanding forecasts.

'Would you run to a cappuccino, Mr Anderssen?' he called to the landlord.

'I can do you an instant coffee.'

'That'll do.'

The last time he had sat at a desk had been that dreadful, hollow hour on the fifth floor at Lane Kaufmann. Phones rang, but were unanswered. Someone threw the switch to kill the squawking klaxon. There was no longer any appetite for its relentless negative call. Silence like this was unnatural. There was a sudden hum of voices from the trading tables. A groan rising from a dozen desks. Another stock must have risen. Joe felt his spirit sinking to depths he had never known existed. He was shaking now. He reached forward to switch off his screen. Across the room, among the brokers, a tall figure was slowly lifting himself up from his seat. Joe could see him out of the corner of his eye. The figure was making his way from the bright lights of the trading desks to the gloom of the quants. He wore a black silk blazer and a tie the colour of raw liver. Halfway across the office floor he took hold of an empty chair, and began to wheel it.

He's coming for me, Joe thought.

The trader rolled the chair right up to Joe's desk. 'Hello, matey boy.' He sank down heavily. His knees were touching Joe's.

'Hello, Julian.'

The trader made a show of adjusting his gold cufflinks. He wasn't in any hurry. 'How's it goin' doon here . . .' There was a hint of Glaswegian in his accent, and his tone was almost friendly. '. . . matey boy?'

Joe proffered a nervous grimace. 'Pretty tense actually, Julian.'

'Pretty tense.' That was an echo. 'Aye. Pretty . . . tense!'

'Yes.'

Julian McEvan wore his hair swept back in layers and so heavily pomaded that it lent him a plastic appearance, like a Savile Row mannequin. He wore a solid gold watch and a signet ring the size of a pound coin. His fingernails were manicured, and his skin looked perma-tanned and polished. His manner seemed engineered to come across as affable, but his eyes burned like ice. 'Pretty . . . fuckin' tense . . . wouldn'a ye say?'

'I guess so.'

'You guess so?' Julian was tapping his knuckles together. 'A lot of guesswork in your job, is there?'

Joe shook his head. He could sense that there was no good answer to this question.

'Do ye see the guys on the desks over there?' The trader nodded his head in their direction.

'Yes.'

'Do you see the wee lassie?' He meant Janie.

'Yes.'

'Do you know how much this job means to them? Do you know how hard they work? Do you know how much they've sacrificed for this bank?'

Joe needed to control his shaking. His mouth felt too dry to speak.

'How well d'you think this floor would do without Janie? Hmm? How well d'you think it would do without the boys and girls? 'Cause if we go tits up who d'ye think they're gonnae blame?'

Joe shook his head. 'I don't know.'

'You don't know? Mr Fucking-clever-mathematician? You can tell me what the market's gonnae do but ye cannae tell me where the shit will fall? Is that what you're telling me, matey boy?'

'I'm not . . .' There was a tear in his eye. 'I . . . I don't know.'

'No.' McEvan leaned back and entwined his fingers. 'You don't know. But guess what? I know.'

'You do?'

'Aye. I do. We've had a wee discussion. You could say we've drawn lots.' The trader started to rise from his chair.

'You've drawn lots?'

'We've drawn names from a hat. From a very short list.' McEvan's eyes narrowed. 'Someone has to take the fall, matey boy. When this goes public – which it will – there'll have to be a villain. Someone whose picture'll appear on the front pages. In handcuffs. Someone to go to jail. Are you with me on this, matey?'

Joe nodded.

'It cannae be Janie.'

'No. No. Of course.'

'It cannae be Helms.'

'No.'

'It cannae be any of us.'

'I know.'

'So you know who it has to be . . . don't you?'

The room seemed to be rolling, as if they were at sea. 'Yes.'

The Scotsman extended his index finger and pressed it into Joe's shoulder. 'It's you, matey boy. We drew your name out of the hat. You're taking the fall. It's you.'

Jacob, the landlord, returned with black coffee in a mug and milk in a bottle. Joe took the drink and settled down at the computer. Was Cassie still there? He needed to know. He set up his log-in codes and tried the network address. The screen gave him an error message. Damn. They'd taken her down. Janie had delivered on her threat and set the system alight. He tried again. No joy. He tapped on his teeth – a bad habit, but it helped him think. They had a back-up system in the cloud. It was the development version. Janie wouldn't have known about it, but would Manesh or one of the boys have taken it offline? He typed in the network code.

'Welcome to Cassie.'

He was in. And suddenly time was flowing again. His heart was racing.

A thought occurred to him. It was surely only a matter of time before this version of Cassie was taken off the network. It surprised him that the boys had left it online for so long. He needed another back-up. He knew an applications-hosting agency in Hemel Hempstead. He called up the forms and fired off the request. It wasn't cheap, almost two hundred pounds a month, but then Cassie was such a beast. And it was cheaper than his rent at Dr Books's, he reflected.

'Upload will take sixteen hours.' Sixteen hours! He found himself looking out of the window. The boats were coming in from the day's fishing. The Robins boys were tying up alongside the harbour wall and the girls from the fish packing station were there to help offload the catch. Even with the pub windows closed the salty smell of landed herring filled the air. Jessie Higgs was closing up her shop. It must be teatime. Casey Limber and Kenny Kennet were negotiating over a tangled nylon net that Kenny must have recovered from a beach somewhere. There was a young woman on the quayside with a baby in a pushchair. Dorothy, he thought. Her name is Dorothy. And that man with the red face is Toby Penroth the lobsterman. The pretty black girl with the red ribbon in her hair – she was Aminata; the noisy lover. He smiled at the thought. She was one of the people who had rescued him from the beach. He hadn't had a chance to thank her yet. Did she know that the whole village seemed to have heard her in the throes of passion? Probably. The plump woman with half a dozen children in tow – he knew her too. She was the schoolteacher. He had called upon her in great haste and urgency, recruiting volunteers to help with the rescue of the whale. Martha. That was her name. Martha Fishburne. All these people, he thought, they are all connected. You could imagine them tied to each other by invisible threads. The children depend upon the teacher. And she depends upon the shopkeeper. And the shopkeeper depends upon . . . what? Weekly deliveries from the wholesaler perhaps? And the wholesaler depends upon fuel . . . and the whole thing becomes Cassie's model all over again.

Now this was ridiculous. Why couldn't he look at a simple scene like a row of children on a quayside without being drawn inexorably back into the tangled mathematics of economic forecasting? He closed his eyes. This, he resolved, should be his first task. He would break this destructive pattern of thinking. He would sever the ties that bound him so tightly to the morass of computer models and economic forecasts that had been his life for eight years. He would make a new start. Here. Today. There would never be another time like this. There would never be a better opportunity to start again, to erase the unwanted memories of a life he had run away from. He had a promise to keep. So damn his thousand unopened emails. He would never read them now. Damn the alert messages from Cassie that would be filling his inbox. Damn the short-sellers with their voracious appetite for corporate failure. Damn Janie Coverdale and Colin Helms and Lew Kaufmann and their myopic focus on profit. Damn the whole wretched lot of them. Damn his whole unfulfilled, unproductive life.

Thus resolved, and infected with a new and refreshing sense of purpose, Joe reached out to close the screen of the computer, but the flicker of an image stopped him. A column of figures was scrolling up the screen with the rhythm and precision of marching ants. And every number was flashing red.

13

I'm thinking about it now, sir

'I have an appointment with Mr Kaufmann.'

The male PA had the thin, unpromising smile of a prison guard. 'You will have to wait. He's in a meeting.'

There was a stillness on the twelfth floor that eluded every level below. The air didn't move. No phones rang. When girls walked the corridors their heels didn't clack. When heavy men in dark suits trawled between offices growling numbers to one another their voices were nothing but murmurs. The deep carpets and panelled walls sucked up the sounds. The volume of the twelfth floor was set to 'low'.

On the walls the paintings were heavy and gilded. And the views from the wide sweep of windows took in an uninterrupted swathe of the city across to the dome of St Paul's and up the river to the west. Joe pressed himself to the window. Imagine if this glass were soft like gelatine. He would lean right through and it would close up behind him. He would drop . . . all the way down. Perhaps he would float. He might drift gently down like a cooling balloon, down past the managers on the eleventh floor, the accountants on the tenth, Colin Helms and his fellow directors on the ninth, marketing and corporate compliance on the eighth, and then human resources and strategic planning and all the trading floors, all the way down to the concrete pavements where he'd settle like a moth. Would they notice him? Would Janie Coverdale look out to see him drifting past? They rarely gazed out of the windows, these men and women of the City. The view held nothing for them. So what if it rained? Or if the sky was filled with red balloons? Or if an analyst floated by?

'Mr Kaufmann will see you now.'

It was a smaller space than he'd imagined. Functional. No white ottoman as there was in Janie's office. Just a desk, a square meeting table, upright chairs, and a shelf of books. His eyes flicked to their spines. He could feel the comfort of familiar titles.

Lew Kaufmann was at his desk. He didn't rise to greet Joe. He just raised his gaze away from a document and nodded towards a chair. Joe eased himself down and waited. Kaufmann was screwing the cap onto a silver pen with careful deliberation.

'Mr Joe Haak.'

'Mr Kaufmann.'

He looked ill, Joe thought. His eyes were filmy, and his skin was dull. He was breathing noisily, as if inhaling was an effort. 'Are you all right, Mr Kaufmann?'

The lines on his face were so deep they seemed to be engraved there. 'No worse than usual,' he said.

But why are you here? Joe thought. He wanted to ask. You must be a millionaire, Mr Kaufmann; a multimillionaire. You must have a fine country home, a villa in France, a yacht in Italy. Why do you travel every day to this castle of glass to struggle with the vicissitudes of share prices and margins? Why wouldn't you be on a balcony overlooking a blue, blue sea, letting the sunshine smooth away the corrugations on your face?

But Kaufmann was tapping the desk now with the end of his pen. 'Talk to me, Mr Haak.'

'What do you want me to say?'

'It was you who came to see me. You have something to tell me?' He lifted a silver eyebrow.

'Yes, sir. I do.' Joe's mouth felt dry. 'If you remember, sir, you asked me to use Cassie to model . . . to model a collapse.'

'I remember.'

In this office there was nothing of the closeness that there had been in their conversation in the wine bar. The desk grew out between them, a barrier to their words. Joe remembered the way that the older man had leaned across to him, had almost whispered the words in his ear. This felt more like an interview. He was the nervous interviewee, Kaufmann the intimidating inquisitor.

'It wasn't easy, sir.'

'The complexity of the task is reflected in the size of your remuneration.'

There seemed no riposte to that. 'I've run a lot of scenarios.'

'And what did you find?'

Joe coughed. 'Well, sir. First, I should really say that Cassie may still not be the best tool to use for this.'

'Spare me the disclaimers.' Kaufmann made a sweeping gesture with his hand.

'But it is *still* important, sir. Cassie isn't a traditional economic model. Not like the Treasury model, for example. It doesn't have algorithms that derive from years of economic research. It's really just a big number-crunching machine that looks at the opinions of a thousand financial journalists who could be wrong a lot of the time. I just thought I should say . . .' He trailed off. Kaufmann was giving him an icy stare.

'I understand all that,' the banker said. He was still breathing heavily. 'Tell me, Mr Haak. You're a mathematician so I'm sure you're familiar with Francis Galton.'

'I remember his name, sir, but I'm not sure . . .'

'He was Charles Darwin's cousin. Did you know that?'

'No, sir.'

'He was a mathematician too. A statistician. One day he was at a county fair and they were holding a competition – to guess the weight of an ox. How much do you think an ox weighs, Mr Haak?'

'I wouldn't have any idea, sir.'

'Take a guess.'

'Well, I don't know. Say about the weight of four men . . . fifty stone?'

Kaufmann nodded. 'So about seven hundred pounds, you'd

say? As it happens, Mr Haak, you were right. But not with your guess. You were right when you said you had no idea what an ox might weigh, and neither did many of the people at the fair. Nearly eight hundred people entered the contest, but not one of them got the answer right. Not one. It turned out that the ox weighed 1,198 pounds. So nobody won the prize, but Galton went away and did some maths. He worked out the average of all of the eight hundred guesses. And do you know what his answer came to? It came to 1,197 pounds. Astonishingly close, don't you think?'

'It's the wisdom of crowds, sir.'

'Indeed it is.' Kaufmann was looking at him closely. '*Rem acu tetigisti*. You have touched the point with a needle. And the amazing thing is that it always works. Always.'

'Yes, sir.'

'You had the courage to tell me this a few months ago, Mr Haak. I asked if you would trust my view, as an expert, over the views of your thousand financial journalists. And you said no.'

'I said *not willingly*, sir.'

'Indeed you did.' Kaufmann was smiling. 'But we both understand, don't we, that you were right. Your thousand financial pundits may be guessing all over the place, and if you take too much notice of any single one of them then you might be pissing in the wind, Mr Haak, but average them out, and you have a very wise crowd indeed.' The old man bent his head and seemed to be closing his eyes. 'So tell me what Cassie makes of this crowd. Tell me about your scenarios.'

Joe cleared his throat. 'Well, it turns out, sir, that equilibrium is very difficult to upset.'

'I would expect this.'

'You can try all sorts of things, and the market just seems to settle into a new state of balance. Double the price of rubber. Lots of companies make huge losses, but others do well. Employment falls in some industries, but goes up in others.'

'I see.'

'And this seems to hold for almost anything we can throw at the economy. Wars. Famines . . . The system is remarkably adaptable.'

Kaufmann's eyes stayed closed. He seemed to be in a reverie. 'But . . .' he said, almost spitting out the word. 'You wouldn't have come to see me if there wasn't a "but" . . .'

'There is a "but", sir.'

Time was slowing down. The hand that swept around the clock face on the office wall seemed to mark each individual second like a precise piece of punctuation. 'If you experiment with the model, then two things seem to have a very volatile effect.'

Kaufmann's eyes flicked open. 'I know the first one.'

'You do?' Joe was surprised.

'Oil!' The banker's hand swung down onto his desk with a thump. 'Everything depends upon oil.'

Joe was nodding. 'Yes, sir, but the economy is still resilient. Even if the price of crude oil doubles.'

'But what if it triples? Quadruples? What if it stops flowing? What then?' The old man was suddenly animated. 'Don't tell me equilibrium can be maintained. The whole complexity of modern life sits on an upside-down pyramid balanced on one small brick – and that brick is oil. Take it away and the pyramid collapses. Without oil farmers can't harvest their fields. And even if they can, well, they can't get the food to market. They can't distribute goods to wholesalers and the wholesalers can't get the goods to the shops. The country grinds to a halt. There are half a million lorries in Britain, Mr Haak. Three million in the USA. God knows how many in Europe, in Asia, in Africa. Now imagine what happens if they stop running. Think of all the businesses that depend on those lorries. Think of all the little vans and all their drivers and all the families that depend upon those drivers, and all the shops and offices that rely upon deliveries from those drivers, and all the people that work in those shops and offices, and all their families.'

'Yes, sir.'

Kaufmann eased himself out of his chair. 'It is the craziest thing in human history, Joe. We've built the greatest society that mankind has ever known – a global society. We communicate across continents, we think nothing of jumping on an airliner for a meeting in Zurich or Seattle or Shanghai. And yet all of this, everything we have created, rests upon a finite fluid resource that we're busy burning away. Did you ever think about this, Joe?'

'I'm thinking about it now, sir.'

'Good. Because we should think about it. We really should. Have you ever been to Easter Island, Joe?' He watched Joe shake his head. 'It's an amazing place. I went there as a young man. Not an easy place to get to. It's the remotest inhabited island in the world. The closest island is Pitcairn and that's well over a thousand miles away. Can you imagine living there?' He pointed up at the wall beside his desk, at a framed painting of an Easter Island statue. It was the only artwork in the room, Joe noticed. The great carved head gazed down upon Lew Kaufmann and all his works. Kaufmann contemplated it for a moment. 'The Rapanui people who lived on Easter Island must have thought their island was the whole world – the only land in a universe of water. Just a few generations after they arrived there, the tales of other islands must have seemed like myths. Maybe they would talk about other islands the way we dream about societies on distant planets. Objects of imagination only.

'But they managed to build quite a civilisation, you know. And they built these statues – "moai", they're called. Over eight hundred of them. Fantastic things. The archaeologists say it was all about ancestor worship, and who knows. Maybe it was.'

He turned away from the painting to look at Joe. 'You're wondering why I'm telling you this, aren't you, Joe?' His mouth turned up at the corners in what may have been a smile.

'I keep this picture on my wall as a reminder, you see. Because the Rapanui people did a very strange thing. They became obsessed with building their statues. And every time they built one, they chopped down a whole set of palm trees, because they used the trees to roll the statues from the quarry. Easter Island used to be covered in forest. Not any longer. Because slowly, tree by tree, the Easter Island people cut them all down. Every last tree. And with the trees went the birds that nested in them, and that was the main food source for the island.' He turned back to look at the painting, the huge impassive moai alone on a bare hillside. 'And without the trees they couldn't build boats to go fishing. I often wonder about the day that they felled the very last tree. What was going through their minds? Didn't anyone protest? Didn't anybody warn them?' He looked back at Joe.

'What happened to them?' Joe asked.

'They died.' Kaufmann gave a shrug. 'They starved. They built their civilisation on a finite resource and when it was gone, so were they.' He looked appraisingly at Joe. 'But we wouldn't be so foolish, would we? We wouldn't build a society totally dependent upon a single expendable resource?' His dull eyes seemed, for a moment, to twinkle. 'And anyway, look on the bright side.' He gestured at the painting. 'They left us some magnificent statues.' He sank back into his chair.

'So you think we'll go the same way?' Joe asked.

Kaufmann sighed heavily. 'I really don't know. We're trying lots of new ideas. Biofuels. Hydrogen. Fracking. They all look interesting in their own way, but biofuels still don't make up more than about three or four per cent of the world's diesel. And every acre we use for growing fuel is one less acre available for growing food. And we're running out of time. And the world is getting more complex and more interrelated than ever. So the answer is I don't know, Joe. I still feel as if we're cutting down the palm trees on Easter Island and we won't start worrying until the last one comes crashing down.'

From elsewhere on the twelfth floor came the murmur of muted voices, the gentle whirr of elevators, the soft tread of footsteps. It was hard to imagine now, just a few floors below, the noise of the trading desks.

Joe looked at his feet. 'Is this really about share prices?' he asked.

'Of course not.'

'Then what is it about?'

Lew Kaufmann's breathing was the suck and blow of bellows, the laboured respiration of a being that evolution never intended to create, the discarded wreck of a human body. He rose to his feet. 'Let me show you something,' he said. He beckoned Joe to join him at the window. They stood together and took in the view, the broken lines of streets and rooftops, the steel and glass buildings of the City, and the sandstone and granite edifices of an earlier age. 'It's never been about money, Joe. When I was a boy London was the greatest city in the world. We were proud to be a part of it. There were eight million people living here then, but we got overtaken.' He paused to let Joe contemplate the vista. 'We were overtaken by New York,' he said. 'Ten million people there were in New York when I first went there. The world's first mega-city. I could hardly believe it. Most people visited to wonder at the tall buildings, or at the lights in Times Square. I went there to wonder how it all worked.'

'How it all worked, sir?'

'How do you feed a city of ten million people, Joe? How many lorry-loads of food do you need every day? How much fuel?' He turned to the younger man. 'How do you feed London? Who organises it all?'

'I don't suppose anyone does.'

Lew Kaufmann was nodding. 'Quite right. Nobody does. It works because of a hundred thousand supply chains. Because thousands of people in two hundred countries get up in the morning and do exactly what they did yesterday morning, and the morning before, planting and harvesting and packaging and transporting, flour and sugar and cocoa and coffee and a great long list of foods and fuels and machine parts and devices. We know this, don't we, Joe? *We* know this because that is what we do, you and I. We follow the supply chains, looking for weaknesses.'

'We do,' Joe said.

'Have you ever been to a mega-city, Joe?' Kaufmann turned away from the window and sank back into his chair. He didn't wait for an answer. 'Of course you have. London is a mega-city now. Twelve million people, but we're way down the list. There are twenty-five cities bigger than London now. Rio is bigger. Lagos is bigger. Tokyo has almost thirty-five million citizens. I once sat in a traffic jam in Jakarta trying to get to the airport. There are twenty-five million people in Jakarta, Joe. How many of them do you think keep a larder?'

'Not many, I should imagine.'

'No. I don't suppose they do. There are half a billion people living in mega-cities now, and most of them live pretty hand to mouth. Even here in London. What happens, Joe, when the supply chains fail? What will happen when twenty million people in Guangzhou or Cairo or Tehran or Paris begin to starve?'

'I've never really thought about it.'

'Not many people do.' Kaufmann gave a long whistling sigh. 'You asked me what this is all about, Joe. And it isn't about the money. It was never about the money. Have you heard of Norman Angell?'

The young man shook his head.

'How quickly the great names are forgotten, eh? He was a writer and a Labour MP. He won the Nobel Peace Prize in 1933. I met him once when I was just a boy, and he was an old man. A thoroughly charming person. In 1910 he published a book called *The Great Illusion*. Have you heard of it?'

Another shake of the head.

'No surprise really. It's fallen out of favour, you could say, but it was a huge success at the time. People around the world read the book in their thousands. You have to remember that 1910 wasn't too different from our world today. All right, they didn't have computers or mobile phones, but they did have the great technologies of the Industrial Revolution, and they had global trade, and they had peace. Peace.' Kaufmann repeated the word, as if it were a concept that he hadn't encountered for quite some time. 'Ah yes. Peace. Apart from a few colonial skirmishes, such as the Boer War, there hadn't been a war between any of the great powers since Crimea – almost sixty years before. And Angell argued that there would never be a major war again. You see, he thought that the global economy was so bound in to the interests of every nation that no country would ever benefit from a future war. So that was it. The end of global conflict. It was an illusion that lasted just four years.'

'I see.'

'Do you know what wars are about?' The old banker raised his eyebrows as if imagining a reply. 'The first real wars were about belief. They were waged to crush and conquer people who believed in a different thing – different gods usually. Then the next wars were all about power. They were fought to bolster the vanity of leaders who wanted to rule bigger and bigger empires. But modern wars . . .' he raised a finger and pointed at Joe as if in warning, 'modern wars are about resources. Food. *Lebensraum*. Water. Oil.'

'What about freedom, democracy, defending human rights?' Joe said.

'It certainly helps to have those things on your side, but they're never especially compelling reasons to start a war in the first place.'

'So is it *war* you're worried about, Mr Kaufmann? Is that what this conversation is about?'

The old man raised his fingers to his lips. 'I don't know if I'm worried any more,' he said. 'I would say I'm resigned to the inevitable. We are past the point of peak oil production. Nobody wants to admit this, but it is true. Over the coming years demand for oil will rise much faster than supply. When will we reach a crisis point?' He lifted his frail shoulders. 'I don't know. I'm sure Cassie could tell us, but I don't think nation-states will risk leaving it that long, do you? Oil is too essential to national security. No country will be able to stand by and watch the taps being turned off.'

There was a moment of eye contact between the two men. The young analyst with the pale pure face, the timeworn banker with his ploughed skin, for a moment they held each other's gaze.

'Mr Kaufmann,' Joe said quietly, 'you're not the person I thought you'd be.'

'And who did you think I'd be?'

'I'm not sure.' Not someone who thought about palm trees, he thought. Or Francis Galton. Or the collapse of civilisation.

'The first time we met, Joe, when you first showed me Cassie, I asked if you could program human nature into your equations. Do you remember that?'

'Human self-interest?' Joe said. 'Yes, I do.'

'Do you understand why I thought it might be important?'

'Perhaps,' Joe said. 'But I'm still not really sure . . .'

'Have you ever read *Leviathan*?'

'*Leviathan*?'

'Thomas Hobbes?'

This whole meeting was turning into an education. 'No, sir.'

'Interesting chap. Came from Malmesbury – somewhere near Swindon. He was born on the night the Spanish Armada attacked the English fleet. Maybe that influenced his philosophy. Who knows? A leviathan is a monstrous sea creature, but Hobbes used it as a metaphor for the state. He portrayed the leviathan as a creature whose huge body is built from the bodies of its citizens. The monarch would be the head, and all the parts would work together only because they had entered into a social contract to do so. But Hobbes believed that, like a true monster, no state, however constituted, would be immortal. There would always be periods of turmoil. Uprisings. Or interregnums. Those were the times when the state would be vulnerable. Hobbes believed that people, without eternal, consistent, strong government, would return, in every age, to a condition of war. That is the true nature of humanity. The natural condition of mankind, in *Leviathan*, is what happens when we have no government, no law enforcement, no civilisation. Hobbes's state of nature is a war of all against all.'

Joe blinked. Where was this heading?

'What is the most powerful force in economics, Joe?' Kaufmann raised an eyebrow. 'It is *self-interest.* Self-interest is the energy source for capitalism. Thomas Hobbes understood this. Self-interest drives everything we do. And we economists, Joe, we're used to thinking of this as a positive force. We like self-interest because it leads to innovation, and investment, and hard work, and the growth of equity. But what if a situation were to arise in which self-interest was a destructive force? What would happen then?'

Joe shook his head.

'No one knows what will happen after a collapse, son. No one. That's because we've never lived through such an event. What happened on Easter Island when the last tree fell and the people started to starve? We don't know. The record doesn't tell us. Did they set upon one another like cannibals? Did they fight to the death over the last scrap of food? Or did they all cooperate peacefully in a communal effort to survive? What do you think?'

'I don't know what to think.'

'Well, that's the most honest answer you can give. None of us knows. If you read novels or watch films about the end of the world, they all seem to take a pretty bleak view of human behaviour. They all depict us carrying guns and shooting anyone who gets in our way.'

Joe tried to think of books he might have read that could shed light on this. 'I'm not sure I've read any novels like that.'

'Come, come,' Kaufmann tutted at him. 'You've surely read *The Day of the Triffids*? No? How about *The Road*? Or *I am Legend*?'

'I've seen the film.'

'Well then.' The old banker allowed himself a smile. 'Mary Shelley wrote a novel in the 1820s called *The Last Man* in which nearly everyone dies in a plague. Law and order breaks down. Violent sects go on the rampage . . .'

'With guns?' Joe asked.

'Oh yes.'

'I'm not sure,' Joe said, 'that I'd know where to get hold of a gun.'

Kaufmann waved that objection away. 'The guns will find *you*.' He straightened slowly, his face betraying a spike of hidden pain. 'What kind of species are we, Joe? Wouldn't it be good if Cassie could answer that for us? Will we cooperate, or will we fight? It's an important question. How many people have to turn violent before we *all* turn violent, just to protect ourselves? Can you program that question into Cassie?'

Joe shook his head. 'I don't think so.'

'Then I don't know how far we can trust your forecasts. Everything will depend on how people behave.'

'I can see that.'

'So if we can't answer for the population as a whole, can we at least answer for ourselves? How will *you* behave, Joe Haak? If the whole world order were collapsing around you, what would you choose to do?' Kaufmann stabbed a bony finger in Joe's direction. 'If you choose to stay honest and law-abiding, you increase the risk that you will starve. Society may find a way to recover. Humanity may bounce back from the edge, but you . . .' he stabbed again with his finger, 'you'll be dead and buried. Choose the path of self-interest and you might well survive, but what kind of world would you find yourself in?'

'I've never considered it before,' Joe said.

'Well, maybe you should.' Kaufmann seemed to be in a reverie again. Then he cleared his throat. 'But there were two things, weren't there, Joe? You said that Cassie had found two simple weaknesses?'

Joe nodded. 'Yes.'

'Then let me tell you now,' Kaufmann said, 'before you tell me. Let me tell you what the second thing is.'

14
I haven't really thought this through

The driveway to the Vicarage looked too steep for his car, so he stopped outside, walked up the slope to the front door, and rang the bell.

Polly Hocking, in denim jeans and jumper, seemed happy to see him. 'Well, well,' she said, 'a gentleman caller.'

'I wondered if you wanted . . . to go into town.' It was harder to say than he'd expected. He should have rehearsed it in the car. It sounded like a pick-up line. 'I mean, I'm going into town.' He stopped and swallowed. 'I just thought I might offer you a lift. If you wanted one.'

She seemed to be thinking about it. A finger was raised to her lips. 'Hmm. Do I need anything from town?'

'Well, I just thought . . .'

'A girl can never have too many shoes, I suppose.'

'I'm leaving now.' He nodded towards his car. 'I'm blocking the road.'

'Well, that would be terrible!' She put a hand over her mouth in mock horror. 'We could have tourists backed up all the way to Penzance.'

'Maybe another time,' he said.

That did the trick. She gave a little skip down the step. 'Honey,' she called back into the house, 'I'm just going into town.'

The disapproving face of the Reverend Alvin Hocking loomed in the bay window.

'We're going in the sports car,' she added, giving him a wave. 'Quick.' She grabbed Joe's elbow and pulled him down the driveway. 'Let's make a getaway before there's a scene.'

He used to be so good at planning. It was one of his strong points. He could draw up a project plan on the computer faster than his team could brainstorm the steps. 'Come on,' he would chide them. 'If we can't plan we can't deliver.' They would laugh aloud at his little aphorisms. 'I'll have that put on a poster,' Jonathan Woodman might say. 'Failing to plan is planning to fail,' Rodney Byatt would cry, and Joe would have to bring them all back down to earth. 'Guys, guys. All I want is a simple plan. Activities, timing, resourcing, dependencies . . .'

'That doesn't sound like a simple plan to me,' one of the boys would say.

But that was his strength. Seeing into the future, identifying the pitfalls, spotting the risks. What had happened to that young man? Just a week ago (was it only a week?) he'd been straightening his tie on the fifth floor in Janie Coverdale's meeting room, talking his team through a project plan in which every eventuality had been captured, every risk had been mitigated, and every hour accounted for. What led that young man to jump in a car, to drive to the end of the world, to walk into the sea? And now what? St Piran didn't appear on any chart he'd ever drawn. There was no dotted line linking Joe Haak to Piran Sands to a stranded whale to Polly Hocking to an unwise car journey into town.

What *was* his plan? Did he even *have* one? He thought about the numbers he'd seen in Cassie's forecast, the lines of red that had filled his screen in the Petrel Inn the day before. He'd been transfixed by them. He had watched, open-mouthed, as line after line of negative forecasts scrolled up the page. There had to be some mistake, some basic error in the programming. If only he could have picked up the telephone to Manesh, he could have tracked down the problem. But that wasn't an option. Why would anyone from Lane Kaufmann take a call from the analyst who'd screwed up so badly? And besides, this was a part of Cassie that even Manesh didn't know about. This was the program he had written for Lew Kaufmann. It was their secret. The supply-chain map. He had punched keys on his keyboard trying to interrupt the program. Something was wrong. He had fired off a database query, and the screen had cleared. Clear all assumptions, he instructed the program. Start with the data and the semantic analyses. Now issue a forecast for forty-eight hours. And another for a week. And one more for a month.

Cassie was thinking. There was a lot to compute. For the heartbeats of time that it took for the calculations to process, Joe sat back in his chair, aware that his pulse was racing. Why was he taking the slightest bit of notice of all this? The last time he had listened to Cassie he'd lost the bank three hundred million pounds, had lost his job, had lost his friends. Why would he give these forecasts a moment's thought? A week in St Piran and his mind was still trapped in a destructive cycle. He resolved to close up the computer, to walk away and never look at these forecasts again. But he hesitated, and it was too late. The message on the screen was clear. 'Category One Alert', the message flashed. And again the screen was filling with numbers, and again they were all red.

Next to him in the car Polly was like a teenager. 'Where are we going?'

'Into town. Treadangel.'

'Oh.' She sounded disappointed. 'I thought that was just a cover.'

'What did you have in mind?' he asked, regretting the question even as it emerged.

'Somewhere intimate,' she said, sliding a hand onto his waist.

'I need to shop,' he said.

'How about St Ives?'

'St Ives it is.'

They parked in the supermarket car park, and Joe knew right away that this was never going to work. Whatever he'd been thinking. However he'd been thinking. This was not a plan. It was a mistake.

'What are we here for, honeybird?' Polly said.

He killed the engine. 'Groceries.'

'Uh-huh.'

He needed a plan. He needed to think more clearly. He needed to come back to earth, to drift down from the cloud of confusion that had swept him up ever since that day on the twelfth floor. To settle like a moth. 'How much food do you think we can fit in the car?' he asked, conscious that he'd never really shopped like this. He'd seen other people do it, throwing tins into trolleys, but he'd never needed to do much more than grab a basket.

'How much do you need?' Polly asked. She had a musky smell about her today, Joe noticed, an earthy smell, the scent of honest toil, of breakfast, of baking, of bed-making. Maybe there was something of the vicar's ascetic aroma there too. Had they tumbled out of bed this morning bathed in each other's sweat? The man of God and the village flirt? He shook his head to scatter the thought.

'If I tell you, you'll probably think I'm crazy,' he said.

'Think?' she said. 'I *know* you're crazy.' She laughed at his expression and poked him with the tip of a finger. 'You drove a hundred miles to try to kill yourself.'

'I wasn't trying to kill myself,' he said. 'And it was more like three hundred miles.'

'So, the first time you took me for a drive I had to bribe you with your keys – and even then you turned back before we reached the main road. The second time I had to come looking for you and promise you good news. And now this time . . .' she gave a sweet smile, 'you came chasing me. If that doesn't make you crazy, I don't know what does.'

'I didn't come chasing you,' he protested, but she wasn't listening.

'You got a hundred people onto a beach, in the rain, to rescue a whale,' she said. 'That makes you pretty crazy.'

'Not half as crazy as this is going to sound.'

She tipped her face and sucked in her lower lip. 'OK then. Tell me just how crazy you are.'

He screwed shut his eyes and tried to erase the image of her. Inside his eyelids the numbers were still scrolling. Pray God they were wrong. They had to be wrong. 'There are three hundred people in the village,' he said. 'In St Piran.' This was going to sound too stupid. He shook his head. 'Never mind.'

'No, no.' She was insistent now. 'Tell me. There are three hundred people . . . so?'

Could it really be this difficult? He opened his eyes and inhaled. 'I have fifty-two thousand pounds in my bank account.'

Her hand flew to her mouth. 'Fif . . .' It was too great a sum for her to speak. 'Fif . . . We could go away. You and me. We could go anywhere we wanted. Rome. Florence. Venice.'

Was she teasing? Her reaction had amused him. 'That'll be Italy then,' he said. 'You want to go to Italy?'

'Yes!' She beamed at him and pressed her hand onto his knee.

'Polly,' he said, 'we're not going anywhere. Nobody is. That's kind of the point.'

'What point?'

'I can't really explain. Listen . . . the world thinks I'm this mad, failed banker, but I was never a banker. I was nothing but a computer programmer. A forecaster. And sometimes forecasts are wrong.'

She was watching him now with wide eyes.

'I don't know if I want to tell anyone what I'm forecasting right now, because the chances are I'm going to be wrong again. And I don't want to be the fool twice.'

'I don't think you're a fool.'

'Thank you, Polly, but you don't really know me. I *was* a fool and I'm probably being a fool again, but I don't know if I can stop myself.' He grimaced. 'Mallory Books says I'm impetuous.'

'Impetuous?'

'He says I take quick decisions and then follow them through, come what may.'

'Then I don't think impetuous is the right word.'

'So what is the right word?'

She seemed to be thinking about this. 'Obstinate,' she said, after a while.

He smiled at this. 'So the obstinate question is . . . how much food can we fit in this car?'

'How much did you have in mind?'

How much *did* he have in mind? 'I'm sorry, Polly,' he said, slowly leaning forward so that his head rested on the steering wheel. 'I haven't really thought this through.'

'Which is why my plan is so much better than yours,' she said.

'What's your plan? We run away to Italy?'

'That's not my plan. That's my dream.' She leaned forward to touch him, fingertips on his neck. 'My *plan* is to buy a picnic in St Ives. A pasty each. A cream slice. A bottle of lemonade. Some chocolate. Then we take a walk. We could walk along Porthmeor beach and up around the hilltop. It's pretty there, a really good place for a picnic. You can sit and watch the seabirds out on the rocks. Sometimes you can see seals basking. Then when the fresh air has chased all the demons out of your head . . .' she took back her hand, 'you tell me all about your worries and we plan together.'

It was warm for an autumn day. The winds that had swept the coast only days before, the day that they rescued the whale, had long since abated. Polly kicked off her shoes on the sands and ran ahead. At any other time, Joe thought, he would have responded to her gaiety, would have let himself be infected by her effervescence. He too should be barefoot on the sands, filling his lungs with the deep salt air. In an effort to show her, to demonstrate his true personality, he broke into a run, but an overflow of ennui ran down into his legs and arms, a lethargy that drained him of energy and will. He petered to a halt after only a few strides. 'I'm sorry,' he said. 'I'm not really in the mood.'

'Yet,' she chided him. 'You're not in the mood *yet*.' And she laughed at him and ran on.

Joe found himself looking at the delicate cast of her footprint in the damp sand. There was a satisfying perfection to the shape of her foot – the absence of her foot. This is where Polly Hocking's foot once was. It had rested here for an instant. It had pressed and moulded the sand, and on it ran, careless and carefree. Yet here in the sand was the intricate curve of her instep, the descending hierarchy of her toes, the determined buttress of her heel. The soft, dissolving pattern awoke within Joe an almost physical wave of remorse. Within the print the sand was rising, and a film of cold Atlantic water was eroding away the outline. What was this? What was happening to him when the achingly beautiful sight of a footprint could almost make him weep?

'I think perhaps you're a little . . . depressed,' she said, when they sat on the rocks to tackle the picnic.

'Maybe I am,' he said. There were birds perching on the rocks, stubbornly fixed to the land, ignoring the splash of the waves. What were they? Guillemots, said a voice in his head, guillemots hunched forward like old gentlemen in hoods. And maybe it's true, he thought. Maybe he was depressed. He had lost his job. He had a right to some melancholy. He was trying to remember the old man, Lew Kaufmann, leaning over the desk towards him, waving his bony hand. 'I will tell you the word before you say it,' Kaufmann had said, and Joe had sealed his lips. 'It's a simple word.' He tipped his head to catch Joe's eye. 'Another three-letter word. What do you say, Joe?'

'It could be.' Was this a guessing game?

'It isn't "war".'

'No.'

'I know. Although we may choose to disagree on this. In

my view, when it happens, it will be war. Remember Hobbes, Joe. Remember *Leviathan. A war of all against all.* A nation will do anything, Joe, *anything* to protect its national security. The only thing more powerful than individual self-interest is national self-interest. And this kind of war is very much easier than sending men and machines.'

'I suppose.'

The old man leaned so far across his desk that Joe could scent the decay from his lungs. 'Even *inaction* can be an act of war, Joe. If one nation needs help and another looks the other way that can be as decisive as an invasion; be it deliberate or opportune, when this thing happens no country will be able to count any other as its friend or ally. Not when it's a war about resources. The time will come when the best way for a nation to protect its own supply will be to devastate other buyers.' He drew in a noisy chestful of air. 'And the word that Cassie came up with, the second great factor that could send us all back to the stone age, that word, Joe, is "flu".'

15
What do people eat?

'I don't understand,' Polly said. They were up on the hilltop now, looking down onto the town. 'There's nothing especially bad about the flu.'

'Isn't there?'

'We have a scare every year. Bird flu. Swine flu. Asian flu. It never seems to do that much. There's another one on its way now. They were talking about it on the news this morning. It won't amount to anything.' She watched for his reaction. 'Is that what frightens you?'

'I'm not frightened,' he said. Or was he? Perhaps, like Kaufmann, he was resigned to the inevitable.

'Then what?'

'We think our society is resilient. We think it can take anything that life throws at it, but we're making one big mistake. Complexity. That's our weakness. In the Middle Ages the Black Death swept across Europe. It killed one person in every three, but civilisation was fairly unaffected. That's how we all imagine it would be if it happened again. Yet when smallpox hit the Romans and did much the same thing – killed about a third of the population – the empire never recovered. It spiralled into decline. So what was different?' He smiled at her. 'Rome was too complex,' he said. 'Key people died and couldn't be replaced. There wasn't the manpower to sustain the armies of occupation. One big epidemic kicked off the decline, and a succession of new epidemics finished it.'

She was looking past him, out across the rocks and the sea.

'Am I making sense?' he asked.

'A little.'

'Just a little. Well, that's more than I hoped for.' He stretched his legs out and lay back on the mossy grass. 'In the Middle Ages, nearly everyone was a farmer. Most farms produced enough food for the family and a little more to trade. When the Black Death came, the farms carried on. Work might have been harder, but there were fewer mouths to feed. The Romans, on the other hand, were city dwellers. They were like us. When smallpox hit the Roman farms, the farms failed, the transport infrastructure failed, and the cities starved.'

'Can I borrow your jacket?'

'If you like.' He pulled it off and passed it to her. She spread it out on the grass and lowered herself down beside him, not quite touching.

'I still think it's nonsense,' she said. 'We have flu epidemics all the time.'

'Not really. Not a strain that kills large numbers of people. More than fifty million people died in the flu pandemic of 1918. Maybe a hundred million people. That's around one person in every twenty all around the world. That's what flu is capable of.'

'But civilisation didn't collapse.'

'No.' But we didn't have the dependencies, he thought. We didn't have the fragile networks, the long supply chains. Industries didn't source components from a dozen different countries; we didn't import most of our food. 'There were fewer than two billion people on the planet then,' he said. 'Today there are seven billion.' He was trying to imagine it now. He had to explain it the way that Lew Kaufmann had explained it to him, up in his twelfth-floor office. 'It won't be the disease that kills us. It will be the *fear*. In 1918 it took people a long time to understand what was going on. They still went to work. They got on with their lives. This time we'll all be watching it on the news channels. We'll watch the first victims die. We'll see the bodies being buried. We'll panic. We'll do the thing that everyone does, we'll look after ourselves. Our families. We'll shut our doors and windows, we'll keep the children inside, we'll stay away from work, but even that won't finish us. Not in itself. What will finish us will be the loss of just a few, a precious few, vital individuals. Critical engineers at the power stations. Truck drivers. Oil refinery workers. People who offload gas from the great tankers. If people are too sick or too scared to go to work, then collapse will follow with frightening speed. Towns and cities will run out of food in three days. Just three days. Maybe sooner if you have panic buying. The country could run out of fuel in two days. Water treatment plants will run out of chlorine in a week. Then what will happen to the water in the big cities? Power stations need people to run them, but fear will keep them away. Or maybe they'll be at home looking after sick families. Perhaps they'll be sick themselves. Or they won't be able to fuel their cars. It won't take much. If just a quarter of the workers at a power station fail to show up for work that almost certainly means the plant has to close. Nearly half our electricity generation comes from gas, and we have less than two weeks' supply of gas in reserve. If the supertankers stop delivering the gas, the lights go off. And as soon as the power stations fail, so too do telephones, mobile networks, TV, radio, and internet. That wasn't a big worry in 1918, but today? Communications will break down quickly. You'll turn on the radio and all you'll hear will be static. You'll try to phone your family but the phones will be dead. Do you think that will help to ease the panic? You'll turn on the taps in your kitchen and there'll be no water. Water doesn't just flow downhill into our houses. It needs power to pump it and there will be no power. You'll have no water to drink, and no water to flush away your waste. You'll go to the supermarket and there'll be no food. It'll be the speed of change that takes everyone by surprise. It could happen in hours. And then the riots will start. Looters first, I expect. People trying to stockpile food.'

He was trying to remember Kaufmann's words, spoken in a wine bar what seemed like a very long time ago. *Society is only three square meals away from anarchy.* It had been easy to picture it then, cloistered away in a dark corner of the great city, surrounded by the commuter swarms. Did it seem so real here on a hilltop, watching clouds drift in an unworried sky?

'Without electricity, people can't get money from cash machines. Companies can't pay their staff or their suppliers. Benefits can't be paid. Credit card payments won't work. Tills won't work. Shops will close, and that will panic people even more. Petrol pumps won't work. People in towns and cities will be desperate for news, but all they'll have will be rumours, and rumours have a tendency to grow more frightening each time they're repeated. They'll see great fires burning on the horizon, plumes of black smoke as rioters get to work. In their fear they'll nail up their windows and doors, and this will just make everything worse. More key workers staying away. More industries closing down. More supply chains threatened. People will have to start drinking untreated water and within days there'll be epidemics of water-borne diseases. Hospitals will run out of key supplies. Within a week we could have reached a point of no return as society collapses and the police and armed forces – what's left of them – find they can't hold things together. Within a month there'll be total anarchy. Freighters and oil tankers bound for our ports will turn back home. They won't dare risk the disease or the lawlessness. People will starve. Armed gangs will rule. Farms will be raided and livestock slaughtered. Arable farms will have no way to harvest their crops, and no way to process their grain.'

Polly was sitting up and looking at him open-mouthed. Whatever she'd expected from his madness or otherwise, it hadn't been this. 'You really believe this stuff?'

'I'm afraid I do.'

'Poor sweet boy.' She settled down, still not touching him. 'And you think it's happening now?'

'I think it might be about to happen.' He twisted his face around to look at her. 'That's why I'm crazy. It isn't just the flu.

On its own that wouldn't be enough to push us over the edge. But I think there's a perfect storm brewing. Iran and Saudi Arabia are facing off in the Gulf. I caught the radio news this morning and already all shipping in the Arabian Gulf has been suspended. There's a blockade at the Straits of Hormuz. One little blockade . . . but it takes an awful lot of oil and gas out of the world supplies. We're losing oil from Saudi Arabia, Kuwait, Bahrain, Qatar, and the Emirates. Seventeen million barrels a day. It also stops Iranian oil going to China and India. This just happens to be less than a week after an explosion took out the main oil terminal in Venezuela, and a very bloody coup took place in Nigeria so no ships are going in or out. You probably don't see any connections between these things, but I do. That's what I was paid to do. I join the dots.' And in his mind he was joining dots. What would the price of a barrel of oil be now, he wondered. Three hundred dollars? Five hundred? Saudi Arabia could pump more oil down its Red Sea pipeline – but no more than a million barrels a day – which would still leave a shortfall of sixteen million barrels from the Gulf States. How much oil does Nigeria ship? He was struggling to recall. Two million barrels a day maybe. The world burns eighty million barrels of oil a day. That was a statistic he could remember. Russia ships ten million barrels a day, but those shipments were at risk. He was trying to do some calculations and wishing he had Cassie. He wanted a newsfeed. He wanted Bloomberg or CNN.

Was this too perfect a storm? He could hear Kaufmann's rattling breath, could picture his yellowing teeth and his wagging finger.

'But what has any of that got to do with flu?' Polly asked.

'Nothing. Or everything.' He looked away. 'There's an epidemic of flu in Indonesia.'

'That's an awfully long way away.'

'Not these days. Not when one person with flu can jet around the world.' His attention was caught by a seabird dropping like a missile into the water. 'Look at that bird.' She turned to look where he was pointing, but seabirds were nothing new to her. This was the landscape she knew. The empty expanse of sea. The falling birds.

But there between the rocks and the horizon was another shape. Polly saw it first. She raised a hand to point but now he'd seen it too. A long grey body, a shimmer, a spill of silver and reflected sunlight and the dark green of the water and the white of the spume and the black of the deep. 'It's the whale,' she whispered. And there was the crest of its back, slick like an eel, carving its path through the surf. 'Do you think it's the same whale?' It was twisting now, showing off its great flipper, slicing through the swell.

'Of course,' he whispered.

Then as quickly as it had appeared it was gone. Just the flukes of its tail and a flick of foam like a goodbye gesture, leaving just a ghostly memory of where it had been. They sat and watched, waiting for it to reappear.

'I think she's gone,' Joe said, after a long while.

'She?'

'That's how I think of her.'

They collected up their things and walked into the town. The appearance of the whale had lifted Joe's spirits. 'My plan,' he said, as they walked, 'is to buy food. And provisions. Just in case.'

'In case it's the end of the world?'

'Yes.'

'You're going to need a lot of food to survive the end of the world.' She was looking at him with a gentle expression of disapproval in the flicker of her lashes.

'I intend to buy a lot of food,' he said.

'And where will you live?'

'In St Piran, of course.'

'So you'll have your own little stockpile of food to see you through . . . while the rest of the village starves all around you.' She began to walk ahead of him.

'You're not listening to me.'

'I am.'

'No you're not. I intend to buy a *lot* of food. Not just for me. I want to buy enough to feed the *village*.'

She stopped walking but she didn't turn around. 'The whole village?'

'The whole of St Piran. All three hundred and eight people.'

'You're mad.'

'A moment ago you thought I was selfish. Now I'm mad.'

She turned to stare at him. 'Well, I can't make up my mind,' she said. She turned back to the path and resumed her walking. 'Why would you do that?'

'Do what?'

'Store up enough food for the whole village?'

He almost had to run to keep up. 'Can I win with you? You were all tetchy when you thought I was doing this for myself.'

'I still want to know. I *need* to know if we're going to plan this.'

'OK.' He was behind her, trying to keep up with her pace. 'I made someone a promise.' He shouldn't have said that.

'Someone in St Piran?'

There was no going back. 'No, no. This was a long time ago. I made someone a promise and I forgot about it. The months and the years went by – and I forgot. Until just the other morning when I was swimming out at sea. When my path was blocked by the whale. When I thought I was going to die it was the only thing in my mind.'

'I see.' Polly stopped walking. 'And what was this promise?'

'Does it matter? It's too long a story. Don't ask me to tell it.' He put his hand on her shoulder.

'You're an odd one, Joe Haak.'

'I know.' He lifted away his hand.

'Who did you make the promise to?'

They were standing face to face now. He felt an ache that seemed to swell from deep inside his chest. He looked away.

It hadn't been a bright clear autumn day like this. It had been cold, midwinter in a gloomy room. A bedside. The lights had been low. The room had smelled of unfamiliar chemicals and decay.

'It was my mother,' he said finally.

'I see.' For a moment she held his gaze.

He could feel a grain of sand in his eye and he rubbed at it with the back of his hand.

'Are you all right?'

'Yes.' He gave her a smile. 'I'm fine.'

'So. How much food do we need?'

'I don't really know. How long will it be after the end of the world before the Tesco supermarket reopens?'

'You tell me. You're the one who worked all this out.'

'The truth is,' he said, 'nobody has any idea what might happen. Maybe the flu will be just another scare. Maybe the world will cope with the oil shortage. We can't tell.'

'But you want to plan for the worst possible case?'

Put like that, it did seem a bleak position to take. He was normally a glass-half-full kind of guy, someone who didn't look on the black side, who never expected the worst. Things usually worked out; that was his motto. That's how his life had always looked. He'd landed a good job, found a great flat, dated some beautiful girls. He was only thirty but he drove an expensive car, lived a lavish lifestyle, and had money in the bank.

But for what? He'd never really asked himself this question before. And where had this sudden obstinate resolution come from?

'I suppose I do. Just don't ask me why.' Maybe the worst possible case was looking like the probable one. Or maybe he'd convinced himself with flawed logic. He'd done that before. He had often seen a string of connections and had laid them all out for Janie, only to see them evaporate. A coup is reported in the Congo and a word pops into his mind – 'tantalum' – a rare earth metal with the chemical symbol 'Ta' and the atomic number 73. He knows about tantalum. It is mined in the eastern Congo and they use it in the manufacture of mobile phones. So his mind settles on Nokia. Too obvious a target. So who stands to lose if Nokia's phone production is jeopardised? A supply chain, he thinks, is as strong as its weakest link. More than a hundred companies supply Nokia, and around six layers of supply separate the company from the mining operation in Congo. 'Short Aftan Components,' he tells Janie. 'They're vulnerable.' But they weren't. His logic had failed him. Aftan Components' stock rose fifteen per cent on news of the coup. It made no sense. He had stood on the trading floor and watched the numbers go red, had listened to the blare of the klaxon and Janie's encouraging words. 'Don't let it bother you, Joe. Sometimes even logic lets you down.'

'So you want to buy fifty-two thousand pounds' worth of baked beans?'

'Not just baked beans.'

'What then?'

'Tins of meat,' he said, 'bags of sugar, rice . . .' He was struggling to make a list. 'I'm not very good at this. What do people eat?'

'What do people eat?' She gave him a look. 'You're a person. What do you eat?'

Into his mind sprang an image of garlic mushrooms, freshly picked and lightly tossed in olive oil. He would eat those. What else did he eat? He ate toasted ciabatta and New York pizzas. Bengalese curries. Danish pastries. He ate crisp Greek salads with olives and feta cheese. He ate wholefood granola with skimmed milk. He ate pistachio nuts, and packets of crisps, and bars of chocolate, and tubes of wine gums. He ate deli sandwiches and bloody eight-ounce fillet steaks. He drank diet colas, and Costa Rican coffees, and Belgian blond beers and wines from the New World. None of this, he felt, constituted a healthy diet. Or a shopping list for the apocalypse. It wasn't what he had in mind for St Piran, but what did he have in mind? 'I'm not really sure,' he said. 'Potatoes . . .'

'They'll keep for a month. Then they'll start sprouting.'

'Bread . . . no . . . not bread. Flour. And whatever else you need to make bread.'

'Yeast.'

He helped her over a stile. 'I think I'm going to need your help,' he said.

She caught his eye. 'I think you are.' She held out a hand to steady herself and he took it. She felt cold.

'Are you warm enough?'

'Not really.'

He took off his jacket and hung it over her shoulders. It looked ridiculously large on her narrow frame. Still, it lent a gamine quality to her appearance. He felt a pang of longing. Did Polly have any knowledge of how beautiful she was? 'It suits you.'

'Don't be ridiculous.'

Proximity to this girl was making his pulse race. They picked their way down the hillside towards the town.

'So your plan is to feed the whole village; for how long?'

He shrugged. 'As long as I can.'

'And what happens when your store runs out?'

He shook his head. 'I can't project that far.' It was a technical answer, he supposed. Cassie couldn't see that far ahead. A day or two was her limit if you wanted accuracy. A week if you wanted guidance. A month if you wanted speculation. He was speculating now. He was betting all his savings on Cassie's one-month predictions. Madness. It had to be madness. And yet . . . we import half of our food, he wanted to tell her. So maybe, as a nation, we could survive if we all ate a little less? But it's more complicated than that. We import nearly half our fertilisers. And the half we don't import relies on phosphorus, and we do import that. And without oil we can't get food to the people. Dots joining dots.

'And what about non-foods?' Polly caught his expression. 'You really haven't thought about this, have you? Toilet paper. Sanitary towels. Soap. Toothpaste?'

'I thought we could manage without those things.'

'Do you want a riot in St Piran?' She slipped a hand into the crook of his arm. 'Walk me back to the car,' she said, 'and I'll tell you how we do this.'

The first plan seemed the most sensible, but Joe wouldn't have it. Polly had suggested asking Jessie Higgs, the shopkeeper, to help out. 'Let Jessie order everything from her wholesaler,' Polly said. 'For a start she'd get a discount. And it would all be delivered.'

Nonetheless the idea worried Joe. 'It's too visible,' he told her.

'Too visible?'

'Yes. At least a dozen people would know. The staff at the wholesalers, the packers, the delivery driver. His mates. They'd tell their friends, and soon half of Cornwall would know, and where do you think they'd come looking when supplies of food go short?'

But a second plan was harder still. 'I'll buy it all myself,' Joe told Polly. 'I can buy it from supermarkets.'

She looked at him as a teacher might look at a truant. 'Do you have any idea how much you could fit in your car? Maybe five hundred pounds' worth if you're very lucky and you fill up every bit of space. Which adds up to a hundred trips. Don't you think that might be a little visible?"

She had a point. He tapped an imaginary tennis ball. 'Love fifteen,' he said.

'And where do you imagine you're going to store all this food? I can't see Mallory Books letting you take it all upstairs.'

'Love thirty.'

The weather was starting to turn as they reached the car. An easterly breeze was bringing in clouds as grey as gunmetal. When he held open the car door Polly put a hand on his neck and planted a soft kiss on his cheek. 'Thank you. I've had a nice day.'

'Me too.'

'We should do it again.'

Could he kiss her back? He leaned towards her, but she was slipping into the car. He had missed the moment. Or maybe there never had been a moment.

'So this is what we do,' she said, once they were on the road. 'We'll borrow Peter Shaunessy's van. It's big. We'll get you a cash-and-carry discount card from the wholesaler in Truro, and I think we could do it in a dozen or so loads.'

'We?'

'No. Just you. I won't be coming. I'm not fond of the Shaunessys' van. It's uncomfortable and it smells of fish.' She dropped her eyebrows to let him know that this was not open for negotiation. There was, in the set of her face, in the substance of her resolve, something of Janie Coverdale. He could imagine her, for a moment, in red heels and a pencil skirt clicking her way among the desks on the fifth floor.

'You'd have made a good trader,' he said.

'We need somewhere to store it all,' she said, making it clear that interruptions were unwelcome. 'The good thing about buying everything from the wholesaler instead of the supermarket is that it should all come in boxes. They'll be easier to stack, and should take up less room. All the same we still need space for several thousand boxes.'

'Several thousand?'

'Did you want to spend every penny?'

He tried not to hesitate. 'Yes.'

'Then there aren't many places in the village where you could stack all those boxes.' She was thinking. 'The fish station, but it's not very secure. It's only made of timber. And it's a mess.' She was tapping on her tooth with a fingernail. This was his mannerism. Had she seen him do it?

'Jessie's storeroom is far too small and you can't even move in there now. There's the schoolroom – but Martha would never allow it. It would be good if you could take a long-term rent out on one of the holiday cottages – but they'll have visitors booked for the odd weekend. Bevis Magwith has some old barns but they're quite a way out of the village and I doubt if they're lockable. And his lambing sheds are going to be needed in the spring. Which only really leaves one place.' She gave him a look that spoke of foreboding. 'I think you had better drive me home.'

PART TWO

Can you make a covenant with Leviathan?

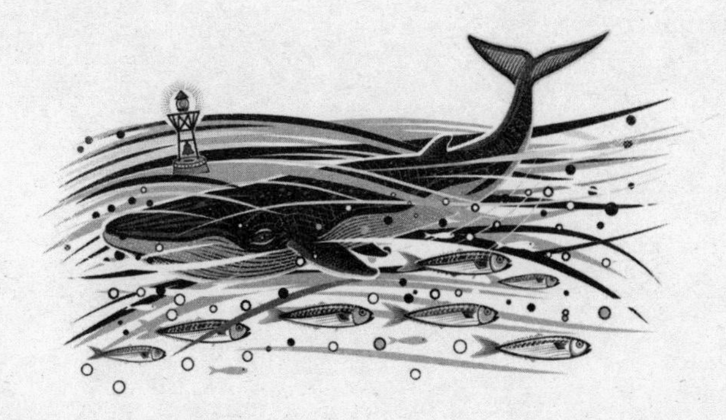

16
When everything changed

In the village of St Piran they still speak of the day when the naked man washed up on Piran Sands. Charity Limber tells the story to her grandchildren, even though they have already learned the details that matter from Casey Junior, their father. And the day is not far off when Charity will have great-grandchildren to tell. She only ever tells the *girls* about the state that the naked man was in, the '*perhaps-ic* state', she calls it, and she leaves this story until they're old enough to understand. 'It were that long,' she says, illustrating with her thumbs apart, and the girls giggle behind their hands. 'But you're not to tell no one. It's our little secret.'

'That was the day,' Charity Limber would tell her grandchildren, 'when everything changed.'

But memory is a fickle lover. When Charity Limber's grandchildren come, one day, to tell their own grandchildren, as surely they will (if Mother Earth will spare them), well, the story might be different then. Maybe there will be more than one whale. Maybe Joe Haak's dimensions will grow beyond human proportions. Maybe it will all have happened on that one autumn day.

Charity Limber takes her grandchildren up to the church on the hilltop. They walk up the churchyard steps and down between the gravestones, and the children run among them, oblivious of the sleepers beneath. There is no vicar any more, but the south door under the porch is always open. The children know this place well. This is where, every year, they hold the Festival of the Whale. 'This is the church of St Piran the Martyr,' Charity tells them. 'When I was a girl, this is where we'd come on a Sunday, all preened up in our cotton frocks. This is where I'd sit.' There are no pews any more, but she shows them the place. 'And when the vicar was a prayin' he'd look at me to see if my eyes were open. And they always were.' Her voice echoes in the nave and drifts into the rafters of the great stone chancel.

She leads the children through the transept to a huge oak door. 'In those days,' she says, her voice dropping to a reverential whisper, 'this door was locked. Always.' She lifts the heavy iron latch. 'Only one man had the key. And that man was Joe Haak.' She pulls the door and it opens with the disobliging squeal of ancient hinges. The children push past.

They are in the Norman tower, the bell tower. The ropes of the bells still hang. One child runs to swing on a rope, but his weight is not enough to tip the distant bell.

'All around here,' Charity says, 'were the boxes. He piled them all the way out from the walls, so that all that was left was a narrow path between them; then he piled them right up to the ceiling. And all the way up these steps.' She takes the hand of the youngest child and they start up the wooden stairway. 'Every step held boxes of food. Tins of meat. Tins of fish. Bags of sugar. Rice. Beans. You had to squeeze your way up. Up to the first floor.' The first floor sits on giant rafters, huge trunks of oak. 'And here there were more boxes and more sacks, high up,' she raises her hands, 'all the way up to the next floor.' Up they go. 'Thirty-eight hundred packages altogether,' she says, and the children try to imagine it, try to picture these bare floors hidden beneath a mountain of tins and packets and bottles and jars.

All the way up they climb, twenty steps northward, then twenty eastward, then twenty southward, then twenty westward, and they emerge out of breath and elated at the top of the tower alongside the bells. 'Careful there,' she calls as they run to the narrow windows. 'There's no glass in them.'

'Thirty-eight hundred packages,' she repeats, 'and to begin

with, he had to carry every one himself. That was the vicar's stipulation. There was no trolley. There were no helpers. Joe Haak had to lift each box, often two at a time, and he had to walk up the steps and through the churchyard just like you did now, in through the porch and right across the nave; and then he had to pile the boxes in here. To and fro. To and fro. Down to his van. Back to the tower. Hour after hour. People would stop and watch him. "What are you doing?" they would ask him. "Why are you doing it?" "I'm storing my belongings in the church," he'd say. "The vicar is letting me rent the bell tower." Belongings? There were soups and casseroles, tinned milk, sacks of flour, all manner of beans, and puddings, honeys and marmalades, sauces, jars of fruits in syrup, dried fruits, purees, bags of dried pasta. There were hot dogs, and tinned carrots, baking powders, pilchards, olives, and boxes of muesli, tins of ham, sacks of peanuts. He bought things in catering sizes whenever he could, so tins of beans as big as buckets, sack after sack of lentils and kidney beans, condensed milk, and powdered eggs.'

It was a superhuman effort, Charity would think. She had seen Joe there several times, the Shaunessys' old fish van parked tight against the wall. The first time she had watched with curiosity as Joe trotted down the steps and swept two heavy boxes from the van. 'Good day to you, Charity,' he had said, and she had blushed. She knew that *he* knew that she had seen him naked, but before she could reply he was off up the steps, grunting under the weight of the boxes. Then back again.

'Can I help you?' she had asked.

'I don't think so.'

Bottles of olive oil, tubs of margarine.

She tried him again when he reappeared. 'I should like to help you,' she said. 'Maybe something light?'

'I'm afraid the vicar won't allow it,' he said as he heaved two boxes from the van. 'It's an insurance thing, you see. Imagine if you were to help me, and you hurt your back. Then whose fault would that be?'

She thought about this as he vanished up the steps.

Boxes of polenta. Soaps.

'I would take full responsibility,' she said, as he came back down the steps.

'It really is kind of you to offer,' Joe said. 'But I can't allow it. If I break the vicar's rules . . . well then?' and he shrugged his shoulders.

Cartons of stock cubes, packets of icing sugar.

Another time she caught him throwing open the door on a fresh vanload of goods. 'More boxes?' she enquired.

'I'm afraid so.'

'Can I help you?'

'No.'

And so it went on. Sometimes when Charity and her dog walked down the hill from her parents' house, the van would not be there. Later she would see it, creeping down the hill into the village. Looking out of her bedroom window in the evening she would see a light glowing from the van, could make out the shape of a man hefting sacks onto his shoulder. How many belongings does he have, she wondered, but she was only seventeen. If a man had that many belongings, well, he would have to store them somewhere.

'Why don't you ask Casey to help you?' she suggested another day as he lugged crates of bottles into the church. 'You could employ him. Pay him twenty pence a box.'

He smiled at this suggestion. 'I would if I could.'

'You could ask the vicar to put him on the insurance.'

But it wasn't a problem of insurance. Not really. If anything, it was a problem of ecclesiastical intransigence. The Reverend Alvin Hocking had not proved easy to persuade. They had met beside the altar, where the vicar was busy arranging some papers. 'I understood you had something to ask me,' he said coldly, avoiding Joe's gaze so thoroughly that he might have been talking on a telephone. He swept away Joe's prediction of Armageddon with a dismissive gesture and a look of contempt. 'Utter nonsense,' he said. 'If you want to play your apocalyptic games you should go and find another village to play them in.'

Joe started his explanation once more, the same one that Lew Kaufmann had used, but the arguments were wasted on the priest. Hocking didn't appear to operate in a world of logical imperatives, and even if he did, he wasn't wired to understand them.

'Do you imagine that God will let us starve?' he asked Joe, his upper lip raised in a sneer.

God seems to have little problem letting people starve, Joe thought, but he was wise enough not to employ this tack. Instead he said, 'God isn't letting us starve,' and attempted a smile. 'He is bringing us a windfall of food.'

'So you . . . *you* . . . are an agent of God?' Alvin Hocking didn't make the proposition sound likely.

'Perhaps.' Joe held out his palms. 'Isn't He supposed to move in mysterious ways?'

'Not that mysterious,' said the Reverend Hocking.

In the end it was a commercial transaction and nothing more. The vicar would not be persuaded that there was any community benefit to the storage of thousands of boxes of foodstuffs in his church, but he did concede that the bell tower had been closed to the public for safety reasons for more than twenty years, and that the space might suitably be used to generate revenue. 'I'm only doing this because Polly insists,' he told Joe. 'You will sign a clear and simple disclaimer absolving the Church or any of its officers of all responsibility for any harm or injury or loss of property that might occur.'

'In return for which I will take possession of all keys for the duration of the lease,' Joe said.

'No other person may enter the bell tower,' the vicar said. He started to descend the steps from the altar. 'And no one may help you with this enterprise or our agreement is void.'

'Agreed,' said Joe.

'You will pay me one thousand pounds in advance, and fifty pounds per week. You will also pay a deposit of five thousand pounds to cover repairs for any damage to the fabric of the building.'

'I will give you a contractual undertaking to make good any damages, but I can't afford a five-thousand-pound deposit. I intend to spend all of my capital on provisions.'

'Then you will have to look elsewhere for your store,' Hocking said.

That was how it was. And for the time it took Alvin Hocking to stalk down the aisle to his vestry, that was the way it might have stayed.

'Very well.'

The vicar stopped but did not look back.

'You may hold my car as a deposit.'

There was a cold pause.

'You may have free use of it until the tower keys are returned.'

'I suggest you transfer ownership of it to me until your tenure of the bell tower is complete.'

'To you or to the Church?'

'To me.'

Well, what would it matter, if the whole world collapsed? 'Very well.'

'That will be acceptable,' Hocking said. 'You may leave the car keys in my vestry.'

Joe could feel a trail of sweat forming around his neck. 'There is one more condition.'

The priest turned around.

'You think I'm a lunatic. Of course you do. Well, you're entitled to your opinion. You think that the future I'm predicting is impossible, so I don't suppose this condition will trouble you.' Joe took a step closer. 'You will agree to make no call upon any of the goods in my store. None whatsoever. You will not accept them, even if given in charity.'

'I would not accept them anyway.'

'Good.'

Alvin Hocking was staring at him now, down the full length of the nave. 'Draw up the document and I'll sign it,' he said.

'I'll include that last provision.'

'You will. And one more.' The sneer returned to the Reverend's lip. 'You will never again speak with my wife.' He held his head back to enjoy the expression on the young man's face. 'You will never consort with her. You will never step out with her, or be found in a private place with her, or pass messages to her.' He stood and waited for a response that he knew would never come. 'If you do, then our agreement is void.' And with a look of smug satisfaction he turned and strode out of the church.

17
You join the dots

'The government is issuing twenty million vaccines,' said Mallory Books. 'Don't they realise we have seventy million people?'

Joe was cooking eggs in a pan. 'How do you like yours?' he asked.

'My what?'

'Eggs?'

Mallory grunted. 'In eighty years I don't think anyone ever asked me that question. I don't even know what a valid answer might be.'

'The usual options are sunny side up or over easy,' Joe said, 'although with me the choices are runny or rubbery.'

'Then I shall have something in between.'

'Good answer,' said Joe. He flipped two eggs onto the doctor's plate, then cracked two more into the pan.

'Have you done with all this larking about?'

'What larking about?'

'They're complaining that Peter Shaunessy's van is always blocking Cliff Street Hill. Apparently it's parked up there all hours of the day and night.'

'Well, they've no reason to complain. There's always plenty of room to pass.'

'That's not what they're saying.'

'Well, I haven't seen the *Ark Royal* sailing up Cliff Street, but I should say that pretty much anything else can squeeze past.' Joe flipped his eggs. 'And anyway it's Saturday. I'm having a day off.'

'Pleased to hear it.' Mallory stabbed at his breakfast. 'Jessie

Higgs is worried that you're opening a shop up there.'

'Tell her not to worry. I'm not. And even if I wanted to, the Reverend Hocking wouldn't allow it.'

They settled to their breakfast in silence. One thing at least, Joe thought, that he'd contributed to Mallory Books's household was the concept of a good breakfast.

'Do you, by any chance, play bridge?' the doctor asked.

'After a fashion,' Joe said, trying to remember the last time he had played. 'Do you have a four?'

'We have a four with you. Jeremy and Demelza play. We used to play with Alfred Moot from the smallholdings but he . . . well, he passed away three years ago. We'll need you in the Petrel tonight.'

'Tea?'

'Yes please.'

There was a symbiosis of a sort in their relationship, Joe thought. Mallory Books would park himself at the table like a garrulous uncle while Joe cooked and waited table, and afterwards cleared away the dishes and washed up, and put the things away. Books's contribution was more subtle. He would offer a running commentary on village gossip, on snippets of news from the radio, on items of interest from his years in the village. None of these things failed to interest Joe. Books had become his newsfeed, his ticker-tape of headlines and highlights. National and international news would sit alongside incidents from Fish Street and the two would be treated with the same attention and deliberation.

'I had Dorothy Restorick in here yesterday,' Mallory said. 'With the baby.'

'Yes, I know her.'

'He's got the snuffles. She thinks it's the Asian flu.'

'Really?'

'I had a chap died of flu once, 1970, I think. Or thereabouts. Corin Magwith. He was Bevis Magwith's great-uncle. Insisted on going out on his tractor in the middle of winter. I told him to stay in bed, but it was no good. They found him dead at the wheel, poor bugger.'

'Oh dear.'

'They're saying up to quarter of a million dead in Indonesia. God knows what the numbers are in India. Nobody's keeping count.'

'I suppose not.'

'They've closed off Singapore, you know. Nobody allowed in, nobody allowed out.'

Joe could feel his antennae twitching. Singapore was a choke point, a shipment hub for goods and oil. How much of the world's shipping went through Singapore? He could picture dots forming in his mind, waiting to be joined. 'What about the Straits of Hormuz?' he asked.

'The what?'

'The Arabian Gulf. What about the blockade?'

'Bad to worse,' Mallory said. 'Japan's got involved.'

Japan? Of course. Ninety per cent of Japan's oil came up through the Gulf. Tick. Tick. Tick. What a time it would be right now to be a short-trader, Joe thought. How the markets must be falling. He caught himself. It was a crazy thought. He had a job to do here, in St Piran.

'They're rationing fuel,' Mallory said.

'Who are? The Japanese?' He wished for a hundredth time that Books possessed a television.

'No, not the Japanese. We are. We're rationing fuel.'

'Really? I must have missed that.' He felt an urge to check up on Cassie. He hadn't logged in for several days. He'd been too busy carrying provisions into the bell tower. 'I think I'll pop down to the Petrel this morning,' he said.

'I don't imagine Jacob will be open yet.'

'I need his internet link.'

It was an almost perfect morning. Joe walked down to the harbour keep and around the wall, standing on the furthest point to look out at the sea. The tide was high, but the wind was low and the waves were gentle. He was looking for the whale. Three times he had encountered her now. He was beginning to think of her as a fixture in the landscape – look out to sea and there she would be, her tail raised in salute; but today there was no sign. He scanned the water. There were boats out fishing, a sailing smack scudding by, a heavy oil tanker close to the horizon. Oil, he thought, unable to escape the mental associations this triggered. Where would this one be sailing from? Libya perhaps. One of the last shipments from Qatar or Kuwait?

He'd been hoarding food now for five days, so there had been plenty of time to do the sums. The Shaunessys' van, he had discovered, would accommodate, on average, seventy boxes from the cash-and-carry warehouse. It took him just under two hours to do the round trip. Loading was easier than unloading. The wholesaler had a loading bay at just the right height for his tailgate, there was an obliging forklift truck driver, and the process was swift; no one paid him a great deal of notice.

In St Piran, it was a lot more awkward. Simply offloading the seventy packages could take him two hours. Every box and sack and crate had to be carried up to the church by hand, and as the store grew the journey became longer. He was having to lift the boxes ever higher onto the burgeoning piles in the bell tower. He had developed a system of a sort. Heavier boxes (tins and bottles and jars) would go along the bottom, lighter ones (packets and sacks) on top; but the packages came in different sizes and shapes, so they didn't stack easily. This is like drystone walling, he thought, more than once, as he staggered into the tower under the weight of yet more boxes. Every stone has a perfect place and every space has a perfect stone. Here would be a good place for another box of tins, there an ideal home for a sack of lentils.

And so the stockpile grew. On the first day he managed no more than two trips to the wholesaler, but he got smarter. On the second day he was there when they opened their doors at nine o'clock, and was back with an empty van at lunchtime. He ate a sandwich while driving. Working flat out, he made it back for a third load just before five o'clock, and he finished work at the bell tower at half past eight in the evening. It had been a long day, but it set the pattern for the days to come. It had come as something of a relief to discover that the wholesaler closed for the weekends. Already Joe had transported almost a thousand boxes of provisions, and had spent around thirteen thousand pounds of his savings.

It was an ill-conceived enterprise. He knew that now. It was foolhardy, impractical, and preposterous. He should have abandoned it at the start. Polly Hocking would probably have called him obstinate. If he'd only had a whiteboard, had thought about it for longer, had drawn out a plan, or had even done any of the calculations, well, he probably would never have started. It hadn't seemed an especially difficult challenge when he had first conceived of it, or even when he'd tried explaining it to Polly. Somehow he had imagined, then, that he could buy all he needed from a supermarket, could bring it home in carrier bags, and stash it all in his room in Fish Street. He hadn't taken time to think about the *scale* of his idea. Still, after a week, the plan had developed a certain momentum. And once he'd made the deal with Alvin Hocking, he had little choice but to see it through. The vicar had his Mercedes, after all. Then, once he'd completed one journey and stowed away one consignment of goods, it had seemed easy enough to set off for a second trip. It seemed the only thing to do. And when the boxes from the second trip were safely stored away, the only thing that beckoned was a third.

It was the recklessness of youth. It was the carefree adventurism of a young man with very little to lose. Thirteen thousand pounds. There were traders at Lane Kaufmann who would earn that much in a week. Joe doubted whether any of them would ever encounter the true value of one week's work represented in tins of custard and sacks of rice. And the thought that any might spend a working week lifting and carrying their earnings in a thousand awkward boxes was monstrous. Yet despite the folly, and the physical effort and the financial cost, Joe had discovered some unexpected benefits to his enterprise. Nonsensical it might have been, but after a week he was feeling fitter. Healthier. Stronger. He had spent eight years bent over computer monitors, growing pale beneath the glow of neon strip lights and plasma screens. He'd never made much progress at the gym before, and had never felt part of a community. Yet here, in St Piran, he was the man who had saved a whale. Here he had formulated a plan to rescue a community from the threat of Armageddon. Somehow, here, among these gentle people, he had discovered a new identity, one that he could never have imagined at his desk in the City. He was sleeping well. His dreams, when he had them, were now free from the visions of his past. In the last five days he had barely thought of the trading desks, or of Janie Coverdale, or of screens flashing red.

The table by the window in the Petrel was beginning to feel like his desk. 'Coffee?' Jacob Anderssen volunteered.

'Yes please.'

There were things he should have done earlier. He sent an email to his father, and another to Brigitha, his sister. 'I'm OK,' he told them. 'I had a personal crisis but I've found somewhere quiet to sort myself out.' He smiled as he wrote this. 'Stock up on food, and take it to the island,' he wrote. 'Please take this warning seriously. I'm not going mad, I promise – but I really advise you to store up at least ten weeks' worth of food in tins. Practically that means around two or three hundred tins for each person. Four hundred if you want to be safe. Please start doing this today. I'm not being alarmist. At least, I don't think I am. We may not have much time.' After he hit the 'send' key he sat back and looked at the view through the window. Was there ever a more agreeable aspect? A fishing boat was steering its way in through the harbour walls and he could see the weathered face of the fisherman at the wheel. How many times would he have made this trip? He could hear the faint noises of the engine chug-chugging to a halt. And there were the Robins boys – Daniel and Samuel – ready on the quay with their ropes. Which one was Daniel and which Samuel? Joe shook his head.

Time for another email. He sent a note to Manesh and copied it to the boys in the development team. 'I'm sorry,' he told them. 'I know I let you down. In the end I couldn't take the pressure. I broke.' Strange how writing an experience down makes it true, he reflected. 'I hope you find success in whatever you choose to do,' he wrote. 'Stock up on food. And don't worry about me. I won't be coming back.'

Someone had entered the Petrel and was sitting down beside him.

'Hello.'

A large round woman in a cotton frock, a wide smile across her rosy features. 'Am I disturbing you?'

'Not at all.' He held out his hand the way that a City boy instinctively does. 'I'm Joe,' he said. 'And I know you, don't I? You're Martha Fishburne.'

'I am that.' She seemed pleased that he knew her name. She took his offered hand in both of hers and shook it warmly.

'Here. I'll move along.' He pushed his computer down the table and slid his chair across to make room. 'Can I get you a coffee?'

'That'd be lovely.'

'Another coffee please, Jacob.'

'Coming up.'

'What can I do for you, Mrs Fishburne?' What a formal City expression that was. Joe wished he hadn't said it. 'What I meant to say was, it's a pleasure to meet you properly. It would be nice to get to know you.'

That was better. Martha smiled even wider. 'I was hopin' to do the same meself.'

'Isn't it a lovely day?' That seemed like a good start.

'My mother would say that every day's a lovely 'un if you can see where tomorrow's dinner's comin' from.'

'Your mother was a very wise woman.'

'She was 'n' that.'

They shared a smile. 'You're the schoolteacher,' he said.

'Bin teachin' here thirty-six years,' she said. 'Not for much longer, I'm afraid. Too few kids.' Her face reflected the chagrin. 'We're just about the smallest school in the county. There's only me now. Me 'n' Modesty Cloke who helps out, and nine kids all the way from four to eleven. Every day I expect that envelope to drop on the mat to say all the young 'uns have to go to Treadangel. Six miles each way. Don't make a lot of sense while I'm still here, still breathin'. Still.' She recovered her smile. 'There in't many faces in this town that didn't pass through my school.'

'I don't expect there are.' Joe nodded.

'Every time I see Benny Restorick comin' down the street in his suit and tie I see the little boy with the gap in his teeth who put an eel down the front of my dress.' Martha grinned. 'An' every time I see Moses Penhallow I see a lad with a stutter so bad he couldn't barely open 'is mouth. And Kenny Kennet – he was so bright but he never cared for learnin'. Only ever happy prowlin' round the beaches. And Jessie Higgs – she was Jessie Magwith then – she couldn't add up to save her life, but now look at her, runnin' the shop, doing all the countin' up in her head as easy as pie.' She gave a laugh. 'Nobody understands this village like me – 'cept mebbe Doctor Books. No one has no secrets from their schoolma'am.'

Joe gave her a smile. 'I don't suppose they do.'

'That Polly Connor – she 'ad no real choice, you know. Her mam, God bless her soul, she was set on her and that vicar from the day he started at St Piran. No matter that he was twenty-six years older, that didn't mean nothin' to her. Not to Nora Connor. Her own 'usband was a drinker, see. And Polly – she were a minx. Nora Connor and Alvin Hocking, they planned it all, they did. I saw 'em. I do the flowers, see, in the church. I knew what was goin' on. One day I'd see 'em deep in conversation and the next Nora would be poorly and Polly would be off up to the Vicarage on some errand wearin' a brand-new frock. I notice these things. And sure enough, Polly weren't much past seventeen, and she's up the aisle with the vicar. That were ten years ago. It made Nora happy, mind. He doesn't touch a drop, that vicar – not even the communion wine – but did it make Polly happy?'

'Why are you telling me this?'

'You look to me like a man who needs to know.'

Joe turned away. 'Is that what you wanted? To warn me off Polly Hocking?'

'Warn you off?' Martha Fishburne looked affronted. 'Who said warn you off?'

'What then?'

'Jus' passin' the time,' said the schoolteacher.

Jacob arrived with the coffees.

'Now 'ere's the thing,' Martha continued. 'When you knows a village the way I know this one, well, there in't too many secrets. If Nan Horsmith has one of her turns, then she tells Jenny Shaunessy, and Jenny tells Jessie when she pops down to get her bread, and Jessie tells the whole community and mebbe that takes half a day, and eventually someone gets a message to Aminata, the nurse, and mebbe she looks in at teatime to see if everythin's well. But I know about it even before Jenny knows. Because I know what time young Thomas Horsmith gets to school, and I see how red his eyes are, and if he's wearing odd socks.'

Joe smiled. 'You join the dots.' She was an analyst too. The only difference between them was the links they saw. He saw the cascade of consequences radiating out from tremors in international supply chains. She saw a much more intimate sequence, but possibly no less complex for all that. Her conclusions drew from a personal knowledge of three hundred personalities and patterns of behaviour that stretched back for half a century. His clues came from CNN and Bloomberg; her clues came from odd socks.

She was nodding. 'I do,' she said. 'I join the dots.'

'So do I.' An unexpected bond had sprung up between them and Joe felt a sudden urge to throw an arm around this woman. There had been a clarity to her story that appealed to his sense of narrative. One thing leads to another and then to a third. 'You could get a job in the City,' he said. Not true, of course. Who would employ this ruddy-faced woman in her cheap cotton dresses, and how would she survive in a world of unfamiliar faces? But she understood the sentiment.

'Thank you.'

'So what do you see now?' he asked. 'When you join the dots?'

She gave him a serious look. 'Not good things.' She shook her head slowly. 'Most people in St Piran, they don't ask questions. Me . . . well, I'm a schoolteacher so that's my job, askin' questions. So lots of people have said to me, see that young man what's livin' with the doctor, that young Joe, he's movin' all 'is stuff into the church tower. And then another 'un will say, tins of corned beef, that's what he's storing. And little Ellie Magwith, she said it were beans. And Benny Shaunessy said it were cans of petrol and you were plannin' to burn down the church. He has imagination, that boy, but me, you see, I join the dots.'

'And what is the picture that emerges?'

'A troubled young man comes all the way down 'ere from London in 'is fancy car and nearly does away with 'isself in the sea. He's a banker, some say, but the next thing he's seen walkin' out with Polly Hocking no less, and there's no surer girl to win a young man's heart than Polly and that's the truth. He's 'ansum and she's very near the prettiest minx ever passed through my class, and when folks see 'em together they looks like rum an' lemonade all mixed up in a glass – you can't see where one of 'em starts and the other 'un begins. You couldn't put a fish-knife between 'em. That's what my Ronnie would say. An' now the vicar is driving 'is car. Reverent Hockin's been up the lane an 'undred miles an hour, folk say, 'is face as black as a March Monday. Louisa Penroth seen 'im in Truro driving down Boscawen Street. Now all that would strike anyone as bein' rather strange, wouldn't you say?' She tilted her head to one side while she waited for an answer.

'When you put it like that . . .'

'An' now 'ere's another thing.' There was something like a twinkle in her eye. 'I remember Peter Shaunessy twenty years ago when he first come into my class. He could never hide a thing from me 'owever much he tried. He's got one of them truthful faces – dun't know how to lie. So now I'm askin' 'im, how long you rentin' your van to that City boy? An' he looks away and tells me how bad business is, how he dun't need a big van like that. So I ask 'im again and he tells me it's good business rentin' out 'is van, he should do more of it. So I says, "Peter – how long?" An' he tells me four weeks.'

Joe smiled wider. 'You're like Miss Marple.'

Martha liked that. 'Do you read Agatha Christie? I think she's wunn'erful.'

'I do too.'

'So 'ere's how I sees it. You've come as far away from the City as you can. No one knows you're 'ere. You *know* somethin'. You know a secret – a very big secret. Somethin' bad is going to 'appen – and it in't good. Now I don't know what your secret is, but what I do know is, your plans got spoiled.' She stabbed him with a soft finger. 'You were goin' to lie up in St Piran and you were going to buy up enough food and drink to see you through whatever it is that's comin'. But two things 'appened to change your plans.'

'Two things?' He was curious now. Had Martha joined more dots than he'd imagined?

'Number one,' she said. 'The whale.'

'The whale?'

'Oh yes. 'Cause one moment you were a stranger in a town where no one in't goin' to give you a second look. An' the next you're a local 'ero. Everyone knows your name. An' what's more . . . you know their names.'

Joe was looking down into his coffee. 'And the second thing?'

'Polly Hocking.'

'I see.'

'So now you're doin' a different thing. A good thing, mind. You're stockin' up enough to feed the whole of St Piran. Am I right?'

There wasn't a lot of point protesting. 'I didn't think I would keep it a secret for long.'

'You're a good man, Joe Haak. I'd love to 'ave taught you. My question is . . . do we 'ave enough time?'

'Enough time?'

'You 'ave three more weeks of that van, which says to me that you 'ave a lot more trips to make.'

Joe let a long whistle escape through his teeth. 'Do you have time for the whole story?'

Martha's face lit up once more. 'When you teach in a small place like this, there's always time for a story.'

They left Jacob looking after Joe's computer and walked together up the quay and round the headland to the sands. 'That's where they found me,' Joe said, pointing.

'I know. Everybody knows.'

He told her about Lew Kaufmann, and about Janie, and Cassie. He told her about oil, and war, and flu. He told her the number of boxes and sacks he could fit in a single vanload. He told her about the Reverend Alvin Hocking and his edict.

Old Man Garrow was parked on the bench overlooking the sands, his pipe smouldering. 'In't seen 'im today,' he said as they passed. 'But I'm lookin'.' He doffed his cap.

'He means the whale,' Martha said.

'Ah.'

They walked for a while without speaking. There were footprints in the sand, Joe noticed. Someone had walked this way ahead of them. Not Polly, though. He would recognise her print.

'Who can I tell?' Martha asked.

'Only people you can trust. If anyone outside St Piran learns about this then we're in danger. Not yet, but eventually we will be.'

'An' 'ow would we be in danger?'

He was remembering the conversation with Lew Kaufmann in the twelfth-floor office. How will we all behave when the food runs out? 'I don't really know,' he said. 'No one really knows how people will react. We could be raided.'

'By who?'

'Hungry people.'

'An' what would they do?'

He shrugged. 'Steal all our food.'

'I see,' Martha said. 'Then we'd be hungry and they wouldn't. Is that so dangerous?'

'Maybe not for them.'

They turned back. 'Would you change your plans for Monday?' Martha said. 'An' not ask me why?'

It was difficult to do anything but nod.

'Get to the cash-and-carry warehouse at four p.m.,' she said. 'An' wait for me.'

'Wh . . .'

She held up a finger to his lips. 'You promised,' she said.

'OK.'

He held out his hand and she took it. Then he let his arm fall across her shoulder and together they walked back into the village.

18
These are they

Imagine a herring gull high above the Cornish cliffs, floating on the warm air currents that drift up from the Atlantic. With a dip of its wing and a turn of its head it tracks the rocky promontories, the secret bays, the hidden coves, the caves and crevices that mark the fragile boundary line between land and ocean. It sees the thumb of land that is Piran Head, a rocky, unforgiving peninsula pointing extravagantly out to sea. It soars over the knuckle and finds the narrow lane buried between ancient hedgerows. Does our seagull follow the lane? Imagine that it does. It picks up the worn demarcations and contours as it twists and turns, as it disappears into a tussock of trees and re-emerges to cross a shallow ditch, as it surges up a steep hill and around a dangerous bend. There are no barriers here for a seagull; no gates, no earthworks, no roadblocks. There is only the warm wind and the sea spray, a place to soar and a place to perch and a place to float on the cold, salty waves. There ahead our gull can see the village – a Norman church with a granite tower, and a wedge of whitewashed, slate-roofed cottages dropped and squeezed into the valley like the work of a casual artist, with barely a perfect corner or a level step or rendering that hasn't been chipped by clumsy vehicles. There are just four boats in the harbour – space doesn't allow for many more – and now, when the tide is out, the boats lie marooned on the mud, the abandoned corpses of once fine vessels that compete with the weathering and the rust and the toil from ten thousand days at sea. There are gulls on the rooftops and the harbour walls, balanced against the winds on pale webbed feet, and they make their presence known. They thrust forward their yellow bills and they call, a hawking, strangled cry – a haak haak haak, a wail.

They are calling his name. This is what they say in the village of St Piran. It is part of the folklore now. You will hear it told, even at the Festival of the Whale. The gulls are calling Joe Haak. Sometimes the children will pick up the call, 'haak haak haak'.

There is no statue, no painting, no photograph even of the man the seagulls call. He lives on in the descriptions of those who remember him, but even these vignettes are slippery. He was tall, says Ardour Cloke, but Ardour was only fifteen when the naked man washed up on Piran Sands. Maybe his memory is capricious. For old Casey Limber says Joe was of medium height – perhaps a little shorter than an average man. Thomas Horsmith says that his eyes were blue, but Ellie Horsmith swears they were brown. Charity Limber says that his skin was pale, that his hair was white, that his voice was deep and low. Jessie Higgs calls his hair a mat of hay and says that his voice was musical and light. Some say he had a beard. Some say he was clean-shaven. Some say only the seagulls truly know.

It was, many would say, the last morning of normality. Charity Limber would call it the end of the beginning. Mallory Books was downstairs at breakfast relaying forecasts of calamity. 'It's here,' he said in a tone laden with import, as he filled the teapot.

'What's here?'

'The flu,' he said, tutting gravely.

'What? Here in St Piran?'

'No, no. Here in Britain. It said so on the wireless. Twelve members of a flight crew at Heathrow apparently. Two of them are already dead.' The doctor was shaking his head.

'Two dead already?' Joe almost dropped the plate he was carrying.

'And one in intensive care. They're closing all the airports to international flights as a precaution.'

Joe let out a slow whistle. 'Closing all the airports . . .' For an instant he was back on the fifth floor at Lane Kaufmann. The consequences of this would be too great to calculate. Even for Cassie. He could imagine Janie Coverdale's voice floating above the trading desks. 'Find me a short, Joe – find me a short.' But everything would be short on this news. Airline stocks first, and airports, and travel companies, and hotels. His head was reeling. Everyone involved in tourism, businesses that thrived on international travel – consultancies, logistics, financial institutions, insurers. He tried to recall similar incidents. Flights were grounded across the USA after the terrorist attacks of 2001. At least one airline went bankrupt. Joe sank into a chair to contemplate the news. 'That isn't good,' he said to Mallory.

'Not good? It's disastrous.'

'Forty per cent of the world's goods, by value, travel by air,' Joe said. He was trying to picture the supply chains stretched to their limits.

'Who cares about goods?' Books snapped. 'People are dying.'

'Yes, I know.' But more will die, he thought. And maybe the flu will be the least of our problems. He could picture Lew Kaufmann's wagging finger. There had been airport closures before, of course, and civilisation had survived. Heavy snowfalls in winter, strikes in summer, dust from distant volcanoes; air travel had always been a fragile link in the web of activity that held up the world's economies. Maybe he was becoming delusional about the threat.

'If it gets as far as Cornwall,' the doctor was saying, 'we shall need to do something.'

'I'm doing something already,' Joe said. 'I'm stockpiling food.'

'Well, I've yet to meet a corpse with an appetite,' Books said. He banged the teapot down onto the breakfast table. 'Food won't be a problem. Influenza will.'

Joe could feel his palms sweating. 'What's the mortality rate?' he asked. 'What are they saying on the news?'

‘They’re not saying,’ Books said. ‘That’s what worries me. Two people died from an aircrew of twelve. You’re the mathematician.’

‘Seventeen per cent,’ Joe said.

‘We can’t really extrapolate from a sample of twelve, but in Indonesia the rate may already be as high as eighteen per cent. And look at the flu pandemic of 1918. That killed almost twenty per cent of the people who contracted it.’

‘As high as that?’

‘By some estimates, certainly. It killed more people in six months than the Black Death did in a century.’

Joe was silent.

‘And anyway,’ Books said, ‘we shouldn’t be talking about mortality rates. As far as St Piran is concerned, a death rate of one person in three hundred and seven is one person too many.’

‘Three hundred and eight,’ said Joe, but he said it too quietly for the doctor to hear.

He drove to the wholesale warehouse and filled the Shaunessys’ van with provisions; boxes of noodles, jars of instant coffee, packets of powdered milk. Mindful of Mallory Books’s comments, he looked beyond the food aisles; detergents and disinfectants, soaps and toiletries. He hesitated on toilet rolls and disposable nappies. They might be popular but they would take up disproportionate space in the van – and in the church tower too. The biscuits looked inviting, but he had a feeling that they wouldn’t last especially long. He had visions of his store of food gradually moving past its sell-by date, one box at a time. That would amuse the Reverend Hocking, he thought. Would he have to carry out-of-date items out of the church and consign them to a waste tip? He put the thought to the back of his mind. What was the difference between plain flour and self-raising, he wondered. The warehouse offered a confusing set of choices. There were 16-kilogram sacks of ‘bread flour’. He took a whole pallet-load.

He was getting fitter. He could jog up the churchyard steps

now, a shrink-wrapped tray of tins beneath each arm. All the same there was no time to fit in a second round trip before his rendezvous with Martha at four. When everything was stowed away he climbed to the top of the church tower and stood looking out. He unpacked a box of oatmeal bars and ate one. It was the first time he had broken into the store. If he was the only one left alive, he thought, he could survive here for years.

The church tower was an open space on four floors, with a central atrium where the bell ropes hung. On the ground floor was a small toilet cubicle – an emergency restroom for worshippers if the services grew too long. On the third floor was another small room, an afterthought, squeezed into a corner of the platform. Joe tried the door. It was a storeroom of sorts. Old bell ropes hung over a rafter. There were some assorted tools laid carefully on a shelf – a lever and a crowbar and some long brass hooks; the paraphernalia, he supposed, of the bell ringers. No one had rung bells in this tower for more than twenty years. They were unsafe, apparently. Surprisingly, there was the narrow wooden frame of a bed in the room, but no mattress. Someone used to live up here. A Cornish Quasimodo perhaps. Joe closed the door carefully behind him. If the food store made it as high as the third floor, then maybe he would need to use this room for boxes.

Still there was time to kill. He left the van parked up at the church and strolled down the hill to the Petrel. While Jacob was making his coffee he logged on to Cassie. The hosting service seemed to be working well. He ran a test search on the database, and sat back looking at the outcome. Time to check the forecasts. His fingers hovered over the keyboard. Did he really want to do this? He could slam the computer shut and never look at Cassie again, turn his back on her fickle prophecies. He already knew what she would tell him. She would tell him a tale of falling stocks and bankruptcies – but these were only numbers. She wouldn't tell him of the drama behind the numbers. How strange, he thought, that he'd never really seen this before. A company failure wasn't just an opportunity for City traders to make a killing; it was heartbreak and ruin for the founders, destitution for the shareholders, unemployment for the workers. Behind every number, he thought, there's a human story. A hundred human stories. And while the traders whooped and corks popped there would be men and women driving home to face their spouses with the news, their faces grim against the threat of tears.

His fingers hovered. Did he want to know? Cassie would know about the flu. She would know about the airport closures. She would have followed the overnight newsfeeds. Would she know how to calculate the impact? Could the wisdom of a thousand commentators really be distilled in a case such as this? Would Francis Galton's ox let them down?

Joe punched the key. There was a pause. Then numbers began to populate the table.

What had he expected? The short-term forecasts were bad, but they weren't apocalyptic. They had worsened slightly since the last time he'd looked. He scrolled down the screen. Almost everything was down in Cassie's forecast; airlines, construction, engineering, mining, telecoms, media. Pharmaceuticals were holding steady. Joe gave a wry smile. Pandemics were good for business, he supposed. Travel and leisure were down, chemicals were down, automobiles too. Oil stocks were steady. Now there was a surprise. Cassie was clearly expecting the price rises to work in the oil companies' favour. Click click, he rolled down the table. This was only a forecast, he reminded himself. Cassie had been famously wrong before, but the numbers were falling steadily. Now he should try a longer-term prediction. This was the feature he had built for Lew Kaufmann. He typed in a code and a search screen appeared. He clicked on the search field. '2 Weeks', he typed, but again his finger hung over the 'return' key.

And then, on impulse, he closed down the screen. What did it matter now? He was too far down this road to turn back. If

Cassie's forecasts were to be believed, then the flu crisis and the oil crisis would act together to shave around eight to fifteen per cent off the value of world shares. In Cassie's view that would be enough to trigger an irreversible collapse. But was it really? It amounted to, what . . . five trillion dollars, but was that *real* money? Did it constitute a real loss? Or was it all relative? Maybe Cassie was wrong. Maybe this *was* a horrible blip, but in a month or two, when the war in the Arabian Gulf had been resolved, when the flu had run its course, well then . . . wouldn't everything spring back?

There was enough time to get to the warehouse and load up before his rendezvous there with Martha. Despite his earlier misgivings, Joe piled the provisions onto the loading trolleys. There was momentum to his project now, and he felt unable to derail it. Sixty-eight boxes or sacks, almost £1,000 in value. As he checked through the boxes, a manager in a cheap suit and half-buttoned waistcoat appeared, hovering near by. Joe glanced unwisely in his direction, and in he swept like a predator, his hand held out in greeting. 'I'm Richard Mansell.'

'Pleased to meet you.' Joe took his hand, but didn't offer his own name.

'And you are . . .?'

'A customer,' Joe said.

'Splendid.' There was an awkward pause. 'Are we looking after you?'

'Perfectly, thank you.'

The manager consulted his clipboard. 'You've been, er, spending quite a lot with us . . .'

'I have,' said Joe. 'You have a very fine store here.'

'Thank you, thank you,' said Mansell, but this flattery clearly wasn't enough. 'Are you buying on behalf of a local shop? Only we'd be more than happy to deliver for you. That would be very much easier.'

'No, thank you. My purchases are private.'

'Private?'

'Yes. I understand that anyone who spends over five hundred pounds in a week is entitled to membership? Isn't that right?'

'Yes, yes, of course.' Mansell looked flustered. It was clear that he didn't want to frighten this customer away. 'But if there's anything we can do to help?'

'Nothing, thank you.'

'Do you have far to travel? Only I understand you were here several times last week and I . . .'

'I'm fine. Really,' Joe said firmly.

'Very well.' Mansell was reversing away. 'Are you sure?'

'Absolutely sure.'

Outside in the car park Joe consulted his watch. There was no sign of Martha and he had half an hour to spare. He found a newsagent and bought a *Financial Times* . . . his first since the day he had fled from Lane Kaufmann. Sitting in the cab of the fish van he folded it open. The news was gloomy. Flu made the front page, but the oil crisis wasn't far behind. America threatens action in the Gulf, read a headline. Of course, he thought, they would have to. Self-interest would be too strong. All of America's own reserves could not compensate for the loss of all that oil. It didn't matter that eight out of every ten barrels of oil shipped down the Gulf was destined for Asia; the impact on world oil prices would be devastating for everyone. He found himself flicking to the financial pages. Oil was up in price by fifty-six per cent. He could imagine Cassie computing this, reading the newsfeeds, adjusting her forecasts. Oil and gas and flu and war – such short words, but words firmly entrenched in her lexicon.

There was a tap on the van window. Martha was beaming at him. He jumped down from the cab.

'I've a surprise for you,' she told him. She took his shoulder and gently turned him around. A small crowd of people was gathered in the car park. Familiar faces, most of them. There was Jeremy Melon, and Demelza Trevarrick, and Casey and

Charity, and the Robins twins. There was Jacob from the pub, and Moses from the B&B, and Benny Restorick, and Bevis and Lorne Magwith from the farm, and the Shaunessy brothers, and the Bartle sisters, and Kenny Kennet, and Modesty Cloke, and pretty Aminata Chikelu, the noisy nurse, and two dozen more whose names he barely knew or remembered. 'Oh my God,' he said, and his hand shot to his mouth. 'You told me you wouldn't tell anyone.'

'I told you I would only tell folk I trust,' Martha corrected him. She threw out her arms. 'These are they.'

Her smile was so wide he could do nothing but return it. 'But my van is already full,' he started to protest.

'That's where we 'ave our secret weapon,' said Martha. She pointed across to the loading bay. Two large furniture-removal lorries were parked there, their tailgates already up against the bay. 'My Ronnie,' she said. 'He works in removals.'

A man in big stained overalls stepped out of the crowd, beaming. He had the same rosy complexion as Martha. 'Delighted to meet you,' he said.

'Thank you,' said Joe. There seemed little else he could say. 'It will be a big help.'

'An' we 'ave twenty or so cars,' said Martha, gesturing, and for the first time Joe noticed how full the car park seemed to have become.

'Dear God.' His mouth felt too dry to speak.

'Well, in't you goin' to say somethin?'

'What . . . what about the vicar?'

'What about 'im?'

'He won't let anyone but me carry things into the church.'

Martha offered a conspiratorial expression. 'I think you'll find,' she said, 'that 'is lovely young wife has taken 'im off to Plymouth.'

'On a shopping trip,' said someone, and a ripple of laughter ran through the crowd.

'An' a show,' said Martha.

Jeremy Melon said, 'I think, Joe, you should give us your instructions.'

'Imagine we're heaving a blooming great whale,' called a voice.

Joe felt a sudden, enormous surge of energy. 'Let's do it then,' he called back. 'Let's shift this bloody great whale, shall we?'

The assembled villagers responded with a cheer.

'I know this will sound mad to you,' Joe said, 'but . . .' He paused, searching for the right words. 'I had a premonition. A dream. I dreamed that a voice was sending me to St Piran. It was telling me to stock up with food – enough to feed the whole village. I dreamed that a terrible famine was coming. So I know it's crazy, but I would never forgive myself if I didn't do it.'

There was a murmur of approval at this. 'I thought it was a computer what told you,' someone said.

Joe blushed. 'That too,' and this made them laugh. 'Please keep this a secret. If anyone in the store asks where you live, please don't tell them.'

'Tell 'em we're stocking up Windsor Castle,' said Benny Restorick, 'in case they all comes down with the flu.'

It didn't seem an especially convincing line, but Joe let it pass. 'OK,' he said, 'you could try that, but only if they push you.'

'What are we buying?' someone called.

'Food,' he said. 'Tins and bottles and sacks. No alcohol please. We don't have room. Nothing that will perish quickly. Nothing that needs to go into a fridge. No pet food, no luxuries. Just good basic food.' Looking at the faces of these honest villagers, Joe had a feeling that they understood this instruction better than he ever did. 'Fill the lorries up to the top. Fill all the space in your cars.' He pulled a credit card from his pocket and held it in the air. 'I'm paying,' he said, and there was a roar of approval.

They moved like an army into the store. Just as they had done on the beach, they acted without further instruction, in unison, like ants on a carcase, spreading down the aisles, heaving boxes onto trolleys, dragging sacks. Joe moved among them like a choreographer, using his new-found knowledge of the warehouse to direct them. 'Get those,' he might say, indicating catering packs of sugar, 'don't bother with them,' waving away the crates of Perrier.

Stalking down an aisle came Richard Mansell, the manager, his waistcoat still unbuttoned. 'Can we help?' he appealed to Joe.

'Can you put all your people onto check-out?' Joe asked. 'We want to process all this as quickly as we can. And we may need extra hands for loading.'

'Of course, of course.'

The swarm of villagers swept through the warehouse like locusts, denuding whole swathes of the store. 'All of those,' Joe would say, 'and all of those.' Mountains of boxes were lifted onto trolleys. Aisles were left bare. 'When you're full go and check them out,' Joe said, but the process had already started. The beep beep of the code readers sounded to Joe like the trading screens at the bank.

It was almost dark when the convoy negotiated the lane back to St Piran. There was a carnival atmosphere at the church.

'We have at least a couple of hours before His Holiness gets home,' Jeremy said. 'But we should work fast.' They formed a human chain. The Shaunessy boys were in the vans tossing boxes from the tops of the piles. The Robins twins were catching them. Then came Benny, and the Magwiths, and Aminata, and two dozen more all the way up through the churchyard and in through the Georgian porch and down past the nave to the bell tower. Then in the tower there was Kenny, and Casey, and Charity, and Modesty, and Martha and her Ronnie, and the Anderssens, and Joe.

'Who's minding the pub?' Joe asked.

'We're closed,' said Romer Anderssen, and she winked. 'But I have a feeling we'll be doing very good business in an hour or so.'

Up the pathway came their purchases. Soups, and soaps, and meats, and grains, fruits, and sugars and pulses and rice. 'Do we need a break?' Joe called at one point. The sweat was running down his face.

'We're nearly done,' came the call back from the other end of the line, but they weren't. There were the cars to empty, and the fish van too. Up the line came the boxes. Kenny, at the end of the line, was climbing like a scaffolder, perching, and balancing, swaying across from pile to pile. 'More here,' he would call out, and up would come the boxes.

Up to the third floor they went, pursued by packages of food. Then up the steps to the top floor. Would they run out of space? Joe felt as if he could lift and carry no more. Several in the line had dropped out. Martha Fishburne and Modesty Cloke were sitting on sacks, exhausted.

Finally, when Joe was thinking they could carry no more, a cry came from outside. 'Last one!'

'Last one,' chorused the Shaunessys. 'Last one,' echoed the Robins. And the call came up the chain. 'Last one!' In through the door of the church came the final package, a shrink-wrapped tray of tins, describing a weary arc as it flew from the arms of Toby Penroth into the waiting hands of Bevis Magwith. 'Last one.'

'Last one,' cried Martha. She had rejoined the line.

'Last one,' called Charity.

How were their limbs still functioning? How were they all still here, moving this mountain of food? Joe found himself shaking his head in disbelief.

'Last one,' called Casey Limber.

'Last one,' called Jacob and Romer Anderssen in unison. And the tray of tins flew into Joe's grasp. Marrowfat peas. He started to laugh. Never in his life had he tasted marrowfat peas.

Yet now he couldn't have been happier to see them. 'Last one.' He passed them up to Kenny Kennet.

'We in't got room for 'em,' Kenny called, and a laugh ran down the line.

'Fifty pints of Seagrass please, Jacob – when you're ready,' Joe said. 'On me.'

The men and women from the chain were making their way up through the churchyard. They wanted to see the store. In through the door of the bell tower they squeezed, wet with the sweat of toil, clasping each other by the shoulders. 'Oh my goodness,' Jeremy Melon said. 'Just look at it all.' The sheer quantity of provisions seemed to stun them into silence, even though they had carried so much of it themselves. They pushed up past the stacks, single-file up the wooden stairway to the first floor, and up to the second. 'Dear God an' Jesus an' all the saints,' Martha said.

When they got to the top there was very little room for more than three or four to stand. 'I've never been up here,' Benny Restorick said. 'Nor me,' said Jeremy. One by one they stood and looked out over the village. It was too dark to see much.

'Jacob has drinks waiting for you,' Joe told them as they filed past.

'We'll be needing them,' said Moses Penhallow.

As the last of the crew clambered down from the bell keep, Kenny found the door on the third floor. 'There's a room here,' he told Joe.

'I know. It's an old bedroom.'

'We could fill it.'

'No.' Joe rested a hand on the beachcomber's arm. 'I need it.'

'What for?' It was an honest question.

What did he need it for? 'I'm going to live there,' Joe said. The answer surprised even him. He hadn't thought of the idea until the sentence had popped out of his mouth, but of *course* he would have to live there. He could picture it already. There was a bed – a narrow one. That would be enough. There was a washroom and toilet on the ground floor. It would be cold, but he could bear it. It might even be a penance, of a sort. 'Go ahead,' he said to Kenny. 'I'll catch up. Make sure everyone has a drink.'

With a clumping of heavy feet the last of the villagers descended the stairs. Joe was alone. Outside, the village was a grey silhouette against the darkening sky. He sat on a box and listened to the disappearing voices, the reversing of vehicles, the faint echo of jovial cries, until all that was left was the silence. Finally he rose to his feet, and went back down to the ground floor. He threw the light switch and the darkness enveloped him. He had spent nearly all of his savings. He had left everything he had ever known and understood. All he owned – almost all – was in this tower, protected by these granite walls. He stood and listened for a while to the solitude seeping from the thousand boxes. And then he made his way down the hill to the village.

19

Some people like the smell of fish

'You have a visitor,' Mallory Books told Joe over breakfast. He pointed to the window looking out onto Fish Street, where someone was tapping on the glass.

Joe went to the front door.

'We're on the news,' Jeremy Melon said, as the door was opening.

'What do you mean?'

'On breakfast TV. Quick.' He grasped Joe's arm and pulled him up the street to where his own front door stood open. They squeezed past his easels and canvases. A small television was visible in the front room among the general disarray of the cottage, its picture frozen on pause. Jeremy was fiddling with the remote control. 'Here.' He wound back the story and pressed the play button.

'Elsewhere in the country,' a newsreader was saying, 'there are signs that families may be hoarding food in anticipation of a possible crisis. One village in Cornwall is reported to have spent over forty thousand pounds at a single wholesaler. Our reporter Jenny Messenger went to find out more.' The picture cut to a young reporter in the car park of the cash-and-carry. 'Now no one in this part of England has yet been affected by the flu scare,' she said to camera, 'and while petrol rationing is surely going to hurt rural communities, there had been little sign that people living here were especially worried. There were no reports of panic buying. Until yesterday. When this warehouse behind me became the site for stockpiling on a massive scale.'

Richard Mansell appeared, his waistcoat neatly buttoned.

'I've never seen anything like it,' he said. 'The car park was full – cars, removal vans, lorries, you name it. They all came at once. Very organised they were. Knew exactly what they wanted.'

'How many people were there?' the reporter asked.

'Well, I didn't count, but there must have been a hundred. Maybe more.'

'There were fewer than forty of us,' Jeremy said, but Joe raised a hand to shush him.

'And what sort of things were they buying?'

'Tins mainly.' The camera switched to a shot of an almost empty aisle.

'And do you know where all these people were from?'

'No. They wouldn't say, but it was clear that they all came from the same village. And it was all paid for by one person.'

'And this wasn't just a new shop stocking up its shelves?'

Mansell was back on camera shaking his head. 'The man in charge told me that this was a private purchase.'

The TV picture returned to the reporter in the car park. 'Whoever it was that came here to buy up food wasn't doing anything illegal. There is no rationing, and the government say they have no plans to impose it, but they're also telling people *not* to panic-buy.' She was walking slowly towards the camera, holding her microphone. 'The shops say that there are no shortages apart from some imported fruits and vegetables. There is still unrestricted fuel for vans and lorries that deliver food, but if this one village in the South West is anything to go by, some people aren't paying too much attention to that message. And if there are many more incidents like this one, then maybe, just maybe, the shops will start running out of food. This has been Jenny Messenger in Cornwall.'

'Oh shit,' Joe said.

'Phew.' Jeremy looked over at Joe. 'Are you buying more today?'

'No.' Joe shook his head. 'I'm just about spent out.'

Back at the doctor's house, Joe told Mallory about his plan to stay overnight in the bell tower. 'I'm not moving out altogether,' he said. 'I still want to keep my room if you're OK with that. I'll be back to use the shower and the bathroom, and to make breakfast and dinner.'

'As long as you're still paying me,' Mallory said.

'Of course.'

'Then why should I mind?' But the doctor was looking away. 'If it gets really cold . . .'

'Then I'll be back,' Joe said.

'You can borrow the mattress from my boat,' Mallory said.

This was the first Joe had heard of a boat. He raised his eyebrows. 'You have a boat?'

'In the harbour.'

'Which one is it?'

'The sailboat. I bought it twenty years ago from one of my patients. Not that I sail very much, but it's perfectly seaworthy. Sometimes I just take it round the bay if the weather's good and there's a breeze.'

Joe gave a respectful nod. 'I'd like to try it some time.'

'Ten pounds an hour,' Mallory said, crunching a mouthful of toast. 'But to you . . . seven fifty.'

There was a boat in Joe's mind. It was an 18-foot sloop, built of wood, and smelling of wet canvas and varnish. Inside the low cabin was the dark odour of pipe smoke. The man at the tiller had a white beard and a way of focusing his gaze on the horizon, and a habit of talking in a voice too low to be heard above the wind. The sails would flap and the man at the tiller would shout a command. 'Come about.' And Joe would snatch at the ropes and slide along the deck, ducking his head beneath the boom. 'Yes, Pappa,' he would say.

'Have you ever sailed?' Dr Books asked him.

'Yes.'

There were more than a thousand yachts in the old harbour at Limhamn. At dawn the forest of naked masts would puncture the skyline like strewn chopsticks, and the clatter of loose ropes in the morning breeze would become a cacophony. To a twelve-year-old the rocking of boats on the swell could easily transform into a familiar solidity. Waking up in a hammock, scrambling onto the deck to see the orange glow of sunrise, peeing into the grey water of the harbour. These were memories Joe hadn't visited for some time. Too long perhaps.

'My father taught me to sail,' he said.

'Where did you sail?'

'In the sound at Oresund.' Joe was smiling with the memory. 'Pappa has an island in the Baltic.'

'Your father owns an island?'

'It isn't as grand as it sounds. There are thirty thousand islands in the Stockholm archipelago alone. Many of them have holiday homes. My father's island is much further south – near Karlskrona. It's about two days' sailing from Limhamn. We would sail there every summer. Just him and me.'

'What about your mother?'

'She lived in London.'

Books made a harrumph noise. He knew when the questions ought to stop. 'Anyway,' he said. 'You can borrow the mattress.'

On the quayside Joe almost collided with Martha Fishburne coming out of Jessie Higgs's shop. 'They'm sayin' we're on the television,' Martha told him gravely.

'Yes. I saw it.'

'There's a lot of talk.'

Joe nodded his head. 'I expect there is. But nobody must talk about it outside the village. Nobody can know where the food is.'

Martha placed a fat finger to her lips. 'You can trust us,' she said. 'In't no one telling.'

What must it be like, Joe wondered, for this remote community to make the national news? Did he really imagine it could stay a secret?

He found Mallory's little yacht – the only sailing boat in the harbour. It occupied the sole deep-water strip, with a stretch of quayside all to itself, but it would require a high tide to sail it out. The cabin, such as it was, was barely high enough for him to kneel in, and the mattress turned out to be little more than a strip of foam in a soiled cotton cover. He rolled it up and carried it up the hill to the church, stopping as he walked, to talk to Jacob from the Petrel, and Benny Restorick, and John Shaunessy, and Toby Penroth. However did anyone walk from one end of this village to another? There were altogether too many conversations waiting along the route.

Demelza Trevarrick emerged from a front door with a cigarette in her outstretched hand. 'Dahling,' she purred. 'Do you have any more adventures planned for us?'

'Not today,' Joe said. He had never had his promised conversation with Demelza, the one he told Jeremy he would have. She was the expert on romance, but he hadn't consulted her yet. Perhaps he had been avoiding her. If he hadn't been carrying the mattress he would have waved at her politely. Without that dismissive gesture she was able to join him as he toiled up the hill.

'Do we have to walk so fast, darling? I was hoping we might talk.'

'Of course.' Joe slowed down.

'Where are we going?'

'To the church.'

'With that dreadful thing? Are you planning on sleeping on it, dear?' Demelza looked at the rolled-up mattress as if it might be infected by the plague.

'It's just a precaution,' Joe said. 'I may have to sleep there if things get . . . well, you know . . . a bit hairy.'

The writer looked worried. 'Hairy?' she echoed. Nothing, she seemed to imply, would ever get *hairy* in St Piran. 'Don't you think you're taking this survivalist thing a little too far? I mean, it's all well and good storing up food. No one is going to mind too much about that. And frankly anything that winds up our good Reverend is always going to go down well in the village, but really? Sleeping in the bell tower on a dirty old cushion?' She sucked at her cigarette and emitted a spirit trail of smoke with a sigh. 'It would be so much more romantic if there was a woman involved.'

Joe looked back at her. 'Well, I'm sorry to disappoint you,' he said. 'There isn't.'

'Are you sure?' Demelza was trying to catch up.

'Of course I'm sure.'

'What about young Polly Hocking?'

Joe stopped. 'Have you been talking to Jeremy?'

'Of course I have, darling. He couldn't keep a secret from me if his life depended on it.'

'Are you still trying to match-make for me, Demelza?'

'I'm trying,' Demelza said. 'But you're making it so difficult. This village is simply brimming with eligible young women. And look at you.' She made a gesture which accommodated his whole appearance from head to foot. 'Such a fine-looking young man. It breaks my heart to see you moving into a draughty old bell tower all on your own when you could at the very least have an orderly queue of ladies ready to join you.'

He had to smile at this image. 'If only that were true,' he said.

'Then why don't you let me help you?'

'The last time we had this conversation we concluded that all the eligible girls were either far too old, were dangerously noisy lovers, or else they smelled of fish,' Joe said.

'Not all of them.'

'Well, most of them.'

'Some people *like* the smell of fish,' Demelza countered.

'In which case,' Joe said, 'St Piran must be a hothouse of opportunity for them.' He set off again up the hill.

'What about the lovely Aminata?'

'What about her?'

'Aren't you interested? She's a darling. And so beautiful. I could set the two of you up with a date.'

Joe grunted. 'I don't want you to think I'm not grateful.'

'But don't you think she's lovely, darling?'

Aminata's face came surprisingly easily to his mind. 'She's gorgeous.'

'Well then . . .'

'Really, Demelza . . . I'm not . . . not actually on the market.'

'It's Polly Hocking, isn't it?'

'What is?' Joe paused again.

'Well, half the village believes that you and she are embroiled in a tryst,' Demelza said. She used the respite to catch another drag on her cigarette and then flicked the stub expertly onto the pavement and stamped it out. 'My dear, it's a perfect story. True love thwarted. The handsome stranger and the beautiful young woman, trapped in a loveless marriage. They meet on the beach . . .'

'. . . beneath a stranded whale . . .'

'. . . their eyes meet. He can sense the unresolved passion of her heart.'

'Can he?'

'Oh yes. And now he is drawn to her. And she to him, but they both know that their love can never be consummated. He moves into the church to be close to her . . . and there he pines away from unrequited love.'

Joe stopped walking again. 'You write romantic novels, don't you?'

She gave him a smile. 'You should read one.'

'I think I just did,' he said. 'And this is what half the village thinks?'

'Oh yes.'

'Then I have to disappoint them. On this occasion the other half is correct.'

'My dear, the other half of the village is convinced you're already at it like rabbits.'

On an autumn day, the sound at Oresund would be busy with boats; sailing yachts like his father's, motor launches, cruisers, ferries, fishing boats, and container ships. It seemed to Joe, when he was twelve years old, as if all the world came through this channel, as if every wave was the wake of a boat. When the sea was still, his father would throw out a baited line. 'Might as well,' he would say. 'We might catch a cod.' They never caught a cod, but there were salmon, and sea trout, and halibut, and eels. Mikkel Haak would strip the fish down on the deck, tossing the heads and tails and guts back into the sea. Joe would fry the fish steaks on the gas ring, and they would sit in the cockpit, father and son, watching the summer lights fade. Somehow, Joe thought, very little had ever tasted so good since then.

Why had this thought popped so strongly into his mind? He hadn't sailed with his father since he was fifteen. Was it to ward off thoughts of Polly Hocking? Him and Polly, at it like rabbits?

'Then both halves of the village are wrong.'

'But *are* they?' said Demelza. They had reached the churchyard and her hand hit the catch of the gate before he could open it. 'There are different kinds of truth, you know.'

'I don't think so. Truth is truth,' he said.

'Truth is beautiful,' Demelza said, 'but so are lies. That's what Emerson said. And do you know what Plato said?'

Joe shook his head.

'He said poetry is closer to truth than history.'

'I don't know what you want of me, Demelza . . .'

She looked at him and gave an exaggerated sigh. 'I'm trying to help you,' she said. 'I just don't think you realise it yet.'

'It's sweet of you.' He lowered the mattress and took hold of her hand, lifting it gently off the latch. 'But I don't need your help.'

'You don't *want* my help,' she corrected him. 'But you do need it. I was right about the girl, wasn't I? The London girl?'

'Not altogether.'

'What was her name?'

He paused. 'Clare.'

'You misread her, didn't you, Joe? You wanted more but she wasn't ready to give it.'

'Something like that. But that wasn't what made me leave the City.'

She squeezed his hand. 'Mallory thinks he understands you. He thinks you're a City hotshot that just got himself into a spot of bother. He thinks you're impulsive. He sees you splashing your money around on boxes of beans, giving your fancy car to the vicar, walking out with young Polly, and he thinks you are an overindulged rich boy just down here for an adventure. I'm not saying he doesn't care for you. I think he does. But he doesn't *understand* you, Joe. I do. That's my profession, you see. That City job doesn't define who you are. It only tells us what you do for a living. You're mixed up, Joe Haak. You're a dreamer. And you're a romantic. You want to fall in love, and you want it to be hearts and flowers and happily-ever-after. But you're making the two mistakes that so many romantics make.'

'Two mistakes?'

'At least two.'

Demelza possessed the face of someone who knew about love. Joe found his resistance retreating.

'Tell me what my mistakes are.'

'Number One,' she said, her eyes lighting up. 'You believe in love at first sight.'

Joe laughed at this. 'Can I believe my ears? A romantic novelist who doesn't believe in love at first sight? I thought that was the basis for the whole genre.'

'Oh, Joe, Joe.' Demelza was shaking her head, her hair swaying across her face. 'You poor dear boy. You have so much to learn. I certainly believe in *lust* at first sight. Heaven knows I've been guilty of that more times than I can remember. God – it's the most powerful force on the planet; hard to distinguish from love when you're the victim, I know. But how many times do you wake up in the morning, look across at the object of your lust, and realise you're not really in love. True love has to cook slowly. It's like a recipe. It isn't a two-minute stir-fry, it's a long, slow simmer. That's why you've never found love in the City, Joe. You think you want to meet a girl, go to bed, and discover you're in love. In that order. But it doesn't work that way.'

'So I've got the recipe wrong?'

'The best recipe for true love is plenty of time spent in close proximity; plus a little jeopardy to face together.'

'Proximity and Jeopardy.' Joe laughed. 'That's the Trevarrick secret, is it?'

'And a generous helping of time. The jeopardy is optional, but it makes for a better story. It's like the grain of sand in the oyster that creates the pearl.' She was looking at him with a serious expression. 'But the time isn't optional. That's essential. Human beings aren't jigsaw pieces. We don't suddenly come upon someone who happens to be the exact match for us. We need to flex our own personalities and our own lives to accommodate another person. And they have to do the same for us. That takes time. It doesn't happen at first sight. Don't make fun of it, Joe.'

'I'm not.' Joe lifted the latch, but her hand still forestalled him from opening the gate. 'I rather like it. Proximity and Jeopardy and a generous dollop of Time. I shall remember that when the right time and the right girl come along. But I'm not here looking for love, Demelza. Really I'm not.'

She arched her eyebrows in disbelief. 'But we're not done yet,' she said. 'We still haven't discussed your second mistake.'

'Ah yes.'

'And this is the more serious one.'

'And what is it?'

'You're chasing the wrong girl.' She released his hand and swung open the gate. 'Think about it, Joe,' she said. 'Think about it.'

*

There was very little to do in the bell tower. Joe turned the heavy key in the lock and closed himself inside. Behind the huge door and the ancient walls he felt safe. He climbed the stairs and unrolled the mattress onto the wooden bed. He tried it out. Not especially comfortable, but it would do. With his hands behind his head he stretched out, looking up at the oak beams of the floor above. There was something cosy about this little room. It reminded him of a tent; cold air leaked in through a hundred small openings. But it was dry, and as long as the night temperature didn't fall too far below freezing, he could survive it.

He was thinking of a night spent in a borrowed tent, in a woodland north of Rouen. It was a night he revisited often in his imagination – more often, perhaps, than he should. He had been fourteen. More than half a lifetime ago. He could picture the glade of trees, the cool shade, the wildflowers, and the tall grasses. It was a sweet memory, yet one of the most painful he possessed. It had been a camping holiday with his mother and his sister Brigitha. They drove to France in Mamma's tiny yellow hatchback; a car that was far too small to reasonably accommodate a two-week camping expedition for three, with all the paraphernalia of poles and pegs and sleeping bags that the enterprise entailed, to say nothing of the wardrobe required by Brigitha (now sixteen) and the luggage requirements of Mamma, who rarely travelled without two large suitcases even for a weekend break. It was to be their last holiday together; if they had known this at the time, then perhaps they would have been more civil to one another. Maybe they would have tried harder. But nothing favourable seemed to be aligned for that trip. Mamma had fretted about the journey for weeks before they left. She was a worrier. Barely two years had passed since she'd separated from Pappa Mikkel. Now she agonised that Joe and Brigitha were drifting away from her too. The magnetism that had held them all together as a family seemed to have dissipated since the separation. She worried about the influence of their father. Joe and Brig were teenagers. Alison Haak knew they would have enjoyed better vacations with their father on his island than they did with their mother in Margate or Southend.

This was the holiday that would put that right.

They didn't plan enough (this was before Joe had developed any of his legendary planning skills, and neither Mamma nor Brigitha was proficient in this domain). And they didn't really have sufficient money for the kind of holiday they wanted. Brigitha was in a bad mood from the start. Sixteen is not a good age for a girl to go camping with her mother and baby brother. They had underestimated the hours of driving; it was a long, tough haul from Calais to the campsite Mamma had booked near La Rochelle on the Atlantic coast. Brigitha sat in the back of the tiny car feigning sleep, walled in by luggage, huge headphones clamped to her head as the miles rolled by. She didn't care for the picturesque French villages they passed, the vineyards, or the fields of sunflowers.

'Look at this lovely scenery,' Mamma would exhort them, a growing sense of desperation infecting her voice.

'I don't want to know,' Brigitha would say.

'But look at this gorgeous little village,' Mamma would reply.

'Just tell me when we're there.'

At the campsite it rained, on and off, for seven days. Everyone was miserable. One morning Brigitha threw Joe's sleeping bag out of the tent without his knowledge while he was off on an errand. 'It was stinking,' she explained sullenly. 'It was making me feel sick. I couldn't share a tent with it for one moment longer.'

But the rains came and soaked it.

'I'm not getting involved in this,' Mamma said. Even *her* patience was growing short. 'You sort this out between you. This is your dispute.'

'Where am I expected to sleep?' Joe protested. 'It's soaking!'

'But Mamma, it stank,' said Brigitha. 'You've *no idea* how

much it stank. I don't know what he's been doing in there.' Brigitha might, in this judgement, have expected some sympathy from her mother. The sleeping bag had truly reeked of adolescent boy, the organic odours of new and untried hormones, the rank excretions of feet and underarms and crotch.

'We'll have to buy another sleeping bag,' Joe said. 'I'm not sleeping in that again.' He was obstinate even then.

'We don't have the money,' Mamma objected. 'You'll have to sleep in mine until it gets sunny enough to hang your bag out to dry.'

Joe tried to sleep in his mother's sleeping bag, but it smelled odd, as if the air in the bag was slowly putrefying. Mamma tried sleeping in the car, squeezed up on the little back seat, covered over with cardigans and towels. Early in the morning Joe woke her. 'I can't sleep in your bag, Mamma,' he said. He didn't tell her about the smell. 'Let me sleep in the car.'

When, after a week, the weather improved, Mamma fell asleep underneath a beach umbrella and burned the backs of her legs.

'You need to keep your legs in the shade too,' Joe told her.

'I did,' she protested. 'But the sun moved.'

It wasn't only the distance from Calais to the Atlantic coast that they'd got wrong. Mamma had hopelessly miscalculated the amount of money they would need. 'We'll be camping,' she'd said. 'What do we need *money* for? We can live on baguettes and cheese and sunshine and fresh air.' Setting off from London there had been an air of romance about this ambition. It would be a back-to-nature trip, canvas above their heads, sand between their toes, long days on the beach, evenings by the pool, campfires, long walks, and healthy, simple fare. But these aspirations were to be short-lived. The budget campsite was a regimented compound of sharp gravel paths with carefully metered pitches for the tents, row upon row of them, precisely aligned and evenly separated. There was barely a blade of grass. It was a long walk to the evil-smelling toilet block and an even longer walk to the beach. 'No fires,' the rules demanded. So right away their dreams had been punctured. Dinner and drinks in the campsite bar on the first two nights accounted for almost a third of their cash. In torchlight, back in the tent, as the rain fell remorselessly above them, Mamma anxiously counted up what was left. 'We're going to have to make this a *proper* camping holiday,' she said, trying to sound cheerful. 'From now on we do all our own cooking. And no more alcohol.'

Brigitha took this edict as an attack on her freedom, as a teenager, to drink as much as she wished. 'In France you can drink from the age of twelve,' she told her mother.

'We'll buy a bottle of cheap supermarket wine and you can have a glass with your dinner,' was Mamma's compromise.

They truly did live on baguettes and cheese. And fresh air. And cheap red wine. For the first week there was precious little sunshine to go with it. Mamma kept an emergency cash reserve in the glove compartment of the hatchback; it was there to cover the petrol costs for the journey home. But Joe and Brigitha discovered it, and gradually, without real malice, they pilfered it. Just a few notes at a time. They used it for ice creams, and for rum and Coca-Cola. They bought fresh-cream choux pastries from the patisserie. They bought after-sun lotion. They went to the Hawaiian-themed disco at the camp pool and they drank piña coladas. When Mamma discovered that her reserve had been raided she sat with her head in her hands and wept. It was, Joe would often think, one of the worst moments in his life. The sight of his mother desolate, in tears, in their pathetic tent on the holiday she had dreamed about, made him feel more wretched than he could ever remember.

It might have been easier if Mamma had blamed them. It might have been more honest. But Mamma blamed herself. Unable to take his mother's remorse, Joe ran from the camp and walked forlornly in the forest for a day, wishing that the pinewoods would consume him.

Perhaps this is what I do, Joe thought, as he lay on the thin mattress in the bell tower. I run. I can't face the consequences of my actions, so I run away. I'm still doing it now.

They had to leave the campsite four days early, just as the heat wave started. Mamma insisted on driving at forty miles an hour all the way back to Calais. 'It's the only way to conserve fuel,' she told them. It may also have been her way of punishing them. Every hour or so they would need to find somewhere to stop so that Mamma could rub lotion onto her sunburned legs. The slow journey, it seemed, was as much a punishment for Mamma as it was for her children. They ransacked every purse and pocket for coins and they used what little they could find to buy fuel. For twenty-four hours they didn't eat. They filled water bottles from a tap at a service station. 'It'll be full of germs,' Brigitha warned. 'It'll kill us all.'

As their irritation and hunger grew, Mamma tried her bank card in a machine in Alençon. 'It won't work,' she wailed. She held her hands over her eyes to avoid seeing the screen with its message of rejection. 'I know it won't work.' Still all three held their breath and waited. The bank machine ejected the card. 'I knew I was overdrawn,' she wept. 'I don't think you two realise how *expensive* it is to look after two teenagers in London.'

'We'll be all right, Mamma.' Joe put his arm around her.

'How will we be all right? How? We should never have come.'

By now Joe and Brigitha had been thoroughly humbled by the turn of events. Back on the road Brigitha made a point of appearing to take an interest in everything they passed. 'Look at that charming windmill. Did you *ever see* such a beautiful church?'

They were never going to reach Calais before midnight. They turned onto a narrow country lane some way north of Rouen, and found themselves driving through woodland. Joe pitched the tent in a clearing within a copse of trees. They had one baguette, a whole fat garlic, and a bottle of sterilised milk between them; it would have to suffice for a meal. Mamma went to find somewhere for a toilet break. She came back with a gleam in her eye and a handful of mushrooms. Ten minutes later they had collected enough for a feast. Brigitha went looking for wood, Joe lit a campfire, and they fried the mushrooms with the garlic and the last of their olive oil. There were two bottles of wine in the car. Mamma had bought them as gifts for neighbours, to thank them for watching their house. 'We can get two more from Asda,' Joe said. A generous splash went into the pan with the mushrooms, and so did some of the milk.

It was the best night of the holiday. They filled themselves with garlic mushrooms, drank much more wine than teenagers should, and sat up late poking the fire and playing cards by the light of a single candle. When they finally turned in they couldn't sleep. They talked into the night. They laughed more than they'd laughed for ten days. They slept in the same tent compartment and they wound their arms around each other for warmth. No one complained that anyone stank, even though, hot and unwashed, they probably all did. Late in the night, when everything was quiet and the only sound was their own breathing, Mamma gave a whisper that broke the silence. 'Did you ever *see* such a beautiful church?' and the three of them convulsed with such laughter that they only stopped because it hurt to laugh any more.

Proximity and Jeopardy, Joe thought. Perhaps that recipe works for families too. If he could relive one night from his whole life it would be that stolen night north of Rouen. He crossed his arms around his chest and squeezed himself. With his eyes closed tight it reminded him of his mother's arms that night. Here and now, Joe thought, he would exchange everything – every bag and box of food, his car, his flat, his career, his friends, every possession he had back in London, every dream he'd ever nurtured, just to be back in that tent, hearing his mother laugh.

And now his eyes stung with tears.

20

There's no flu in Cornwall

At sunset Joe was back at the quayside. There were butterflies inside his head. Or so it felt. His heartbeat was wrong. As if there was too much air inside his lungs, or insufficient lungs for the air. When he was a boy Pappa Mikkel had taught him how to stay calm in a crisis. 'Give the crisis a score,' the old man would say. 'Mark it out of one hundred. Then look at the horizon as if nothing mattered, and ask yourself how much it would score tomorrow. And how much next week. And next year. Will they write about this matter in your obituary? Will anyone die? If not, you can turn to face it once again and recognise it for the impostor that it is.'

Joe tried to look at the horizon. A soft mist had risen from the sea and there was no sharp line to mark where the ocean ended and the sky began, only the amber glow of the western sun. I score this crisis fifty, he thought, and just thinking about it started to calm him; but tomorrow it might score sixty. And next week ninety. And next year one hundred. People would die. And there might be no obituaries to read.

Unless of course he'd got it all wrong. Unless the Reverend Alvin Hocking knew a greater truth – that God would not permit His children to starve. Or Cassie had her conclusions wrong. Again. Sometimes, perhaps, the wisdom of an army might fail to guess the weight of an ox.

Down on the harbour-front by the Pay-and-Display car park, where once his own car had been abandoned, a high-performance car had appeared from behind Jessie Higgs's shop. It was now creeping along the narrow roadway searching for a space between the boat moorings and the lobster pots and the wet nets. He could hear the grumble of its engine; a Porsche convertible by the look of it. He turned away. Cars like this were trophies of success in the world he'd left behind, but it was rather late in the evening for tourists to be calling. He found himself looking back at the car. It was manoeuvring awkwardly into a space. Who would be driving to St Piran in a car like this? He could feel the butterflies returning. He watched the driver's door swing open, and the figure of a woman emerged in slow motion, just a leg first, then an arm, then a gradual and difficult rise to a standing position. An older woman then, unused to low seats. Or a younger woman who wasn't well? There was a gaunt familiarity to the figure. She hunched over the car like a wounded creature, thin, out of place among the lobster traps and moorings in her magnolia suit and hair that bobbed precisely at her shoulders.

Could it be?

Now his heart was rebelling in its cage. Look at the horizon. This scores no more than a twenty. And next year who will remember it? Was she here to exact some kind of revenge? Had her life been destroyed by the crash? Should he run? But he had no car to flee to; and where would he go? He should welcome her then. He owed her that. She had, after all, driven all this way, and it could only have been to find him. Should he welcome her with a hug, with a smile? Should he show surprise? 'Good Lord, it's you!' Or nonchalance? 'I wondered how long it would take you to find me.' His legs were taking him down the harbour-front towards the car. Janie Coverdale was looking his way. Her face looked drawn.

'Have you eaten?' Joe asked her. 'Because if we're quick we might persuade Jacob Anderssen to cook you up a lobster.'

She seemed to be seeing him for the first time. She took a step away and held out a forbidding hand. 'No,' she said. 'Don't come any closer.' And then, when he seemed to be ignoring her instruction, she snapped at him the way she sometimes did to the younger traders on the fifth floor. 'DON'T COME CLOSE.'

He stopped. 'Janie? It's me.'

She was looking at the ground. 'Hello, Joe,' she said.

'Hello, Janie.'

'I'm ill,' she told him. 'You mustn't come too close.' And then she was deflating like a punctured toy, folding down onto the harbour-side, her knees at unnatural angles.

Joe lifted her up, but there was nowhere to put her. He walked around the car and managed to open the passenger door, then slid her down onto the seat.

'Where are we going?' she asked. She was blinking at him.

'Somewhere safe.' He went around the car and squeezed into the driver's seat. The position was all wrong. He was far too close to the wheel, but it hardly seemed worth resetting the controls. He started up the engine. 'There's virtually no petrol.'

'There isn't a drop to be had this side of Exeter,' Janie said. 'They're queueing for five miles at Bristol. Five miles! I had to pay a man in a driveway a thousand pounds to siphon petrol from his tank and I think he thought I was robbing him.' She coughed.

'How did you find me?' he asked.

'Joe . . . I have the flu,' she said. She was like a rag doll collapsed in a hammock.

'It may not be the flu. It could be anything.'

'It is the flu, Joe. It's the Asian flu. Colin Helms brought it back from Singapore.'

'Helms?'

'He was on a flight where they all got sick.'

'How is he now?'

'He's dead.'

Joe almost drove the car into the window of Jessie Higgs's shop. 'Dead? Colin Helms?'

'And Martin Lawrie. And Harriet Adlam.'

He shook his head slowly. 'Martin Lawrie?'

'And Harriet Adlam.'

'I don't know them.' It seemed an almost heartless observation.

'You know Harriet. From the ninth floor. Tall girl with glasses. Wears red suits.'

He did know her. He could picture her alongside him in the lift, swaying as if listening to a secret tune. When he stepped off at the fifth floor she would give him a little wave with red-nailed fingertips. 'Toodle-oo,' she would say.

'Toodle-oo,' Joe whispered.

'That's her.'

'Dead?'

'They found her at home this morning.'

'Jesus God.'

He turned the Porsche up the hill. Someone waved. Casey, walking a poodle. Another wave. Modesty Cloke.

'They seem to know you here,' Janie said, weakly.

'How did you find me?'

'Oh, you know . . .' Janie gave a long, painful-sounding cough. 'Manesh found you,' she said when the coughing was done. 'Someone here got insurance on your car.'

They pulled up outside the church. Joe tried to pass her the car keys.

'Keep them, Joe,' she said. 'If I die of the flu you can have the car.'

'Don't say things like that.'

'I want you to have it.'

'You're not going to die.' He pushed the keys into her pocket. 'Don't move,' he said. 'I'll carry you.'

'No, you mustn't.' But she had no strength to resist. He lifted her like one of his sacks of pulses and carried her up the steps and into the churchyard.

'Where are we going?'

'You'll see.'

He lifted her into the church and carried her towards the bell tower. 'I need to put you down,' he said, sliding her onto hesitant feet, 'just while I find the key.'

The key to the bell tower was made of heavy wrought iron, and was as large as a dinner spoon. As he slid it into the lock a voice interrupted them both. 'What have we here?' The voice of the Reverend Alvin Hocking echoed around the Plantagenet walls. He had emerged from his vestry and was facing them down from the far end of the nave.

'Good evening to you, Reverend,' said Joe. He was struggling with the awkward key.

'Visitors are not welcome in the bell tower,' the vicar intoned. 'This is a house of God, not a knocking shop.'

Not any kind of shop. Joe couldn't get the key to turn.

'We have an agreement,' said the priest. 'No guests.' No hookers, he seemed to be saying. He started towards them down the aisle.

'Please don't come any closer,' Joe said. 'This lady is ill. She has the Asian flu.'

'I am,' Janie said in a weak voice. 'I am ill.'

'Then you need a doctor, not a draughty church.' The vicar's tone bore still more than a hint of contempt. 'We have an agreement.'

'Sod our agreement.' The key turned and the heavy door swung open. But there wasn't going to be time to thwart the Reverend Hocking. Enraged and suspicious, he stormed towards Janie and Joe.

'Please.' Joe blocked his way. 'Janie is sick.'

'That's a cock-and-bull story and you know it. There's no Asian flu in Cornwall.'

Janie Coverdale was sliding down onto her haunches. The red soles of her Louboutins were showing and her mascara had run down one cheek like the damaged reputation of a drunken party girl.

'Tell me what I've done to upset you,' Joe said. He was

standing in the aisle so that Hocking couldn't pass. 'I've given you my car. I'm paying you handsomely for space in your bell tower. I've filled the place with food in case you have a hungry congregation to feed. I've obeyed every letter of our agreement.' I haven't spoken a word to your wife, he might have added, but to raise this point might have been to suggest that the sanction was justified. Half the village think we're at it like rabbits, he could have said.

'I told you no guests,' Hocking said. He moved so close to Joe that their lungs were sharing the same air.

'Then sod it,' Joe said. 'You're coming with us.' His hand flew out and snatched the vicar's wrist. 'I'm sorry. You've given me no choice.' He twisted the wrist fiercely and the older man buckled. 'Get in.'

His arm bent up his back, the Reverend Hocking stumbled forward into the bell tower. With a kick to his pants Joe sent him tumbling into a heap of boxes.

'Wait there.'

Joe helped Janie through the door and locked it behind them. Then he scooped her up and carried her up the three flights of stairs, leaving the vicar looking bruised and intemperate on a sack of dried fruits.

'Who is he?' Janie asked. Joe had laid her down on the narrow mattress he'd taken from Mallory Books's boat. He'd made up the bed with sheets and a duvet from the doctor's house.

He started to tell her the story. When he reached the part about Polly Hocking she managed a smile. 'Are you fucking her?' she croaked.

Ah well. Perhaps poetry really was closer to the truth than history. 'Some would say we're at it like rabbits.'

'Joe Haak, you're a rogue.' She wagged a disapproving finger, then sank back onto the mattress. 'Oh God,' she said. 'I feel awful.'

'You're not going to die,' he said. 'It's only the flu.' But he was thinking of Harriet Adlam waving her fingernails like a sine wave. Toodle-oo. He sat down heavily on a box of tins and watched her breathing. Her face was wet with sweat.

'Talk to me, Joe,' she said, after a while. Her voice was almost too thick to understand.

'Do you want some water?' he asked. When she nodded he went to fetch a jug. He had carried it upstairs – not to drink, but to wash with. She wouldn't know. She drank from the spout. A lot of it spilled on her blouse. She didn't seem to care.

'Why did you come looking for me?' he asked.

She was shaking her head slowly. 'I didn't know I was ill when I left London,' she said. 'I thought I was running away from it. This . . . this fever . . . only started an hour or so ago.'

'That quickly?'

She nodded.

'But why me?'

'Kaufmann said.' She gave him a very weak smile. 'He said to come and find you. He said you'd be prepared.' She glanced around at the wall of provisions. 'I think he was right.' She broke into a spluttering cough that lasted for too long.

'I'm sorry,' Joe said. 'For what I did.'

'What did you do?'

'For Lane Kaufmann. And Cassie. For breaking the bank. For losing all that money.'

For a moment her forehead crumpled and her eyes squeezed shut. When she opened them again there was something of her original fire back in them. There she was, the girl who had commanded the fifth floor, who had once run an empire and traded a hundred million dollars a day. 'You silly ass,' she whispered to him. 'You didn't lose us money.' She closed her eyes again. 'Why did you run out on us?'

He shook his head. 'I was scared.' They'd drawn my name out of a hat, he could have said. I was taking the fall.

'By the time you made it to the door the market was already falling,' she said. 'I told you all to keep your nerve. And everyone did. Except for you, Joe. You were the only one to break.'

Was this true? 'I'm sorry,' he said.

'By the time you were racing down the Embankment we'd clawed back twenty-five million. Oh God.' She blinked and screwed up her face. 'I'm dying, Joe.'

'No you're not.' He moved to sit on the edge of the makeshift bed and took her hand. 'You're not dying. I promise. I won't let you die.'

'Sixty people died of the flu in London last night,' she said. 'Didn't you see it on the news?'

Sixty people! 'I might have done.' Had he missed that bit? Surely the only item on the news was the one about the villagers in Cornwall. The greedy villagers who were hoarding food.

'Julian said it was because you'd gone. That was why our position was recovering so fast.'

'Did he now . . .?'

'It'll be OK now the geek has run away. That's what he said.'

'I'm sure he did.'

'I tried to call you but you'd left your phone behind.'

'I know.'

'By the time you'd have reached the M4, we were almost even,' Janie said. 'God, it was exciting. Cassie was right. So right. We should have had more faith.'

'But still you shut her down,' Joe said. 'You shut Cassie down.'

'Just for a few days, Lew wanted some more controls, but I've never come closer to wetting myself on a trading floor. You, Joe, you were like the football fan who can't bear to stay and see his team go down three–nil, so he flees the stadium, and misses the four goals that give them the cup.' She opened her eyes again. Almost playfully. 'Did you and me . . . Did we ever . . .?'

'Did we ever what?' A silly question. He could picture the

white leather ottoman and the bones of her knees and the half-smile that played around her lips as they rocked together.

'I'm sorry,' she said. 'I shouldn't have asked.' Perhaps she didn't remember. 'By the time you'd have got to Bristol,' she said, 'the market was in free fall. The world was offloading stocks. When Hong Kong closed it was like the January sales. Every bank in the City was taking losses. Huge losses.' She stopped to cough, and to drink again from the wash jug. 'Colin Helms said brokers were leaping off the top floors all the way down Threadneedle Street. But not at Lane Kaufmann. Because we had Cassie.' She squeezed his hand and seemed to relax against the pillow. 'My blue-eyed boy.'

It may have been the last time she spoke coherently. She slept then. Joe could hear Alvin Hocking's heavy footsteps climbing the stairs. He braced himself for the inevitable row, but when Hocking entered there was a long, uncomfortable silence. The vicar, still breathing heavily from the climb, stood looking at Janie. Eventually he spoke.

'I think I need to ask your forgiveness,' he said.

'That's OK.'

'I may have misjudged you.'

Joe looked up at him. 'I didn't make it easy for you,' he said.

'All the same.'

The only sound now was Janie's broken breathing.

'They say six hundred people died of the flu today in London,' Hocking said.

'Jesus! I thought it was sixty.'

'Sixty last night. Another six hundred today.'

'Dear God.'

'Indeed.' Hocking seemed to have shrunk in size, a small man now, standing by the pitiful bed. 'Should I pray for her?'

'If you like.'

The priest lowered himself onto his knees. 'If this makes you uncomfortable,' he said, 'you could search your store for some brandy.'

Joe gave a smile. 'Martha told me you were teetotal.'

'There are some things that even Martha Fishburne doesn't know.'

'There's just one box,' he said. 'For emergencies only.'

'Well then. I think this qualifies, don't you?'

21
Yea, though I walk through the valley of death

Janie Coverdale died some time before five o'clock in the morning. There was nowhere else to sleep, so Joe and the vicar sat up together and watched as the delirium took her. For a while her fever was so high that Joe was sure she would die of heat stroke. He descended the stairs to the church and brought back a bucket of cold water, and they soaked her, but still her body burned. 'She needs electrolytes,' Hocking said with some authority. They spooned glucose and painkillers into her water and she drank when she was conscious, but by midnight she was in a coma, sweating with the fever, and shaking with cold. Joe had a medicine chest, stocked up from the cash-and-carry, but there was nothing that seemed strong enough for Janie. 'I wish we could ask Mallory,' he said. 'I don't know what to give her.' But they didn't need to voice their fears. Locked away in the highest room of the tower, they were quarantined from the village. There was no way to ask Mallory Books for his advice. And anyway, what could he have said? They gave her aspirins and ibuprofen, crushed into water – a cocktail of analgesics. They gave her a sleeping draught and a syrup for the cough. They took it in turns to sit alongside her and wipe her brow with a flannel. Hocking recited Bible verses. Joe struggled to find things to say. He talked about the fifth floor. Did she remember that day when every stock was climbing and nothing wanted shorting, and between them, the two of them, they'd fastened on Eurotunnel shares, on nothing more than a hunch? Did she remember how the stocks had fallen? How sweet the champagne had tasted, and Cerys Kenworthy saying she brought the bottles all the way to London on the Eurostar and the whole office collapsing with mirth? Did she remember the day when, ten minutes before trading ended, a freak storm disabled an oil rig and with seconds to go they had turned ten million loss into a profit?

'Does she have any family?' Hocking asked.

'Three husbands.' Joe nodded slowly. 'All divorced. No one else.'

'No kids?'

'None that she's ever mentioned.'

It was cold in the bell tower after midnight. They found a box filled with clerical robes and wrapped themselves in them for warmth. Joe wore his coat. Around three in the morning Hocking began to sing. 'Oh Lord my God, when I, in awesome wonder, consider all the works Thy hands have made.'

'That is one of my father's favourite hymns,' Joe said.

'I see the stars, I hear the rolling thunder, Thy work throughout the Universe displayed.'

'Then sings my soul, Oh Saviour God, to Thee,' both voices sang. 'How great Thou art. How great Thou art.' There may have been acoustic resonance in the old bell tower. The great bell seemed to hum along to the tune. 'How great Thou art. How great Thou art.'

'Are you a believer?' Hocking asked.

'Not especially.' There didn't seem to be any point in lying.

'Is Janie?'

'Perhaps.'

They sang 'Abide with me, fast falls the eventide', and Joe found himself, much to his surprise, remembering the words. Then they sang the twenty-third psalm. 'The Lord is my Shepherd, I'll not want.' Afterwards the vicar recited the words slowly. 'Yea, though I walk through the valley of the shadow of death, I shall fear no evil.'

After this they were silent. Joe turned off the lights and they were left with the faint glow of the moon through the Norman arches. 'We could take it in turns to sleep,' Hocking suggested, but there was nowhere to sleep. By 4 a.m. Janie was cold, and they covered her over with everything they could find. Joe took off his coat, but her breathing was shallow. He lay down alongside her and covered her with his arm, and imagined that she was relaxing into his hold.

At five in the morning Hocking woke him. He, Joe, had fallen asleep. 'She's gone,' the older man said.

Surely goodness and mercy shall follow me all the days of my life, Joe thought. Thy rod and thy staff, they comfort me still, but not today. Not here. Not for Janie Coverdale. Click click, her heels would go along the polished tiles of the trading floor. All the boys' heads would turn, young and old, married and single, trapped by her magical allure. 'Find me a short, my blue-eyed boy,' she would murmur, would ruffle her rings through his hair. 'Let's go make money, boys and girls. Let's go.' One button open on her blouse. Just to keep them guessing. And the white leather ottoman. Perhaps that was all the passion she had left in her after three husbands and countless lovers. Perhaps that should be her memorial at Lane Kaufmann. The white ottoman and the paintings of the Charente.

They swaddled her in the clerical robes and laid her on the floorboards alongside the bells. Joe cried and Hocking put an arm around his shoulder. They watched the sun come up over the eastern hills.

'I think I broke our agreement last night,' Hocking said.

'Did you? How?'

'I had some of your brandy.'

'Oh.' Joe waved the point away. 'I should never have suggested it.'

'All the same. I think our agreement is void.' There was a long pause. 'You may have your car back.' Hocking drew the keys from his pocket and passed them to Joe.

'Thank you. We need to survive first.'

They hadn't discussed this, but it was clear all the same. First, they had to survive, and they'd seen what this disease had done to Janie.

'And whatever becomes of us, you may talk to Polly, if you wish.'

'Thank you.'

'If only one of us survives . . .'

'Then what?'

Hocking was in a reverie. His eyes seemed to focus on the far horizon where the sea became the sky. 'Nothing. It's OK.'

What was he going to suggest, Joe wondered. If only one of us survives . . . then he should take care of Polly? Did that need saying? But what if they both survived? Or neither?

'I didn't know flu could kill a person. Not like that. Not so fast,' Hocking said.

'It's just how it happened after the First World War,' Joe said. 'They called it the Spanish flu then. People would go to bed feeling fine, and wake up dead.'

'We need to tell the village. We need to warn them.'

'I think the media is doing that for us.'

'No, really. We really *do* need to warn them. They think we're safe down here in St Piran, but all it takes is one young woman . . .' The vicar let the thought hang in the air.

'How?' Joe asked. 'We can't go downstairs.' If we go into the village, was the unspoken message, we'll spread the infection.

They ate a breakfast of corned beef and tinned tomatoes. They had no spoons or forks, so they ate with their fingers, and used the plastic lids of caterers' margarine packs as plates, but neither man was hungry. They made orange squash with some of the water from the bucket. It was beginning to dawn upon them that they might be together, here in this bell tower, for quite some time. Proximity and Jeopardy, Joe thought. And a generous helping of Time. Just not quite the company either he or Demelza had envisaged.

'Polly will be wondering where I am,' Hocking said once

the sun was up. 'My car . . . *your* car . . . it's still parked at the Vicarage.'

'Perhaps you're out comforting a parishioner.'

'All night?'

'Are there any other keys to the bell tower? Apart from the one I have?'

Hocking nodded slowly. 'One more,' he said. He dug deep into a pocket and retrieved a key. 'I have it.'

'Then no one else can get in?'

'Not without a battering ram.'

'Then I think I know what we have to do.'

There were herring gulls above them, out along the ramparts, resting up, readying themselves for the sun to warm the morning air. When the clap of the first bell sounded the gulls scattered like confetti in a gale, hawking and screaming in a halo of beating wings. Dong . . . ong . . . ong. A second clap, louder than the first. This one caused a stir all the way along Cliff Street, down as far as the dock where Toby Penroth was untying his boat, and where Casey Limber was rolling out a net. Jessie Higgs appeared at the door of her shop. 'What in God's name?'

Dong . . . ong . . . ong . . . onggg.

Martha Fishburne, not yet at school, flung open a window. It must be one of the children playing a prank, but which one would do such a thing? Jeremy Melon stepped outside to knock on the doctor's door. Kenny Kennet, halfway down the quay with a sack to fill, turned back to look up at the church.

And now a second bell. A higher pitch. And now the first again. And now the second. Two ringers then. What could this mean? The church bells hadn't been rung in two decades. Benny Restorick and Daniel Robins, coming from two directions, met at the corner of Harbour Hill and Fish Street, and neither man needed to say a word. Benny pointed up the hill and they fell into step, with young Thomas Horsmith behind them, and Jacob Anderssen, and Martha, and Charity, and Jessie some way behind. Old Man Garrow followed in slow pursuit, waving his stick. Jeremy Melon and Mallory Books appeared, scuttling down the lane, and then came the Shaunessys and the Bartles, and more who stepped out of their front doors to swell the crowd. Charity and Ardour Cloke were there, and Modesty, and Valour, and Faith. Abel O'Shea the harbour master, too deaf to hear the noise, tottered into the fray looking unsettled. The Penhallows were there, and a clutch of children nearly ready for school. 'What *is* that racket?'

Old Man Garrow waved his stick. 'Eez an omen,' he prophesied. 'An omen.'

Polly Hocking was in her dressing gown. She came to the door of the Vicarage and looked in consternation at the bell tower. A crowd was sweeping up the hill.

Dong. Dong. Dong.

'Someone's stealing all that food,' said Benny Restorick boldly.

'Well, they won't get away with much if that's the car they came in,' said Jeremy. The Porsche was sitting forlornly by the gate.

This observation bemused them. 'What then?'

'Try the church door,' someone said.

Daniel Robins ran ahead. 'Locked,' he reported back.

'Then it must be Joe,' Jeremy said. 'What is he playing at?'

The ringing had stopped.

''Tiz the very devil,' Old Man Garrow warned. He leaned heavily on his stick. The hill had tired him out.

'Joe?' Polly Hocking called up to the tower. 'Alvin? Are you there?'

'Mebbe they've locked 'emselves in?' Martha said. 'It's the sort of thing boys do.'

'Can we get a ladder?' someone suggested.

'Don't be soft.'

And then there was a cry. Someone had been spotted on the

high rampart. A man with a cloth mask tied around his face. A murmur infected the crowd.

'It's Alvin,' shouted Polly.

'Dear God in heaven,' said Demelza Trevarrick. 'He isn't trying to kill himself?'

That suggestion drew a collective gasp. The narrative was almost clear. Demelza would tell the story later, as she saw it then. She would lean back in her seat in the Petrel Inn and drop her voice to tell the tale that had come to her in that moment. The vicar, wounded by his wife's infidelity, had confronted her lover in the tower. They had fought, but the young interloper had tempered his resistance and a blow from the cuckold had sent him crashing through the ancient banister and left him swinging on the bell rope. It was almost over. The wounded lover had tried to scramble down the rope and the bell had sounded out his distress to the village. But the vicar was ahead of him. With a slice from a convenient knife he had severed the rope and the young philanderer had fallen to his death. The bells were silenced, but now, confronted by his deed, the wronged husband had come to seek his own salvation. With a single leap he would break free of the bounds of Earth, soar out over the churchyard, and for a moment at least he would be there with the gulls, until, in an instant, gravity would prevail and he would fall to his death before his own congregation. A sermon on the fragility of life that none would ever forget.

But Demelza's fancies were short-lived. High on the roof of the tower a second figure had emerged. Joe, also masked, a torn shred of a clerical cowl tight around his face. He placed a hand on the vicar's shoulder.

'Can you hear us?' Hocking called down. There was a shuffling in the crowd. Maybe this was an excuse for a sermon, but it wasn't a Sunday. No one had time for prayer.

'Listen please,' Joe shouted, and the crowd hushed. They could hear him clearly. 'We've got a dead woman in here. She died last night. Her name was Janie Coverdale. She was a friend of mine. She died of the flu.'

This generated another gasp.

'That's her car by the churchyard.'

Evidence then. A babble of voices started up.

'Wait, please.' Joe let the hubbub subside. 'The Reverend and I sat up with Ms Coverdale all night. We were with her when she died. This time yesterday Janie Coverdale was fit and healthy. This morning she's dead.' Joe straightened up. 'I've never seen anything so fast, but I have to warn you. Janie won't be the last person to seek refuge here. They'll be fleeing from the cities as we speak. They'll get in their cars with all the fuel they can lay their hands on, and they'll drive as far and as fast as they can, until they run right out of fuel, or out of road.' Any further, he thought, and their tyres would be wet. 'It will only take one person,' he said, 'just one person with the flu to make it here. And half of us could be dead by the end of the week.'

The crowd was growing. More people were climbing up the hill to swell the numbers.

'You have to close the road,' Joe shouted.

'A gate,' called Moses Penhallow. 'We could gate the road.'

'Good idea,' said Joe. He was looking down at the sea of faces. Familiar faces now. The faces of a crowd that had rescued a whale. Such a very short time ago. Polly was there. He could see her anxious expression. 'Reverend Hocking and I might be dead in two days,' he said. 'We're both infected.'

The crowd fell silent.

'You need a strong gate,' he said. 'A high gate. People will climb a low gate. They'll break through a weak gate. We're looking at very desperate people here. They'll be scared. And hungry. Block the harbour too. And the cliff paths.'

The voices were starting up again.

'Go,' Joe shouted. 'Go!' He put his arm around the vicar.

'Go,' Hocking called. He waved them all away. He and Joe ducked down beneath the ramparts. And they were gone.

22

It's your perfect storm

'How long does it take?' Hocking asked.

'It varies with the virus,' Joe said. 'But typically the cycle takes around three days. You get infected, but you won't know about it for the first day. And you won't be infectious. The second day you'll be infectious yourself, but you won't have any symptoms. You'll feel fine, but anyone coming into contact with you could catch the virus. Then forty-eight hours or so after your first contact, your symptoms will start to appear. After that it depends on the strain of flu.'

'How do you know all this stuff?'

'It was part of my job.' His job. So long ago. Hiding in the shadows at the back of a trading floor, punching numbers into keyboards. He felt a sudden ache.

'So we're not really infectious yet?'

Toodle-oo, Janie Coverdale. Toodle-oo, Harriet Adlam. Toodle-oo, Colin Helms. He tried to focus. 'Probably not, but I don't think we should take any risks. Who knows how quickly this strain works.'

'I wish I could talk to Polly.'

There was very little to do. 'We have only one bed,' Alvin Hocking said. So they constructed a second out of sacks of chickpeas, cardboard boxes and bubble wrap. There was no room for it in the little third-floor bedroom.

'I'll sleep on the landing,' Joe said. He walled his new bed in with packages and sacks. It was almost cosy. He sat on a stack of crates looking out through the open window, out over the rooftops, down to where the cobbles ended and the sea began.

How would they block off the harbour, he wondered. Was it even possible?

There was a sudden, urgent noise: the ringing of a mobile phone. Joe sprang to his feet. 'Do you have a telephone?'

Hocking shook his head. 'There's no signal in St Piran.'

'There is . . . *up here.*' He was hunting for the sound. It rang again. 'Here!' Janie's jacket lay discarded on the floor. From the pocket Joe withdrew her phone.

'Hello?'

The voice sounded a thousand miles away. A hollow, empty voice; an echo, overladen with static, forced from damaged, ancient lungs. 'Is Janie there?'

'Mr Kaufmann?'

'Joe?'

His turn, now, to break bad news. He broke it starkly. 'Janie's dead, Mr Kaufmann.' Were there other words? Was there an easier way? He could feel Janie's death occupying the space around him like a malign vapour, like a black ink stain on the light of morning. He could picture her cold wrapped body on the floorboards, by the bells, close to where he stood.

Kaufmann was quiet. Had he heard? Perhaps he had. Joe waited.

'Are *you* all right?' Kaufmann asked at last.

'I think so. I'll be infected . . . I suppose.' Another long pause. 'Can you tell people? Her family.'

'Of course.'

'Can you . . . tell everyone on the fifth floor. Tell them how brave she was.'

'I will.' Kaufmann was breathing noisily. 'But there's no one in the office today. I've told everyone to stay at home. It could be weeks before we open again. We've been hit hard, Joe. We've already lost five.'

Five? He didn't dare ask. He didn't want any more names. 'How about you, sir?'

'I'll be OK, Joe. I'm with my family, somewhere we'll be safe.'

'That's good.'

'Did you see the news, Joe? They say this virus is the same as the Spanish flu of 1918. It's identical. So we know how it behaves.' Kaufmann gave a noisy cough. 'One of the things we know about the Spanish flu was the way it took fit, young people and left the elderly unaffected.'

Joe's head was swimming. He supposed that *he* was a fit, young person. Was he going to die too? 'It's your perfect storm,' he said. 'Just as you feared. A flu epidemic and an oil shortage all rolled into one.'

'This is no random storm, Joe,' Lew Kaufmann said, from a long way away. 'This is war.'

'War?'

'Of course. Nations have been trying to recreate the Spanish flu for some time. Didn't I tell you about this?'

'Maybe you did, sir. I don't remember.'

'Well, it isn't a new idea. A few years ago American scientists dug up the body of a woman who had died in the 1918 epidemic. She was buried in permafrost in Alaska. They called her Lucy. They were able to extract flu viruses from her lungs and do you know what they did? They published the genome sequence on the internet for all the world to see.' Kaufmann snorted. 'After that, this epidemic was just a matter of time. What was interesting was just how few differences there were between the 1918 virus that killed so many millions of people, and the flu viruses that are out there infecting people all the time. Just twenty-five base pairs in the DNA. That's all.'

Joe was finding it hard to think now. He wanted this conversation to end. 'So you believe someone has . . . recreated this virus?'

'What do you think, Joe?'

'Sir. Janie's dead. Tomorrow I'm going to be sick. In two days' time I could be dead too. I don't know if I even care any more.'

'I understand.' The line went quiet. 'You will phone me, Joe?'

'If I can.'

'Good luck.'

'Thank you, sir.'

Hocking was standing, watching. Joe passed him the phone. 'Do you want to call Polly?'

The priest nodded.

'Do it now. There's hardly any battery left.' Joe left the vicar typing numbers into the phone, and climbed slowly down the steps to the ground floor. As he descended he could hear Hocking's voice, soft, murmuring, like a background conversation in a bar. At one point he seemed to raise his voice. 'No! No . . .' It was a moment of sharpness. Joe dropped down to the stone floor.

There was a job he could do, he thought. He had planned to take an inventory. What better time to start than the present? If he could find a pen, he could compile a list of all the food in the bell tower, every tin, every bottle, every jar. He sat down on a box, but could summon up no enthusiasm for the task. These could be his final few days. Was he destined to spend his last hours imprisoned like a ghost in a tower? He could leave now. Who would stop him? He could set off up the hill, and over the cliffs. Surely he would meet no one. Maybe he could take refuge in a cave? Or else, perhaps, he could run down to the harbour, to Mallory's boat, and sail it out to sea. He could cough the influenza phlegm out of his lungs and spit it into the Atlantic swell. Maybe he would drift a thousand miles. Maybe they would find his body washed up naked on a beach in Hawaii. Another beach. Another adventure. That might be fitting, he thought.

But instead he waited for all sounds of Hocking's voice to stop, for the conversation to end. And he tried not to think about Polly.

They lunched on potted ham and cold tinned potatoes. With no way to boil water in the tower they opened jars of fruit to drink the juice. And there was always the brandy.

As the day wore on, reminders of Hocking's less tolerant nature were starting to surface.

'In a way this is all your fault,' he said to Joe as they sat splayed out on the floorboards, hemmed all around by boxes.

'All my fault?'

'If you hadn't run to St Piran in the first place, we wouldn't be sitting here now.'

True, he supposed. And a fair point to make as you stare down death. If he hadn't panicked when the market looked set to destroy them, if Janie hadn't told them to write out their wills, if Julian McEvan hadn't threatened him, if his name hadn't been drawn out of a hat, if a wall of faces hadn't looked his way with such terror in their eyes . . .

'If you'd had the courage to turn around and go home.' The vicar was persisting now. 'If you'd had the good sense . . .'

He wouldn't let it bother him, but it was cold in the bell tower. The wind leaked through the arches and found its way into every corner. Cold can make a man intolerant, he told himself.

'Come to think of it,' Hocking was saying, 'why did you bring her to the church at all? Madness. You should have driven her as far from the village as you could.'

Which may not have been far. There might not have been enough fuel to get as far as Treadangel. He would have had to visit the church tower to fetch one of his cans of petrol, and there he would have met Alvin, and there they would have talked, and how would anything be any different?

'You know the trouble with people like you . . .'

Who *were* the people like him? Young people? Young men? Young men with raging hormones? Young men with too much money and too little sense? 'I think perhaps I do,' he said. 'I *do* know the trouble with people like me.'

There was a doctor he had seen in Wimpole Street, a lady doctor with a fake tan, and real jewellery, and half-moon spectacles that hung around her neck on a cord. Dr Marcia Brodie was her name. She had an animated face that exaggerated every expression. 'Helloooo, young Joe,' she would exclaim when he came in through the door of her consulting room, and every muscle in her face would work to create an aspect of delight. 'What have we here?' she would enquire with foreboding as she peered into his eyes with an ophthalmoscope, and her face would mould into a look of magnified concern. She acted as the in-house therapist at the bank, responsible for the physical and mental health of the staff – or so it seemed. She would see all the bank's employees, twice a year, in an office on the ninth floor, and there she'd measure blood pressure, and pulse rate, and cholesterol, and she'd ask probing questions, and peer into eyes and ears with instruments designed for that sort of thing, and her wonderfully kinetic face would provide an animated narrative to the whole consultation.

'I want you to come and see me in my clinic,' she told Joe one year, handing him a card. 'Phone that number and make an appointment. The bank will pay.'

So Joe did as he was told and found himself, days later, in a basement consulting room with parquet floors and Arab furnishings. Dr Brodie made him lie on a cold examination table without his shirt. She pressed him here and there with cold hands and listened to his breathing with a cold stethoscope. Medicine is cold, Joe thought. It's a series of cold interventions.

'Breathe in,' Dr Brodie said, her eyebrows flickering. 'Breathe out. Breathe in. Breathe out.'

Later, while he was putting on his shirt, she told him that his blood pressure was high. 'Are you under any stress?' she asked him.

I work on the trading floor of an investment bank, he could have told her, but she already knew this. 'Perhaps.'

'Then we will have to fix you,' she said. 'You know the trouble with people like you? You don't respond well to stress.'

You know the trouble with people like you . . .?

'. . . you think you know it all,' Hocking said. 'You think

because you earn all that money and drive a fast car, there's nothing more you need to learn. Well, you're wrong.'

Dr Brodie had given him pills and breathing exercises. Breathe in. Breathe out. His father had made him look at the horizon and count. Janie and Julian had given him stress, and he'd cracked.

'I don't respond well to stress,' Joe said. 'That's the trouble with people like me. I have it on good authority.'

The vicar looked at him, surprised. It wasn't the expected answer. 'Is that your excuse?'

'It's the only one I have.' And that was true. But how was it that numbers on a screen could make him stressed, while the death of a friend and the fear of death, his own death, seemed to instil in him a profound sense of calm? 'I have breathing exercises,' he said. 'They're good if you're stressed. Would you like to try them?'

'No thank you.' It was a curt reply. Perhaps Polly's husband needed the exercises more than he did.

An hour later and Hocking was contrite again. 'I'm sorry,' he said. 'I didn't mean to blame you. It isn't your fault.'

'Thank you.'

'Will you forgive me?'

'Of course.'

No symptoms yet, Joe thought, as he lay on the makeshift bed that night. No temperature, no cough, no mucus.

There were bats roosting at the top of the bell tower. As it grew dark they took flight, each one a flicker of motion, each one catching the moonlight for a blink of time. Bats in the belfry, Joe thought. It seemed fitting.

He lay and listened to his heartbeat amplified through the bubble-wrap blanket. Every beat, it seemed to him, was sending the virus through his bloodstream, an invisible regiment of malign forces, an enemy set on killing him. Would he die?

He had been asleep when Janie died. Barely asleep, but asleep. He'd been lying next to her. For an hour he had felt her shaking, sweating, trembling, battling the demons in her bloodstream. For the next hour she had started to relax. He had imagined that this was the recovery, but it wasn't. Her body was letting go. That was when he slept. If he had stayed awake, would Janie still be alive? It was a foolish thought. He knew that, but he couldn't help thinking it. It reminded him of a saying of his father's. 'Do you know how to stay alive for ever?' Pappa Mikkel would ask, grinning beneath his beard. 'Just keep breathing,' he would say. 'Just keep breathing.' Some time last night Janie had forgotten this simple command. How could it be so hard? Breathe in. Breathe out. Breathe in. Breathe out. But death cheats in this game, Joe thought. It comes in your sleep.

A bat flew by so close he could feel the cold whip of wind from its wings. He pulled his covers up over his head.

Death, he felt, was no stranger. Not any more. He'd seen him out there in the bay, when numb with the cold, and torn apart with anguish and regret and guilt, he'd looked into the abyss. Death was there to be sure, waiting in the dark waters. Death was patient. What was a week to death? A month? A year? No matter that the whale had saved him, had carried him ahead on a bow wave, had dropped him safely on the sand; what did death mind? He could die in the inky black waters, or be dashed on the rocks, or cough himself to death in a belfry, it was nothing to death; the outcome would be the same. Joe felt himself collapsing slowly beneath the force of this thought, beneath the artless recognition of his own fragility.

On the other side of the wall, he could hear Alvin Hocking praying.

23
No power 'n' no phones

Some say, of the bats that live in empty churches, that each one is a departed soul, caught between this world and the next; and when they fly their roosts at sunset, they flee to petition the next world for admission; and those that return at dawn have been denied. Some say the bats are the spirits of those who were lost to the plague, for they were many.

But not in St Piran.

The Magwiths took up one of their field gates and deployed it at the top of the lane. Bevis Magwith supplied it with a padlock and a chain, and all through the first day, one of the Magwith brothers stood guard to admit only those that he knew, or could vouch for. But the system was imperfect. When young Corin Magwith deserted his post for twenty minutes to help bring in the cows for milking, Aminata Chikelu and Elizabeth Bartle were left waiting at the gate, unable to get home.

'We shall have to cut a key for every villager,' Aileen Magwith complained.

A solution appeared on the second day. Jeremy Melon offered up a padlock with a combination lock. 'All we have to do,' he said, 'is to post a sign on the way *out* of the village telling motorists the secret number, so that anyone leaving can manage the lock themselves, but anyone coming from *outside* the village won't know the number.'

The system worked for the second day, but there were few, in practice, who braved the lane. Most stayed at home in the village – even those who would normally make the trip for work. Schools and colleges throughout the county had been closed anyway: a temporary precaution to cope with the flu pandemic and the fuel shortage. Benny Restorick came back to the village after a fruitless search for petrol. 'There's none to be had anywhere,' he told anybody who would listen, and the news soon found its way around the village. 'Every filling station between here and Plymouth is closed,' he said. 'I queued for four hours at a station in Redruth but they were only giving customers two litres each. Two litres! And that ran out before I could get any.'

Around dawn on the second day, the lights in the village went out. Radio alarm clocks were silenced. Kettles wouldn't boil. Demelza Trevarrick appeared outside Jessie Higgs's shop at breakfast with a gin and tonic in her hand.

'Well, we have to drink something,' she said.

No one in the village had gas for cooking or heating; there was no gas main in St Piran, but Jacob Anderssen at the Petrel had a camping stove, and he deployed it, making urns of coffee and tea. A queue soon formed out onto the quayside. The water wasn't boiling fast enough to quench the thirst of an entire community.

'How long do you think this will last?' Demelza asked, watching the line of people grow.

'We've had power cuts before,' said Moses Penhallow. 'We used to have one a week when I was a lad.'

'Is it *just* a power cut, though?' Demelza said.

'I expect they're rationing electricity,' said Jeremy. 'It might go off for two or three hours, then come back on again.'

'Two or three hours?' someone said. 'I've got my washing to do.'

But by late afternoon the power had not come back. A cluster of villagers was still collected around the Inn, and Jacob was churning out hot drinks. 'We should pop up the hill and raid some of Joe's soups,' Kenny Kennet said, but angry faces turned his way.

'No one goes in or out of that tower until they've both fully recovered,' said Dr Books. He was there too with a whisky and soda.

Or until they're both dead. That was surely a thought that many shared.

'Hands up everyone who thought young Joe Haak was mad,' said Martha Fishburne, always unable to resist classroom commands. 'An' now 'ere we are wishing we 'ad some of his soups.'

Polly Hocking came down the hill from the Vicarage. 'Any sign?' Jeremy asked.

'Not a peep,' she said. She looked tired.

'Someone should telephone the electric company,' Hedra Penhallow said. 'This in't right.'

'The telephones are down too,' said Jessie Higgs. 'I tried to call the dairy this morning but there's no dial tone.' Her statement was supported by a dozen others.

'Well, there in't many saying young Joe is mad any more,' Martha said. 'No power 'n' no phones. There'll be no water soon enough.'

'They say there's flu in Plymouth,' Benny Restorick told them. 'And in Redruth, and in Truro.'

'What about Penzance?' someone asked. 'What about Treadangel?'

'Don't know, but it won't be long.'

'We shouldn't be coming and going,' Mallory Books said. 'We should all stay in the village until the epidemic is over.'

'There won't be any comin' or goin' if we can't get fuel,' Benny said.

Daniel and Samuel Robins arrived with a boxload of fish – hake, and pollack, and a dozen crabs. The Bartle sisters set to work stripping out the backbones and lopping off the heads. Jacob and Romer Anderssen tossed the fish into pans. 'You may as well knock on doors,' Jacob told Thomas Horsmith and Benny Shaunessy, 'tell everyone free dinners.'

'But no free ale,' added Romer.

And within a half an hour, the crisis in St Piran had become a party. Old Man Garrow vanished into his cottage and emerged with a squeeze-box. Kenny produced a penny whistle from one of his bags, and the strains of a sea shanty sounded out. Aminata sat between them and sang the lyrics. The fish was frying, and feet were tapping, cider and ale were flowing, and a balmy autumn breeze was drifting in from the sea. Moses and Hedra were lighting candles, Charity and Casey were wound in an embrace, Martha and Ronnie were dancing, Demelza was lighting a French cigarette, Kenny, when he wasn't playing his whistle, was whispering into Elizabeth Bartle's ear. There were children running, and women gossiping, and men sharing stories; there was a poodle snuffling for fish heads and scraps, and Jacob with his big voice calling out over the heads of the crowd, turning the fish steaks in the huge pans, families coming down the hill with folding chairs and tables, and you might have thought this was a jubilee party or the coronation of a king; all that was missing was the bunting and the souvenirs and the cake. And if, as it grew late and the music carried on, one figure broke away from the celebrations and slipped into the shadows on Harbour Hill and ducked around the corner onto Fish Street, then who would have noticed as the shadows grew long? And if that figure pulled a coat around herself, and flicked a strand of hair from her face, and looked up at the grey silhouette of the Norman church, then maybe that was as it should have been. 'Some folks weep while other folks dance,' as Martha used to say. Not everyone was in the mood to tap their feet.

'Polly?' At least one person had seen her slip away from the party. 'Would you like me to walk up the hill with you?'

Polly turned. The nurse was already wearing her uniform. 'Aminata?'

'Do you feel like some company?' Aminata slipped her hand into the crook of Polly's arm.

'It's OK really. I think I need to be on my own.'

'We have a saying in Senegal,' Aminata said. 'It is never good to be alone. But if you really *have* to be alone, then be alone with a friend.'

'A village,' Martha Fishburne would say, 'is more'n a row of houses. It's a whole network of connections.' In another life, Joe might have been able to model them on his computer. The nurse who works night shifts is connected to the girl by ties of friendship; the girl is married to the vicar; the vicar is locked in a tower with the analyst; the analyst is listening to the vicar praying. Tug a cord at one end of the network and the whole village responds. It was how a hundred people managed to save a whale. It was how one arm slipped into another and a walk up the hillside could matter so much.

On the morning of the third day there was still no power but by now the party spirit had waned and a new problem threatened. Martha Fishburne had turned on the taps in her bathroom to be met by nothing more than the hollow echo of empty plumbing. She had stepped out into the street, and there was Jessie Higgs's husband Jordy, newly home from the navy.

'Bo'sun,' Martha said, 'you're back.'

'We've all been sent home on shore leave,' he told her. 'To help with the National Emergency.'

'Is that what they're callin' it? A National 'mergency?'

'Seems so.' Bo'sun Jordy Higgs was a weathered young man, his face square and red, like a raw steak.

'Well, I've a national 'mergency of me own,' Martha said. 'I've no water.'

'None of us has,' Higgs said. 'Bevis is taking the boys out to the pumping station to see if it needs fixing.' His shrug betrayed his opinion on the futility of this mission.

'How am I to wash? How are any of us to wash?'

'In the sea?' Higgs suggested.

Mallory Books, in his overcoat, with blankets under his arms and a five-litre bottle of water, made his way up to the church and rapped on the door of the bell tower.

'They never answer,' came a voice. It was Polly, sitting alone in the pews.

'I expect they're upstairs,' Books said.

'I imagine so. I don't suppose they can hear us.'

'Have you tried calling them?'

'From time to time.'

The old doctor put his eye to the keyhole. There was nothing to be seen but boxes. 'Joe, if you're there,' he shouted, 'I need you to hear this.'

From the tower there was silence.

'Joe, I'm leaving some blankets by the door. The church will be empty in ten minutes' time. You can come down and get them.' He beckoned to Polly. 'And a bottle of water,' he shouted. 'Joe, I need to know if you can hear me. If you can hear me, please give one ring of the bell.'

There was a long silence from the bell tower.

'Joe!' Mallory called again. 'Ring the bell for me.'

Another long pause. And then a single, weak tap of the bell.

'Good boy. Now listen to me, Joe. You'll need the blankets. Keep yourselves warm. Drink plenty of fluids. Do you hear me, Joe? You'll be infectious for at least seven days *after* the symptoms disappear. You need to allow eight or nine days to be sure. Make yourselves comfortable. Polly and I will bring water and we'll leave it here every day at this time. We'll bring clean clothes. Make sure no one is around before you come out to fetch them. Do you hear me, Joe?'

A second weak tap on the bell.

Mallory lifted himself away from the keyhole and looked at Polly. 'Did you hear that?'

She nodded.

'I shall write it all down for him, so he won't forget.' Mallory disappeared into the vestry and returned with a pen and some notepaper. When he had finished writing he folded the paper carefully into an envelope and placed it on the blankets. 'Come with me, my dear.' He held out his hand and Polly took it. Then they left the church, and locked the door behind them.

24

Curry paste, one hundred, forty-eight

It was a way of coping perhaps. Besides, it was cold in the bell tower. Joe was exercising by moving boxes around. He had started his audit. Alvin was looking on, wrapped in his clerical robes, blowing out misty breaths. 'I hope you're not going to ask me to help,' he'd said to Joe. 'I have a weak back.'

'I'm only doing it to stay active,' Joe said. He was shifting boxes from one pile to another, and writing a list of what he found in each pile. 'We have to do something.'

'We could pray.'

'Thanks, but that doesn't keep you warm. At least not the way I do it.'

'If you like,' Alvin said, 'I could scribe.' He held out his hand for the paper and pen.

'Thanks.' Joe started to call out the inventory. 'Twelve jars of sliced beetroot at 560 grams.'

'Twelve beetroot 560,' echoed the vicar, writing it down.

'Twelve vegetable soups 400 grams.'

'Twelve veg soup 400.'

They had thirty-eight hundred items to record. This wasn't going to be a short exercise.

'Didn't they give you receipts?' Alvin said. 'Surely this is all on the receipts.'

'It probably is,' Joe said. 'But I lost them.'

'You lost them? How could you lose them?'

'I threw them away,' Joe said. 'Don't ask me why.' He hadn't liked the receipts. They had seemed like a paper trail. He didn't like the numbers on them, the prices, the totals. He couldn't think about this food store as a financial transaction.

He didn't want to think about how much it had all cost.

All the same, his fecklessness irritated his new companion. 'You're a silly ass,' Hocking told him.

'I am,' Joe agreed. 'I'm a hopeless case. Shirataki angel-hair pasta, thirty-six packs, 150 grams.'

'I can't even spell that.'

'Just put pasta.'

'I can't get used to the idea that you just threw away the receipts.' It was clear that the Reverend found it hard to let things go. 'Just threw them away!' With an outstretched arm he threw away imaginary papers.

'You don't have to help if you don't want to.' Joe reached out, offering to take back the list.

'No. It's all right. I just think you're an ass. That's all.'

And I think you're an ass, Joe thought, but he simply said, 'One-pint bottles of corn syrup – twelve.'

'Corn syrup. Pints. Twelve. What's that in litres?'

'I have no idea. It doesn't really matter.'

'Of course it matters.' Hocking was in a tetchy mood. 'You can't have some things in litres and some in pints.'

Joe exhaled very slowly. 'Just write it down.'

Hocking snorted. 'I still think it matters.'

'Two-and-a-half-litre tins of cold pressed extra virgin rapeseed oil,' Joe said. 'Four.'

And so they progressed. After an hour they had recorded fewer than two hundred items. 'This could take us all week,' the vicar complained.

'We may have all week,' Joe said. 'We have to do something to fill the time.'

'Who would have thought,' Hocking said as they started on a new pile of boxes, 'that flu could be so deadly?'

Who indeed? 'It's the most deadly disease known to man,' Joe said, and he found himself smiling at the vicar's look of disbelief. 'We've just become complacent about it, that's all. If we want to take a day off work, we phone in and say we've got the flu. That's crazy when you stop to think about it. We're more frightened of diseases like ebola or lassa fever or SARS but that's because we don't really understand risk. Some ebola strains kill around seventy per cent of victims, so that frightens us. We suppose that even the worst flu is nowhere near as deadly as that. Seasonal flu kills only one person in a thousand, so that isn't really worth worrying about, is it? But it still means that seven thousand people in Britain die of flu every year; thirty-six thousand people in the USA; half a million or so worldwide. There aren't many infectious diseases that kill half a million people a year, but flu does. Now what if a flu virus comes along that kills a much larger percentage of its victims? Somewhere between ten and twenty per cent? That's the fatality rate you might expect with a really bad flu. And flu has a very big edge on diseases like ebola or anthrax. It's so much easier to catch. That's the genius of the flu virus. It's worked out the fastest possible way to spread. If you want to catch ebola you have to come into contact with body fluids, but if you want to catch flu you only need to breathe the same air.'

Hocking looked uncomfortable at this. 'I don't think you should use words like *genius*,' he said. 'And you can't say that flu has *worked out* how to do this or that. It's a virus. It doesn't work anything out.'

'Maybe not in the sense you mean,' Joe said. He wanted to say more, but found himself stalling. 'Forty-eight bars of soap.'

'Soap, forty-eight.'

There is some comfort in the discipline of a routine task. It takes away the need for conversation. It leaves little room for deliberation. If you dawdle, well, the job doesn't go away. The boxes will still be there. And a task like this one could develop a rhythm, and so it did. Twelve tins of peas. Peas, twelve. Nine jars of pineapple jam. Jams, pineapple, nine.

'Twenty-five-kilogram sack of peanuts,' Joe called out.

'Not for human consumption,' came back the vicar.

'Of course they are.'

'No they're not. They're for feeding birds.'

'Who in their right mind would buy a great heavy sack of peanuts just to feed the birds?'

'Who indeed?'

'Well, they're for human consumption now,' Joe said.

'Assuming that anyone apart from you and me will ever touch any of this stuff,' Hocking said. There was a slight acidity to his tone.

'Let's hope they don't have to,' Joe said. He would have been happy to leave it there.

'Did you ever stop to think,' the vicar pressed on, 'when you were storing up this little warehouse of yours . . . just how much fish is landed in St Piran every year?'

The question was immediately disarming. Joe could feel the familiar flutter that he felt when a stock they had been shorting at Lane Kaufmann defied his analysis and started to rise. He didn't want to hear the answer.

'Twenty-four tonnes last year,' Hocking said. He was enjoying this. 'Shall I save you the trouble of working out the sums?'

'If you like . . .'

'Enough to feed the village quite comfortably. Almost half a pound of fresh fish for each person every day.'

There had been days at Lane Kaufmann when everything he touched had turned to lead. None as bad as the day he'd fled, of course; but days all the same when faces had turned his way with accusing looks, when losses rose to six-figure sums. The time he advised them to go short on platinum. 'You never short a precious metal,' Jonathan Guy advised him, but the forecasts looked so good. 'Do we do it?' Janie had asked him. 'Are you sure?'

And sometimes it had gone the other way. 'Are you sure?' Janie asked him when he pinged her to take a short position on coffee. 'You know what commodities are like, Joey boy.' And he had shaken his head – no, Janie, I'm not sure. But either way his bloodstream thickened when the numbers started rolling in. 'Shit shit shit,' Janie said. 'You should have stuck to your guns, Joe.' Or, 'I should never have listened to you, Joe. I should have listened to my gut.' You couldn't win when you were an analyst.

Half a pound of fish. He tried to picture it. What did half a pound of fish look like?

'Think of a half-pound steak, Joe. It's a meal.'

'Not enough to live on, though,' he said.

'But what about Bevis Magwith's farm? Did you ever stop to think about how much milk his cows produce? He has sixty cows, forty cows in milk. He told me they give him over eight hundred litres a day. I've worked that out in pints for you, Joe, because I know you'll appreciate this. That's five pints for every person in St Piran. Every day.'

Did he ever stop to think about anything? He was thinking of the fish that he and his father pulled out of the sea in the shallow waters round the island. Fried in butter they would melt in the mouth. 'What are you trying to say?'

'I'm telling you that you've just wasted your life's savings on a load of cheap food that no one really needs. You'd have done better buying up the fish catch for a year.'

'This is about human nature,' Lew Kaufmann had told him, the day that they had sat in the old man's twelfth-floor office under the gaze of the moai.

'Is it?'

'Of course it is. All economics is about human nature. Individual self-interest. Every economic model works on the assumption that human beings will behave selfishly.'

'Cassie doesn't work that way.'

'Doesn't she?' The old man had leaned back and raised a weathered eyebrow. 'That's not what you told me the first time you showed her to me. Don't you remember? You told me she works by averaging the forecasts of economic experts; every one of them believes in selfishness. So self-interest will inherently be part of every forecast she makes.'

'I suppose so,' Joe had conceded. 'Still, it's a rather bleak view of humanity, isn't it?'

The old banker had shaken his head. 'Not really. Self-interest is simply another way of describing the survival instinct, and that is one of the most positive traits we possess. When the collapse comes,' he said, 'you can count upon self-interest coming to the fore.'

'Twelve jars of Arrabiata sauce,' he said to Alvin Hocking.

But his mind had been drawn away from counting foodstuffs to that conversation with Kaufmann. The old man had been in an apocalyptic mood that day. 'When the collapse comes,' Kaufmann had said, 'the survival instinct will be powerful.' He had given a long, watery cough, and Joe had reflected that perhaps the ancient banker knew more about the survival instinct than he'd ever stopped to imagine. 'People will stay at home, but only for so long. When the water stops flowing, they will flee the cities. They will flee in their tens of thousands, in their tens of millions. That's when self-interest will start to trump community interest, or even national interest.' Kaufmann had fixed Joe with an icy look. 'It would be better for everyone,' he had said, 'if those millions were to stay at home; if the key workers at the power stations, and the water treatment plants, and the fuel depots, and the transport networks, were to be protected and helped back to work. Because the instinct for survival won't recognise that the man people are mugging in the street for his last litre of fuel is a driver distributing food. No one will stop to ask if the woman they just robbed of her last loaf is an engineer in a power plant.'

'Arrabiata sauce?' Hocking was sounding contemptuous. 'What is that anyway? Who in St Piran ever cooks with Arrabiata sauce?'

'It goes well with fish,' Joe said.

They stopped for some lunch. Tuna from a jar, and cold tinned potatoes.

'How are you feeling?'

'OK. It's too early to expect symptoms anyway.'

Afterwards Joe climbed to the top of the tower. Janie was still there. Janie's body. He felt an urge to unwrap her just to make sure. What if she was only sleeping? He called down the stairs to Hocking, who was resting on the third floor. 'Alvin?'

'Yes.'

How cold it was up here. He reached into the folds of the shroud and found Janie's hand.

'Yes, Joe. What is it?'

'Nothing.' How could her hand be so cold so quickly? Where does all the warmth go?

Half a pound of fish. Milk, and butter, and cream, and cheese. Could you live better than that? The finest meal of his life had been garlic mushrooms cooked over a campfire. Did anyone really need marrowfat peas or Arrabiata sauce? Surrounded by all these cold preserves and still tasting the soft gelatinous texture of the cold tinned potatoes and the oily chemical flavour of factory tuna, the thought of fresh clean food, fish pulled that very day out of the sea, milk still warm from the cow, seemed like a dream from another world.

'I feel I ought to apologise,' Hocking said. He had climbed the stairs and emerged silently onto the top-floor landing.

'What for?'

'I called you an ass.'

'I am an ass.'

'Maybe, but I shouldn't have called you one.' The vicar placed his hand on the young man's arm and slid it down towards where Joe's hand was buried in the shroud. He disentangled the cold dead hand of Janie Coverdale. 'Leave her be, Joe.' He drew Joe's arm slowly out.

'I think . . .' Joe said, 'I think . . .' Did he ever think? Could he think? 'I think . . .'

'It's all right, Joe.'

Why was he shaking so much? 'I think we should bury her.'

'That's against the law. She can't be buried without an inquest. Trust me, I know about these things.'

'Then what should we do?'

'We need to report her death formally. She needs to be seen by a doctor. Mallory Books won't do. We need a proper doctor.'

'But how can we do that? We're infected with the flu. We can't even go into the village.'

'Then we shall have to wait. The law will overlook our delay in reporting the death given the circumstances.'

'If there still *is* any law.' Joe's shakes were subsiding.

'There are some things we can always rely on, Joe. The sun will always rise tomorrow. We are all mortal. And there will always be laws to obey.'

And human self-interest, Joe thought. We can always rely on that too.

Aside from eating there was very little else to do. 'Shall we carry on with the stocktaking?' Hocking asked.

But now it was Joe's turn to shrug. 'What for? It seems we have all the fish we can eat. We have milk and butter and clotted cream. Are there hens in the village?'

'Toby Penroth keeps a dozen. And the Moots, and the Shaunessys.'

'Eggs too then.'

'And lamb. Bevis has a hundred ewes.'

'A hundred? How much meat do you get off a ewe?'

'Well, I wouldn't know, but I reckon enough for a good village barbecue.'

Joe sighed. 'Why did no one tell me this?'

'They probably expected you to work it out for yourself. We don't ask a lot of questions in St Piran, you know. If a young madman turns up in a slick new car and wants to fill the church tower with food, why should anyone try to stop him? That's not what we do.'

'Well, I wish maybe someone had.'

They sat for a while, but it was cold just sitting, especially as the wind seeped in through the open vents. 'What are we doing?' Joe asked after they'd sat in silence for minutes. 'Are we just waiting to die?'

'Of course not. We're being responsible. We're not letting this infection get into the village.'

'But it *will* reach the village. Eventually. Someone is going to find their way to St Piran and when they do it will just have to run its course.'

'You don't really think that.'

'I don't know what to think.' Joe was on his feet now, pacing. 'What if we save one life? Just one?'

'I know.'

'What if it was Polly?'

Funny how a name can be a weapon. How a name can disarm you, how it can trip you up. Did he react to the name? Did it make him stall? Was Alvin Hocking watching him for evidence?

But evidence of what? He'd never even kissed her. Yet half the village thought . . .

'There is nothing between me and Polly,' Joe said, and then he wished he hadn't spoken. How can a man feel guilty when he's committed no crime?

But the older man wasn't watching him. He was sitting with his head in his hands. 'I know,' he said. 'Polly told me.'

'Told you what?'

'She told me there was nothing between you, but I've seen the way she looks at you. And I've seen the way you look at her. If you drop sodium into water you *will* get a reaction. The sodium doesn't choose to react. Neither does the water. The laws of nature just take over.'

'I thought you didn't believe in the laws of nature.'

'What? Because I'm a priest? My dear boy, I have to believe in the laws of nature. I believe God created them.'

'And did He create the flu?'

'Ah.' Hocking lifted his head from his hands. 'We would need a week for that conversation.'

'We may have a week.' Or we could both be dead in two days.

At least they weren't talking about Polly. 'Tell me, Joe, do you believe that nature *has* to be so cruel? So red in tooth and claw? What if God took away the predators? Wouldn't that make a nicer world?'

'Perhaps.'

'But then we'd be overrun with rabbits. And rats. And grazing creatures. And all the grasslands would be overgrazed, and all the forests would be consumed, and the world would perish.'

All the world would perish. All the supply chains would collapse. 'So the lion will never lie down with the lamb?'

'Only in a zoo.'

'And flu is just another predator?'

'Well, isn't it?'

'So God created flu to help maintain the balance?'

'I don't know. But I know that flu exists so it must be part of God's purpose.'

'So this is the world that Leibniz described, then?'

'Leibniz?'

'Gottfried Leibniz. He was a mathematician.' Like me. 'He was responsible, more or less, for setting out the rules for binary arithmetic. I knew a programmer once who had a picture of Leibniz on his desk. He's the father of our science, he used to say. But Leibniz had some weird ideas too. Like you, he thought that everything we find disagreeable in the world, like flu, wasps, earthquakes, war – well, they're all there because without it the world would be a worse place. And Leibniz thought we lived in the best of all possible worlds.'

The priest rose slowly to his feet.

'So do we?' Joe asked him. 'Do we live in the best of all possible worlds? Is that what you think?'

'If you mean do I think God is going to let this world go to hell in a handcart, then no, I don't. I don't think this flu, or this war in the Gulf, is going to do anything more than cause a little discomfort. For a few days or so. You, of course, think differently.'

'Do I?' No one likes to be told what they think.

'Of course you do. Otherwise why all this?' Hocking waved his arm around, taking in the boxes and the sacks.

'Forecasting the future is like forecasting the weather,' Joe said. 'You can't look very far ahead. And even when you think you can, you can still be wrong.'

'And you foresaw this, did you?' said Hocking. 'You saw St Piran going hungry?'

'Not me,' Joe said. 'I didn't see anything. It was Cassie.'

'Who is Cassie?'

Joe gave a shrug. 'Someone who can see into the future. Just a little way. This isn't a science, Alvin. This isn't like sodium and water. This is just guesswork.'

'I see.' The older man had thrust his hands deep into his pockets for the warmth. 'So this is all just a guess?'

'Of course.' How could it ever be anything more? 'There are four scenarios,' he said, 'you look at them and you take your pick.' He could hear Lew Kaufmann's febrile voice. 'Scenario one says Leibniz and his friend Dr Pangloss are correct. Everything just gets better and better. Our cars get faster, our dinner plates are filled higher, we all live longer, women get more beautiful, and we all have a lot more sex. Scenario two says Leibniz sucks. Everything gets slowly, progressively worse. Harvests fail. Deserts expand. Coral reefs die. Forests are felled. Oil slowly runs out. It's a long, slow descent back to the dustbowl poverty of the 1930s, back to the pitiful subsistence lifestyle of the Dark Ages. Scenario three can't make up its mind. Life stays very much the same in scenario three. We all jog along happily and nothing much changes. But scenario four is the one that my friend Lew Kaufmann talked about, and once you learn about scenario four, well, you just can't stop wondering. Ever since he sat opposite me in a wine bar and spelled it out, it's been part of my consciousness.'

'It's become an obsession.'

'If you like.'

'And what is scenario four?'

Joe was thinking now about Kaufmann – about the fourth future. 'We think that complex systems last for ever.' For some reason, into his mind had swum the image of the whale. 'Do you remember the whale?' he said. 'Had you ever seen such a creature? Could you imagine the complexity, the vastness of organisation, the systems all in synchrony that keep an animal like that afloat? How many trillion cells are there in a whale – every one a tiny engine, manufacturing proteins, reproducing, burning energy? Think of the work the kidneys must do. Think of the lungs processing all that oxygen. How big must the heart be? How powerful its beat? Now there's an animal with no real predators apart from humans, but what else could hope to touch such a creature? And yet . . .' Joe looked across at Alvin Hocking. 'And yet . . . for a short while on Piran Sands, all those biological systems were good for nothing. That's scenario four. That's what the whale was facing. If it hadn't been for us, then all of those complex systems would have closed down, one after the other. First the lungs, and then the heart, and then the brain, and then the other organs, one after another in quick succession. And after that, all that would be left would be the trillion cells, but just imagine *you* were one of those cells. Your supply chains would be gone. You wouldn't get new oxygen, and you wouldn't get fuel. So one by one, the cells die too. Once the whale stops breathing it doesn't matter if you're a cell in the heart or a cell at the tip of the tail. There is no scenario that sees you survive.'

'So that's scenario four? Death?'

'The funny thing is, I've never understood it in quite that way before now, but yes. Complex systems all have the same four futures. They can grow, they can decline, or they can chug along unchanged. Or they can die. That's scenario four. That's what happens to each one of us. And that's what's happening to the world, Reverend Hocking.'

'The world is a whale on a beach?'

'Yes. I truly think it is.'

'But the whale didn't die . . .'

'Only because we were there to save it.' The two men shared a glance. 'I'm a forecaster,' Joe said. 'That's what I do, but there's a weakness when we forecast the future. We tend to build our visions of the future using our knowledge of the past. That's been my weakness too.' He was remembering Lew Kaufmann and his story of the turkey on the day before Christmas Eve. 'You can't use today to predict the future.'

Alvin Hocking reached into his robes and drew out his little Bible. 'God uses the same metaphor,' he said. He was flicking through the pages. 'He's warning the prophet Job. Don't underestimate God. That's his message. He uses the image of a leviathan – a great creature from the deep as something too monstrous ever to contemplate resisting it.'

'A whale,' Joe said.

'Probably a whale. Or something more fearsome.' The vicar ran his finger down a line of text. 'Canst thou draw out Leviathan with a hook?' he read. 'Or his tongue with a cord? Canst thou put a hook into his nose, or bore his jaw through with a thorn? Will he make a covenant with thee? Shall the companions make a banquet of him? Shall they parcel him among the merchants? Behold, the hope against him is in vain.'

'I like that,' Joe said. 'A warning that some forces are so elemental that humanity has no power over them.'

'If you like.'

'And does Job warn us about the end of the world?'

'Ah . . .' Hocking was flicking through his Bible again. 'Not especially. If we want to understand Armageddon then we have to read St John the Divine. He gives us the four horsemen of the apocalypse, the biblical harbingers of the end of the world.

The first one rides out on a white horse. He is Pestilence.'

'Disease?'

'Yes. Like the flu perhaps. Then comes War – on a red horse.'

It will be war, Lew Kaufmann had said.

'Then Famine riding a black horse.'

'I think we may be close to that.'

'And finally the pale horse. We depict the rider with a scythe.'

'And that one?'

'His name is Death.'

They went down the stairs together. 'Shall I take a turn calling?' Hocking said. He picked up a case of tins from the top of a pile. 'Rice pudding, twelve tins.'

'Rice pudding,' said Joe, scribbling it down. 'Twelve.'

'Curry paste, one hundred grams, forty-eight sachets.'

'Curry paste, one hundred, forty-eight.'

'I like curry,' said the Reverend. 'Good call.'

25
I liked her

In the dark, quiet hours of the second morning, they buried Janie Coverdale in a cardboard coffin made from packing boxes, brown tape, and old bell ropes. They crept into the churchyard and the priest opened up the sexton's shed. There they found two sharp spades, and a pickaxe, and a shovel. They worked hard, by torchlight, in a corner of the graveyard where Hocking said that the soil was easy and the rocks were deep. They dug a very shallow grave. 'It will do,' the older man said. 'We'll move her when this is all over.'

If this is *ever* over, Joe thought.

When the hole was deep enough to take the body, they lifted Janie in. She seemed as light as a box of oatmeal.

'I am the resurrection and the life, says the Lord,' intoned Hocking. 'Those who believe in me, even though they die, will live, and everyone who lives and believes in me will never die.'

Joe's head was beginning to swim. He was dizzy from the sweat of digging, and disoriented by the hour. It may have been four in the morning. 'Those who believe in me, even though they die, will live.' Had he ever thought about those words before? He looked across at Hocking, but it was too dark to make out the man's expression. Was the vicar aware of the doublespeak? But of course he was. That was the point of the verse, after all.

'Almighty God, you judge us with infinite mercy and justice, and love everything you have made. In your mercy, turn the darkness of death into the dawn of new life, and the sorrow of parting into the joy of heaven, through our Saviour, Jesus Christ.'

In the pause that followed Joe muttered, 'Amen.' It was a reflex.

'Let us commend our sister Janie to the mercy of God, our maker and redeemer.'

'Amen.' It may not have been the right response.

'We who are born of woman have but a short time to live,' Hocking said. 'Like a flower we blossom and then wither. Like a shadow we flee and never stay. In the midst of life we are in death.' He paused.

'We should cover her over,' Joe said. 'In case anyone wakes up early and comes upon us.'

'The day of the Lord will come like a thief, and the heavens will pass away with a roar, and the heavenly bodies will be burned up and dissolved, and the earth and the works that are done on it will be exposed.'

It seemed like an apposite verse. Joe picked up a shovel. 'You recite your scripture,' he said. 'I'll dig.' He scooped up a shovelful of soil and dropped it into the grave, onto the cardboard package that was Janie.

'Behold, the day of the Lord comes, cruel, with wrath, and fierce anger, to make the land a desolation and to destroy its sinners,' chanted Hocking.

'A little quieter if you can,' Joe said. Another shovel of earth. 'We don't want to wake the village.'

'Wail, for the day of the Lord is near; as destruction from the Almighty it will come.'

It will come. Joe was shovelling fiercely now. In the dark, each load of earth vanished into the void that was the grave; but it was easier work than digging the hole had been.

'But understand this, that in the last days there will come times of difficulty. For people will be lovers of self, lovers of money, proud, arrogant, abusive, disobedient to their parents, ungrateful, unholy, heartless, unappeasable, slanderous, without self-control, brutal, not loving, treacherous, reckless, swollen with conceit, lovers of pleasure rather than lovers of

God, having the appearance of godliness, but denying its power.'

Joe was breathing heavily. 'That's quite a verse to commit to memory. St John the Divine again?'

'The second book of Timothy,' Hocking said.

Together they mounded the grave with soil.

'Would you like to say a few words?'

A few words? Could you sum up a human life in a few words? 'There's nobody to hear them,' Joe said.

'God will hear them.'

God will soon be weary of words, Joe thought. He tried to picture Janie in her Armani suit with her Hermès bag, and Louboutin shoes, and her Tiffany necklace. 'I don't know what to say about her,' he said. 'She was good at what she did.' But what *did* she do? She shorted stocks. She bet on failing companies. She celebrated when others mourned. She seduced young traders working late, lying back on the white ottoman, rolling up her skirt. She walked out on three husbands. Or maybe they walked out on her. What did it matter any more? What did anything matter?

'I liked her,' he said. It seemed the most honest epitaph. 'Working with her was . . . fun.' No, not fun, not exactly. Exciting perhaps. Like being perched on the edge of a precipice. Some would fear the fall, but Janie relished the view. He thought of Colin Helms, and Harriet Adlam. 'Toodle-oo, Janie,' he whispered. He waved his soil-stained fingers. 'Toodle-oo.'

'How are you feeling?'

'OK.'

They tossed the spades back into the sexton's shed. A soft glow was touching the eastern horizon. 'You were right,' Joe said, 'the world may end, but the sun always rises.'

'It does.'

Had they been up all night? Probably. In the face of death an hour of sleep seemed like the loss of an hour of life.

In the church, close to the door that led to the bell tower, they found a neat pile of provisions and an envelope marked 'Joe'. There was a clear plastic container filled with water. There were blankets, coats, and clean clothes. 'Someone has been thinking about us,' Joe said, smiling. He picked up the blankets and coats. 'More blankets! Do they think we're freezing to death?'

'Maybe we are,' the priest said.

Joe picked out the envelope and gestured at the water. 'Can you bring that?'

'It's nice to be remembered,' Hocking said as they returned to the bell tower. He flicked the light switch that should have illuminated the stairs. 'The bulb's gone.'

They stood in darkness contemplating the gloom.

'I don't think it's the bulb.'

They found their way upstairs by torchlight. 'There isn't a single light on in the village,' Hocking said, looking from the open window.

'Maybe they're all still asleep.'

'It's a power cut.'

It's *the* power cut, Joe thought.

They sat wrapped in the blankets and drank fruit juice from a tin. When the sun was high enough, Joe tore open the envelope. 'It's from Mallory,' he said. Just reading the doctor's words made him smile. He could hear the old man's voice clearly. 'Now listen to me, Joe,' he read aloud. 'These are doctor's orders. You'll need the blankets. Keep yourselves warm. Drink plenty of fluids. You'll be infectious for at least seven days *after* the symptoms disappear. You need to allow eight or nine days to be sure. Make yourselves comfortable. Polly and I will bring water and we'll leave it here every evening. If there is anything else you need, write a note and leave it for us. Don't leave soiled clothes. They could be infected. And there's one thing you can do for us, Joe; every day around breakfast time, ring the bells. One ring of each bell will do. The low bell for Alvin and the high bell for you. That will tell us that you're both still alive and well.'

He passed the note to Alvin, who read it again, then passed it back. 'We could be in here for two more weeks.'

'It's looking that way.' If we survive.

At the bottom of the tower they untied the two bell ropes. 'Which one is which?' Joe asked.

'It doesn't matter, does it?' Hocking said. 'We're both still here.'

'It might matter tomorrow.' Could they really be this matter-of-fact about the possibility of death? But strangely the observation made them both laugh.

'I'm glad you find it so funny,' Joe said, but he was laughing too. 'One of us could ring the wrong bell; just think of the anguish that could cause.' He pulled one of the ropes and a distant bell sounded, the clear tones echoing all around the tower. 'The high one,' he said.

The vicar pulled the second rope. A deeper, fuller tone. They let the vibrations fade until the church was silent once more.

'I'll tie this rope shorter,' Joe said. 'Then we'll know.' He knotted the rope. 'That's mine.' He was wondering what the mood was in the village. Mallory would be happy to have heard the bells. It would prove that they had read his note.

'People always laugh after a funeral,' Hocking said. 'It's something I've noticed. Once the body is dispatched, and the verses have been read, it's never too long before the first laugh.'

'Something the Irish understand, I suppose.' Joe was imagining an Irish wake.

'And the Cornish too.'

When Mamma died, had there been laughter? Joe couldn't recall any. His father had shaved. He remembered that. A strange beardless man in the hallway in an unfamiliar suit, hunched, and gaunt, and foreign. A stranger at the funeral. 'Who is that *man*?' someone whispered. 'It's Joe's and Brigitha's father.' But it didn't feel like his father. Mikkel Haak was a man who *could* laugh, but the clean-shaven man in the hallway with the ancient suitcase had no laughter in him. He looked as cold and loveless as an accountant. As a banker perhaps. Joe had seen him from the landing, bent, like a damaged interloper in a home that used to be his own. When he, Joe, had descended the stairs, Mikkel had hugged him like a bear. They had cried together. And when Brigitha had come out from the kitchen, they had all hugged, six arms entwined.

Where was Brigitha now? The memory of the funeral had brought back the scent of her hair and the dampness of her tears. He felt an urge to see her, to see Mikkel, to recreate that six-arm hug. 'Would you look at that beautiful church,' he would whisper into her ear. 'Look at those amazing windmills,' she would say. And then they might laugh, remembering a night half a lifetime ago.

They hadn't buried Alison Haak. Perhaps if they had, it might have been easier, but instead of resting in the cold, dark earth, she had rolled away, concealed within her coffin, transported on a mechanical conveyer, and clumsy curtains had closed behind her. That was the way they disposed of bodies now. A crematorium orderly would whisk her body away to be consumed, but in a corner of Joe's mind he'd been waiting for her to re-emerge, like a girl in a magic show, reappearing with a flash of light and a drum roll, and applause.

'I was seventeen when my mother died,' he said.

The vicar nodded slowly.

'My sister was nineteen.'

'It can't have been easy.'

'It wasn't.'

He knew how to remember Mamma's face. He'd practised, so that he would never forget. He could see her opening a gift at Christmas, her eyes wide with pleasure, her teeth so white, her face so smooth. It was a silent memory; she was kneeling on the hearth rug, hair tied back with a ribbon. He could replay the moment now, in slow motion, frame by frame; the way she turned her face towards him, the way her mouth fell open with delight, the way her lip curled up almost over her gums. The whites of her eyes as she glanced this way, and that. 'I can picture her,' he said. 'My mother. It was fifteen years ago, but in my mind she's still there. She's still real.' There were other pictures too, but none so sharp. Mamma weeping in a tent. The day Pappa Mikkel left – a day when she wouldn't weep. Mamma's face on the pillow of her hospital bed, so thin she didn't look like his mother any more; and all around her bed the faint scent of putrefying flesh, the odour he'd detected in her sleeping bag three years earlier.

Hocking was wise enough not to speak.

'If I die, that picture of her dies too. No one will remember that moment the way that I do.'

'Then don't die.' The older man put his hand on Joe's shoulder. 'At least not yet.'

They counted more boxes.

Mamma had died in a hospice bed, in a room of her own, with flowers all around, a view of the lawns, and feeders outside the window for the garden birds. She had asked for *The Beatles* to be playing. When the end was very near the hospice nurse told Joe he could put the music on. Joe had plugged in his mother's music player, and played it softly so that it wouldn't be heard in the neighbouring rooms. It played random tracks. 'Strawberry Fields Forever'. 'Across the Universe'. It didn't seem likely that Mamma would be able to hear it; her coma was too deep. But it was her wish. Joe held one of her hands, and Brigitha the other. The nurse sat with her arm around Brigitha. The clock hand on the wall counted out the final seconds of Mamma's life. Keep breathing, Mamma, Joe had thought. Breathe in. Breathe out. But her breaths had been so shallow it was hard to tell if she was breathing at all.

No one was quite sure which song had been playing when the end finally came. But when the nurse took Mamma's wrist to check her pulse, and when she gave them the look that would tell them the waiting was over, the Beatles were singing 'She Loves You'.

'It's her message to us,' Joe said. He didn't believe it, but he knew it was true all the same.

'Are the people we loved still watching us?' he asked Alvin. 'Are they watching us from beyond the grave? Is that what we should believe?'

'It's what I believe,' Alvin said.

'But is it true? Does believing it make it true? Or could the whole world believe in a lie?' Could poetry really get closer to truth than history? Did the wisdom of crowds extend to insight about life's greatest mysteries? If you average out the opinions of seven billion people, then God exists, as surely as an ox weighs 1,198 pounds, as surely as oil prices will soar after a war in the Middle East, or the sun will rise in the morning. But could the crowds be wrong?

'I want to write a note to Mallory,' Joe said to Alvin, after a while. They broke from their stocktaking task, and Joe sat down with paper and pen.

'Thank you for the water,' he wrote, 'and the blankets and the clothes. We are both still well. No symptoms.' Although now that he came to write that line, he became aware that he was sweating. Perhaps it was from the long exertions of the morning. 'From everything I've learned, St Piran is well placed to weather any crisis. We have fish, milk, even eggs, but we must avoid infection at all cost. I don't need to tell you how much damage one infected refugee could do to the village.' It felt and sounded like a memo to his junior analysts. He shook his head slowly, disliking the words he'd written. He had a headache now. How had it come on so quickly? 'Ask Bevis to close off the road until the crisis is over. That won't be until the electricity and water come back.' If they ever do. 'Ask the Robins and the Shaunessys to pool their catch to feed everyone.' He laid down the pen.

'I can't write any more,' he announced. He signed the note

and passed it to Alvin. 'Can you leave it out for the doctor? I'm feeling groggy. I think I ought to have a lie-down.'

'Good idea.'

It was early afternoon. Joe lay back on his makeshift bed and pulled up the blanket. A pulse was throbbing in his temple. Above him were the floorboards of the bell platform. Around him were boxes. If he focused on the ceiling he could feel the oak boards moving closer. He tried to close his eyes, to listen for sounds from the village, but there was nothing but an eerie silence. Even the gulls were quiet today. Only his heartbeat was noisy; it was gushing thick blood up through his veins, and every beat brought a needle of pain. When he looked up, he saw Janie. She was sitting upright, pale and shocked in her cardboard coffin; she was speaking, but her words were lost to the wind. 'Take no notice of her,' the vicar was instructing him. 'The dead will try to convince you they're alive.'

'But she isn't dead,' Joe said, with a terrible urgency. 'She isn't dead. She's alive.'

'Dead bodies can do this sometimes,' Alvin said. 'It's a nervous reaction.'

'But we buried her. How did she get back up here?'

'It's amazing what the dead can do.'

Janie was reaching out to him, her thin fingers burdened with rings. If she touched him, he knew, then he would die too.

'NO!'

'Are you all right?'

Had he called out in his sleep? 'Yes,' he said, his heart still racing. 'I'm thirsty.'

And then, it seemed, he slept again. 'Dear God in heaven,' the vicar was saying, 'do I have to bury everyone myself?' Perhaps this was a dream vicar, not the real one. Yet the churchyard was littered with bodies. They lay in rows waiting for the earth to consume them. Jessie Higgs was there. He could see her plainly. And Colin Helms. Brigitha was there. And Mamma. She was lying on her own beneath a yew tree. She was wearing white.

Manesh Patel and Jonathan Woodman and Harriet Adlam were piled in a heap. No one could untangle them. 'These are the people from the bank,' Joe told Hocking. 'They must be buried together.' 'I could never dig a hole deep enough,' the vicar said.

He woke for a moment and there was Alvin Hocking looking sternly down upon him. 'You've got the flu,' he was saying.

He, Joe, had a spade in his hand. 'I can help,' he said. 'Then dig over there,' the vicar told him.

Over where? He crossed the churchyard, but the path was blocked by the body of the whale. How had it come this far up the hill? But of course. A wave had carried it. 'We have to get this whale back into the sea,' he shouted, but too many of the villagers were dead. There was the body of Martha Fishburne. And there lay Old Man Garrow. Joe leaned with all of his weight against the whale. He could never move it.

'You have to *bury* it,' someone said.

Of course. The spade felt cold in his hand.

And then there was a face close enough to touch, close enough to kiss. She looked dead too, but as he approached her eyes flickered open. 'Polly?'

Her face was as fresh as a plucked peach. 'I have a plan,' she was saying. 'We'll drive out to the cliffs. And there we shall have a picnic.'

'No. No. No. We have to bury this whale.'

'We'll have a pasty, and a cream slice, and lemonade.' She was standing up now, and taking off her coat. Slowly. She was pulling the belt through the loops. 'Polly,' he called. 'Don't do that.' If she took off her coat she would catch a cold. If she caught a cold she would die. Look at the death all around them. Look at the bodies. 'Polly! No!'

She was wearing a cotton frock. She was flicking her fringe away from her eyes. She was twirling for him. 'Do you like what you see, Joe?' He was backing away now, but there were too many bodies. Altogether too many bodies. 'No, Polly. No.' She was naked now, as pure as a painting. She was coming towards him, but he would infect her. He knew this now. 'POLLY!'

He was awake again. Sweating, but cold. 'Alvin?'

He was there, but a long way away. 'You called her name,' he said.

'I'm thirsty.'

'There's nothing to drink.'

Of course there wasn't. He knew that, but his mouth was so dry. When he closed his eyes the room was turning like a Ferris wheel.

Then it was dark. His tongue felt too heavy to speak. He looked for Alvin, but no one was there. In a moment of lucidity he tried to sit up. Perhaps Hocking, too, was ill. He tried to call out, but his throat would not obey. Something stank. It was vomit. There was the acid taste in his mouth. 'Water?' he managed to say, but no one was there to hear him.

He lay back down. Breathe in. Breathe out. Breathe in. Breathe out. He could picture Pappa Mikkel giving him instructions. Just keep breathing, Mikkel would say.

He had to have some water. He lifted himself up again. Could he stand? Not really. His head and his limbs protested too much, but he could shuffle on hands and knees. He pushed his way out of his bed and onto the floor, and with an unlikely effort, out onto the landing. There was someone there, sitting in a chair. A silhouette of a man framed against the pale glow of an evening sky. Or was it morning?

'Help me,' Joe said.

'I can't help you, Joe. You have the flu.'

'I know.' All of his energy seemed to flee his body, and he lay down on the wooden boards. 'I want water.'

'Water won't help you, Joe.' The man had turned away and was looking out into the gloom.

Breathe in. Breathe out. He was looking for a glass. A bottle. A vessel. Anything with fluid in. An opened tin loomed close. He snatched at it.

'It's empty, Joe,' the voice said. Joe looked at it. He had to check. He held it to his lips, but nothing emerged. 'Go back to bed, Joe.'

'Water?'

'There isn't any water.' Human self-interest. Survival of the fittest.

Joe closed his eyes. He was wet with sweat. No wonder he felt so thirsty. And yet he was cold. A shiver came across him like a gypsy curse. He twitched, and started to shake. 'Oh God.'

'Go back to bed.'

But he wasn't sure where his bed was any more.

'I'm ill,' he said.

'Of course you're fucking ill.'

It wasn't all confusion. There was clarity too, and it came in moments like a vision. He tried to picture the water bottle that Mallory had left. What had they done with it? Surely they had left it on the ground floor, just inside the door?

'Where are you going, Joe?'

'What do you care?' He tried to lift himself to his feet, and for a second he balanced. At the top step he hovered, thinking as clearly as he could. Then he sank down. He would go down the staircase on his backside. One step. Two. And then a cascade of steps. At the bottom of the flight he lay in a heap. Breathe in. Breathe out, but still alive. Still breathing. He looked around for something to drink, but it was too dark to see anything. Nothing. Another flight of stairs then, but somehow the activity was sharpening him. He stood up more easily this time. His heart was sending the blood around his body, and the blood was feeding his muscles, and his muscles were still alive. This flight of steps he would walk down. His legs were trembling. One step. Two. There were boxes all the way down, piled high on every step. He would have to tread carefully. He leaned on the banister. Pappa Mikkel Haak was at his shoulder. Keep breathing, boy, he was saying.

Two flights down, and one to go.

The man was behind him. 'Why not just push me?' Joe said. 'Save us both time.' But when he looked, the man was gone. Or was he in the shadows? One more flight. His legs felt useless now. He bumped down the first step. 'Don't fall,' Pappa Mikkel said. 'Don't fall.'

Had Janie felt like this? Had she sweated so? Had she shaken like this? He was going to fall. He could see that now. It was the only way down. If he survived, he would drink. If he didn't . . . well, death wasn't such a bad thing, was it? The black void of the stairwell was welcoming. If he leaned forward just so . . . just so . . .

But there was a hand on his shoulder. 'Don't be a bloody fool.'

He was lifted up and hefted over a bony shoulder. 'Don't struggle, you silly ass, or we'll both fall.' And then he was back in his blankets, back on his mattress.

'I'll get you something to drink.'

Time passed. He may have slept again. He woke to find a glass of water being held to his lips. 'Thank you.' It was going to make him sick, but it was sweet.

'Get some sleep.'

Thick blood moves slowly in tired veins, and as it slows, so does the power of thought. A notion that might have come quickly on any other day now congealed slowly in Joe's mind like a blood clot. On his father's island was a cabin. Brigitha would sit in one big armchair with a sheepskin cowl wrapped around her, and he, Joe, would sit in another, and Pappa Mikkel would stoke the fire until the glow from the flames warmed their faces. 'Can we sleep *here*?' Brigitha would say. 'No, no, my dear,' their father would reply. 'But it's cold in the bedroom, Pappa.' 'We must be a *little* cold at night,' Pappa would say. 'If we are too warm, we cook; and anything that cooks goes soft. And we wouldn't want that to happen, would we?'

Joe pulled away his blankets and let the chilly air touch

him. 'I'm cold now, Pappa Mikkel. I won't cook.' He was shaking, but the fingers of icy wind that ran down his limbs felt like friends. They would keep him awake, would keep him breathing.

And so they did, for a while, but close behind them rolled a fog, a numbing, grey fog – he could sense its tentacles curling around him. It had no personality, this fog. No face. No voice. It could be death, but death without teeth. If this was death, Joe thought, then death lacked a presence. If this was death, then death was like switching off the lights in a big house; first the farthest rooms, then the dining room and the kitchen and the landing, and then the living room, and then, with the house almost in darkness, there's time for a last look around, a farewell moment, perhaps, to see if everything is in order; and then the final switch in the hallway. Death, Joe saw, was nothing more than darkness. But it wasn't a fearful darkness. Sinking in was almost a pleasure. Count backwards from ten. Isn't that what they would say to patients before an operation? How easy that should be. Ten. Up the nostrils like smoke from a pyre. Nine. Upstream into the lungs searching out the secret recesses. Eight. Dissolving like bubbles in a bow wave. Seven. Elastic tendrils slipping into the brain. A pale light growing brighter. Six . . .

When he awoke he was thirsty again. He ached like a man who'd been dragged for miles behind a stampede of horses. Every muscle protested as he tried to sit, but the throbbing in his temple had subsided, and the needles of pain were gone. He needed to pee.

Standing up was easier than he'd expected. His feet were cold on the hard wooden floor. Unsteadily he made his way down the stairs and peed. The toilet wouldn't flush. It stank. Where was Hocking? He fumbled his way back up to the third floor. 'Alvin?' He pushed open the door to the little storeroom. 'Alvin?'

The older man was in his bed. He seemed to be asleep.

'Alvin?'

There was a low moan from the dark space where the bed should be.

'Alvin. Are you OK?'

'I'm thirsty.'

26

There are other jobs

Dr Marcia Brodie spoke in a soft Welsh voice, and her tone had a musical quality that became reflected in her face; up in pitch and her eyebrows would rise, down in pitch and she would tip her face forward and bury her chin in the folds of her neck. 'What do you dream about, Joe?' Eyebrows up.

'I'm not sure what you mean.'

Eyebrows down, chin down. 'Easy enough question, Joe. When the alarm clock rings, what are you dreaming about?' Eyebrows slowly up.

Why was he remembering this? They were sessions he'd tried to forget. He'd almost succeeded.

'Look at me, Joe.' Her eyebrows were hovering halfway up her animated forehead. 'Listen to me carefully.' Listen to my musical voice, focus on my mobile features. Hypnosis, or so he'd read, was a willing submission to a mind game. It was consent to play along, to participate in a fiction that a human being could be coaxed into a trance. 'You have to collaborate, Joe,' Dr Brodie would say – an unfortunate choice of word perhaps. 'Some people are *difficult* to hypnotise. You must relax, Joe. Relax.'

But how could you relax in a cold surgery, with a stranger with cold hands? How much less could you relax with the unspoken fear that you might reveal secrets in your sleep?

Still, he had tried. He'd seen stage hypnotists at work; he knew how he ought to behave. He had let his head drop forward and allowed his eyes to close. His body had flopped like a puppet with cut strings. 'Good boy, Joe, good boy.' Still, he knew it was an act, and so, probably, did she.

'You are in a *light* trance,' Dr Brodie would say. A very light trance, they would both think. 'You may open your eyes.'

But it had never helped to open his eyes.

'I'm going to take you back in time,' she would say, but already his mind would be wandering dangerously. He'd be thinking about work. He did that a lot. 'How old are you now, Joe?'

'Twenty-eight.'

'So we're going back in time. I want you to go back, Joe. Back in time. When I click my fingers you'll have gone back fifteen years.' But now he's trying to do the mental arithmetic. She would click her fingers. 'How old are you now, Joe?'

Twenty-eight minus fifteen would be . . . would be . . . she'd made him sleepy, too sleepy to do the sum . . . add two to make thirty, take away fifteen to make fifteen, add two . . . 'Seventeen.' No. That was wrong. 'Fourteen. Thirteen. I'm thirteen.'

But now she would know he was faking. 'Some people are difficult to hypnotise,' she would sigh.

Still, they did work some things out, over half a dozen sessions in the basement clinic in Wimpole Street. 'I've written a report for the bank,' she told him one day, waving a brown envelope at him.

'Don't I get to see it?'

'If you want. Do you want?'

He hesitated. 'Why does the bank get to see the report anyway? Aren't these sessions supposed to be confidential?'

'Normally they would be.' She tore open the envelope. 'But your employer paid for these sessions, and you signed a waiver.'

'Did I?'

'You did.' She withdrew a single sheet of paper from the envelope. 'To whom it may concern,' she read. 'Confidential report of counselling sessions with Jonas Mikkel Haak.'

He snorted. 'Not really that confidential, is it? Not when you address it to "whom it may concern". It really only concerns me.'

'Good,' said Dr Brodie, and she handed him the page. 'Because it really only *does* concern you.'

Joe took the page. The introduction that Dr Brodie had read aloud had been a fiction. Instead the page was a handwritten note.

Dear Joe.
I've enjoyed our sessions. I hope you have too. You should not worry that you could not succumb to hypnosis. Many patients cannot. I find it an encouraging sign of independence of mind.

You may like to keep this note. Most people who come for counselling very quickly forget the advice they were given, but you can keep this letter in your pocket, and reread it any time you want.

At heart, Joe Haak, you are a fine young man. You have a warm and loving nature. You are a romantic. You want to believe the best in everyone, and this is endearing. For you it is a defining quality; but you work in an environment of conflict and suspicion. Every day you encounter the reality of human nature, and it rarely matches the model of humanity in your mind. As an economist you face a world in which human behaviour is defined by selfishness. This sets up a conflict in your personality. A cognitive dissonance. It makes you uncomfortable. It forces you to act and to take decisions that violate your basic nature and beliefs. And this, Joe, is causing the stress that you are suffering from. You have been anxious and irritable. You find it hard to concentrate. Your thoughts race and your imagination works overtime. You imagine the worst. You worry. These are all symptoms of stress. And you do not manage stress well.

But take heart. For the time being, stress can be managed. Anyone can learn how to do it. And you are an able learner. Use the techniques we have worked on together. I would prefer you to learn to manage stress than to develop a cynical attitude, or to discount your powerful sense of humanity. Believe me, I've seen too many honest, well-meaning people in this city turn into misanthropes. Please don't let this happen to you. Keep hold of your sense of optimism. Treat the bitter assumptions of the trading floor as an exercise in mathematics and not as an insight into your fellow humans. Continue to believe in the essential goodness of the world. It becomes you. I really don't want to see you evolving into the kind of hard-bitten, grumpy grouch that the bank so often produces. You are worth more than this Joe. Never forget it.

But beyond the short term, I have some wider advice. Lane Kaufmann may not thank me for writing this (and since they pay my fees I trust that you'll be kind enough to conceal this from them); but one day, I believe, it will all get too much for you. When that day comes, don't hesitate. Get up from your desk and walk away. Don't bother to gather your things or say goodbye. Walk out of the office and don't look back. You've often spoken with me about the promise you made to your mother. You won't keep that promise by desperately holding on to a job that destroys your health. There are other jobs, and other careers.

Stress can be managed – but only up to a point. It can be good for some of us, but not for you. You weren't born to be a City banker, Joe. One day you will wake up and realise that you don't enjoy it any more. When that day comes, it will be the day to move on.

Make plans for that day, Joe. And don't leave it too long.

Your friend,

Marcia Brodie

The sunrise was spectacular. Joe sat on the very edge of the rampart, on the roof of the bell tower, scaring away the gulls that had slept there. He let his legs dangle perilously over the wall. In the eastern sky the sun emerged sluggishly, a cold glow over the autumn trees, but still it rose. It rose. Every day the sun must rise, he thought. And yet it so nearly hadn't. He might have been lying, today, on the cold, oak floor beams, wreathed in a blanket, never to see another sunrise. The sun must rise, he realised, but only if you're there to see it. If you're cold and dead then no sun ever rises again.

He breathed in the misty air of the morning. Had he ever felt so alive? Had the colours of autumn dissolving out of a low cloud ever seemed so sharp or so beautiful? The ache of the infection that still pained his limbs was changing into a different kind of ache, a gnawing longing, drawn from the physical beauty of the world around him, from the soft blue of the sky, the granite grey of the sea and the gentle greens of the meadows. He heard a cry from the lane below him. Someone was waving; someone in a blue fisherman's smock and a red pompom hat. Joe couldn't recognise the face from this distance, but he waved in return. 'Good morning!' What honest words those were. This was a truly good morning.

When the sun had fully risen, he descended the stairs to the ground floor and joyously rang both bells. He opened up a box of muesli and a can of evaporated milk, and took them up to the third floor. 'Breakfast?' he said.

27

There'll be shootin's and killin's

On the fifth day after Janie Coverdale arrived in St Piran, the fishermen Daniel and Samuel Robins spotted a fishing smack out in the bay. They were less than two miles out, fishing for herring. Samuel gave a call and pointed towards the west. Coming towards them, under full power, was the smack. 'There was no time to flee,' Daniel told the village later. When the newcomer cut his engine, no more than twenty yards separated the two vessels, and momentum drew the boats even closer.

'Robert Batho out of Newlyn,' called a voice from the deck of the smack. 'Who are you?'

'Daniel Robins,' came the reply. And then, because Daniel was wholly without the means to dissemble, 'Out of St Piran.'

'Welcome back to sea, stranger,' said Robert Batho of Newlyn. The two boats were drawn up almost alongside each other. 'How's it bin for you?'

'It's been . . . well, the same as for everyone, I guess,' said Daniel.

'Has the flu reached you?'

'Not really. Not yet.'

'Then you're lucky. We've lost nearly a hundred in Newlyn.'

'A hundred?' Daniel was genuinely shocked.

'And it's still bad. *Really* bad. There'll be more dead when we get home, that's for certain. More burials. My neighbour 'as it now. And 'is son. We lost two from one fishing boat. Brothers they were.'

'Dear God,' said Daniel.

'Don't let the boats get too close,' said Samuel Robins under his breath, moving up from the rear. Perhaps it was the talk of brothers dying that had got to him. Daniel touched the throttle very slightly and the two boats drifted a little apart.

'How are you for fuel?' the Newlyn fisherman asked.

'Not too good.' This was true. 'Maybe enough for a week. Maybe two. We're fishing close to shore.'

Batho was nodding. 'Good plan,' he said. 'As far as I know there in't a drop o' diesel to be 'ad in all of Cornwall.'

The Robins brothers digested this remark.

'There was talk of the army bringin' in supplies of fuel for essential services. That's us, but I've not seen an army man yet. You?'

Daniel shook his head.

'Have you got any electric?'

'No.'

'Water?'

'No.'

Robert Batho out of Newlyn started to throttle his engine. 'Then you're as buggered as we are,' he called over the noise of the engine. 'Good fishing.'

'I've 'ad pollack up in the channel,' Daniel said, 'a mile or so.' He pointed. 'Going for herring here.'

'There's mackerel by the ton out there,' Batho said, pointing off to the horizon. 'Go three or four miles if you've enough fuel and you'll catch 'em on the line.'

'Thank you,' Daniel said.

The seaman revved his engine. 'Be seeing you soon.'

'Yes. See you soon.'

Peter Shaunessy had a shortwave radio on his boat. He brought it into the village complete with the battery and all the wires. 'There's no one broadcasting on the main frequencies,' he told a small crowd in the Petrel, 'but we'll find out everything we need to know with this.' It was entertaining for a while. Peter twiddled knobs, and Kenny Kennet took the aerial out onto the roof, on the end of a long wire, and waved it about, and eventually they started to pick up signals. They spoke to a radio ham in Shropshire who told them that things were bad in the county, and another in Brittany who was broadcasting an appeal for help. 'We need medicines,' he was begging in poorly accented English. 'And food.' A man in Ireland bemoaned, 'We're right out of the black stuff.' 'Oil?' Kenny asked. 'Not oil, you eejit. Guinness.' The shortwave frequencies were humming with conversations, every one of them detailing deprivation and disease, and many of them offering up advice, helpful or otherwise. 'Don't drink the water,' instructed a radio enthusiast from somewhere in the north of England. 'Which water?' Kenny asked him. 'The contaminated water,' said the northerner. 'Don't drink the water.' 'We should put him in touch with that Irish feller,' Jacob Anderssen said. 'What a conversation they'd have.'

After an hour, most of the crowd in the Petrel had drifted away. 'We still don't know what's going on,' Aminata Chikelu complained to Elizabeth Bartle. This was, perhaps, the most common sentiment in the first days of the crisis. 'Won't someone please tell me exactly what is going on?' was Martha Fishburne's appeal. It was a heartfelt cry that echoed the helplessness that everyone in the village felt, a sentiment that was not in the least assuaged when they discovered, through the medium of Peter Shaunessy's radio, that much of the rest of the world felt the same way. When the electricity had failed, Mallory Books had mounted a one-man campaign in the village to encourage the storage of water. 'The pipes may dry up soon,' he had warned them. They filled baths and saucepans, bottles, and jars, and within a day the old doctor's prediction had proved accurate. Bevis Magwith had appeared in the village within an hour, complaining loudly, and his shouting attracted a crowd.

'You should've filled up your bathtub, Bevis,' Louisa Penroth the lobsterman's wife told him.

'Bugger the bathwater,' said Magwith. 'I've got forty milking cows needing water, and a dozen heifers, and a bull, and I've only enough in the troughs for one day. If we don't get water in the next twenty hours I'll have to start shooting cows.' This was a sobering thought. 'And then sheep,' he added.

'Is there a stream in the village?' Aminata asked.

The villagers shook their collective heads. 'None as I've ever seen,' Martha said.

'Then how did the village get water before the pipes?' said Aminata. 'Every old village has to have had a source of water. They didn't carry it here.'

'There was a well,' said Old Man Garrow, and all heads turned his way.

'Where was it?' said Magwith. 'Show me.'

A trail of villagers set off down Fish Street. 'It were right there,' said Garrow, pointing with his stick.

'Underneath the phone box?'

'They covered it over, zee.'

Half an hour later the Magwiths were back with a JCB. It made short work of the phone box and all the wires.

'They put down a big slab of concrete as I remember,' Old Man Garrow said. 'I were only a nipper.'

Sitting in the digger, Bevis Magwith was already directing the big scoop at the ground. The crowd stood back. Sure enough a disc of concrete came up as easily as a spadeful of sand. Afterwards they all stood around and looked at the hole.

'That's the well all right,' Garrow said, unnecessarily.

One of the Robins boys appeared with a bucket and a rope. They sent it down, and back it came full of water.

'Someone should taste it,' said Jeremy Melon, moving away as he spoke in case he might be selected.

Lorne Magwith stepped forward and took the bucket. Without saying a word he took a long draught. The crowd around the well were silent, awaiting a verdict. 'It'll do,' he announced, and he received a rousing cheer.

'We'll be back with a pump and a tank,' Bevis Magwith told them. 'If you all wants milk then the cows get first call.'

No one chose to argue with this, but in the bar of the Petrel that evening the prognosis delivered by those who gathered in the candlelight was not good. Jeremy spoke for them all when he aired a common fear. 'What happens when the fuel runs out?'

Jacob Anderssen was rationing beer. A quarter-pint per person was all he could offer. Romer Anderssen was keeping a tab. 'We've never been so busy,' she complained to anyone who would listen. 'And we've nothing to sell.' There were spirits in bottles, there was even wine in the cellar, but Romer wouldn't part with any of this except at the usual prices. She still expected normality to return. 'We have a tab for beer,' she told the crowd of drinkers, 'and that's only because Jacob's got less sense than he has money. If you want more, you'll have to pay.' Some, like Mallory Books, seemed to have cash in generous supply, but after a few rounds of whiskies, even his generosity started to run short. Candles were scarce, so a single candle was used to light the bar. There was, at least, a log fire. This blessing may have been the principal attraction that had drawn the crowd indoors. In the early evening it seemed that half the village was there. The Petrel had become a refuge, even in the dark, from cold unlit homes. Romer opened the upstairs function room they used for weddings and parties, and lit another candle. There weren't enough chairs for even half of the drinkers, so most of the men leant up against the bar, while others stood in little clusters, packing out the corridors and the annexe room. Annie Bartle and Charity Cloke helped behind the bar. The Shaunessys and the Daniels brought baskets of fish, Toby Penroth brought five lobsters, Kenny Kennet a bucket of mussels. A dozen people in the small kitchen cooked on an assortment of camping stoves. Jessie Higgs arrived with more candles and there was a cheer.

Those villagers who stayed late, after most of the crowd had gone, sipped very slowly at their meagre drinks. Oblivious to the absence of law-keepers, Romer insisted on ringing the bell at 10.30. 'Time please, gentlemen, time, ladies.'

'Darling, can't we stay for one more teensy drink?' begged Demelza Trevarrick, who had run out of cigarettes and was now forced to beg them from a dwindling number of smokers.

'We have our own beds to go to,' came the curt reply. 'Drink up please.'

Back out on Harbour Square a soft rain was falling. 'God, it's dark,' Demelza complained. 'And it's cold. And now it's pissing down.' This was strong language for the romantic novelist. She took hold of Jeremy Melon's arm. 'Darling, you're going to have to walk me home.'

'I can't see any better than you can.'

'Well, if one of us stumbles then the other one can catch them,' Demelza said. They set off up Fish Street, feeling their way along the walls. Some of Mallory's generosity with whisky had found its way into her system and she was unsteady. 'Doesn't anyone in this godforsaken town possess a torch?'

There seemed to be no answer to this question.

'We'll never make it as far as my cottage,' Demelza said. They had barely walked twenty yards, but they were already close to Jeremy's front door. 'Jeremy, darling, please don't abandon me here. I shall never find my way home.'

'You could always spend tonight with me,' Jeremy said.

For a moment the rain seemed to stop and a sliver of moonlight appeared from behind a cloud. It would be light enough now to carry on up Fish Street without a torch. If Demelza needed an excuse, she had one. Still, moments of passion are all that some ever have, as she'd once explained to Joe.

'I didn't think you liked girls,' she said now. It was a valiant piece of final resistance. 'You've lived in this village for fifteen years . . .'

'Sixteen . . .'

'. . . and I've never seen you with a girl.'

Jeremy sighed. 'In some places,' he said, 'it's difficult enough to be gay. Imagine trying to explain "bisexual" to St Piran.'

The cloud that had released the moon began to recapture what little light there was, and a fresh burst of rain began to fall. 'Well, don't just stand there,' Demelza said. 'Let's get inside.'

Very late that same night there was a raid on the village. A heavy truck drove straight through the gate at the top of the lane and came tearing into Harbour Square, ramming right through the window of Jessie Higgs's shop. By the time Jessie and Bo'sun Higgs had come tumbling downstairs to investigate the commotion, the thieves had already left. They'd emptied several shelves of packets and tins.

'They're looking for Joe's store,' Jessie said darkly.

In the cold dawn light, villagers gathered to inspect the damage. Toby Penroth came with planks of wood to nail over the broken window. 'Do you think the glazier in Treadangel will be back at work?' Jessie asked.

'No one's coming into this village until the flu has gone,' said Bo'sun.

It wasn't the end of the troubles for St Piran that morning. As the village was still contemplating the damage to the shop, rustlers, with livestock lorries and dogs, drove down the lane, broke open a gate, and took sixty-one of the Magwiths' ewes. Lorne and Bevis were both at the village pump fetching water, Forrest and Corin were milking. Aileen spotted the raiders quite by chance from the bedroom window while she was making the beds. She ran out towards them waving Corin's shotgun, but the thieves calmly closed up the tailgate of the final truck and sped back up the lane. No shots were fired, and the shotgun, it later turned out, was unloaded, but still the incident, following so closely after the raid on the village shop, would rattle the village considerably.

'There'll be shootin's and killin's afore we know it,' Old Man Garrow warned them.

'We should call the police,' Aileen told her husband, but no one thought this was a workable idea. Instead Bevis took matters into his own hands. He drove the big JCB up to the Penzance to Treadangel road, and there he dug a metre-deep trench right across the top of the lane. The spoil from the dig he heaped where the St Piran lane started, blocking off the lane from the main road. For good measure he tore up some of the verge, and piled it onto the mound. He stopped to admire his work. It would only take a few hedgerow trees, he realised, to conceal the road altogether. The single-track lane to St Piran had never been easy to spot, even at the best of times, even when there used to be a sign; now it would vanish altogether.

It took Bevis less than an hour. A few metres of hedgerow were translocated from somewhere down the St Piran lane to the mound of earth and rubble that now transected the T-junction. A local person would surely spot this unexpected barrier where once a road had been, but any stranger would drive straight past. St Piran had effectively been erased from the map.

Had Bevis Magwith been a reflective man, he might have pondered the significance of what he had just accomplished as he drove his digger back towards the farm. Only one road ventured down the headland to St Piran, and now that fragile lifeline was closed. In a single headstrong act of petulance, Bevis might have ruminated, he had effectively executed a divorce for the whole community of Piran Head. He had severed their link with the county, and with the world that lay beyond. Jeremy Melon would recognise the import. They were now, he might have said, little more than a rock pool abandoned by the tide.

In the pale grey skies over Piran Head that day, no planes flew. In the waters there were no large ships. No walkers broached the cliff paths. Not a vehicle navigated the lane. No voltage flowed down the wires, no water down the pipes. On the airwaves there was no music. Villagers awoke, on this dull October day, to nothing more than the cry of the gulls, the whistling of a cold north wind, and the ringing of two church bells.

28
I'd kill for a hot meal

'I was in Truro last week,' Alvin Hocking said. 'There was a man wearing a sandwich board. Do you know what it said? "The End of the World is Nigh". I hadn't seen one of them for years.'

Joe smiled. 'Maybe he was right.'

'Do you think so?'

'It's starting to look that way.'

They were sitting on the roof of the bell tower looking out over the ocean. In a short while it would grow too cold and they would have to move indoors, but for the time being it seemed better to be outside.

From a narrow street below arose the sound of a voice, a woman's voice singing, lifting and curling over the slate rooftops. From this far away the words were indistinct, but the melody was familiar, and such was the purity of the voice, so perfect was its tone, that for a few brief moments the two men were mesmerised by its beauty.

'It's the voice of an angel,' Joe whispered. Was he still affected by his brush with death?

'It's our village songbird.' Alvin smiled. 'Funny how her voice carries so.'

'Who is it?'

'Her name is Aminata.'

'The nurse?'

'I'd love to have her in the choir. But she works nights, and sleeps during the day.'

'It's a Diana Ross song,' Joe said, closing his eyes to concentrate. '"Close To You".'

'It's a Carpenters song too.'

'When you think about it,' Joe said, 'that chap with the sandwich boards was only doing the same thing that I used to do – warning everyone that collapse was on its way.' A picture had popped into his mind of the fifth floor at the bank. He was there in his suit and sandwich boards. 'Go short on Samsung,' they might say. 'Beware of publishing stocks.' And on the back, 'The End of the World has a 68% Probability of being Nigh'.

'Only nobody was listening to him.'

'They didn't always listen to me either.'

'In a sense that was my job too,' said Hocking. 'What is a priest for, if not to warn of Armageddon?'

Joe smiled again. 'We may have more in common than we ever imagined.' He let the thought settle in his mind. Perhaps it was true? They both studied their holy documents, and both peddled a liturgy of fears.

And both loved Polly Hocking.

But was that still true? Had it ever been true? There had been a time when he'd felt much the same way about Clare Manners from Corporate Communications. She was a flirt too. She wore jeans to the office, and blouses that were an inch too short for her torso, exposing a ribbon of tanned skin around her waist that had tormented him. She had a laugh that carried clear across the fifth floor. She would wiggle her backside when she walked past his desk, just enough to make her message clear. There had been days in the gloom of the fifth floor at Lane Kaufmann when the only relief from tedium had been the wiggle of Clare Manners's bottom, and the music of her laugh. He had dreamed about her, had fantasised plans for asking her out. They would fall in love. They would dine in a different restaurant every day on the way home from work, and would stumble back, arms wound around each other, to his flat for sex. They would holiday in Kalimantan, would sleep on the deck of a klotok boat drifting upriver at Tanjung Puting. They would buy a yacht and sail every summer to Oresund.

But it wasn't to be. The first time they dated it had been an awkward evening; the first hour was spent hunting out a restaurant that would serve gluten-free dishes, and the second struggling to settle on a subject for conversation. She talked about horses and skiing; he talked about almost anything else. 'You will have to compete for my affections with Geordie,' she told him. Geordie was her horse, although that hadn't immediately been clear. In the bustle of the restaurant her laughter hadn't sounded so musical. Too soon they found themselves back out on the pavement, and what now? A club perhaps? Or back home for something more biological? They had opted for the sex. Back in his flat he tore off her clothes, knowing this was what he'd dreamed about for so many months, but puzzled that he wasn't more excited. She had been cold and awkward. 'Do you really want to do this?' he'd asked her, trying to soften her with kisses while attempting to unclasp her underwear.

'Only if *you* do,' she'd replied.

Did that constitute a 'yes'? Legally perhaps, but could you have an ambiguous affirmative in the bedroom? And Joe sought reciprocal passion; so maybe that meant he didn't really want it either. Would that make her answer a 'no'?

'I love you, Clare,' he'd told her, when the sex was done and her face was on his shoulder. Where had those words come from? They'd escaped from his lips as if they'd been pupating inside him for a year or more, waiting for their moment to emerge.

'Now you're being scary,' she'd said.

'Will I see you again?' he'd asked her in the morning as she had disappeared into his bathroom.

'Of course.' Her laughter was almost musical once more. 'You'll see me in the office.'

'That's not what I meant.'

They dated again and this time he found what seemed like the perfect restaurant overlooking the Thames at Chiswick with beautiful views and just the right dietary regime. He booked a table by the window. To follow he bought tickets for a show-jumping event at Olympia. But despite these preparations the evening wasn't the success he had hoped for. Clare didn't enjoy the meal. She ordered a sweet potato and cashew nut curry with wild rice, but it was too spicy for her palate and she left most of it on the plate. 'Let's order you something else,' he pleaded, but she wouldn't have it. 'It's put me right off this place,' she said, as she watched him eat. They sat in the arena at Olympia and watched horses jumping. Joe had imagined it would be the perfect diversion and, at first, Clare had seemed truly excited by the prospect. But once in the venue, she grew critical. She didn't like the course. She didn't rate most of the riders. She took issue with the scoring. One of the riders was rather free with his use of the whip, and Clare announced that she'd seen quite enough. 'I'll see you in work tomorrow,' she said to Joe as they walked back to the Hammersmith Road. She permitted him the most cursory kiss. 'I won't come back if you don't mind.' She offered him a grimace. 'Time of the month.'

That had been fifteen months ago. He'd struggled to keep the flame alight, but they had never dated again. It hadn't been for want of trying – at least not on his part. He'd written her a note ('I'm sorry you didn't enjoy the horses . . . let's meet up again') but she hadn't replied. And she stopped walking past his desk. He had bumped into her in the office lobby once, and they had stood too far apart while he asked her out for lunch. 'I'm too busy,' she told him, and wouldn't catch his eye. 'Next week then?' But she was busy the next week too. And the week after. From time to time he would picture her face, would imagine her sashaying past the quants, teasing them all with glimpses of her midriff. He would find himself sitting at his desk, staring into the middle distance as if, perhaps, she was there. She turned up in his dreams, forever out of reach. He needed a gesture – some extravagant, symbolic act that would recapture her attention. But his courage and his imagination had failed him. One day he saw her on the fifth-floor landing and they passed each other with nothing more than a nod, the minimal shake of the head you might give to an acquaintance, not the knowing smile of lovers. Standing in the lift the very same day he overheard a conversation that wasn't intended for his ears; Clare Manners was dating Julian McEvan. Fancy that! Clare and Julian! They were flying off to watch the Grand Prix in Monaco. Burning with hurt and indignation, Joe had walked out of the office and all the way up the Embankment onto Waterloo Bridge, his body awash with emotions. He'd leaned against the guard-rails, watching the riverboats struggling up the Thames. A heavy barge slid beneath the bridge, gliding effortlessly downstream. Joe found himself watching as it sliced its way through the murky waters. Something about the vessel struck him as a metaphor for his relationship with Clare. As he stood and watched, she was drifting away from him. Already her features were becoming indistinct. Already she was disappearing into the river mist, becoming silently swallowed by the arches of Blackfriars Bridge; and then she was gone.

Clare Manners was Clare McEvan now. She'd left the bank and they hadn't kept in touch beyond the social media messages that everybody shared. She'd posted her wedding pictures online; Clare and Julian as glossy as their photographs, every hair in place, every smile perfect, every blemish erased. They had married in a castle somewhere. All the men wore kilts. And they had honeymooned in the Seychelles on Desroches Island and they posted photographs taken at sunset of the two of them alone on miles of pure white beach.

Clare. Clare Manners. Peach-like and perfect. But how could a girl who could wiggle her rump so suggestively be so cold? How could the chemistry of sodium and water fail them so thoroughly? And was there something of her in Polly Hocking . . . the hint of a performance in her teasing, the shadow of a different, hidden person behind the flirtatious mask?

'There is a fundamental difference between us,' Hocking was saying.

'Is there?'

'Your forecasts are self-serving. They're designed to help you make money – to help your bank make money. My forecasts are aimed at helping people. Helping them to prepare for the next world.'

Joe nodded. 'You're right, of course.'

'I worship God, and you worship Mammon,' Hocking said, warming to the theme.

'Indeed.' There seemed little point in arguing.

'If the world does go to hell in a handcart, it won't be the fault of religion; it'll be the fault of you and your kind.'

'Me?' The priest's provocation had worked.

'Not *just* you.'

'That's a relief.'

'But people like you.'

There it was again. *People like him*. Draw a Venn diagram where this circle represents people, and this smaller one is men, and this third one is young men, and this circle that intersects is bankers, and so this space represents young male bankers . . . and how far down do you want to go? Young male computer programmers who work in investment banks, with Danish surnames, and dead mothers, and mild phobias, with no clear faith, but with stockpiles of food in seaside churches? That would catch him. Romantics unable to chase the right girl? That would narrow it down.

'You're generalising,' Joe said.

'No I'm not. I'm classifying. I'm making taxonomic observations about a socially distinct group of people of which you are one.'

There was nowhere to go with this. Joe resisted giving an audible sigh. 'Make another observation for me,' he suggested. 'From your wide knowledge of human behaviour, tell me . . . what do you think is going on out there?' Did that sound sarcastic? He hoped not.

'What do you mean?'

'We've got no electricity and no water. We can see for ourselves that the whole of St Piran has been without power for a week. I'm guessing that means the whole of Cornwall has no power, and that means it has no water . . . and maybe this goes even wider. Maybe the whole country is affected; maybe the whole world.'

'It won't be that bad,' Hocking said.

'But what if it is? Imagine there's no oil being shipped from the Middle East or Nigeria or Venezuela. I think that's probably the case right now. Imagine that Russia and Kazakhstan are holding onto their oil for the duration of the crisis, and that means that Europe is effectively out of fuel. Even gas generating stations rely on deliveries of some supplies by road. And maybe the Qataris and the Russians have turned off the gas. And everything has been hit by the flu epidemic. Key workers have stayed at home long enough to bring down the whole infrastructure. Shops are empty of food and nobody is delivering any more. Imagine it, Alvin. Now tell me, in your opinion, how are people behaving?'

Alvin Hocking was staring into the distance.

'It's important, Alvin. It's the one unknown quantity in our computer model.'

'I've never had much faith in human nature.' Hocking paused. He was watching a boat out near the horizon. 'Is that an oil tanker?'

'I hope to God it is.' Joe was looking too. 'Which way is it going?'

'Away.'

'Still. They come in full and they go back empty. That's the way it works.'

'The Bible warns us about forecasting the end of the world,' Hocking said. 'St Matthew says, "of that day and hour knoweth no man, no, not the angels of heaven".'

'I don't think my employer would have approved of that line.'

The priest pulled a Bible from his pocket. He was searching

for a verse. 'He also said nation shall rise against nation, and kingdom against kingdom: and there shall be famines, and pestilences, and earthquakes, in divers places.'

'Well, we seem to have been spared the earthquakes.'

'Don't make light of this, Joe.' The vicar frowned.

'I'm sorry. I didn't mean to.'

'Isaiah says, "Howl ye; for the day of the Lord is at hand; it shall come as a destruction from the Almighty".'

'I don't much like the sound of that.'

'Who would? Mankind has fallen, Joe. That's our problem. All have sinned and fallen short of the glory of God.'

'But what does that mean in practical terms?'

'It means we can't trust anyone. If law and order breaks down then everything collapses. It's the law of the jungle. If a man knows he can kill with impunity, with no fear of retribution, then he *will* kill.'

'Will he?' A memory was surfacing. The silhouette of a man at the top of the stairs. A terrible sensation of thirst. 'The way you tried to kill me?'

Alvin's expression was a volatile mixture of fear and contempt. 'I didn't try to kill you, Joe. I saved your life.'

How much of that was true? 'I don't believe you.' Somehow the elation that had accompanied his return to health had buried his memories of that night.

'You were delirious.'

'I know.'

'You were calling for something. I don't know what.'

'I was calling for water.'

'How was I to know? You were making no sense.'

They sat for a while in silence.

'Don't do this, Joe,' Hocking said. He had turned his face away. 'We were both close to death. We're both alive. Don't complicate it with conspiracy theories.'

If a man knows he can kill with impunity . . . he will. Was that Alvin Hocking's message for humanity? Would a hungry man kill his neighbour for a loaf of bread? Would they need to barricade the village from murderous marauders?

'It's a bleak view of humanity, Alvin,' Joe said. 'Does the Bible really give us such a pessimistic prognosis?'

The priest turned back to face him. He couldn't conceal an expression of relief that Joe had let the subject go. 'Have you never read the Old Testament?'

'Not recently.' Not at all, but he knew some of the stories. 'Perhaps I should have programmed the Old Testament into my computer model.' What difference might that have made? Never mind crowd-sourcing opinions from CNN or Reuters. What about Abraham, or Elijah, or Zephaniah?

It was time to go inside. Joe got to his feet. His limbs still ached. 'Are you ready for something to eat?'

'How about some cold ham and cold potatoes? Washed down with cold soup?'

'Sounds perfect.'

'Do you know what?' Hocking said. 'I'd kill for a hot meal.'

PART THREE

Can you make a banquet of Leviathan?

29

How will we all behave?

It barely seemed the same village. Bearded, and unwashed, Joe and Alvin released themselves from their self-imposed confinement some time around midday on the eleventh day. Hocking went directly to his vicarage in search of Polly. Content to be free of his company, Joe walked down to the harbour. There were very few people on the streets. He knocked on the door of the old surgery in Fish Street and let himself in.

'Is there anybody home?'

'My dear boy!' Mallory emerged from his surgery room and embraced Joe. 'It's good to see you.'

'It's wonderful to see you too.'

Mallory stretched out his elbows, holding Joe at arm's length to survey him. 'I'm just seeing to Mrs Restorick,' he said, 'and then we must have a small whisky to celebrate.' He nodded in the direction of his surgery, and Joe saw the beaming faces of Dorothy and Benny, here evidently for a consultation of a medical kind.

'Oh, I'm so sorry,' Joe said. 'I didn't mean to interrupt.'

'Lovely to see you again, Joe,' Dorothy called.

'Yes, good to see you, mate,' said Benny.

'You too,' Joe said. He made to close the door.

'Shall we tell him our news?' Dorothy said. Her eyes were shining with excitement. 'We're having a baby.'

'Congratulations. That's wonderful news.' Joe gently closed the door. Life goes on then. Stock markets rise and fall, supply chains snap, civilisations crumble into dust, but the magic of human reproduction overrides everything. Sodium and water. The chemistry of life is unstoppable. This sudden confrontation with human biology gave him an urge to see Polly. He was free of any obligation not to speak to her now, but what would they talk about? Where would they find privacy in the goldfish bowl that was St Piran? He would like to visit the beach with her, to see her footprints on the soft sand, but would that be enough? Could it ever be enough?

The surgery door swung back open, and out came the happy couple, all smiles and hugs, with Books following on behind. 'Do come and see me if anything worries you, anything at all,' the doctor was saying. 'But you've done this before so you know the ropes.'

'I can't thank you enough, Doctor,' Benny said. He pulled a bottle of red wine from a carrier bag. 'We didn't know how to pay you, but I thought . . .'

'That is very generous, Benny. Very generous indeed.'

Barter has become the currency of exchange, Joe thought. 'Gift economics'. He wondered if there might have been a time when Books would have refused a gift of wine, happy to be performing a service for the community; but now, perhaps, even the doctor was, at some level, aware that every currency has to operate through the principle of fair exchange. The payer has to be happy with the price, and the seller happy to accept it. He hadn't thought about the sociology of exchange for quite a while. These were links in his brain that already seemed to belong to an older, less relevant world.

Mallory closed the front door and came back into the hall, triumphantly brandishing the wine. 'It seems we don't need to raid the whisky,' he said. 'Come, come, my boy.' He led Joe into the front room. 'Tell me everything.'

'Everything? What do you want to know? We've been shut up in a church tower doing an inventory of groceries.'

'My dear boy, I'm not interested in that. Not in the least.' The old man recovered a corkscrew from a sideboard and started to tackle the bottle. 'You will find,' he said, nodding at the wine, 'that we have to make this last. Just half a glass is as much as we should drink. John and Lucy Thoroughgood are brewing up some cider apparently, but that won't be ready for weeks. Months even. And it could be vile. Kenny Kennet has some recipe for seaweed wine that Old Man Garrow swears is drinkable, but I can't imagine anyone is looking forward to that with any enthusiasm. This,' he tipped the bottle towards Joe, 'this may be the last bottle of decent French wine that you and I will ever enjoy . . . unless I can diagnose a lot more pregnancies. *Symptoms*, my boy. I want to hear about your symptoms.' He pulled out the cork with a soft pop and deposited a splash of the precious wine into two glasses. 'Don't spare me the details.'

The Harbour Square was barely recognisable. On the cobbles had sprung up an assortment of tables and benches, some hastily assembled from rough-cut lumber and empty oil drums, others clearly transported from gardens and balconies. In the middle of the Square, right outside the Petrel Inn, the Magwiths had installed three old cast-iron feed-troughs. 'What are those?' Joe asked, when they finally ventured outside.

'That's the village barbecue,' Mallory told him. 'It's smoky, mind. No one has any charcoal, so we're cooking with wood.'

'It's enormous,' Joe said. 'You could feed the whole village with this.'

'We *do* feed the whole village. Every teatime, two hours before it gets dark. The boys go out all day collecting wood. There's their pile.' Mallory pointed at a huge stockpile.

'Good Lord.' For some reason Joe was still constructing economic models in his mind. How did this work? he wondered. Who was paying whom, and how much, and with what?

'Every able man and woman and child is part of the effort,' Mallory said. 'Some are fishing in boats right now – in every boat they can lay their hands on. Others are angling off the quay, some are collecting shellfish.' He pointed out to the harbour wall, where a dozen or more people stood pressed against the ancient stones with rods and lines. 'Right now there are folk up at the farm helping the Magwiths with the afternoon milking. They'll be back up there before dawn for tomorrow's milking. The farm does have a generator to power the milking machine but we're trying to conserve fuel for the boats. So they're milking by hand.'

Milking by hand. Mallory made it sound like an ancient custom.

'What happens to all the milk?'

'We drink it. We poach fish in it. We churn it into butter and cream. Corin is making cheese.'

How long had it been? Eleven days? Joe found himself nodding with admiration.

At the far end of the Square stood the crushed remains of the telephone box. Where it had stood, an old iron hand-pump had been lifted into place and bolted onto heavy wooden sleepers. Bo'sun Jordy Higgs was manning it. Wearing no more than a summer shirt he was rhubarb-red and sweating as he hauled on the handle. Jessie and Martha and half a dozen more were passing buckets and tubs down a chain.

'I could take a go doing that,' Joe said.

Heads turned to welcome him. 'Well, hello, *stranger*!' said Martha, delivering a voluminous hug. He was passed down the chain, receiving an embrace from every person. How many years had he worked side by side with colleagues at Lane Kaufmann and how often had he been hugged? Not often. He let himself return every squeeze, and it felt good.

'I won't say it's not good to see you,' Jessie said. 'We're more'n ready for that food store of yours.'

Joe tried to make his grimace look like a smile. 'When the time is right,' he found himself saying. The uncomfortable image of a trailing queue of villagers carrying away the hoard of food that he'd so painstakingly assembled, stored, and catalogued surfaced in his mind.

Jordy Higgs had used the interruption to stop pumping. 'I won't hug you,' he said, lifting his arms to show the circles of sweat. 'I'm stinking.'

'Then let me take a turn,' Joe said.

'Are you sure you're well enough?'

'I'm fit as a fiddle.' Was that true? Possibly not, but surely he could man a pump?

'There you go then.' Higgs stood aside and Joe took the handle. The iron shaft was cold in his hands, and it was heavier than he'd imagined. He lifted it high and then leant down, letting his weight do the work. A satisfying stream of water emerged and was caught in a bucket by Aminata Chikelu.

'Good work,' she said.

For an instant they shared a smile, and then he looked away. What would Polly be doing now? he wondered. Were she and Alvin in bed together, making up for lost time? He hauled on the pump. It was easier this time. Would they be wound together in some sort of celebratory passion? He pressed down the handle with all the force he could muster. Maybe he wasn't the only person pumping, he thought. Up. And down. Up. And down.

Higgs was grinning. 'Take it easy,' he said. 'Leave some water down there.'

When it was Higgs's turn again to pump, Joe sat on a wall to recover his breath. Martha came over to him. 'Can we 'ave a word?' she asked.

'Sure.'

'Shall we walk a little way?'

'OK.' He dropped next to her and they strolled away from the pump and all the action.

'We bin' thinkin', it might be 'bout time to open up that store of yours.'

'I see.'

''Tin't just a thought, Joe. I'm here to ask you properly. Can we open up the store?'

Now that the question had been formally asked, Joe felt another wave of panic. 'Are you sure?' he said.

'I wun't be askin' if I weren't sure.'

Why did he feel this sudden reluctance? This was why he'd bought all the food, surely? 'You do understand it's an emergency store. I thought perhaps we'd wait until people were really . . . starving.' Those were the words he said, but surely he didn't mean them. They felt wrong in his throat.

There was a long pause and Martha was looking at him strangely. 'They all 'elped you with that store,' she said, her nod accommodating the whole village of St Piran.

'I know.'

'An' they *are* starvin',' she said.

'What about all the fish? The milk?'

''Tin't enough. The boys don't have near enough fuel to fish. The catch is way down. Besides – 'ave you ever tried livin' on fish 'n' milk?'

She was a woman who joined the dots. She was like him. This was why she'd drawn him aside from the others, to allow him to display his uncharacteristic reluctance before her, and her alone. The battle between his natural charity and his sense of possession had to be allowed to happen. She understood.

'It won't last long,' he whispered. 'The store.' He'd done the calculations often enough these past dark days. To feed three hundred people, they had enough food for eight weeks. Maybe four months with the help of the fishing, and the dairy herd, and the lambs.

''Tin't your food no more,' she said, but her eyes were still kind.

'Of course,' he was gulping now, 'of course.'

'What's the word then, Joe?'

He looked at his feet. 'Let's open up the store.' And with each of these five words a weight seemed to lift from his shoulders. '*How will you behave, Joe Haak?*' The words of Lew Kaufmann seemed to echo in his ears. '*How will we all behave?*' 'You're right, Martha,' he said. Every one of these people had welcomed him with an embrace, and here he was equivocating. 'You're right! By God you're right.' He almost gave a skip. 'Let's open it now.'

Martha's face was almost split in two by her smile. 'Now let's not go mad,' she cautioned. 'We don't want to eat it all at once.'

'No.'

She linked her arm through his. 'Come with me,' she said. 'Let's go 'n' meet the cooks.'

The crowd began to form well before teatime. Children arrived first. The boys came to light the fires, the girls came to watch. Then came the women carrying plates, and mugs, and cutlery, and the men with pint glasses, and more fuel for the fires, and meagre offerings of food. Half a dozen eggs from the Thoroughgoods, a tub of margarine from the Clokes, carrots from Nate and Rose Moot's smallholding. 'I hear we've got a proper dinner tonight?' said someone, and the word spread among the gathering numbers.

''Tis all down to our Joe,' Martha told them proudly.

It was smoky in the square as the fires began to take. Joe and Casey Limber carried a twenty-kilogram sack of rice from the church tower and they emptied it into nine huge tureens that were starting to simmer. Romer Anderssen and Rose Moot cooked up a sauce in a collection of borrowed saucepans. They used the carrots, two dozen tins of tomatoes from Joe's store, twenty jars of his ready-mixed sauce, and a bucket of well water. The Bartle sisters stripped the flesh from fish, and tossed the fillets to Jacob and Kenny, who blackened them, thirty at a time, on a flat iron griddle. Moses and Hedra Penhallow and the Shaunessy brothers poked the fires, and turned the fish, and still the crowd grew. Kenny cracked open mussels and dropped them into the sauce. The rich aroma of woodsmoke and cooking filled the square.

The light of the afternoon was fading. From up the hill came the growl of an engine, heralding the arrival of the Magwiths and their volunteer milkers, all squeezed together onto a farm trailer and towed behind a tractor. They came with several churns of milk, and these were lifted off the trailer with a great deal of noise and barracking. With one of the Magwith brothers in charge, the milk was poured into jugs and set on the tables.

How do you feed so many hungry mouths? Joe thought. He was remembering Kaufmann's question. *How do you feed a city of ten million people?* Here in this square, just three hundred seemed an almost insuperable task; all that wood to burn, all the superhuman effort to gather in the fish, and to milk the cattle, and to fetch, and to carry, and to cook. He should have understood all this. This was the very essence of the models he'd built for so many years, the detailed mathematics of supply and demand, the dependency chains he'd studied, the human interactions he had learned. Yet nothing in this village made sense. Where was the currency of exchange? How were the milkers rewarded for their time, or the fishermen for their catch?

The first full ladles of fish, rice and sauce were being heaped onto plates, milk was being decanted into glasses, and people were taking their seats around the tables, when Alvin and Polly appeared in the square. The villagers rose up to greet them.

'Reverend Hocking, thanks be to God,' declared Eileen Magwith.

The lean grey face of the vicar assumed an avuncular smile. 'My dear Mrs Magwith.' He shook her hand with both of his. 'My dear Mrs Fishburne, Mrs Horsmith, Corin – how very good to see you.' He began to work his way through the swell of people, touching them, hands upon shoulders, making eye contact. 'Mrs Cloke, thank you so much for your prayers. Jacob, Romer, Joshua, Mary . . .'

Left behind as the melee swallowed the vicar, Joe found himself standing next to Polly, feeling the soft electricity that surrounded her. She hadn't especially looked his way. 'Are you all right?' he asked her.

She was looking at her shoes.

'I have Alvin's permission to speak to you,' he said. He felt an urge to grasp hold of her.

'Not here,' she said, and she looked away. Someone had caught her eye and she was waving. 'Another time,' she said.

There are cold dynamics in a human crowd, especially for a single person. Whom do you greet and whom do you ignore? Do you stand in one place and hope that the party will come to you? Or do you circulate with jovial bonhomie? Can you risk being isolated out on the margins, standing alone with your empty glass? Joe found himself squeezed out to the periphery as preparations for dinner reached their climax and families and groups of friends began to congeal. He found room on a bench at the far end of a table, alongside a heavy man whose acquaintance he had yet to make. 'I'm Joe,' he said, offering a handshake across the table to an elderly couple he also seemed to be meeting for the first time.

'I understand we have *you* to thank for the rice.'

He tipped his head to deflect the remark.

'Joe, good to see you.' A hand fell on his shoulder. 'Do you have room for two more?'

He looked up to see Jeremy and Demelza.

'I'm sure you can squeeze us in, darling.' Demelza's arm was around Jeremy's shoulder, her hand flat on his breast; it looked to Joe like an almost sexual embrace.

30
There are always other girls

They remember that winter well, in St Piran. It rained so hard in November that Bo'sun Higgs declared he would build an ark. They tried moving all the tables and chairs from the Harbour Square into the fish packing station so they could eat without being rained upon. It was never going to work. They could maybe squeeze in a hundred people, but no more. 'We won't all fit in the Petrel,' Jacob Anderssen said, gloomily. 'Nor the schoolroom,' said Martha.

'We could all fit in the church,' Joe said, but even the big men looked doubtful. Peter Shaunessy shook his head gravely. 'Vicar'll never let us,' he said.

But they walked up the hill, a delegation, carrying tables and benches.

'What about the pews?' objected Alvin Hocking, when it was clear that his sanction could not prevail.

'Firewood,' said Joe.

They cleared space in the churchyard for the cooking. Gravestones made splendid ovens. In heavy rain, for a day, they hefted gravestones, and iron railings, and benches, and tables, and before sunset they had a cafeteria with ovens and tables and more barbecue space than they could possibly manage.

'Please spare the pulpit,' Hocking begged, and they did. The iron railings of the choir stalls were commandeered for fire stacks. The pews became benches, and the backs of the pews became tables.

Polly stood and watched, her arms folded across her bosom. Joe tried not to catch her eye.

As November progressed, food supplies fell. Joe watched as

the boxes and sacks from his store were lugged outside to be added to the broths and the stews. He would strike the items off his register. There should, he felt, have been a committee of villagers for him to consult. He wanted to tell someone, 'We should go carefully.'

'Who's in charge?' he asked Jeremy one evening as they squeezed together onto tables in the candlelit church for dinner. 'Who do you think is in charge of all of this?'

'In charge of all what?'

'Of all the organisation? Who marshals the resources for the cooking and cleaning? Who plans the menus? Who rations the food?'

Jeremy shrugged. 'I thought you did,' he said.

The daily fish catch was well below the half-pound of fish per person that Alvin Hocking had predicted; this despite the growing numbers of people angling from the rocks and the harbour wall. 'The catch is never high this time of year,' Daniel Robins told him. 'It's normally half in November what it is in July. There's too few hours of daylight. And besides, we don't have the fuel to go out far enough.'

The milk ration from the Magwiths was also lower than they'd expected. Hand milking drew less milk, and the farm had run short of food concentrate for the cows, so the Magwiths were feeding the livestock on silage. One wild night, Eileen Magwith was woken by the sound of gunshots. The dogs were barking. Out in the fields at first light they discovered they were now down to nine ewes. Raiders had come across the cliff paths and taken the rest overnight. They'd been shot dead and carried away. There were bloodstains on the grass where the ewes had fallen.

Joe became a fisherman. He borrowed Mallory's sailing boat, but he rarely raised the sails. He and Jeremy would row it out to the middle of the bay and there they would sit with a dozen lines in the water. There was a small inboard motor, but they were careful to use it only sparingly. On the first day they caught eight small mackerel. It didn't feel like much reward for nine hours spent at sea. 'Dinner for eight,' Jeremy said as they moored back up in the late afternoon.

Dinner for twenty, Joe thought.

Peter Shaunessy rigged up his radio in the church where the signal was excellent. 'What's happening with the flu?' Mallory Books would ask him, and Peter would throw the question out at everyone who came on air. They spoke to a husband and wife in Plymouth who had eaten nothing for six days apart from sachets of cat food. 'We don't care about the flu any more,' the man told Peter. 'I wish it would come and take us.' They spoke to a cruise liner in the Channel. 'We've had twenty-four die of flu,' the radio operator told them. 'We want to come ashore.'

'Wait for seven days,' Joe told them. 'Give the infection a chance to clear.'

'We can't wait. We need water.'

The rain eased in early December but it gave way to a fierce north wind. Out in the sailing boat Joe and Jeremy were churned between the waves like butter in a can. One day they caught no fish at all but the next day they pulled in a John Dory and two dogfish and a huge conger eel. They would all go in the pot.

'Yellow as gold,' Jeremy said as they gutted the John Dory. 'It's French . . . *jaune doré*.'

'You're a well of information,' Joe told him.

They opened up the crates of corned beef and hams, and they soaked the dried chickpeas and lentils and beans. Evening dinner in the church had become an institution, one that Joe had begun to enjoy. Romer and the cooks had learned to bake bread in the gravestone ovens. Nate and Rose Moot would churn milk into butter and bring it every evening in a wooden bucket. There was no cider yet, but the Thoroughgoods had samplings of a hot apple punch. Dinner might be a scrap of hot bread, and fresh butter, and a tankard of warm milk with a chaser of apple punch, and a goulash of fish and beans and oddments from tins, and even a mouthful of fruit. These were the best meals Joe could remember since the garlic mushrooms north of Rouen, or the fish he used to fry with Papa Mikkel. He would think back to the way he ate in the City, but it all seemed so long ago.

Nonetheless, there was only one meal a day, and still the whole village was hungry. After dinner Joe would take a candle, and check the contents of his store. Could it be disappearing so quickly? The stairs were empty of boxes already. The sacks were vanishing fast. From time to time a knock would sound on the door of the bell tower and there would stand a villager with a basket. 'Can you spare any milk powder? Do you have any soap?' Joe would swing open the door to admit them and they'd leave with a basket of provisions. Already they were coming to the end of some of the tinned vegetables and soups, and fruit had to be carefully rationed. Pasta and rice were disappearing rapidly. There was plenty of bread flour, but for how long?

The weather grew colder. Polly was ignoring him. The fish catch did not improve. Jeremy stopped joining him on the sailboat. 'I've got chilblains,' he complained. 'And we're catching so few fish, I don't see how it helps having me there.' It helped to have company perhaps, but Joe didn't say this.

'I'd do better collecting fish from rock pools,' Jeremy said. 'There are blennies and gobies and butterfish if you know where to look for them. We could be collecting more edible seaweeds too.'

And so the days passed, and the days became weeks. On a day close to midwinter, with the sky as grey as old linen, Joe took the boat out alone and tied himself to the wheel. Impetuously he raised the sails. A strong, steady wind filled them, and before long he was far out, further than he'd ever sailed from St Piran, almost beyond sight of the land. There were other boats; in every direction the ocean was dotted with fishing smacks, and rowing boats, and yachts. But they kept their distance. Every boat in Cornwall is out at sea, Joe thought. He dropped the sails and let the yacht bob in the water as he threw out the lines. Without Jeremy he caught two full buckets of herring. He tacked back against the wind. He had almost lost sight of Piran Head, but there it was, the rocky headland and the whitewashed village, the stone harbour and the Norman church. It would take some time to sail back, but he had a couple of hours until dusk. He set to the task, letting the ropes run through his palms, feeling the secret power of the breeze, enjoying the solitude and the freedom of the water. He used to do this with his father. Pappa Mikkel would go below to smoke a pipe. 'Take her home, Joe,' he would say, and they would tack between the rocky islands along the coast, past Sölvesborg and Karlshamn with Joe at the wheel. Sometimes the wind could be as solid as an elk. 'Trim down your sails, Joe,' Mikkel would call from below, and sometimes he would, but often he would disobey, and he'd feel the little yacht rising up in the water like a racer, scudding between the waves.

A slick of black slid beneath the water in front of Mallory's little boat, and at once Joe was alert. He pulled on the wheel, and swung a few degrees to starboard.

There it was again. Grey this time, uncommonly fast, just a foot or so beneath the surface.

'The whale,' he whispered. And there it was, only metres away, breaking above the swell like a submarine released from a tether. With a great thrust of hidden power it lifted almost clear of the rolling ocean, turning as it did so. There, for the smallest instant of time, it hung in the unfamiliar air, defiant of gravity, until with a further twist it fell into the gulf between the waves and a huge cascade of spray and foam rose in its place.

Joe's hands were tight on the wheel. The bow wave from the breaching whale lifted the boat, and for a heartbeat Joe thought it might capsize, but down it sank again, safely. Now the whale was cresting again. Up it rose, and again it turned, and this time it held steady with an eye towards the boat, and down it slapped, lobtailing its flukes against the milky foam behind it.

'Oh my God,' Joe whispered.

Where had it gone? He scanned the surface of the sea as the impact tossed his boat for a second time. The whale must have dived deep. There was no sign that he could see. He loosened the sails and let the crosswind pull him forward. Then there it was again, another breach, a hundred metres away. This time it fell backwards into the water, with what could have been a wave of its fin. A minute later and there it was again – a long way off this time, heading away.

'Goodbye, old friend.' Joe raised his hand. 'Goodbye.'

There were flecks of snow in the darkening sky as he turned in towards St Piran harbour. He allowed himself a short burst of the motor, and scrambled forward to throw out the fenders. Annie Bartle in her aprons was there to help tie up the ropes, her hair hidden behind a polka-dot scarf. 'Any luck?' she asked him.

'Two buckets of herring.'

'My word!' She looked at them. 'That's better than the boys did today.'

'I was lucky,' he said. He swung the buckets ashore. 'And I saw the whale.'

'Some of the boys saw it too. It's been out in the bay all day. Here . . .' She held out a hand to help him ashore.

You're ten years too old for me, Annie, Joe thought, but the touch of her hand on his arm was warm and it made him remember how long it had been since he'd been close to a woman. 'Some people *like* the smell of fish,' Demelza had told him. He probably smelled stronger than Annie did today. Maybe she was enjoying *his* smell. 'Can I walk you to dinner?' he asked, and he kinked his elbow.

'I'd be delighted,' Annie said, linking arms. They took a

bucket of herring each, and swinging them with exaggerated rhythm, they set off up the hill.

There was no fishing the next day. The wind was blowing a blizzard of sleet off the sea. Dinner was a stew of seaweed and chickpeas and it tasted foul. The following day was no better. A storm swept in during the night, and now it was too wet for the barbecue fires to burn and the ovens had been flooded. Romer and Jacob and Martha raided the store for oatmeal and sugar, and dinner was a milky porridge. No one complained. It was a relief not to have seaweed.

'We need the weather to pick up,' Joe said, but the following day was almost as bad. The Robins brothers took their boat out and landed a modest catch of pollack, which they stewed up with seaweed and beans and tins of vegetable soup.

That night, as the church was emptying of diners, Bevis Magwith lumbered up towards Joe. 'It's three days until Christmas,' he said. 'What are we going to do?'

'Christmas? I hadn't really thought . . .'

'All the same,' Magwith said, 'we should do something.'

'Yes,' Joe said. 'We should.' Who was in charge? he wondered again. Why was Magwith coming to him?

'I've a barren cow you can have.'

'Thank you.' Joe didn't know what to add. What was a barren cow? Beef, he supposed. Hardly traditional festive fare, but very welcome all the same.

'I'll get Nate Moot to butcher it tomorrow.'

'Thank you. How do you suggest we cook it?'

Magwith shrugged. 'That's up to Romer and Jacob, I suppose.'

Joe went to hunt out the Anderssens. They were clearing up the pots and pans and helping to quench the fires. He told them about Bevis Magwith's offer.

'He always were a kind man,' said Martha. 'He were a kind boy too.'

'We should do something special,' Jacob said.

'I'll get the children to make decorations,' said Martha. 'And they'll sing some carols.'

'How much meat do you get off a barren cow?' asked Romer. No one knew the answer to that.

'It'll be tough and chewy,' Jacob said.

'Another big stew then.'

Joe remembered a Christmas once, on his father's island, when Mikkel and his mother were still together. How old would he have been? Seven perhaps? Possibly eight, but no older. It snowed hard all night and Pappa had to dig a passage out from the cabin door. Outside it was as perfect as a greetings card, crisp and clear. Pappa went all around the cabin snapping the icicles off the awnings. Joe and Brigitha built snowmen. Mamma spent the day in the cabin cooking, but what a feast! A duck roast, with caramel potatoes and red cabbage; and *ris ala mande* – rice pudding with almonds and cinnamon. He could still remember it today. They sat around the log fire and sang songs. They sang English songs, because these were the ones that Mamma had taught them, but Pappa sang Danish songs too, 'Det Er Hvidt Herude', he sang, and a mournful song about lost love. And they all sang, 'Wonderful, wonderful Copenhagen, friendly old girl of a town', because this was Mamma's favourite song about Denmark, and Mamma sang a descant on the final line, 'wonderful, wonderful Copenhagen for me'.

Stepping outside the church into the December night, thinking about that Christmas on the island near Karlskrona, Joe nearly missed the hooded figure in the porch. She was standing so still she might have been a shadow. 'Polly?' It was too dark to see her face, but there was no mistaking her magnetic field. 'Polly?'

'Hello, Joe.' Her breath was a fine mist.

'Can we talk?' His hand was on her arm already. 'Come.' He led her into the churchyard. She stumbled alongside him. It was as dark as a mine.

'Where are you taking me, Joe?'

'Somewhere we can talk without being seen.'

'Why would we do that?'

They stopped beneath the yew tree. He wished he could see her face. He held her at arm's length, his hands on her upper arms. 'I've missed you,' he said.

'I haven't been anywhere.'

Was she smiling at him? Was she letting her face drop forward the way she did? Was her hair falling over her eyes? He released her shoulders, slowly. This should be sodium and water. He should be kissing her now. He thought of little Clare Manners and her tantalising ribbon of flesh. Could it be happening again? Was it possible that the chemistry wasn't working?

'Have you been OK?' he asked. 'We haven't really had a chance to talk . . . you know . . . since . . .'

'I know.'

'Did you miss me?'

'You shouldn't have to ask that, Joe.'

What did that mean? 'I do have to ask. I need to know, Polly. Did you think about me . . . all those weeks?'

'Of course.'

'I know it's difficult for you,' he said. 'I know Alvin makes it difficult.' He could hear her breathing, could feel her breath on his face.

'What do you want, Joe?'

What did he want? I want you, he could have said. I want the warmth of your body next to mine. I want to feel your face between my hands. I want to lie beside you. I want to wake up every morning and see your face on my pillow. 'Can I kiss you?' He whispered it, and was suddenly fearful that his voice would carry away from the churchyard to waiting ears beyond.

Instead of an answer she leaned towards him. He felt her face brush up against his. She placed a soft kiss on his cheek, and pulled away. 'Take me back, Joe.'

But he'd seen the kiss as an invitation, and now he was pulling her closer.

'No,' she said, and he released his hold. 'Take me back.'

They picked their way between the graves. 'I'm sorry,' Joe said. 'I didn't mean . . .' But what didn't he mean? There seemed no truthful way to end the sentence.

'That's OK,' she said. There was the dim glow of candlelight from the church window. 'Find another girl, Joe.' She held out her hand and touched his cheek; he let his face turn it into a caress.

'There are no other girls.'

'Oh, there are *always* other girls.' She pulled away her hand.

He shook his head. 'It wouldn't matter if there were a thousand.'

'You don't need a thousand, Joe. You only need one. You just haven't found her yet.'

'I thought perhaps I had.'

They stood together in the silence. Joe could feel his heart filling his ribcage. 'Now you're scaring me,' Clare Manners had said. He found himself rehearing some of Demelza's words. Human beings aren't jigsaw pieces, she had said. We don't neatly fit together.

'Where were you going?' Polly asked him.

He shrugged. 'Just down to see Mallory.'

'Go then.' She stood for a moment and looked at him in the thin light. Then she turned and went back into the church.

31

I think she's been shot

He didn't feel like taking the boat out. He rose, and washed in cold water. He didn't breakfast from the store any more. It might, once, have seemed like *his* food, but that was in another time, when different rules applied. Today his breakfast was a draught of well water, and nothing more.

He was cold all the time these days. If we get too warm we start to cook. That was what Pappa Mikkel would have said. If we start to cook we go soft. It was bitterly cold in the bell tower, but it was cold at Mallory's too. No one had spare wood for a fire; they needed it all for cooking. So he wrapped up as warm as he could, a T-shirt, a shirt, a pullover, a duffel coat, and a woollen hat.

There was no one on the quay. It could have been the morning when he first arrived, alone in his car with all his fears. But the sea was warmer then, and the wind kinder. He pulled up the hood of his coat. He had no plan for the day. Find another girl, Joe. Find another girl.

Perhaps he could find a fish in a rock pool. Jeremy and Kenny seemed to find a few. He pushed his hands deep into his pockets and walked the length of the harbour wall, and around the headland path. This was where it all started, he thought. This was the beach.

He was no longer alone. A thin figure was scrambling along the rocks at the water's edge. It could only be Kenny, in his gendarme hat and canvas coat. 'Hey!' Joe raised his arm to call, but something had distracted Kenny. The beachcomber's attention was elsewhere, out to sea. He stood like a man transfixed, and then he turned and climbed the rocks, choosing a higher position to watch the surf crashing in.

'Hello!' Joe called.

Kenny turned his head and saw him, and then he beckoned. 'Come here. Quick.'

Joe started forward.

'Quick!'

He broke into a run.

'Look.' Kenny was pointing at a dark shadow in the water. 'There she is.'

Joe clambered up the rocks to join him. 'What's brought her back in again?'

'God knows.'

There was something strange about the whale. She was barely moving. Floundering perhaps, rolling haphazardly, tossed this way and that by the waves. 'What's the matter with her?' The great beast seemed comatose – asleep perhaps. 'Do whales sleep?'

'I don't know.'

'She's bleeding,' Kenny said. The water around the whale was swirling an oily brown. 'I think that's blood.'

'Dear God . . .'

'I think she's been shot.'

'Shot?'

'Look.' Kenny pointed at the long head of the whale. A dozen flesh wounds seemed to pepper the top and one side of the animal's skull. Could they be bullet holes? 'Someone's been trying to pop her with a shotgun,' he said.

'I saw her a few days ago,' Joe said. 'She was in the bay. Who could have shot her?'

'Anyone. She could have travelled twenty miles. There's a hundred boats out there. Anyone could have taken a shot at her, but she probably dived and swam away. And came back here to die.'

Somehow the suggestion seemed appropriate. Perhaps the

whale felt as connected to this stretch of sand as he did. 'Maybe she thought we could save her again.'

'Maybe.'

A wave caught the body of the whale, and rolled it up towards the shingle. 'She's going to beach again.'

'It looks that way. How is the tide?'

'High as it's been for a few days.'

Another wave deposited the creature in a crevice between two long fingers of rock. The men stood and watched, feeling helpless this time as the tide sucked out from beneath the beast. This wasn't a clean stretch of sand and shingle as it had been the last time she beached. This time the whale was tangled in a knot of rocks.

'We won't get her out of there.'

'A hundred men wouldn't get her out of there.' The two men made their way to the rocks, and the beachcomber placed his hand on Joe's arm. 'I think she's dead, Joe,' he said gently.

And so she was. The lustre seemed to have left her body. She wasn't lying on her belly the way she had done before; this time she had rolled over and her head had subsided into a cradle of rock. This was scenario four, Joe reflected. There was no way back for this whale. Even now the blood flow would have stopped; the highways that fed and nurtured the great organs had ceased to operate. Trillions of cells would be crying for oxygen, but none would ever come.

'We should cut her up,' Kenny said.

'Should we?'

'What else can we do? If we leave her on the rocks she'll slowly rot until she stinks out the whole village.'

'I suppose you're right.' But neither man moved. It seemed to Joe like the end of a chapter in his life. This was the whale that had saved him, had lifted him, had sent him scudding up onto the beach in a wave of its making. This, in turn, was the whale he had saved. He had mobilised a village of people and together they had hauled it back into the sea. Now here it was, like a gargantuan specimen from a carnival of horrors, a greased and folded carcase. As they watched, the whale sank into its lodged position between the rocks and Joe saw the eye of the creature, still open, staring sightlessly at him. And then, with great finality, the eye closed, and the whale was still.

'I'll go for help,' Joe said. 'You wait here.'

The previous time he had sprinted around the headland, calling upon everyone he could see. They had all been strangers then. This time he walked heavily along the sea path. There was no one on the harbour. No one in the square. He turned up Fish Street towards the stile where the cliff path started. At the top of the road three figures were in conversation. He recognised Peter Shaunessy. Just the man to talk to, but who were the others?

'Peter!' he called.

The big fisherman turned around and returned his wave. The couple to whom he'd been talking looked anxious. A young man and a young woman, their faces unfamiliar to Joe. Peter was passing across a package of some description. The young man snatched at it and clutched it under his arm. 'I'll be with you now,' Peter called down towards Joe. He gestured to the young couple, and with what seemed like unnecessary haste, the pair turned and headed away, up the cliff path.

'Who were they?'

Peter looked sheepish. 'Just a couple from Treadangel,' he said. 'They came here over the cliffs.'

'What did they want?'

Peter shrugged. 'What do you think? Food. They're saying Treadangel ran out of food three weeks ago.'

Joe tried to absorb this. 'What have they been eating?'

'Anything they can lay their hands on. They've been trapping gulls, fishing off the rocks, boiling up acorns . . .'

'Dear God!' Joe was assailed by an acute sense of discomfort. Life in St Piran had been easy compared to this. Trapping seagulls? 'What did you give them?'

Peter looked away. 'What could I give them? If we start sharing what little we have, where will it end? It isn't just Treadangel, you know. What about Penzance? What about Truro? If we share our sea-catch with Treadangel, then why not with them? Why not with Bristol or London?'

'So you didn't give them anything?'

Peter shifted a little from one foot to the other. 'I may have given them a brace of lobsters.'

'Lobsters?'

'And a bass. A small one.'

'And?'

'Half a dozen crabs.'

Joe rested his hand on the fisherman's shoulder. 'Peter Shaunessy, you're a good man.'

'They won't be saying that tonight at dinner.'

'They will in Treadangel.' A thought was surfacing. 'How many people live in Treadangel?'

Peter shook his head. 'No idea. A thousand perhaps?' He looked at Joe's face as if they might work this one out together. 'Five thousand?'

Joe turned towards the cliff path where the pair from Treadangel were making their way up the hill. 'Wait!' he called. 'Wait!'

'What are you doing?' Peter demanded. 'You in't going to give them food from your store?'

'Not the store. No. Wait!'

The Treadangel man turned back, trying to spot the source of the noise.

Joe waved wildly. 'Come with me,' he said to Peter. He set off up the path at a run.

The couple looked thin. There was something shiny around the girl's mouth. Fish scales. She'd been biting into the raw fish that Peter had given her.

'Wait!' Joe ran up to them and held out his hand. 'I'm Joe.'

The pair stared at his hand with suspicion. 'We're looking for food,' the girl said. 'That's all. We can trade.'

'We can work,' offered the man. 'We can work on ships. Or in the fields.'

'We have food,' Joe said.

The young man glanced over at Peter. 'He told us you didn't.'

'Well, he didn't know everything. We *do* have food. Look . . . I have a proposal.'

'Anything. We'll do anything.' The man extended his arm and took Joe's proffered hand.

'Do you still have any cases of flu in Treadangel?'

The girl shook her head. 'None for four or five weeks.'

'Good.' Joe was a little out of breath. 'Can you get everybody in Treadangel here tomorrow at midday?'

The man raised his eyebrows. 'The whole town?'

'Yes. The whole town. Young and old. We're going to cook you a banquet.'

The couple returned his smile with a look of disbelief. 'A banquet?'

'Of a sort. Yes.'

'What's the catch?' the girl asked.

'There is no catch. Tomorrow is Christmas Day. Think of it as St Piran's Christmas gift to its neighbour.'

Still the man looked suspicious. 'What do you want in return?'

'Nothing. Just be here at midday. Come to the church. Bring everybody. Everyone who can walk. Bring knives and forks and plates and spoons and mugs. And bring baskets in case there are any leftovers.'

'Leftovers?' The Treadangel girl's face had turned from a smile into a sob. 'Promise me this isn't a trick,' she said, her words almost swallowed by her tears.

Joe took her hand. It felt cold. 'I promise. We will feed you. It won't be Christmas turkey or mince pies, but we will find food for everyone.'

'What is this?' asked Peter in a low voice as the two visitors turned and walked away. 'Are you out of your mind?'

'No more than I've ever been,' Joe said. 'No more than you were when you gave them that fish and those lobsters. Thank you for trusting me, Peter. Now I think you need to come with me.'

32
Permission to come ashore

They rang the bells on Christmas morning. Joe and Alvin, ignoring the fears of the safety inspectors who had kept the bell tower closed for so long, hauled on the ropes until it seemed that the reverberations would echo out across all of Cornwall.

'They'll hear that in Treadangel,' Alvin said.

'I hope they do.'

Down on the beach work was under way on the carcase of the whale. Two dozen men or more were there, taking direction from Peter Shaunessy. They wielded knives, saws, axes, even a chainsaw. Daniel and Samuel Robins were there with crates and barrels.

'Try not to waste a single scrap,' Peter called. 'Put all the blubber and oil into the barrels and all the meat into the crates. We can use it all.'

The tide was low now and the whale was a long way out of the water. Despite Peter's encouragement, the beach was already a charnel house of blood and grease. The shingle was slippery with oil, and out to sea ran a broth trail of blood and whale-skin and fragments of flesh. Joe stood and watched from the safety of the path. This was his whale. His whale being dismembered before his eyes.

'This is nothing like any animal I've ever butchered,' Lorne Magwith told him. 'The fat is so tough it blunts your knife. The muscle is so dense it doesn't want to cut through . . .'

'But is it edible?' Joe asked.

'It'll likely taste awful.'

'I don't care what it tastes like.' Joe was thinking of the

Treadangel girl with her mouth full of raw fish. 'As long as it doesn't poison us.'

'It's freshly dead,' Lorne said. 'It should be safe for a day or so.'

'Good.'

Up at the church the cooking had already started. Romer Anderssen in a leather apron had taken charge. The fires were burning, a low smoke hung over the churchyard, and the smell of roasting meat leaked out into the lanes.

'What can we take from the store, Joe?' Romer called, when she saw him.

'Anything,' he said. 'Everything. It's Christmas. Take whatever you need.'

They were garlanding the church with holly branches. Boxes of decorations, recovered from attics and garages, were being unpacked and strings of tinsel were being hung between the trees.

'Dun't it look festive?' Martha said. She came up to Joe and slid an arm around him. 'We've got every child in St Piran 'anging out decorations. By the time them Treadangel folk get here they'll not recognise the place. And nor'll we.'

Inside the church, Alvin Hocking seemed to have taken charge. This was his space, after all. He was supervising the arrangement of tables. Polly was unfolding chairs. She avoided Joe's gaze.

Eileen Magwith was playing carols on the piano. She stopped, looking up guiltily when Joe appeared. 'I shouldn't be doing this,' she said, apologetically. 'I should be helping.'

'Eileen, you are helping,' Joe said. 'This is the very best thing you could be doing. Please don't stop.'

'Are you sure?'

'I've never been more sure.'

In the churchyard Bevis Magwith had arrived on his tractor with churns of milk and the butchered cow. The army of people on the barbecues and ovens were helping him to offload.

There were boys struggling up the hill with barrow-loads of whale-meat. John and Lucy Thoroughgood were decanting cider from a barrel into a huge tureen. 'Come and have a taste,' John called. He held out a ladle to Joe as he passed.

'Thanks.' Joe took the ladle. 'Not bad.'

'It could have done with a few more weeks to mature,' John said. 'But we're warming it up with cinnamon and cloves. It'll be mulled cider.'

Had the village ever seen such industry? Had anyone ever seen such joyous faces on a Christmas morning? Joe stepped out of the church and filled his lungs with the clean, fresh air. It was a perfect day. A little cold perhaps, but then it was Christmas.

'I hope these Treadangel folk show up,' Demelza said. She was helping Aminata and the Bartle sisters to crack open mussels and fillet fish.

'I'm sure they will,' Joe replied.

'I think we have visitors already,' said Aminata. She pointed down towards the harbour. 'I saw three ships come sailing in. Well, one ship.'

All faces turned to follow her gesture. Sure enough, a vessel under full sail appeared to be making its way towards the harbour.

'That's one hell of a swanky yacht,' Jeremy said. 'Someone should go and see who they are.'

'Maybe they're from Treadangel,' said Aminata.

'I don't think so. Treadangel is inland. It could be from Penzance perhaps.'

'I'll go,' Joe said. 'Why don't you come too, Jeremy. Let's make sure they're friendly.'

The two men made their way down Fish Street to the harbour. Abel O'Shea, the harbour master, was already waiting on the dockside, and with him was Casey Limber. 'Who is it?' Joe asked them.

'Nobody we know,' Casey said. He was watching the boat

through binoculars. 'Looks to me like a Poole registration. It's a catamaran. Quite a yacht. Ten metres I'd guess.'

'Twelve,' said the harbour master. 'A metre and a half draught.'

'Will it make it into the harbour?'

'Only just, with the tide this high.'

They stood and watched the boat draw closer. The sails came down, and a figure on deck was throwing out fenders. Under motor power it edged towards the harbour walls. Now there were three people visible on board.

'Permission to come ashore,' called a man's voice.

'Are you clear of the flu?' Joe shouted back.

'Quite clear. How about you?'

'We're clear.'

'We've not been lettin' anyone in,' O'Shea said. 'That's what old Doc Books told us.'

'And he was right,' Joe said. 'But it's Christmas Day.'

'You can back up to here.' Casey pointed at a mooring.

The catamaran slid past the harbour wall into the steady water of the quay. Gently the skipper eased it around until the stern was close to the wharf. A young woman on board, no more than a teenager, her hair a mass of curls, threw out a rope and Casey nimbly caught it. He wound it tightly around the capstan. A second woman, a generation older than the first, pulled up a gangplank.

'Welcome to St Piran,' Joe said. 'Happy Christmas.' He reached out his arm to help the younger woman step ashore.

'You don't know how good it feels to be back on dry land,' the girl said as she took Joe's hand and shook it warmly. She was shaking the curls out of her hair as if this might free them from the ocean spray. 'We've been at sea for months. Grandpa wouldn't let us make landfall until now.'

'You have a sensible grandpa then,' Joe said. 'But you're quite safe here. Perhaps you'd like to join us all for a Christmas meal?'

The teenager gave a squeal of excitement. She called over

her shoulder. 'Did you hear that, Mother? We're invited for Christmas dinner.'

'It won't be turkey, I'm afraid,' Joe said.

'So long as it isn't fish and lentils I really don't mind.'

Joe made a face. 'There may be some fish and lentils.'

'But it'll be on dry land. That'll make all the difference. By the way, my name is Cassie.'

'Cassie?'

'And I don't know if you can help us. We're looking for someone called Joe Haak.'

33

The opinions of an aged Jewish banker

The doors to the Petrel were open, even though no one was home. Joe and the Kaufmanns sat around the table by the window, the table that Joe had once called his office. 'I can't offer you anything to drink,' he said.

No matter.

There had been four people on the yacht. Cassie, her parents Tom and Kate, and Tom's father Lew. Joe had held out a hand to steady Lew Kaufmann as he gingerly crossed the gangplank, and once on land they had embraced.

Now safely ensconced in the Petrel, Lew told Joe their story. The catamaran was one of several yachts he owned, all of which had been moored in the big marina at Sandbanks, near Poole. This one was the smallest of his fleet, but it was, he thought, the steadiest in the water. He had started to fit it out for a long ocean voyage soon after Cassie – the computer program – had started its predictions. He named the yacht *Cassandra's Dream*. They had filled the on-board store cupboards with food and fresh water, and when the flu had started its dreadful course the family left their home in Sandbanks and set sail. They made for the Azores. Kaufmann, it emerged, owned a home in Angra do Heroísmo on the island of Terceira. The crossing to the mid-Atlantic islands took four weeks. It was not the time of year anyone might have chosen for such a trip, but the yacht was made for these conditions. She bore the Atlantic swell and several storms, but the wind was rarely greater than a force four. In due course they tried to make landfall at Ponta Delgarda on the Azores island of São Miguel. The Portuguese authorities, however, anxious to quarantine the island, would not allow them to disembark, or even moor up. The family sailed on, from São Miguel to Terceira, a two-day passage. The sheltered marina at Angra was full of yachts. *Cassandra's Dream*, the Kaufmanns discovered, was not the only vessel to have fled continental Europe for the Azores. Once again the harbour authorities forbade anyone to disembark, but they did, at least, allow visiting boats to tether themselves together. It was a refuge, of a sort, from the unrelenting swell of the open ocean. The result of Angra's limited hospitality was a huge knot of small vessels, lashed one to the other, floating like a tangle of flotsam in among the jetties. Containers of fresh water were thrown from the quay to the nearest boats and were passed along the chain to the latecomers. *Cassandra's Dream* found itself at the end of a string of twelve. And there she stayed, protected from the worst of the weather, but unable to dock or to deposit passengers ashore. After some days the harbour authorities relented. Many occupants of the flotilla had flouted the quarantine by swimming ashore, and it no longer seemed likely that anyone still represented a health risk. The Kaufmanns, liberated from their yacht, took up residence in Lew's comfortable villa overlooking the Baia do Morgado.

'So what made you come home?' Joe asked.

'The news,' Kaufmann said.

'What news?'

On board *Cassandra's Dream* was a communications desk worthy of an ocean liner. While Tom and Kate had busied themselves sailing, Lew had been below decks working the radio. This was not the ham radio of Peter Shaunessy; conversations with Irishmen on hilltops bemoaning the shortage of Guinness were not for Lew Kaufmann. His connections were altogether closer to the heart of government. 'I've been in daily touch with Toby Maltings,' he said, 'at the Home Office.'

'Do we still *have* a Home Office?' Joe asked.

'Oh, my dear boy, very much so. What did you imagine?

That the government of the country would just evaporate in the face of a minor crisis?'

'A minor crisis? It may have felt like a minor crisis in the Azores. You told me once that this was a war . . .'

'And so it is. And so it has been. I've been speaking with COBRA . . .'

'Cobra?'

'The government's emergency committee. They've been planning for this eventuality for a very long time, Joe. Long before the first flu victim in Bandar Lampung, before the first shots were fired in the Gulf, they had it all worked out. I did some work for them before the crisis so they've kept me in the loop, so to speak.'

'You did some work for the government? What kind of work?' Joe knew, as he asked this question, that he could never have asked it on the twelfth floor of the Lane Kaufmann building. But here, at his table in the Petrel, he felt empowered.

The old man's eyes were twinkling. 'Well, the truth is, it wasn't really *me* who did the work for them. But you know that, don't you?'

Joe was shaking his head, genuinely puzzled. He'd never seen Kaufmann so animated, or, it should be said, in such clear good health. Three months at sea seemed to have smoothed out many of the creases on the old man's face.

'My dear boy, ask yourself this. Why would the COBRA committee be the slightest bit interested in the opinions of an aged Jewish banker? I've been a government adviser for thirty years, but only at a very low level. Once a year or so, they invite me to a workshop at the Treasury to talk about ways of protecting the banking industry in the event of a collapse. All very flattering, of course, but I'm not sure my ideas were ever listened to. Then everything changed in this last year. All of a sudden we had something they wanted. Or perhaps I should say we had *somebody* they wanted.' The banker's eyes gleamed. 'And that wasn't me, Joe Haak; it was *you*.'

'Me?' Joe's head began to swim.

'Of course. Last spring I showed them Cassie. You should have seen their reaction! Half an hour after we started the demonstration the Home Secretary herself came down to have a look at it, and the next thing you know we were trying to find diary slots to show it to the Cabinet Secretary and the Secretary of State for Defence.' Kaufmann leaned forward. 'Cassie saw all of this coming.'

'I know,' Joe said.

'And I dare say you thought her predictions were wrong. So did I, at first. But she wasn't. It was Francis Galton's ox, Joe. No single person saw it coming, but aggregate a thousand opinions and ten thousand forecasts and your map of dependencies and the picture couldn't have been clearer. Five days after we first introduced Cassie to COBRA there was a code red alert.'

Joe was trying to take all this in. 'They used Cassie to help plan for this?'

'Of course. What Cassie did was give us a clear understanding of the way that supply chains would fail, one after the other. She showed us the dependencies one industry had upon another. Oil, transport, power, water . . . it was like lining up a domino cascade with every domino in its correct position. And once we knew that, we could plan.'

'So what was the news that brought you home?'

Kaufmann said, 'It's over.' He stretched out open hands.

'Over?'

'It may not seem like it here at the very tip of the country, but it's true. The lights are going on again. They've been on in London for two weeks. The crisis in the Gulf is over. They've started shipping oil again. The first shipment should be at the refineries within days.' Kaufmann leaned back in his chair and gave Joe a wide smile. 'New vaccines are going into production immediately; we're confident they'll hold back the flu epidemic.'

'But thousands must have died?'

'Millions, I expect. We won't know the full extent for some time. But it hasn't come anywhere near the worst of Cassie's projections. Do you remember the forecasts you showed me back in my office all those weeks ago?'

Joe nodded.

'According to that original projection, the collapse should have been irreversible. Those were the predictions I shared with the COBRA team. We were expecting this to be a one-way process, like the tower of wooden blocks collapsing onto the floor. We thought there was no way back.'

'But there was?'

'One of the clever things about Cassie, Joe, was the way you built it to allow us to test different scenarios. That was very useful. I remember the first time you showed it to me, you varied the temperature of the relationship between Saudi Arabia and Iran. That was clever. It meant that we could take Cassie's predictions and vary some of our assumptions. Sometimes when we did, it didn't make much difference. We could see what might happen, for instance, if we were to alter the price of oil; but it was already so high that nothing we could do would make a difference. But one day, soon after the crisis started, when *Cassandra's Dream* was halfway to the Azores, I took a call from Toby Maltings. What would happen, he asked me, if we changed our assumptions on human nature?'

The ghost of a smile was starting to play over Joe's face.

'I told him to try it. We'd been assuming that hunger and desperation would set neighbour against neighbour. We'd thought that the failure of the currency, the collapse of law and order – all of these things – we thought they'd lead to anarchy. It seemed inevitable.'

Three square meals away from anarchy,' Joe echoed.

'And anarchy was part of the equation. It was what made the collapse irreversible. If society collapses, then workers won't go back to work. Delivery drivers won't risk their lives to deliver fuel. Power station workers won't walk twenty miles to work, risking injury or assault, just to get the machinery working. It's simple self-interest. Networks collapse. Confidence dives. Currencies go up in smoke. We had no reason to expect anything else. Self-interest is the most powerful force in economics.'

Joe was nodding. 'Perhaps it is.' He could picture the algorithms, could see it the way that Lew Kaufmann saw it, red lines on graphs plunging unstoppably downwards. But human beings could confound equations. 'Perhaps it is the most powerful force . . . in *economics*.'

There were raised voices outside in the Harbour Square. Someone was calling his name. Through the door of the pub came Casey Limber and Mallory Books. 'I said you'd find him here,' Casey was saying.

'Friends of Joe?' asked Mallory, crossing the pub and extending a hand to Tom Kaufmann.

'Yes.'

'Then . . . welcome to St Piran.' Mallory shook each of the Kaufmanns' hands in turn. 'I'm sorry for this, but I'm going to have to take him away from you.' He turned to Joe. 'We need to get going, my lad. Your visitors are arriving.'

Together they climbed the cobbled hill to the church gate, stopping once or twice to allow Lew Kaufmann and Mallory Books to gather their breath. A crowd of St Piran villagers had collected at the top of the lane. The church bells were ringing. From the stile alongside the church, the clifftop path snaked away from the village, following the twists and turns of the coastline. From here it was possible to see almost a mile of the footpath; and all the way down the pathway into the valley and up from the other side, like a trail of refugees from a conflict, came a column of people, walkers, in twos and threes, in family groups, carrying babies, holding hands, clutching baskets and bags.

Joe and the Kaufmanns made their way through the throng to the stile. Waiting there was Martha Fishburne and a choir of children from the school, all lined up beside the dry-stone wall.

'Here 'e is!' called Martha, and a 'hurrah' went up from the children. The cheer was picked up by the crowd. 'And not a moment too soon. We've bin waitin' for you,' Martha told Joe. 'Now we can start.'

She nodded to the lines of children. From the back row a clear melody emerged from a clarinet – Emily Horsmith proving to be a musical talent – and in the perfect beat of silence that followed this introduction, the singing started.

'Oh little town of Bethlehem, how still we see thee lie.'

Leading the long retinue of Treadangel visitors was the couple Joe had met the day before. They greeted Joe with an embrace, as if they were old friends.

'Above thy deep and dreamless sleep, the silent stars go by . . .'

'Welcome to St Piran,' Joe said. 'Merry Christmas.'

'Merry Christmas to you.'

'But in thy dark streets shineth the everlasting light . . .'

And then the visitors were pouring through the gate and over the stile, pale and cold, panting from the climb, thin from weeks of deprivation. But every face wore a smile.

'The hopes and fears of all the years . . .'

Alvin Hocking appeared from within the crowd like a ghost, wearing his full clerical gowns. He laid a hand on Joe's arm. 'Merry Christmas, Joe.'

'. . . are met in thee tonight.'

'And to you.'

'Shall I take over?'

'If you wish.'

As the line of visitors began to build up behind the stile the vicar planted himself by the churchyard gate and set to embracing each person in turn. 'God bless you, my child,' he said warmly. 'Happy Christmas. Welcome to St Piran.'

In due course he was joined by Polly, who slid her hand into his. 'Don't hold them up,' she whispered. 'The food is ready.'

'Of course. Of course.'

In the churchyard the barbecue fires were blazing. The lines for food began to grow, plates held in outstretched arms for ladles of meaty stew.

'God rest you merry, gentlemen. Let nothing you dismay,' sang the choir.

It was a hubbub of people, and they swarmed through the churchyard clutching plates and spoons. In time there was insufficient room in the church or in the churchyard to accommodate them all, so the crowd spilled out into the lane, and down the hill, and still they came up the cliff path and through the gate; older people now, toiling weakly up the track. 'Greetings,' Alvin was saying. He'd stopped trying to hug every visitor by now. 'Happy Christmas.'

'Happy Christmas, Vicar.'

'Good King Wenceslas looked out, on the feast of Stephen . . .'

Jeremy Melon squeezed through a press of people to find Joe and the Kaufmanns. 'There's our Good King Wenceslas,' he said, poking Joe lightly in the ribs and pointing at Hocking. 'The good king distributing his Christmas largesse to the needy.'

Joe smiled at this. 'He's doing a good job.'

'All the same . . . you'd think it was his idea. His whale.'

'It wasn't anybody's whale. I used to think of her as my whale, but of course she wasn't. She was a wild creature. Nobody owned her when she was alive, and no one owns her now.' Joe put his hand on Jeremy's arm. 'I'm sad she's dead. I wish she was still out there, where she belongs. She saved my life once.'

'But now she's feeding all these people.'

'Yes,' Joe said. He found himself looking out towards the ocean. He had become used to looking for her there, his whale, out among the dark rocks and the rolling waves. 'Yes, she is.'

They found a stretch of low wall where Lew and Mallory could sit, and one by one they took their turns in the queue to join the banquet. The Anderssens and the Magwiths were ladling broth out of twenty-gallon drums, Jessie and Bo'sun Higgs were piling dishes with mounds of rice and beans,

Charity, Casey, Kenny and the Bartle sisters were straining noodles and pasta. Aminata and the Penhallows were spooning out vegetables.

'Plenty to go around,' Bevis Magwith said when he saw Joe. 'When they're all done, send folk around for second helpings.'

'I've never eaten whale before,' Cassie Kaufmann said. She looked a little hesitant, hovering over the plate with her spoon.

'Well, I hope you never have to eat it again,' Joe said.

'Think of it as beef,' Jeremy suggested. 'There's a whole cow in there somewhere.'

'Don't think of it as anything,' said Mallory Books. 'Just fill your stomach.'

Demelza Trevarrick joined them, her plate heaped high. 'It isn't exactly cordon bleu.' She pressed up close to Jeremy. 'But it's perfectly edible.'

It took more than two hours to feed everyone for the first time, but by mid-afternoon the cooking still hadn't stopped. There were changes of shift at the cauldrons. The Thoroughgoods and the Moots took over from the Magwiths and the Anderssens. Throughout the feast the Shaunessys and the Robins never stopped barrowing whale-meat up from the beach. The cooks were searing steaks over the fires and dropping the blackened pieces into the stew as fast as the queue could file past to fill their plates. The boys were still arriving with firewood. Fresh barrels of mulled cider and blackberry wine were being poured, smoke was billowing between the gravestones and up through the yew trees, and still the choir sang.

'Time for a break,' Martha finally announced once the full repertoire of carols had been exhausted for the third time. But by now a rival Treadangel choir had formed. They took their places, children and adults, and started on 'The Twelve Days of Christmas'.

Joe drifted away from the Kaufmanns. He was looking for Polly, but wherever she was, she didn't appear to be in the crowd outside the church.

A hand touched his arm. It was the girl from Treadangel. 'I'm Susannah,' she said.

'I'm Joe.'

'I know. You introduced yourself yesterday. How can we ever thank you?' A red-eyed toddler was sitting on Susannah's hip, and she bunched the child up with a hug as she spoke.

Joe shook his head. 'You don't need to.'

'You didn't have to feed us all. You could have kept it for yourselves.'

'It was a *very* big whale.'

'All the same . . .'

'And it's Christmas.'

He had seen Polly. She was talking with a Treadangel man, a tall youth with a thin beard and heavy eyebrows. Her elbow was resting against his chest, her tongue idly playing around her lips.

He looked back at Susannah. Yesterday she'd been biting into raw fish. 'I'm sorry it wasn't Christmas turkey and roast potatoes.'

'It was better.' With her free arm she pulled Joe's head forward and kissed him.

'Have you had a second helping?'

'I've had thirds.'

What a party this was. Joe slipped away and made his way over to the fires, where the cooks were still at work. There was still a queue, still plates to fill.

'Four calling birds, three French hens, two turtle doves . . .'

'It's the feeding of the five thousand,' came a voice from behind him. He turned. Alvin Hocking was grinning.

'Well, it certainly feels like a miracle.'

'It's the closest thing to a miracle I've ever seen,' said a Treadangel man, joining the conversation. 'They say the chap who did this filled the whole church tower with food.'

Alvin smiled across at Joe. 'So they say.'

'And they say he's used the whole lot of it for this meal.'

'Apparently he has.'

'And he caught the whale himself.'

'Now that,' said Joe, 'might be going just a bit too far.'

In the smoke underneath the yew trees Polly had attracted more men. She was doing a little dance, wiggling her waist to 'The Twelve Days of Christmas'. Joe turned away. 'I need to find my guests.'

Mallory Books and the Kaufmanns were still on the wall where he had left them. 'I've sent young Thomas Horsmith down to my house to fetch the Clynelish,' Mallory said. 'They've run right out of cider.'

Joe laughed. 'I thought the whisky was for emergencies. What's the emergency?'

'The emergency is – there's no whisky!'

The singing ended and the sound of Old Man Garrow's squeeze-box rose up from behind the churchyard wall, joined by Kenny Kennet's penny whistle and Bo'sun Higgs's banjo. The time for carols had passed. It was time for dancing. But not before an announcement. 'One moment please, Kenny, Arwen!' Alvin Hocking was climbing onto a tombstone to speak. The musicians obliged and parts of the crowd began to fall silent.

'Everybody . . . everybody . . .' The vicar was used to having a crowd's full attention, but it was clear he wasn't going to get that here. He raised his voice to compensate. 'Everyone . . . I have some short announcements.'

The hubbub dropped to a hum.

'We want to wish everybody from Treadangel a very merry Christmas from the villagers of St Piran,' he announced.

'He already did that,' Jeremy whispered caustically to Joe. 'When they all arrived.'

'I want to thank everyone who worked so hard to make this fine meal. Too many people to mention, and if I try to name names then I'll probably miss some out, and that wouldn't do. So let me just say a very big thank-you to everyone here in St Piran.'

There was a huge cheer at this.

'He should thank the whale,' Jeremy said. 'It made the biggest contribution.'

'As most of you know, I run the ministry here in St Piran as well as St Luke's in Treadangel. Of course, as we all know, it hasn't been possible to run services at both churches these past few weeks, for reasons we all understand.'

'There was nothing to stop him,' muttered Jeremy. 'He'd *had* the flu. He could have gone back and forward without any problem. It was just the thought of a four-mile walk across the cliffs that put him off.'

'But I'm glad to say that I shall be back in St Luke's for the service on Sunday morning. I do hope as many of you as possible will be able to join me there.'

'They'd come if he offered them a slap-up meal.' Jeremy was clearly intent on offering a running commentary on the vicar's contribution.

'Jeremy!' Joe chided.

'Sorry.'

'We'd like you all to stay a little longer. We have rice pudding and fruit – enough for everyone but only a small helping, I'm afraid. And then there'll be time for more . . . socialising.'

'I see young Polly's been doing some socialising already.'

Joe found himself smiling at this remark.

'But we can't have everyone walking back over the cliffs after dark. It would be far too dangerous. So we have another little surprise . . .'

'A helicopter?' Jeremy ventured.

'Mr Magwith is reopening the lane.' The vicar paused as if expecting a cheer. When none came, he soldiered on. 'Mr Magwith has a cattle lorry with enough diesel for half a dozen round trips to Treadangel. We think he can take fifty or sixty people at a time, so anyone who has difficulty walking, please avail yourselves of a lift home.'

This announcement did earn a cheer, and Hocking smiled at the response.

'For everyone else, we will be lighting lanterns all the way down the lane to light your way home.'

'Please, whatever you do, don't pray,' Jeremy said in a low voice.

'I know some of you want me to say a prayer . . .'

'No, we don't.'

'But what I suggest is that each one of us makes their own silent prayer.'

'Good idea.'

'I'm told that there is still plenty of meat from the whale. I'm also reliably told that it must be eaten fresh. So please, before you leave us this evening, if you have baskets, take them down to Piran Sands and fill them. The best of the meat may be gone, but what is left is still nutritious. We should thank God for sending us the whale.'

'God must be a pretty dab hand with a shotgun then.'

Joe put a hand in front of his mouth. He was at risk of laughing.

'I leave you with Mr Garrow, Mr Kennet and Mr Higgs, and their very individual musical style. Thank you once again. And Merry Christmas.' The vicar beamed widely, and stepped down from his podium.

'He can never resist a platform,' Jeremy muttered. 'Is there any more of that cider left?'

'If we're patient, Mallory might let us have a drop of his Scotch.'

'That's the best thing anyone has said all afternoon. Lead me to him.'

34

A heart as big as five men

They hold a special party every year in St Piran; they call it the 'Festival of the Whale'. Whatever the weather, on Christmas Day, the villagers climb the hill to the empty churchyard, and a choir of children forms, and they sing the carols, just as they have always done, and the families all gather around and applaud. They never cook a whale, of course. These days they manage with fresh fish and baked potatoes, slices of Christmas cake, and mince pies. The children draw a whale on a huge roll of paper and they hang it on the wall of the empty church as a reminder of the apocalypse and the whale. Those that were there on that day sit heavily on the stones and tell the story. Thomas Horsmith tells them about the whale. He demonstrates its size and he shows them how the men hacked away at it with saws and knives and axes to strip away all the blubber and the meat. 'We et its liver,' he tells them. 'Its liver were as large as a house. Its heart were as big as five men. Good meat on that heart, mind. And we barrelled up more blubber 'n you can imagine.'

When it starts to get dark they turn off every light in the village. 'This is how it was,' Charity Limber tells the crowd as they look out over the grey rooftops and black windowpanes. 'When night fell, there wasn't a light in the village. Not a glimmer. The darkness would come down, and folk would light candles, or they'd huddle around fires. That's what we did that night. That was when it happened.'

'Tell us how it happened,' a child will ask. The children know that the men are in the village, waiting for the sign.

'It were the very end of the party,' Charity says. 'All the food had been eaten, all the plates cleared. Old Bevis had pulled up in the lane in his lorry, ready to take the Treadangel folk home. But it weren't quite over. We had one last carol to sing.'

'And who sung it, Mrs Limber?'

'It was supposed to be me. That was how we'd practised it. But when the time came I couldn't do it. I was holding my Casey's hand and he says to me, "You're on now, Charity," and I shook my head. I says, "I can't sing. Not in front of all these people." "But you have to," he says. And then a voice says, "I'll sing . . ."'

'Who was it, Mrs Limber?'

'Her name was Aminata. She was an African lady, a few years older'n me, but just about the sweetest and prettiest girl in the whole village. She had a smile that would light up a room. A nurse, she was, but a singer too. She climbed up on this stone here, and all the crowd fell quiet. They knew this was the last song of the night.'

And on this cue, every year, one of the village girls climbs up onto the tomb where Aminata had stood, ready to replay that moment.

Charity is pausing. She does this when she tells the tale. She wants to use the silent seconds to create the effect. She looks around the crowd of faces. Young and old, they are quiet now, holding their breath. The youngest have their hands in front of their mouths. 'There was . . . a short note on a clarinet,' Charity says.

A clarinettist alongside Charity recreates the note. The villagers of St Piran know what's about to happen.

'Then two things occurred at the same time. Aminata opened her mouth, and out came the most beautiful voice you can imagine . . .'

The girl on the stone tips back her head and starts to sing. '*Silent night*,' she sings, '*Holy night* . . .' And even now, half a century later, the magic of that moment is preserved every year at the St Piran Festival of the Whale. Even now that perfect note sends a tingle down every spine. Even now it is possible to believe, for that briefest of spells, that there was never any sin in the world, that hardship is an illusion, that the great mysteries of birth and death, of love and loss, of consciousness and being, can all be distilled into a single clear voice. On that first banquet in St Piran, there was hardly a couple who didn't hold hands in that moment; barely a child who didn't look up at a parent's face; scarcely an eye that didn't blink back a tear. No one moved. No one breathed.

And in the village of St Piran, every Christmas day, as the singer hits the end of the first line, the lights start to go on in the village; just as they did so many years before. Today the men are throwing switches, all the way down the streets, so that in every window a light will glow, and the dark shadows of the houses will be transformed. Today the villagers wait for that moment. A great cheer goes up when the first light shines, and all around the village windows are illuminated, until the whole valley seems like a carnival of lights.

On that first Christmas night there was no such expectation.

'All is calm,' Aminata sang.

And all was calm.

'All is bright . . .'

The stained-glass windows of the parish church of St Piran the Martyr illustrate scenes from the lives of the apostles. When illuminated from inside they cast a multicoloured blush of light across the yew trees and the gravestones outside. Someone had left the light switch on, so when the power came back to the village, the crowd was bathed in a kaleidoscope of warm light. And if anyone wondered, just for a moment, if this had been planned (perhaps a generator was lighting up the church), there were suddenly lights all the way down the valley. The street lights shone. The harbour lights shone. There were bulbs burning in attic rooms and front rooms, in bedrooms and bathrooms; every switch that had been left on was channelling electricity. And as it dawned upon everyone what had happened, a cry went up.

'*Sleep in heavenly peace*,' sang Aminata. '*Sleep in heavenly peace*.'

The switching-on of the lights marks the end of the Festival of the Whale. Villagers pull their coats tight around themselves, and they make their way out of the churchyard gate and back down the hill to their homes. It was the end, too, of that first Christmas celebration. There were thanks, and goodbyes. The advance party set off along the lane with armfuls of lanterns, and behind them came the walkers in their family groups, and Bevis with his first lorry-load of passengers. It was the end of a day of revels. Joe found himself alongside Alvin and Polly at the church gates. Hands were being shaken. 'Thank you, Vicar, thank you, Vicar . . .'

'God bless you, my child. God bless you.'

It felt like an ending, Joe thought. Like emerging from a very long tunnel; like stepping onto dry land after a voyage across an ocean. Sometimes life could do this. It could draw a line. Beyond this line, life would say, nothing will ever be the same. The sun will rise tomorrow but it will rise onto a different world.

The line had been there when Mamma died. The Beatles sang 'She Loves You', and somewhere between the opening chords and the closing chorus they had all crossed it, Joe and Brigitha and Mamma too.

The line was there too when Janie died. He'd been asleep when she crossed that particular line. On this side is the world you know. On the other . . . is something else.

Mamma used to love Christmas. In his mind Joe unfolded the picture of his mother. There she was, opening gifts, skin as perfect as alabaster, teeth as white as chalk. There was the tear-drop in her eye, where it always was, and there was the smile. Five months after the camping trip, after the night north of Rouen. She looks up at him and she meets his gaze. Had there been wrinkles around her eyes? He couldn't remember any. No wrinkles then. Just pure, perfect eyes. But a voice in his mind had lodged a disagreement. She *did* have lines around her eyes, the voice said. Did she? And what colour were her eyes? They were green, Joe remembered. They were grey, said the voice.

Could he be forgetting? Could he possibly ever forget Mamma's face?

He had crossed another line. Mamma's face was fading. Like every line that life draws, Joe thought, there is never a way back. There is only forward. He could not re-remember the image. He could only lose it.

He had crossed a line too the morning that he woke in the bell tower and felt the disease gone from his body. That was a different sort of line. That was a second chance. Perhaps, Joe thought, it was a third chance.

And now another line. He knew it as he saw the last Treadangel family wave goodbye. His store was almost gone. The whale was gone. The lights were back on. But what did the future hold for Joe Haak?

Hedra Penhallow sought out Joe and the Kaufmanns. She bustled up to them as they were readying to leave the churchyard. 'We can offer you rooms in the B&B,' she said. 'Free of charge.'

'That's kind of you,' Tom Kaufmann said. 'But we can sleep on our boat.'

'I won't hear of it,' Hedra said. 'You'll sleep on dry land. Now that the electricity is back on we may even have running water.'

'Thank you,' Tom said. 'But we can't put you to that trouble. Besides, we may want to sail at first light.'

'I wish I was in my own bed,' Cassie said. 'My own bed at home.'

They walked back down the hill. Mallory said goodnight and disappeared into his cottage. Jeremy and Demelza slipped away into the shadows. There was only Joe now, and the Kaufmanns.

'Does this mean the crisis is really over?' Joe asked Lew.

'It's exactly as I told you, Joe. It has taken a while. But yes. It *is* over.' Lew Kaufmann looked tired. It had been a long day for him. Kate came across to support him.

'Can we have this conversation on the boat?'

The tide was low and the catamaran was floating several feet below the level of the harbour wall. The gangplank sloped down at an intimidating angle towards the rear deck.

'Dear God,' Lew said, 'I'll never get across that.' He sank heavily down onto a capstan.

'We'll help you, Father,' Tom said. But even he seemed to hesitate at the prospect.

'We could still get you a room in the B&B,' Joe suggested.

'No thank you. No.'

'Then we shall all lift you aboard,' Tom said.

'No.' Lew held up a hand. 'I won't be lugged around like a sack of fish. I'm too old for that. Please hear what I have to say first.'

'Very well, Father.'

'Mr Haak?' Lew turned towards Joe. 'Mr Haak, we need a conversation.'

'Do we, sir?'

'We do. We have important things to discuss.' The old man was breathing heavily. 'Tell me something, Joe. What happened here today?'

'Pardon, sir?'

'You heard me, Joe. What happened here?'

'I'm not sure what you mean, sir. You were here.'

'Yes, Joe. I was here.' Lew was regaining his breath. 'And you are an economist. And so am I. And that is why I'm struggling to make sense of this.'

'I'm still not sure . . .'

'Come and sit down, son.' The old man gestured at a pile of empty herring boxes. 'We can't do this with me sitting and you hovering.'

Joe lowered himself gingerly onto the boxes.

'They tell me you spent your whole life's savings on food, and you stored it away in the church tower . . .'

'Well. In a manner of speaking . . .'

'. . . and that you shared it out among the people of the village?'

Joe nodded.

'And today that same village squandered the windfall of a whole whale, and the entire contents of your food reserves, on a party for another village altogether?'

'I can see how it might look . . .'

'How it *might* look? Tell me how it *should* look, Joe. I'm keen to understand.'

How should it look? Joe turned towards the ocean. It was too dark to see. I made a promise, he thought. A long time ago I made a promise to Mamma. And it did seem like a long time ago now. On a cold, fresh morning he'd abandoned his clothes on the rocks close to here, and walked out into this ocean. He could recollect the sting of the icy water and the pull of the undertow; and that moment when he'd given in to the cold and fallen forward into the surf. He remembered swimming, feeling the sea enveloping him like a monstrous, living being. He could recall it scouring, cleansing, and bleaching away every last shred of stress and anxiety from his bones. But when he'd tried to turn around, his way had been blocked. For there had been the whale. And as she plunged into the depths, so he was drawn down with her. That was the way with whales. That was the way, he realised, with the bank. As it had plunged, so had he.

'Why are you here, sir?' he asked. 'Why did you come to St Piran?'

'We came for you, Joe.'

Of course. They hadn't come to visit him. They had come to collect him.

'Where do you want to take me?'

'Back.'

Back to the City? Back to the bank? Back to his desk on the fifth floor? But Kaufmann seemed to read his mind. 'It won't be back to the bank,' he said.

'Where then?'

'They need you at the Home Office. At COBRA. They need your skills.'

'Did they send you to fetch me? Is this why you left the Azores?'

Kaufmann looked uncomfortable.

'You don't need me,' Joe said. 'Really you don't. There are a million computer programmers in London. Pick any one.'

'No one else has your insight, Joe. No one else knows how Cassie really works. We need to fix her. So much has changed; we need to update her. Most of all we need her to understand this.' Kaufmann lifted a thin hand to indicate the village.

'This?'

'Cassie would never have factored in what happened here. Even with the wisdom of a thousand economists and a million news reports, she would never have predicted this. And it wasn't just here. Similar things have been happening in every village, town and city that we know of. And it wasn't just the whale. Nor was it just *your* food store. You weren't the only benefactor in St Piran, Joe. I've been speaking to people today. The farmer gave his milk. The smallholders gave their vegetables and their cider. The fishermen fished. The doctor gave his time and skills. Some people worked all day carving up that carcase, some carried firewood, some cooked. Where is the currency for all this? What is the medium of exchange?'

Somewhere in Joe's head he could hear the purity of a single voice.

'There is no medium of exchange,' he said. 'Cassie wouldn't understand it.' He was thinking of the algorithms, the mathematical cog-wheels that constituted Cassie's brain. The columns always had to add up. Credit always equals debit. Self-interest always applies.

'That's why we need you, Joe. We need you to change that.'

'We can't make Cassie predict everything,' Joe said. 'There are too many uncertainties. Too many unknowns.' He gave a shrug of submission. 'After all, who could have predicted that a whale would end up on our beach?'

'Or that a crazy man would fill a church with food?'

Or that a promise I made to Mamma would have to be kept, Joe thought.

Lew was breathing heavily again. 'But some things we *have* to predict. There's too much at stake if we get this wrong. This isn't about share prices. It was never really about share prices. You know that, don't you? This is about planning for . . . if . . . when . . . this happens again. It's about trying to save lives, Joe.'

'I know.' Joe was looking out to sea again now, trying to picture how it might work. 'Look at the ocean,' he said. 'It rises and it falls. I can forecast with complete confidence that in just a few hours from now the sea will fill this harbour, and the yacht will be level with the quay. But look at that man.' He pointed across to the figure of Daniel Robins coiling up ropes on the deck of a small boat. 'Where will he be in a few hours? Will he be tucked up in his bed, or will he be out at sea? Or somewhere else? I can predict the movement of a great ocean, but not that of a single man. What software could predict that, eh?'

For a while the two of them sat and contemplated the great ocean. Then Lew spoke again. 'The thing is, we don't need to know what one man would do. We need to know what a hundred people would do.'

Or a thousand. Or a million. Or three hundred and seven.

Joe said, 'The funny thing is, we shouldn't be surprised by what happened. Think about the people you know. Think about your friends, your family, your neighbours. How many of them would you describe as violent or dangerous? Why did we ever imagine that when the crisis came we'd suddenly all change into different people?'

'Maybe we listened too closely to our old friend Thomas Hobbes.'

'Maybe we did.'

'*Where every man is enemy to every man . . . there is no place for industry . . .*' Lew was quoting. '*No knowledge of the face of the earth, no account of time, no arts, no letters, no society, and which worst of all, the continual fear and danger of violent death.*'

'I remember,' Joe whispered.

'*And the life of man solitary, poor, nasty, brutish, and short.*'

'I'd forgotten how bleak Hobbes's vision was.'

'But perhaps we didn't read him carefully enough. Hobbes's Leviathan survives because of a social contract that binds us all together. When Hobbes said that our natural condition was nasty, brutish, and short, he also showed us that we can rise above our situation and build societies that support each other.' Kaufmann rested his thin hand on his knees. 'Perhaps it isn't the behaviour of others that we fear. Maybe we're frightened that we'll be the ones who will change.'

'Maybe.'

'Then come and help us teach Cassie that.' The old man beckoned to his granddaughter. 'Help me up, will you, child.' He rose ponderously to his feet. 'Understand me, Joe, I don't expect you to come today.'

Joe lifted himself off the herring boxes. 'You don't?'

'No. I know you better than you think I do. You're not ready yet. But when you are ready, you should come to the Home Office and ask for Toby Maltings. Tell him Lew Kaufmann sent you.'

Joe nodded slowly.

Lew turned to his granddaughter. 'Do you still wish you were in your own bed?'

'Wouldn't that be wonderful!'

'If we left now, you could be in your bed before midnight,' Lew Kaufmann said.

Tom came over and placed a kindly hand on his father's elbow. 'There is no way we could do that,' he said. 'The tide is too low, it's way too dark, and we're still two days' sailing from Sandbanks.'

But Lew Kaufmann was grinning. In the cool glow of the harbour lights his ancient lined face seemed animated. 'Who said we had to sail?' he asked. 'They've reopened the road. And we're only four hours away by car.'

Tom looked confused. 'But we don't have a car . . .'

'No. But Joe does. And I'm betting he can find enough fuel to get us home.'

A strange silence seemed to have settled upon the group.

'Please, Grandpa . . . let's do that,' Cassie said.

Joe was shaking his head. 'It's a coupé. It won't fit five people . . .' But it might work, he was thinking. Alvin had given him back the keys. And there was still fuel in the store.

'Will it fit four?'

'Well, yes, but . . .'

Lew held out his hand. 'When currencies break down,' he said, 'we need other mediums of exchange. Would you swap your car for my boat?'

35

It's called moving on

A hazy morning mist had settled over the village. Something similar had settled over Joe. He sat on a bench in the churchyard. Where had he learned this patience? An hour passed. Then another. And there was Alvin Hocking stalking down the hill towards the village, a Bible tucked beneath his arm.

He tried the door of the Vicarage. 'Polly?'

She was there in hipster jeans and a man's rugby shirt.

'Joe!'

They stood, one at each end of the hallway, an uncomfortable gap stretching out between them.

'Happy Christmas,' Joe said. 'I don't think I had the opportunity to say it properly yesterday.'

'They're saying it's all over,' Polly said.

'Yes,' Joe said, 'they are.'

'Is it true?'

'I expect so.'

'Were you looking for Alvin?'

'No. It's you I wanted to see.'

Neither made a move to close the gulf between them. The long hallway with its gilded mirror, its polished table and heavy Bible, the plain crucifix that hung on the landing – all seemed like barriers that could not be breached.

'We don't have anything to talk about, do we?' Polly said. 'Not any more.'

Joe drew a step closer, but she retreated back into the shadow.

Joe let out a sigh. 'I'm thinking of leaving.'

Her face was as still as a painting. 'Leaving St Piran?'

He nodded. Wheels were turning in the carriage clock as it contemplated chiming.

'With those friends?'

'No. They left last night.'

She considered this. 'Where will you go?'

'That might depend.'

She moved forward just a step, and a shaft of light from the landing window caught her. There was a glow to her face, a bloom in her cheeks; in the cold December light she seemed almost radiant.

'I want you to come with me,' he said.

They were frozen in a fresco, he hesitating, she retreating. The carriage clock began to strike.

'I can't,' she said.

'Why not?'

Her face seemed to tell him the answer.

'I don't understand,' he said.

'What don't you understand, Joe? I've already told you. Find another girl.' God, she looked beautiful in the shadows. The big shirt hung on her loosely like a tent, yet still she seemed all curves and mysteries beneath.

'Why are you being like this? Before Alvin and I went into the tower, you and I were friends. I thought we were more than friends. I thought you liked me.'

'I do like you, Joe.' A very small voice.

'Then why have you been avoiding me? Why did you brush me off that night in the churchyard?'

She shrugged. There was something petulant in her expression.

'You deserve better,' he whispered.

But Polly shook her head and her face became a scowl. 'Do I? Do I *really* deserve better? What have I done to deserve better?' She stepped a little closer and held out her hands. 'Have I done great works? Am I a wonderful humanitarian? Am I a teacher? Or a healer? What have I done? Hmm?' She looked at him and her eyes were sharp enough to cut. 'Or do I deserve better because my cheekbones look like this, and my tits push out just this far, and my eyes, and my hips, and my waist look just this way?'

Joe was shaking his head, but he couldn't find any words.

'You don't even *know* me, Joe. Not really. You think you do because one day we took a drive together. Because I took an interest in you when you were feeling low. But that doesn't mean you know me. Not really. So why do I deserve better? Is it because I'm a fine and wonderful person with a mind that everyone overlooks? Or is it because I'm a flirt who can hook men the way that Dan Robins hooks fish? Or is it just because you want to bed me, Joe Haak?'

He found himself looking away, uncomfortable with the question. 'It isn't that,' he said.

'Isn't it?'

He wanted to say the words. I love you, Polly Hocking. I love you, but the words stopped before they reached his tongue. 'Now you're scaring me.' That was what Clare Manners had said. And he wasn't even sure if the words were true. He *wanted* them to be true. But maybe his eyes told a different story. Half the village think we're at it like rabbits. 'I do want you.' That at least was true. He did want her.

'Do *you* deserve *me*, Joe Haak?'

He shook his head and suddenly there was a tear in his eye.

'Everyone in the village thinks you're a saint, Joe, but I know it's not true. You know it too. This isn't a shopping trip to St Ives, is it, Joe? This isn't a road test in your new car?'

He shook his head. 'No.'

'Then what are you asking me, Joe? Exactly what?'

When the gap between them closed it was Polly who moved. 'Maybe neither of us deserves the other, Joe.' Now her hand was behind his head pulling him forward, but the kiss was a short one. It was a goodbye kiss. 'Not as good as you expected, was it?'

'Better,' he said, but it wasn't.

'I'm a flirt, Joe. That's who I am. I enjoy the company of good-looking young men.'

'Is that all I was?'

'Of course not.'

'But?'

She turned her face away.

'The whole village . . .' he started to say, but his voice trailed off. How could he finish this?

'I know,' Polly said. She squeezed his hand. 'The village thinks we're wanton, lustful teenagers. They think we steal away together every night. They imagine we spend the night screwing each other down on Piran Sands.' She held his gaze. 'Do you remember that day in St Ives?'

He nodded.

'You told me how your computer worked. Do you remember?'

'Yes.'

'If enough people think a thing is true, then it probably *is* true. Isn't that how it worked?'

He blinked back a tear. 'Something like that.' It may not have been an explanation that Francis Galton would have recognised, but wasn't that what the wisdom of crowds was? Ask a large number of people and average out their answers. Ask them if this share price will rise. Ask them the weight of an ox. Ask three hundred people in St Piran and they will tell you that Polly Hocking and Joe Haak were lovers. Shouldn't that make it true?

'But it doesn't always work that way, does it, Joe?'

It doesn't always work. Three hundred people can be wrong. A thousand people can be wrong. The whole world can be wrong. Even poetry can be wrong. 'I don't suppose it does,' he whispered.

She pulled him close again. This time it was a longer kiss. She felt soft in his arms.

'Do you wish it *was* true?' he asked, when their lips finally parted.

'Do I wish we were making love all night down on the sands? In December? We'd freeze to death.'

'What if it was summer?'

'Then it would be far too light. There'd be holidaymakers all over the beach. Walkers. People in boats. Teenagers getting stoned.'

'What if we went to Florence? Or Venice? Or Rome?'

She smiled. 'That's not a plan. That's a dream.' She was moving away. 'I'd love to be in Florence with you, Joe. But you wouldn't. You'd hate it. You'd hate me flirting with Italian men. You'd get bored by my whims and fancies. You have your own dreams to follow. You don't want to spend your life following mine.'

'I wouldn't mind.' He was shaking his head. 'If it meant we were together.'

'And you'd never forgive yourself for taking me away from Alvin.'

'Wouldn't I?'

'No, Joe. I know you. Alvin isn't a bad man. You know that more than anyone. You're the only person in St Piran, apart from me, who has lived with him. He has his problems. But we all do, don't we?'

'He has more than most.'

'Which is why he needs me.' Polly released his hand.

'Does he?'

'More than you'll ever know.' Her expression told him the conversation was coming to a close.

'I think perhaps there *is* a saint in St Piran,' Joe said softly. 'And it isn't me. And it isn't Alvin.'

'I don't think they'll be renaming the village.' She smiled at him. 'I would like to say come back to St Piran and see me some time.' She looked down. 'But I can't say that, can I?'

'Why not?'

'Do I have to tell you, Joe? You disappoint me.' She looked back up at him.

'I would rather you did.'

'Because I don't want to spend the rest of my life looking out for you. I don't want to watch every car that comes down that lane and wonder if it's you. I don't want to have to look twice at every blond-haired tourist. I have to be able to get on with my life. So I need you to promise me that if you go – *when* you go – you'll never come back.'

'Never?' The suggestion shocked him. This was his home now, this haphazard collection of houses, this bay, this harbour, this church. He knew the best places in the cove to fish. He knew the winds and currents and eddies of the shoreline. He knew every face. He knew the names. Leaving for ever wouldn't be easy.

'Never.' There was sorrow in her face, but she raised her hand again to touch him. 'I can't spend the next ten years waiting for you to show up on the harbour with a girl on your arm.'

He shook his head. 'I wouldn't do that.' But the suggestion stung, with its echo of the truth.

'Even so. I can't live two lives, Joe. Alvin isn't always easy. You know that. If I'm waiting for you to reappear in the village one day, will I try quite so hard to make things work between us? Or will I give up too soon? Either you and I run away together now and make babies on a beach in Spain, or we build new lives without each other in them.'

'Let's do that first one then,' he said. He tried to smile. 'I could do Spain.'

'No, Joe. We already did that conversation.'

'Then why? Why, if we don't care a jot about each other, would you mind me coming back? Why would you give it a moment's thought? I'd just be another stranger on the beach.'

She looked at him. 'You already know the answer to that question. And if you don't, then you need to work it out for yourself.'

Joe wiped his arm across his face; her words were hard to digest.

'No letters,' she said. 'No messages. No emails.'

'None?'

'It's called *moving on*, Joe.'

Moving on.

'Don't look back,' Dr Marcia Brodie had told him. '*When the day comes, don't hesitate. Get up and walk away. Don't bother to gather up your things or say goodbye. Walk away and don't look back.*'

'I have something for you.' He reached into his pocket, enjoying the expression on her face. 'Think of it as a Christmas present.' He pulled out a set of keys. 'It's Janie's Porsche. She told me I could have it if she died.' He held the keys out and Polly took them hesitantly. 'It's a sports car. When the summer comes you can put the roof down.'

'Won't you need it?'

'Not where I'm going.'

Her hand closed on the keys.

'Remember me,' she said.

'And you me.'

He went to the bell tower and let himself in. He had planned to take some time. To set a date, maybe a month ahead. To have a farewell dinner with Mallory, and with Jeremy and Demelza. But life had drawn another line. You can never go backwards, he thought.

He collected up his few belongings, the clothes he had bought on the shopping trip with Jeremy, and a few provisions from what was left of the store; a few dozen assorted tins, some rice, some oatmeal, some dried beans. He packed them into boxes and tied them into bundles. Then he hefted the first package onto his shoulder and made his way down to the harbour.

'What time is high tide?' he asked Kenny, who was sitting on the harbour wall whittling some wood with a knife.

'You missed it,' Kenny said. 'Are you off fishing?'

'I thought I might,' Joe said.

'This fancy boat yours now, is it?'

Joe nodded. 'I swapped it for my Mercedes.'

'And we thought you'd already swapped that with the vicar . . . for young Polly.'

How the stories grew. And they wouldn't improve once Polly was seen out in the Porsche.

'There's a tide tonight at ten to seven. You wouldn't want to sail then. Next high tide is at a quarter past seven tomorrow morning. Or thereabouts.'

'Thank you.' How did this beachcomber always know the times of every tide?

'It'll still be dark, though. Sun won't be up until after eight. But you could sail out into the bay and watch the sun come up.'

Joe loaded up the catamaran with the contents of his bundle. He looked around the well-appointed cabin. How much more comfortable it was here than in his austere hideaway in the bell tower. He lay back on a bunk and gazed up at the low ceiling. There would have been room here for Polly, he thought. They could have fitted together on this bed. Snug but comfortable.

He collected the rest of his belongings and as much food as he could manage from the bell tower, found five big water containers, and filled them from the village pump. There was no one else at the pump today. The water must be flowing in the pipes again.

He did a check of the boat . . . ropes, and sails, and fenders, and anchors. He pulled tight the mooring ropes, enjoying the familiar feel of them running through his hands.

It was dusk. On the quayside he could hear voices whooping with excitement. He climbed the ladder and peered out over the deck. There were lights on in the Petrel, and in the B&B, and in the fish station, and the shop, and in the harbour master's office. And now strings of Christmas lights were flickering all along the harbour wall, and the old lighthouse was ablaze. A day late, he thought, but welcome all the same. And it wasn't the End Of The World. There were tears in his eyes. He climbed back down the ladder into the cabin. Sounds of laughter were drifting out along the quay, and he was laughing too. How strange it felt to laugh alone. By the light of an oil lamp he folded down the map table and pulled out some of Kaufmann's charts. He'd start by sailing directly out, out of sight of land, away from it all. Maybe, he thought, he could go to Tahiti; or any one of a thousand tropical islands. He could, but the island that beckoned wasn't one with sandy beaches and coconut palms. It was an island with rocky bays and a small woodland of tall pines, and a log cabin with a stone fireplace and a tunnel to the front door through the snow. Brigitha would be there. And Pappa Mikkel. They could roast up a duck and eat *ris ala mande*. They could enjoy a late Christmas. They could raise a glass to Mamma.

He did an inventory of the boat. The Kaufmanns had taken as many of their personal belongings as they could fit in the car, but there were plenty of things left; all manner of tracking devices, crockery and cutlery, sou'westers and waterproofs hanging in a cupboard, books, some food, bottles of fresh water, some red wine, and a whole case of Pedras Brancas – brandy from the Azores.

There would be no goodbyes. Marcia Brodie was right. And so was Polly. Instead Joe sat at the chart table with a shallow glass of wine, and pulled down the charts for Fastnet and for the Irish Sea, and he pored over these until the voices on the shore had grown silent and the fresh new lights had been turned off. When he had exhausted the charts he found some paper in a drawer.

'Dear Mallory,' he wrote.

This brandy is my gift for you. I'm sure you will share it with Jeremy and Demelza and Martha. Alvin Hocking also has a taste for brandy despite anything Martha might tell you. Maybe you could spare him a bottle. I'm leaving in much the same way that I arrived. Alone, in the early morning, and unannounced. Please forgive me for this. I need to find my father and my sister. I miss them more than I ever thought I could.

I owe so much to you and to the people of St Piran. And I've realised that the Christmas banquet was the perfect leaving party. I'd be happiest for it to be my parting memory.

Do take care.

All my love

Joe

He took the letter and the case of brandy to Fish Street and slipped them into the hallway. Mallory was already in bed.

Joe woke before dawn, even before the gulls. He had slept surprisingly well.

Mamma would never sleep well on Pappa Mikkel's boat. She would complain about the rocking. She would grip the sides of her berth and her knuckles would go white from the effort. 'I have to hold on,' she would say, 'or I would fall out of bed.' Pappa would laugh at this. 'You won't fall out of bed.' He would try to release her fingers one by one. 'You have to learn how to let go,' he would say.

Mamma learned how to let go. But Pappa, Pappa was still breathing somewhere, Joe was sure of that. The flu wouldn't have taken Pappa Mikkel. He would have fled to his boat, would have sailed to his island. He didn't mind the cold. 'We have to stay a little cold.' Stay cold and keep breathing. It was the way to defeat death. Breathe in. Breathe out.

Pappa would release Mamma's grasp on the bed, one finger at a time. 'Let me tuck you in,' he would say to her. 'I will tuck your blankets in so tight you could never roll out; not even if we have Jonah's storm.'

That was how she died too; her blankets tucked in tight.

From time to time Joe would hold her hand and would whisper Pappa Mikkel's words back to her. 'Just keep breathing, Mamma. Keep breathing.' Sometimes when she was awake, she would purse her lips to let him see her exhaling, and the gesture would always look to Joe like the blowing of a kiss.

In the days before she died, Mamma's skin seemed thinner than tracing paper. He would have to be careful, even holding her hand. She looked fragile enough to rip in half.

'Mamma spoke to me today,' Brigitha told him, very soon before the end.

'What did she say?'

He was sitting with his sister in the little hospice tea room. They were changing shifts. Brigitha was nineteen now. She could drive. She would drive Mamma's car, the hatchback that had been all the way to the Atlantic coast of France, back to their little house in Blackheath, and she would sleep. It was Joe's turn to sit. To wait for the inevitable.

The walls of the hospice tea room were decorated with the handprints of children, each dipped in a different-colour paint and pressed onto the magnolia walls, each labelled with a name and a date. The mural was only half complete. 'Would you like to add your print to a wall?' a nurse had asked him once. 'The handprints are made by the children of our guests.' They talked about the dying patients in the hospice as *guests*. It made the place sound like a country hotel.

Mamma might have been a guest, but Joe wasn't a child any more.

'Mamma made me promise to be strong,' Brigitha said. 'She told me that life is wonderful. She told me to enjoy my disappointments as well as my achievements, because these will make me stronger.'

'Mamma said all that?'

'Yes.'

'She made you promise?'

'Yes.'

'That's quite profound for Mamma,' Joe said.

'She told me to fall in love, and never to hold back.'

'Is that what she did, do you think? With Pappa?'

'I don't know. Maybe not. She made me promise to enjoy every day. "There is nothing not to enjoy," she said.'

Joe pondered this. 'She hasn't asked me to promise anything,' he said in a low voice.

'Oh, she will. She will.'

When he went in to take his turn, Mamma was asleep. The lights were very low in the hospice room – so low there was barely the brightness of a candle. It would be hard for anyone to stay awake in that gloom. Maybe that was the point; to send the dying to sleep, so then they could stop breathing. Joe fell asleep too, in the straight-backed chair. When he awoke, Mamma's head was turned and her eyes were open. 'I'm sorry, Mamma,' he said. 'I fell asleep.'

She was mouthing something at him. 'What is it, Mamma?' He moved closer. 'Do you need water? Anything?'

She shook her head.

'What are you trying to tell me, Mamma?' He held his face right up beside her and she blew the words into his ear. Just three words. They were the last words she would say in this world.

'Make me proud,' she said.

'I will, Mamma.' He squeezed her hand. 'I promise.'

36
She joined up the dots

Joe dressed, climbed up the boat ladder, and stepped across onto the dock. He started to untie the moorings. It was still dark, but there was a light breeze, a southerly, and the sun would soon be up. Perfect for sailing, he thought. He drew the fresh St Piran air into his lungs, remembering the morning when he'd first stepped out of the doctor's house and done the same thing, scenting the tang of salt spray, and fish scales, and wet rope. This would be the perfect time to leave, he thought. Now in the shadow of darkness, with the glow of the rising sun waiting just below the horizon. Now while the villagers of St Piran were in their beds.

For a moment he didn't notice the figure sitting there, legs dangling off the side of the harbour.

'Who's there?' The mystery figure had made him jump.

'Just another traveller hoping for a lift,' came a voice. A woman's voice.

'Who *is* that?'

The woman on the dockside was rising to her feet. 'Another outsider,' she said. She stepped towards him and he saw her face illuminated by a sliver of light from his oil lamp.

'Aminata?'

'Aminata Chikelu,' she said, holding out a hand. 'Permission to come aboard?' She was wearing embroidered jeans and a ski jacket zipped up tight to the neck.

'Of course.' He held out a hand to steady her, but she leaned so shakily towards him that he found himself almost picking her up and lifting her onto the deck.

'Thank you,' she said, finding her feet. 'I was hoping you might take me along.'

'Along where?' He was experiencing a sense of disorientation.

'Wherever it is you're going.' She let herself sink into one of the cockpit seats. Then, catching his eye, she screwed up her face at him. 'Were you expecting someone else perhaps?'

He shook his head. 'No.'

'Good. Because I understand you invited her, and she turned you down.'

'Who?' But that was a silly question. Joe sat heavily in the seat opposite. 'Who told you that?' He held up his hand. 'No. It's all right. You don't need to tell me.'

'This *is* St Piran,' she said.

'Exactly.' He gave a shallow sigh. 'This is St Piran.'

'And we are friends.'

'I know.'

Aminata seemed to be watching for his reaction. 'She belongs here, Joe.'

'I know.'

'They *all* belong here. Everyone belongs here.'

'Except for me,' he said softly, and she fixed him with a look.

'And me,' she said.

'I don't believe we've ever been properly introduced,' he said, after a while.

'Does that matter?'

'Perhaps not. But you were one of the people who saved me. At the beach. I've never really thanked you.'

'That's OK.' She waved a hand. 'It wasn't me who found you. That was Charity.'

'All the same. You helped to carry me . . .'

'All part of the job.'

'You gave me the kiss of life . . .'

'Did I? I can't remember.' There seemed to be twinkle in her eye.

'You're from Senegal?'

She smiled at this observation. 'There you are,' she said. 'You know everything you need to know about me.'

'I'm sorry,' he said. 'I think that came out wrong.'

She put a hand out and touched him gently on the wrist. 'Not at all,' she said. She looked out beyond him to the harbour wall, and maybe beyond that her eyes were gazing towards a distant ocean. 'My father was Senegalese, but my mother was a Cornish girl. I'm like you. I'm a hybrid.'

'A hybrid . . .' he echoed.

'Or a chimera.' Aminata swept the hair away from her face and gave him a long look. 'I come from a town called St Louis,' she said. 'It's on the coast of Senegal, on the west coast of Africa, right up north, near the desert border with Mauritania. Not too many people ever come across that border. Only Tuaregs and a few madcap travellers. It's an out-of-the-way place you see, but it's beautiful. A colourful place. A place filled with music and laughter. And it has beaches.'

He smiled. 'A bit like St Piran then?'

'Not really, but I know what you mean.'

'I wasn't just off on a fishing trip. I'm sorry. I was planning . . . a longer trip.'

'A longer trip?'

'And I was planning . . . on sailing alone,' Joe said.

'Alone?'

'Yes.'

'Then you need to know a saying that we have in Senegal.' Aminata rose slowly out of the seat. 'It is never good to be alone. But if you *have* to be alone, then be alone with a friend.' She took hold of his hand and squeezed it gently before releasing it. 'I've never been on a sailing boat before.'

'I'm not sure that's a great qualification for coming with me,' he said.

'Oh,' she said airily. 'I have other qualifications.'

'I look forward to finding out what they might be.'

She was climbing down the ladder now to the cabin. 'Can you get my bag?'

'You have a bag?' He was surprised.

'Of course.'

He swung the lamp, and there it was on the dockside where she had been sitting, a large canvas sports bag. A little heavy perhaps. He carried it aboard feeling unsure quite what was happening.

'Aminata . . .' he said.

'Yes.'

'Why do you have a bag?'

In the low light of the cabin her smile seemed able to engulf them both. 'Ah,' she said. 'Martha said I should pack for a long journey.'

'Martha did?' His head was starting to spin. 'Martha Fishburne? The teacher?' How did Martha know he'd be on the boat? How would she know he was planning a long journey?

'Of course.' She was inspecting the cabin. 'Not as much room as I'd expected,' she said, testing the weight of a saucepan.

'It can sleep six.'

'And there's only the two of us . . .' She opened a cabin door and slid down onto the bed, '. . . in very close proximity. Will that be a problem?'

'Not for me,' he said. 'But how about you?'

'I'm a nurse,' she said, standing back up. 'Nothing bothers me.'

He nodded. 'That's good.' He was thinking about that word – *proximity*. That was Demelza's word. Proximity. Jeopardy. And a generous helping of Time.

'There are a few things I need to warn you about, though,' she said. 'If we're to share a boat this size. For how long . . . exactly?'

He cleared his throat. 'Well, I'm not sure . . . exactly.'

'Then approximately?'

He tried to imagine the trip. Would they go up the Channel

or the Irish Sea? What would the winds be like in January? 'A couple of weeks,' he said. 'Maybe more.'

'Ah,' she said, and she moved close enough to him that they might touch. 'Then you need to know my two bad habits. If you can't live with them, then we may need to rethink this whole adventure.'

'Two?' he said. 'Is that all?' I might need to compile a list of mine, he thought. I might need a fat notebook.

'Are you pretty tolerant?'

'I can live with most things,' he said. I shared a bell tower with a half-mad priest. He found himself hoping that nothing would stop her coming with him.

'Number one then.' She held up a single suggestive finger. 'I have a tendency to sing.'

He smiled. 'I heard you on Christmas Day.'

'While I work usually. It sometimes drives my colleagues mad. My patients enjoy it, though. Well, some of them do.'

'I see,' he said. 'And this is a *tendency*?'

He was teasing her and she saw it. She showed him her smile, a perfect curve of perfect teeth.

'What sort of things do you sing?'

'Oh . . .' she gave a dismissive wave, 'all the popular classics. The Beach Boys. Motown.'

'Well, maybe we could do with a little music at sea. It can get quiet out there.'

'Would you like to hear me sing? Just in case you can't take it?'

'No, that's OK.' He held up a hand. 'I heard you.'

'Are you sure?'

'Absolutely.'

'Not even two bars of "Baby Love"?'

'Not necessary.'

'Well. Good.' She gave him a nod and her hair bobbed in rhythm to the gesture. 'Are you ready for number two?'

'I'm braced,' he said.

'Are you very broad-minded?'

'Of course.' Something in the air around this girl was affecting his pulse.

Her smile widened into a grin and her arm slid around his waist. 'They may have mentioned this one in the village. I make a lot of noise. In bed. Apparently. Or so I'm told.'

So she did. 'There won't be anyone around to hear you.'

'Except for you.'

They untied the fenders and he started up the little inboard engine.

'I thought this was a sailing boat,' she said.

'It is,' he said, 'but first let's get out of the harbour.'

'So it wasn't the end of the world after all?'

'Wasn't it?' he said, and he felt her giving him a gentle pinch. 'Maybe not yet.'

'It was just a very long power cut,' she said. 'And everything's back to normal. You know something?' She was nodding at him gently. 'We get things like this all the time in Senegal. A whole district can go without electricity or water for months. Years even. And nothing ever collapses.'

He wanted to answer, but too many objections assailed him. Still, maybe she was right. We kept on breathing, he thought.

There was only a very slight swell as they rounded the inner harbour wall. The dawn light was sufficient to see by. She stood beside him, and like pilot and co-pilot they broached the first wall.

'I think you ought to wave,' she said.

'Wave goodbye to St Piran?'

'Yes.' Aminata had turned slightly and was waving her hand at the quayside.

He found himself turning to follow her gaze. The string of Christmas lights was twinkling all along the harbour, and there were figures waving back. Dozens of them. They lined the wall, and they were cheering. He recognised Mallory Books. What was he doing here? At six in the morning? And Kenny Kennet, and Casey Limber, and Charity Cloke, and Jeremy Melon. These were the people who had saved his life, who had carried his frozen body from the sea. The Higgs family were there, and Old Man Garrow leaning on his stick; and the Magwiths . . . a dozen or more of them. And the Bartles, and the Horsmiths, and the Anderssens and the Penhallows. Joe found himself lifting his arm and waving.

'How did they know?' he said. 'How did *you* know?'

'It was Martha,' Aminata said. 'She told me to tell you she joined up the dots.'

Of course she had. Kenny would have told her about the boat. And Polly would have told her about their meeting at the Vicarage. Someone would have seen him filling his water containers. And Kenny would have told her about the tides. And there she was with Ronnie, waving.

And there was Demelza, shouting, but her words were lost to the sea.

'What did she say?' Aminata asked.

'I didn't hear it.' But I think I know. Poetry is more truthful than history perhaps. Or maybe she was just wishing us a happy ending.

Two figures stood on the very end of the harbour – Polly and Alvin Hocking, holding hands. Alvin would be happy to see him go, Joe thought. And maybe Polly too. He waved, and they waved back. And slowly the harbour fell away and dissolved into the darkness of the dawn, and the cries and whistles of the villagers of St Piran evaporated into the stillness of the ocean and the slap of the waves.

Author's Postscripts

1. The quotation 'Any society is only three square meals from anarchy' appears to derive from a dialogue exchange in the British TV comedy series *Red Dwarf*. 'They say that every society is only three meals away from revolution. Deprive a culture of food for three meals, and you'll have anarchy.' That conversation was in *Red Dwarf*, Series III, premiered in 1989. Online suggestions on Wikiquote.org throw up some alternative derivations. 'Any society is only three square meals away from revolution' may have been said by Dumas (1802–1870) or Trotsky (1879–1940).
2. For a detailed account of the way that civilisations can collapse, readers with stamina might wish to try *Collapse* by the Pulitzer Prize-winning author Jared Diamond. The book explores the events on Easter Island, as well as the collapse of societies in Angkor Wat, Greenland and South America. I had no sooner finished reading *Collapse* when I had a chance encounter with Professor Jared Diamond at a remote forest lodge in Sumatra. I am grateful to him for engaging in a dinner conversation about the plot for *The Whale at the End of the World*. 'How realistic is the collapse scenario?' I asked him. 'Perfectly realistic,' he told me. 'It's one of the scenarios we work with.'
3. Much of Lew Kaufmann's speculation about social collapse derives from an article by Deborah MacKenzie that was published in *New Scientist* in April 2008. The article was entitled 'Will a pandemic bring down civilisation?' Joe and Lew's examples draw unashamedly from this.
4. The man who sequenced the virus that caused the 1918

flu epidemic was a US military pathologist called Jeffrey Taubenberger. His first attempt to isolate the virus led him to specimens of human tissue stored in blocks of wax at the Armed Forces Institute of Pathology. He searched through samples taken from more than seventy soldiers who had died in the epidemic, eventually isolating the virus from the lungs of an army private called Roscoe Vaughn. Taubenberger was able to sequence some of the genome from this sample, but there wasn't sufficient tissue to finish the job. The breakthrough came when Taubenberger was contacted by a Norwegian researcher, Johan Hultin, who had been working in Alaska looking for the buried remains of victims of the 1918 flu. Hultin got permission from native Alaskans to dig up the body of the woman they would later name 'Lucy'. Lucy had been particularly obese, and the fat around her lungs had slowed down the rate of decay. In 2005 a team at the Centers for Disease Control and Prevention in Atlanta, led by Dr Terrence Tumpey, announced that they had successfully recreated the virus that infected Lucy. Ten vials of the virus are now kept at the centre. This might have been an end to the story but for the rather disturbing fact that full details of the gene sequence were later uploaded onto an online database. In December 2011 a Dutch virologist, Ron Fouchier of the Erasmus Medical Centre in Rotterdam, told a scientific convention in Malta that, using this online data, he had created a live flu virus that could well be deadlier that any contagious disease that humanity had ever faced.

5. On 2 July 2014 the *Independent* newspaper was one of many that reported on the development, by Dr Yoshihiro Kawaoka of the University of Wisconsin-Madison, of a genetically modified version of the 2009 strain of pandemic flu that would effectively allow it to 'escape' the control of the human immune system. The human population of the world would be defenceless against this strain of flu.

According to the article by Steve Connor, many scientists are horrified that Kawaoka was allowed to deliberately remove the only defence against a strain of flu that has already demonstrated its ability to create a deadly pandemic that killed as many as 500,000 people in the year of its emergence. One researcher is reported as saying, 'He took the 2009 pandemic flu virus and selected out strains that were not neutralised by human antibodies. He repeated this several times until he got a real humdinger of a virus.'

6. I am grateful to Michael Fowle and also to those members of the online 'Quants' Network' who volunteered to sanity-check the City trading passages in the story. In particular Emilie Pons and Johan (Hans) Beumee read the whole manuscript and both were forthcoming with helpful comments and suggestions. Where I could, I have taken their advice to make the trading floor of Lane Kaufmann as realistic a City environment as possible. In some cases, however, I was happier to leave the story as I had imagined it, even though this has probably compromised accuracy. Emilie told me that Joe would not be called a 'quant' because he wasn't strictly a trader. I've left the term in, because I rather like it. Johan helped me understand short trading but advised that most traders have the possibility to go short. The fifth floor at Lane Kaufmann would be more likely to be a floor devoted to 'exotics and leveraged deals', rather than to short selling. The kinds of losses that Janie's short-traders make would be unlikely, he advised. These kinds of losses would be more likely from other forms of trading. In the end I ignored what was probably excellent advice here, partly because I didn't want to complicate the story with too many financial processes, and partly because I was drawn to the dark symbolism of short trading. I hope that real quants and traders will forgive me for this.
7. It takes courage and a particular set of skills to read the

first rough draft of a novel, and then to suggest a whole raft of changes and improvements to the author. I am lucky in this regard to have an utterly brilliant and fearless editor, Kirsty Dunseath, whose advice always comes with extraordinary insight. I owe Kirsty a huge thank-you. An equally big thank-you to Mark Stanton and Sue Ironmonger, who both saw the promise of that first manuscript, but who helped me recognise and address the flaws. I owe them all a great deal.

8. The annual sea fish catch in Cornwall is over 15,000 tonnes, with a market value of £35.5 million. Many of the fish caught are bottom-dwelling fish, such as haddock, hake, monkfish and sole. Two-thirds of the catch comes into Newlyn, Cornwall's biggest port, where monkfish, sardines and crabs are the three biggest catches. In Mevagissey (where I once lived) fishermen catch around 800 tonnes of fish a year, mainly haddock, sardine and pollack. St Piran has a far smaller catch.
9. Fin whales very rarely beach. Most of the 2,000 or so whales that die on beaches around the world every year are toothed whales. The fin whale is a baleen whale. But there have, nonetheless, been some recorded incidents of fin whales beaching. A 19-metre fin whale, described by vets as 'incredibly undernourished', died after being stranded on a beach near Carlyon Bay in Cornwall in August 2012 (I also lived for a while in Carlyon Bay). Three years earlier in January 2009 an 18-metre fin whale died after being stranded on a beach in Courtmacsherry in Ireland.
10. It is really not wise to eat the flesh of a stranded whale. Whale blubber is a very effective insulating material (one of its functions is to protect the living whale from the cold of the oceans) and it continues to provide insulation even after the whale dies. A dead whale will maintain a high body temperature for several days, slowly cooking in its own body heat, and providing a perfect environment for

bacteria to thrive. In 2002 eight people contracted botulism after eating the blubber of a whale that had become stranded on a beach in Alaska. The villagers of St Piran and Treadangel were lucky in this regard.

11. Readers will appreciate that the whale in the story represents an unexpected bounty that could be shared to good effect. Real whales are beautiful, sentient creatures that deserve our love and respect. They are certainly not a potential source of food. We can share the bounty of these animals by giving them the freedom of the oceans, by visiting them on whale-watching trips, and by opposing, through organisations such as Greenpeace, any nations that still hunt whales.

12. Here are the first nine verses of Job Chapter 41 (from the 21st Century King James Version):

    1 Canst thou draw out Leviathan with a hook? Or his tongue with a cord which thou lettest down?
    2 Canst thou put a hook into his nose, or bore his jaw through with a thorn?
    3 Will he make many supplications unto thee? Will he speak soft words unto thee?
    4 Will he make a covenant with thee? Wilt thou take him as a servant for ever?
    5 Wilt thou play with him as with a bird? Or wilt thou bind him for thy maidens?
    6 Shall the companions make a banquet of him? Shall they parcel him among the merchants?
    7 Canst thou fill his skin with barbed irons, or his head with fish spears?
    8 Lay thine hand upon him; remember the battle, and do so no more!
    9 Behold, the hope against him is in vain. Shall not one be cast down even at the sight of him?

13. An account of Jonah and the Whale appears in both the Bible and the Qur'an. In this story, Jonah is ordered to prophesy hard times for the wicked city of Nineveh, but he struggles against this edict. Eventually, he flees from the city. He finds himself on a boat in a storm, where the only remedy appears to be for him to be thrown overboard. (The seafarers all cast lots, and Jonah loses.) He volunteers for this sanction, and sure enough, his sacrifice calms the storm. But it isn't the end for Jonah. As we all remember, he is then swallowed (and rescued) by a very big fish. Here is the Qur'an story from Sura 37 (translation by Muhammad Asad):

And behold, Jonah was indeed one of Our message-bearers when he fled like a runaway slave onto a laden ship. And then they cast lots, and he was the one who lost; [and they cast him into the sea], whereupon the great fish swallowed him, for he had been blameworthy. And had he not been of those who [even in the deep darkness of their distress are able to] extol God's limitless glory, he would indeed have remained in its belly till the Day when all shall be raised from the dead: but We caused him to be cast forth on a desert shore, sick [at heart] as he was, and caused a creeping plant to grow over him [out of the barren soil]. And [then] We sent him [once again] to [his people], a hundred thousand [souls] or more: and [this time] they believed [in him] – and so We allowed them to enjoy their life during the time allotted to them.

And not forgetting . . .

Jonas (Joe) Haak a computer programmer

Harriet Adlam, a banker
Jacob Anderssen, a landlord
Romer Anderssen, a landlady
Annie Bartle, a fish filleter
Elizabeth Bartle, a fish filleter
Robert Batho, a Newlyn fisherman
Dr Mallory Books, a doctor (retired)
Dr Marcia Brodie, a City doctor
Rodney Byatt, a computer programmer
Aminata Chikelu, a nurse and a singer
Ardour Cloke, a teenage boy
Charity Cloke, a teenage girl
Modesty Cloke, a teaching assistant
Valour and Faith Cloke, children
Janie Coverdale, a City trader
Martha Fishburne, a teacher
Ronnie Fishburne, a removal man
'Old Man' Arwen Garrow, a fisherman (retired)
Jonathan Guy, a City quant
'Mamma' Alison Haak, Joe's mother
Brigitha Haak, Joe's sister

'Pappa' Mikkel Haak, Joe's father

Colin Helms, a senior City banker

Jessie Higgs, a shopkeeper

Jordy 'Bo'sun' Higgs, a sailor

Reverend Alvin Hocking, a vicar

Polly Hocking, a vicar's wife

Emily Horsmith, a girl

Nan Horsmith, a mother

Thomas Horsmith, a schoolboy

Cassie Kaufmann, a teenager, Lew's granddaughter

Lew Kaufmann, a bank director

Tom and Kate Kaufmann, Cassie's parents

Kenny (Kenver) Kennet, a beachcomber

Casey Limber, a net-maker

Aileen Magwith, a farmer's wife

Bevis Magwith, a farmer

Corin Magwith, a farmer

Ellie Magwith, a schoolgirl

Forest Magwith, a farmer

Lorne Magwith, a farmer

Clare Manners/McEvan, a City marketeer

Richard Mansell, a cash-and-carry manager

Julian McEvan, a City trader

Jeremy Melon, a naturalist and writer

Jenny Messenger, a TV reporter

Nate and Rose Moot, smallholders

Captain Abel O'Shea, a harbour master

Manesh Patel, a City analyst

Hedra Penhallow, a B&B owner
Moses Penhallow, a B&B owner
Louisa Penroth, a lobsterman's wife
Toby Penroth, a lobsterman
Benny Restorick, a council worker
Dorothy Restorick, a mother
Daniel Robins, a fisherman
Samuel Robins, a fisherman
Benny Shaunessy, a schoolboy
Jenny Shaunessy, a villager
John Shaunessy, a fisherman and fish dealer
Peter Shaunessy, a fisherman and fish dealer
John and Lucy Thoroughgood, smallholders
Demelza Trevarrick, a writer of romantic novels
Amelia Warren, a City barista
Jonathan Woodman, a computer programmer
The villagers of St Piran in the County of Cornwall
The townspeople of Treadangel

and not forgetting

a fin whale

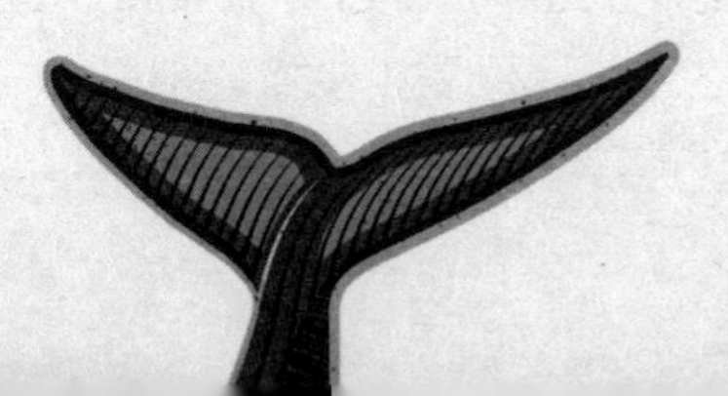

READ A CHAPTER FROM

THE MANY LIVES OF HELOISE STARCHILD

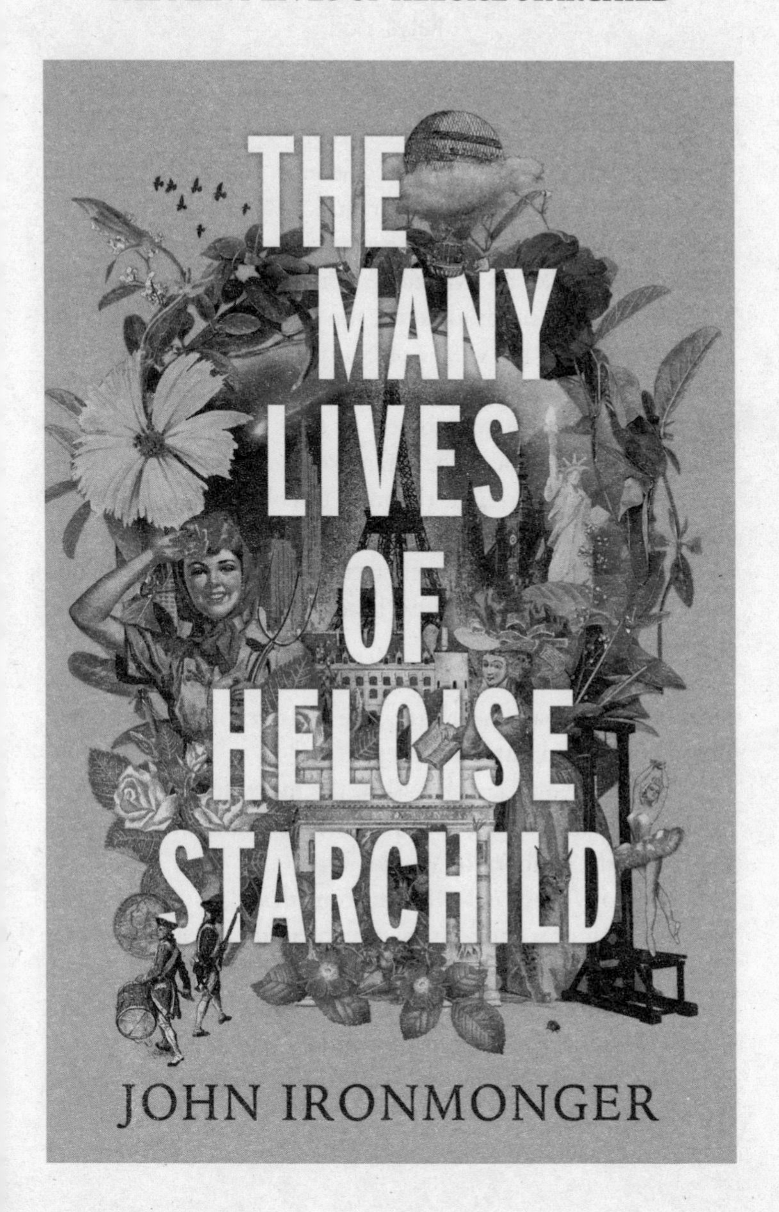

1

Katya, 1952

It rained like the storms of Genesis the night Katarína Němcová was born. The Tatrzańska River burst its banks, and a tide of mud and debris swept along the dirt lane to the Němcov farm like an avalanche. The midwife's bicycle stuck stubbornly in the mudslide at the top of the track leading down the river valley to the village of Nová Vyšný, and the midwife, unwilling to launch herself on foot into the deluge even for the birth of a baby, was forced to ring her bell furiously to announce her presence. The infant's father, Jaroslav, ran all the way up the track through the mud to collect her, and he carried her back to the homestead over his shoulder like a sack of corn, with no boots on his feet and nothing more than a strip of tarpaulin held over his head to shield them both from the rain.

Katarína's mother had been in labour for fourteen hours. She had been awake for thirty. She had very little energy left. Blood vessels had burst in her eyes.

'What kept you?' Jaroslav asked the midwife.

'Twins in Stará Lesna,' the midwife told him, 'a rainstorm in Poprad, and a stillborn in Vysoké Tatry.'

When baby Katarína (known from that day as Katya) was born, an hour or so later, a tiny grub of an infant, underweight, blue, slick with mucus and blood, her mother Frantiska died. Baby Katya took her first breath as her mother took her last, like the blow and suck of an accordion – out, and in. One soul departed, and the other gave voice to the trauma in a wail, a cry to the gods.

*

In the foothills of the Tatras the rain would often fall as snow in November. In the winter of 1952, the village would say, it fell as tears. Every household sent someone to the funeral of Frantiska Němcová and the weeping was as loud as had ever been heard in the graveyard of the small white church on the hillside where the young woman was laid to rest. Baby Katya's grandfather Krystof (Frantiska's father-in-law) slipped on ice on the morning of the burial, cracked his skull on the cobblestones, and came to the funeral with bloody bandages swathing his head. Six young women from the academy in Štrbské Pleso, friends of the dead woman, wearing white-and-black uniforms, looking cold against the snowscape of the High Tatras, sang a lament that started quietly like a whisper but grew into a crescendo, and the grey-coated crowd around the grave held hands with one another and murmured along with the chant. Many of the women wept. There were so many in the churchyard that latecomers had to stand behind the wall along the roadside, taking shelter under the oaks.

Snow began to fall as the bearers lowered the coffin into the ground.

Baby Katya's father, Jaroslav, like a frozen statue at the graveside, wore the same black greatcoat his grandfather had worn when he came back from the war in 1918; even stripped of all insignia and colours, and faded from years of wear, it lent him a military bearing. The long-faced priest with heavy eyebrows who swung incense over the mouth of the grave was Jaroslav's brother Paul. He laid a hand on Jaroslav's shoulder when the words had all been spoken, as the crowd pressed forward to throw soil.

Thunk. Thunk. The earth was rocky in the Tatras. It fell onto the coffin like shrapnel.

'She only lived here for nine years, and yet they loved her in this village,' the priest told Jaroslav.

'They did.'

Wiping cold dirt from gloved hands, mourners lined up to pay their respects, blowing lungs of steam as they waited. 'We are so sorry,' they said, each one clutching young Jaroslav's hand, some of them offering a kiss to his cheek. 'She will be missed,' said others. 'God will bless her daughter,' many said.

A woman bent with age, her head buried beneath a black wool shawl, cupped Jaroslav's hand into her own. 'Does the infant have the gift?' she asked, her voice a watery cough.

'She is only five days old,' Katya's father said. His eyes were red from weeping and from the cold. 'How would we know? We will not know for a dozen years or more.'

'Do her eyes shine?'

'Yes, they shine.'

The old crone kissed Jaroslav's hands. 'Then she has the gift,' she said.

'Perhaps,' Jaroslav said. He returned the kiss.

'I pray to God for it.'

'You should not. It did not bring Frantiska joy.'

'But I will pray all the same. It will bring her back.' The woman released his hands.

The priest took the old woman's shoulder. 'Veruska Maria, you should get out of this cold. It will kill you.' He steered her away, her feet crunching on the newly fallen snow.

By the time the line of mourners had shrunk to a straggle, the snow was drifting down in flakes as big as roses. 'We should get inside,' the priest said. 'We should get warm.'

'She shouldn't be buried like this,' complained a farmer from Starý Smokovec. Beneath his coat he was wearing the blue one-piece boiler suit he wore to milk cows at the collective farm. 'All this . . .' he waved an intolerant arm, '. . . all this religion. This chanting. It is not the communist way.'

'Her family was from the West. It is what she would have wanted,' Jaroslav said. His eyebrows hovered low over his eyes.

'Well, it's too late to ask her now.'

A man wearing no hat, the tips of his ears glowing purple in the cold, whispered something into Jaroslav's ear, so quietly, Jaroslav had to lean close to hear it.

'Is it true she was in Lidice?' he asked.

The farmer nodded, a faint drop of his head. 'She was.' This reply, too, was a whisper.

'How did she survive?'

'By the grace of God,' Jaroslav said. 'The grace of God and a stubborn will.'

A Russian GAZ-M20 automobile, like an overweight cockroach, was parked at the top of the lane, as close as it would dare come without running into deep snow, and the driver, a jowly man with a Bolshevik *budenkova* cap, sat watching the funeral stony faced without once leaving his vehicle, or turning off the engine.

'Look at him,' Krystof said to the priest, nodding up towards the man in the motor car. 'NKVD.' He spat into the snow as he spoke the words. 'Russian secret police. Just in case Frantiska was a spy. Someone has been telling them stories. What do they imagine she can do, now she's dead?'

A tractor from the collective farm came to sweep away snow but it left a landscape of grey mud beneath its wheels. Mourners found themselves picking their way up the hill to the church hall along a perilous trackway of snow and mire. Jaroslav's sister Marta, wearing impractical high heels, carried baby Katya, swaddled in so many blankets only the infant's eyes showed through. In the warmth of the Tatry Kostol hall everyone wanted to see the child, but Marta was sparing. 'She is sleeping,' she told almost every person who tried to lean in for a closer view.

It was almost an hour before the baby opened her eyes and cried. The hubbub in the hall died away and the cry of the tiny infant rose above the heads of the mourners like the call of a wild bird.

'It's Frantiska,' said Verushka Maria, the old crone, her voice heavy with age, and many heads turned her way. 'It's little Frantiska reborn. I know that voice,' she said. 'I would recognise her anywhere.'